crush

a novel
laura susan johnson

Beaten Track
www.beatentrackpublishing.com

crush

First published 2011 PeachHam-Beach Publishing
UK Edition published 2012 by Beaten Track Publishing

A CIP catalogue record for this book
is available from the British Library.

ISBN: 978 1 909192 11 9

Cover design and all images by the author.

Fiction/Romance/Gay Men/Relationships/Erotica/Child Abuse/Sexual
Dysfunction/Emotional Problems/Hate Crimes/Animal Rights

PeachHam-Beach Publishing,
Hammett Valley, Idaho.
peachhambeach.jigsy.com

Beaten Track Publishing,
Burscough, Lancashire.
www.beatentrackpublishing.com

this book is dedicated to:

my parents who love me as I am,
my Uncle Lionel Clyde "Bob" Purkey,
the memory of Matthew Shepard,
and all of the "Tammys" and "Jamies" out there.

This book is a work of fiction.
Any resemblance to any persons,
living or dead, is purely coincidental.

Warning:
Contains sexuality, adult subject matter,
profanity, disturbing content and violence.

Intended for readers aged 18 and over.

author's notes:

It should be noted that although there may be similarities between "Crush" and the true story of Matthew Shepard, whose brutal attack in Wyoming made headlines in the Autumn of 1998, "Crush" is entirely a work of fiction. Like many bystanders, I had heard about the hate-crime by watching CNN, but I never learned any of the details or followed the trial of his killers. I have only recently read Judy Shepard's inspiring tribute to her beautiful gay son, *The Meaning of Matthew: My Son's Murder in Laramie, and a World Transformed*, two months after the completion of "Crush". Any similarities to Mr. Shepard's story are completely coincidental.

There are four hospitals in this book: UC Davis Medical Centre is a real hospital and is located near downtown Sacramento, California, not in the town of Davis, CA. For clarity's sake, I created the fictitious "Davis Hospital" to which Tammy drives Jamie, after Jamie is attacked by classmates. "Saint Paul's Hospital", also a fictitious creation, is located in West Sac, CA. "Yolo County Hospital" in the city of Woodland is also fictitious.

Laura Susan Johnson

crush

book one:
love's first kisses

prologue:

thames lee mattheis
(december 30)

Interrogation room, Sommerville Police Department

"Please state your full name," the first officer says, and I do, as it reads above.

It's like the English river, pronounced "Tems". Everyone calls me "Tammy", but it's *not* the girl's name, it's pronounced "Temmy" (as if they even sound all that different from one another!). Mom's made life a lot harder than it has to be. First of all: she named me after a *river*. The woman isn't even English! Our ancestors were French, Greek and Irish. Second: she decides to nickname me "Tam" or "Tammy", which is an Irish form of the name "Thomas". Third: I get teased constantly that "Tammy" is a girl's name. And fourth: the way it's pronounced "Temmy". My life has been spent spelling it for people, teaching them to pronounce it correctly, and fending off the guys calling me, "Tammy, Tell Me True"! Mom could have named me "Thomas", so I could be nicknamed "Tommy". She could have named me "Timothy", so I could be nicknamed "Timmy". But no, I'm named after a river, with a weird nickname that's perceived as girlish, which everyone has to be taught isn't even pronounced phonetically.

As I sit here in this claustrophobic grey cubicle, my eyes tracing each graffiti-carved inch of the metallic table before me, I contemplate how much my life has changed in the past few weeks since I came home from L.A. to help Mom.

How different I am.

In spite of how love once touched me in high school many years ago, and before discovering an unforeseen tender-heartedness for stray cats not many years ago, I used to have only one true goal driving me, and that was to *hurt* people. It was my only real source of joy and fulfilment.

Disregarding the chill in the air drawing this year to a terrible close, a conclusion I never in my wildest dreams would have imagined, large beads of clandestine sweat are forming on the nape of my neck.

No, it *wasn't*.

I only *wanted* it to work that way.

And since it didn't, I couldn't keep it up. Deceiving women and men didn't really give me the thrill I wanted.

I had become evil.

And I wanted to be *happy* being evil.

But I could not.

I continued to love someone I'd left behind, and I saved a kitten from certain death. Saving Bootsy was a catalyst, an act of kindness that sparked my heart back to life.

And I could not ignore the real me, the longing in my heart to be human again.

To care, to love.

To love and to be loved back.

I *didn't* love being mean. I *didn't* love hurting people the way I'd hoped I would.

And I missed my friend. I didn't get away from him by moving three hundred miles away. He was always with me, day after day, year after year, always in my dreams, asleep and awake.

I missed him. I had never stopped missing him, from the day I left him behind to try to "find myself", to the day I was called home.

He means more to me than anything.

6

No matter how mean, selfish and narcissistic I had wanted to be, I loved him.

I still love him.

And he loved me.

I want him to *love* me, present tense.

But I think he's going to die.

I want to go back in time, not years, just hours, just a day. I want to do what my instinct told me to do.

I can't. I can't do what I want to do. I can't go back in time.

I didn't try to end his life, contrary to what the police think, but he wasn't safe to be left alone that night. I had a premonition.

I failed him.

Dozens of bodies at my feet, in a wasteland I'd created, women and men, crawling blindly and weeping for me to assuage their pangs. I sat above, smiling down at them like an evil goddess, like Kali, luxuriating, listening to them wailing their misery, their cries dying slowly until every last voice quieted and all the bodies stilled.

"Address?" the policeman barks.

He's just my type, or what I had once thought my type. Big, tall and craggy like Huey Lewis. No delicacy about him. I had fun once or twice, bringing down a guy looking like this. It gave me a heady feeling, to conquer the kind of man that everyone assumes, by his looks, is "manly".

I'm pretty. I don't mean to sound conceited. It's just something I've been told too many times not to believe.

Jamie's pretty too. Prettier than I am.

Because he never has *cared* about that kind of thing. Not like I have.

And I used my prettiness to harm people.

The first time I took down a "man's man", I was twenty-eight. I thought I'd have a hell of a challenge. I thought he'd beat the shit out of me for hitting on him. I was wrong, wrong, wrong. He fell like a leaf in October, the big brute.

But by then, the thrill of soul hunting had passed. I had thought that I could resurrect it, and find nothing more titillating and satisfying than snatching him, body and soul, and then leaving him desolate and aching for more of me.

Deliberate, precise, just plain heartless, I'd made capturing and collecting people's love without giving anything back my supreme objective in life.

I'd toppled many women, the number somewhere in the sixties or seventies, before I'd moved on to men. I hadn't had more than maybe four or five guys before I decided I was finished playing games with their lives and mine.

It was those kind of men... players, fratboys, meatheads, the kind of men who eat like pigs and burp loudly, drink beer and then piss on pavements, worship both playing and watching football and stack themselves on 'roids until they become butterball turkeys in their later years, that I'd practised on.

But always, there was something in the way of me enjoying myself totally.

Always that beautiful little face in the way, obstructing my view. That delicate, refined visage, the face of an angel, the face of a child-man, a face so exquisite, so unique, so unforgettably beautiful, that not even the most glamorous movie-star can begin to compare...

"Please state your current residence!" squawks the second cop.

"809 Truckee Street, Sommerville."

The tape recorder in his hand has a little glowing red light on top. I lick my lips, knowing that the words that are about to slip through them will be sucked onto the shiny entrails of the audio cassette. Forever.

My mouth is dry, tastes bitter, like I've been chewing on a bar of Ivory soap.

I fell in love for the first time, ever, sixteen years ago. I ran away from that love. And I stayed away, for a long time, before Mom fell, before I was called home.

"Please, can I have a soda? I'm so thirsty." The moisture trickles down my back, cooling it, before being absorbed by the elastic of my Jockeys.

I'd never been in love with anyone before him, and I've never been in love with anyone since.

I finally received... no... I finally accepted, truly accepted his love only days ago.

The second police officer leaves for a moment and returns with an ice cold can of Dr. Pepper. "This okay?"

"Anything," I mutter through sticky lips, popping it open with a refreshing "sssst!" sound and gulping several freezing swallows before releasing a quiet belch.

"So," begins the rugged-faced cop, "These... uh... journals..."

Now, I'm in jail, accused of a violent crime.

"Pretty sick stuff, wouldn't you agree?" Rugged Cop asks.

"Yeah," the second cop shudders.

I tell the cop that I didn't do it, that I didn't hurt Jamie, that I've never hurt anyone, at least not in the way they're *thinking*. Guilt rears its head again, and I begin to confess my sins. I tell them that I've killed many people *emotionally*, not physically, that I was a serial soul stealer.

"A *what*?" sneers the Rugged Cop.

I repeat myself and he says, "No, what you are is a pathetic piece of *shit* who deserves to burn in hell." I wonder if it's because of the crime I'm being accused of, or because of who the victim of the crime was... is...

"I wrote in those diaries when I was twelve, thirteen years old! I was angry... I was a *kid*!"

"The way these are written," the second cop says with a repulsed shiver, "I'd say you're capable of committing a crime this violent."

"I was only a kid!" I reiterate angrily.

"Keep your temper," warns Rugged Cop.

"I didn't do this, I swear it!"

"I'd like to ask you about the bruise on the back of the victim's neck," Rugged Cop scowls. "What's that from? It almost looks like a hickey or something."

They don't laugh, they don't spout innuendoes. Still, under the surface, I feel the attitude, and it has me wondering just how many allies we even have around here in the wake of this brutal beating of which I have been named the chief suspect. Do they *care* about Jamie? Do they care about him at all? Or do they think he deserves it, like I deserve to "burn in hell"?

I try to tell the police that I love my boyfriend, present tense, that I'd never, ever hurt him.

That I'm not that boy anymore.

That when I *was* that kid, I was in pain, and, yes, I acted out, but I've never hurt anyone... not physically.

I try to tell them, but my despair muzzles me. My natural propensity to blame myself for all that has gone wrong, even after I tried to get Jamie to take the fateful night off, even after I begged him to let me go to work with him, asserts itself, and my uncooperative lips crumple.

I don't think they believe me anyway.

two:

james michael pearce
(aged three to thirteen)

I never find out why they hate me. I've always wanted to know. I love them. Why do they hate me? I am three—that's my earliest memory—when they start hitting me. My mom reaches back and slaps me hard at the table during breakfast. I don't know what I've done to make her slap me. When I am old enough to be in school, I remember my preschool teacher taking me aside and asking about the bruises, welts and burns. Nothing comes of it, or my life would be different than it is.

My kindergarten teacher calls a meeting with Mom and Daddy because I've slapped a boy in class for calling me an ashtray.

Before the Child Protection people come, my parents cram me into the car and drive north, from our house in south Sacramento to Oregon, to live with people on Mom's side of the family. Arguments erupt between Mom and a lady I believe is my Grandma. None of the people in that house talk to me or pay any attention to me.

I prefer never to be left alone with Mom and Daddy. I always am.

From what I can scrape together from my memories, Mom is

dark-haired and slender, with bright blue eyes. In earlier years, she is elegant, projecting an image of a well-groomed professional at her job as a secretary for an attorney somewhere in Salem. Later, she turns stringy-haired and wild-eyed. She scares me.

Daddy is fair-haired with large brown eyes. He's quiet. I never hear him raise his voice, but he's susceptible to suggestion and battles several addictions.

The folks in Oregon kick us out after Daddy gets busted shoplifting at a Payless, and we move back to the Florin neighbourhood of Sacramento. My first grade teacher calls the cops when she sees how I look one morning—a black eye and blood drying in my hair. I have no idea how my parents manage to sneak me out of the police station.

We move to the small town of Sommerville, a hamlet of less than eight thousand people, just east-north-east of Davis off the interstate, into a two bedroom house that has some measure of privacy. It is on a corner parcel surrounded by weed-infested, loamy-soiled reject lots. The walls are of plaster, which has much better soundproofing than sheetrock.

That's when they decide that in order to avoid having to move around, I should stay hidden. I'm locked in my room. At first, I get fed two or three times a day. Then there comes a time when I don't get a crumb for at least four or five days. I remember crying for them to let me out to go to the toilet. They bring me a bucket, and they beat me because I have to use it, because they have to dump it every now and again. They lug it out to the real toilet across the hall, cursing me and covering their noses at the stench I've caused.

Once a week, sometimes every other week, they let me out to shower and stretch my legs. My muscles ache. Daddy begins to make me accompany him when he showers. He tells me I mustn't run away and to do what he asks. I've tried to forget that first shower he made me take with him, and I do try to run. I prize open the stubborn, splintery window in my room, and I have almost wriggled halfway out when they catch me. Mom rips chunks of my hair out while lashing me with a thick black

12

belt with round metal studs in it. When it's over, I try to hide from the hot, throbbing pain by curling in a ball and rubbing my bloodied body against my filthy bedsheets, praying for another chance to escape.

"Why you wanna run away, Pretty?" asks Daddy with sad, dark eyes. "I *love* you."

And then they put the chains on my legs, and I can't even leave my bed to see what time of year it is, what colour the sky and leaves are.

After the first shower, Daddy shows me how to do the things he likes the right way. At first I close my eyes. I don't want to watch what he's doing to me, but Mom yells, "Pay attention!" So I have to watch. I watch, and I learn, but I hate the sight of him down there—the weird, crazy, scary faces he's making at me. I hate that part of my body—I hate it even more when he's down there, because he's doing things that feel good, and my body begins to do funny things in response.

I'm afraid.

I know this is wrong.

It's so wrong.

I hate myself.

When I'm seven or eight, they begin to make the videos, usually one or two a month.

I've tried to bury those years deep inside my mind. I'd be lying if I said I don't remember. I remember liking some of it, and feeling dirty and guilty. I remember hating other things. The truth is I remember so much that I shudder and cower down like I'm caught in an ambush. Any moment, a deadly memory will strike home and kill me. When I'm awake, it's easier to be in control. I can shoo the memories and the visions away. I can stay busy at work, with friends. Asleep, the nightmares are brutal, impossibly as graphic and horrific as the real thing so long ago. I relive those seven years every night in my sleep, my senses functioning perfectly in dreamstate. I see everything, I hear everything, I smell everything, I feel everything, I taste everything. Every so often, when I'm just waking, cosy in my bed, the dreams seemingly over, I'll see it, and it's so real, and I'll hear his soft voice. "Come on, pretty baby. Show Daddy you love him. Show Daddy..."

I should die in that room, but I don't. When Daddy's not loving me, I feel so alone. When I don't see him for a few days, I cry and beg him to come. Of course, he never comes in without her. Sometimes they ignore me. Sometimes my cries only anger them, and Mom hits me with the studded black belt until I'm covered with glowing red welts for days after.

So I try harder to please them. I'm so hungry.

I want to die, but every day I'm still breathing. The food they bring me becomes less and less in amount and frequency. When my daddy finally returns to my bed I'm so happy I readily service him, loving his presence, his warmth, his soft solidity, the closeness, the way I feel so safe...

My skills improve and I not only get used to it, I *want* to do it. Because I don't want to be left alone. He can't stay away from me very long, he says, I'm too good. He taught me so well.

Mom videos Daddy as I do the things he showed me, and then he puts me on my stomach—I wish she would stop recording, stop watching and go away. But she stays. "You're a nasty boy, Jamie," she says, her mouth pulled into a snarl-smile that still scares me in my dreams, her vulva wet. After Daddy comes, he takes the camera from Mom and she uses the big flashlight on me, or the whisk broom, or whatever she can get her hands on that's shaped right.

I get used to what Daddy wants, and pleasing him is second nature. And he always praises me when I'm finished. He's as gentle as he can be, unless Mom tells him to do it harder.

The flashlight I never get used to. It hurts. They trade laughs and comments like they trade the camera. It hurts when they say those things about me, even worse than when Mom uses the flashlight.

And when he videos her burning me with her cigarette, calling me names as I scream, I don't understand what I've done wrong. I'm doing what they *tell* me to do. I don't want to, but I

14

love them. Why does she burn me? Why doesn't Daddy make her *stop*?!

They only ever change the sheets when they want to make a new video. Otherwise, my bed stays soiled. While Mom tucks in the nice smooth clean sheets, I huddle down on the floor as far away as the chains will let me go. I don't want to do this. It's the same every time, a story they have to tell over and over again. When he has all his clothes off, Daddy squats down naked beside me. "You ready to make another show with Daddy?"

"No," I cry. "I don't want to do the show." I really don't. Though I've said I've gotten used to it, even gotten to like it, I really don't like doing these videos. I'm so mixed up inside. I want Daddy to love me, but I don't want to do things to him, I don't want him inside of me, and I especially don't want Mom to do the things she does with her flashlight, belt and cigarettes.

But when Daddy smiles and kisses me, and says, "I'll bring you mac and cheese, your favourite," my stomach clenches and churns. I'm so *hungry*.

"How about green beans? And Ding Dongs for dessert! With the creamy stuff in the middle!"

So I do the shows with him. Sometimes the mac and cheese is hot and creamy, with plenty of salt and pepper. It's so wonderful that I beg them for seconds and thirds. Other times it's cold and tastes like it's a few days old, but it stops the cramping in my tummy.

I'm the centre of their attention a couple of times a month. Otherwise, I'm a nothing behind several locks and chains, they ignore me except to bring food now and then, and to dump my bucket into the toilet.

It takes a few more years, but I learn to stop screaming. If I stop screaming sooner, she'll stop burning me sooner. I learn other things too. If I don't scream, they're not as fun to watch. They finally stop making videos when I'm eleven or twelve, when I become too skinny and weak to do what they like. I've become so weak I don't even care when Mommy hits and burns me. So they stop. They no longer come into my room, not even when I beg them to bring me food.

I'm in a dark forest. I can see myself, my skin reflected in the meagre light. I can't see ahead or behind me. There are no sounds in the wood, not even the howling of coyotes or the hooting of owls. I'd rather hear anything than this thickening silence.

No-one is here. No-one, and I'd rather have to do the videos, and I'd rather be burned with her cigarettes, than be here with only myself.

But I'm too skinny and weak to make their friends happy now.

I'm all used up...

They don't come back.

April 23rd.

My thirteenth is my last birthday in that room. Daddy opens my door, peeks in at me for a second. I don't notice him. I haven't eaten—I've lost count after six days or so.

He hasn't brought food. He doesn't come in. He just closes the door softly.

There is no mirror in my room. I've never liked mirrors. I see my father in my hair and my mother in my eyes. Now, even without a mirror I look down, and I see myself. My hair is falling out. My eyes are about to sink into my brain. My skin is grey. I feel so light.

The loud reports from outside my room are the last sounds that make my body jump, the last stimuli I respond to in that house. And then the house is quiet. I've been praying to die. I'm crying. I'm in pain. I'm unbearably thirsty. I hate the silence. It's horrifying, the silence.

Please God, let me die. Sleep drapes itself over me like a heavy wool blanket, and I surrender. The endless hours in that stinking bed meld together, the chains eating into the skin of my ankles forgotten.

I'm alone in this thickly wooded wilderness. The trees close in around me, as always, but the difference now is, they seem friendly, like they feel sorry for me being all alone, and are bending down to tell me everything is going to be okay.

I stop being hungry. I stop being thirsty. I stop being afraid of the deafening silence. I stop being angry at Mom and Daddy for leaving me for so long without food, for not emptying my commode so I can use it.

I stop loving Daddy. I did everything I could to let him know how much I loved him, how much I needed him.

And still, he left me.

Alone, in the dark.

I hate him.

My most recent and frequent companions come to visit, buzzing in through the slit of the open, screenless window that I once tried to crawl through to freedom—shiny green flies that have followed my repulsive aroma for miles. As I sleep, their tiny black tongues lap at the sweat, vomit and other ungodly waste that's leaking out of me unbidden.

I stop praying for God to come get me.

three:

tammy mattheis
(aged four to fourteen)

The memory is there. It's buried far, far below millions of grey and white molecules, beneath bundles upon bundles of nerve fibres and synapses. It's there. But I don't remember it right now.

I'm in a grocery shop with my mother, somewhere in Sacramento. I'm going to be five in a few months, so I'm too old to ride in the baby seat. I'm a big boy now, and a good boy, for I never run off on my own when I'm shopping with my mom. I walk beside her quietly, like the good boy I am. We get in the checkout line behind a dark haired lady dressed in a powder blue business suit and shiny patent high heels. Her black hair is piled neatly on her head. She never looks to see any of the people around her. She has a baby in her cart. He's sitting in the baby seat like he's supposed to be, his curly blonde hair like a halo, his soft baby legs dangling, one chubby little hand holding the railing in front of him, the other clutching a piece of Red Vine liquorice. He's looking at me, his face and hands coated in sweet, sticky liquorice residue. The woman with him finally turns to face us briefly, a red vine hanging out of her

18

mouth as well. Her sour face doesn't match her nice clothes and pretty hair.

The little boy reaches out for me as if to say, "Come here!" And I go to him, which is something I never do. I don't talk to strangers, no matter how old, or young, they may be. But I go to the little boy in the cart. I don't even like Red Vine liquorice, but I go to him. "You have big eyes!" I tell him, and he smiles and laughs at me. "How old is he?" I ask his mother.

"Two," the woman grunts, grabbing several more packs of Red Vines, along with a bunch of beef jerky packs. "These too," she tells the cashier. She seems unfriendly. She won't look at me. I glance backward to my own mom, who smiles gently.

I turn back to the blue-eyed baby boy and he reaches for me again, the little pink bow of his mouth curling up in a smile. I shake his gooey hand, "I'm Tammy. How do you do?"

The baby giggles. "What's his name, please?" I ask the woman whose eyes match his. She ignores me. My heart stings, and I look at my mom again. She just smiles and shakes her head. I turn back when the baby babbles musically, his relatively new and unabused vocal cords manufacturing the loveliest sounds I've ever heard as he jabbers and coos like a magpie. "He's so sweet!" my mother exclaims. The baby's mom continues to disregard everything we say and everything her baby does.

I wish I knew what he was trying to talk to me about! I stand on tiptoe and take his sticky pink hand in my own. "You don't say!" I gasp. "Is that right?" The more I respond to him, the more the baby loves it, filling my ears with enchanting gurgles and coos of delight.

His mother finishes paying for her groceries and says flatly, "Come on, Jamie. Let's get out of here."

"Jamie? Is that his name?" I ask desperately. The dark-haired woman blinks her blue eyes rapidly at me and in her grown-up-irritated-at-annoying-child voice, says, "Yeah, Jamie. What do you care? You won't ever see him again!" Tears crowd in my eyes as I turn back to my mother. She looks like she's likely to say something to this rude, haughty, dark haired lady who now turns to look for the bag boy. As her attention is taken *from us, I stand on tiptoe again and kiss the baby's liquorice-coated cheek. He smiles, leans down over the safety bar in front of him, and kisses my mouth.*

Love's first kisses.

Then she takes him away from me.

In the car on the way home, I cry, tears mixing with the sticky stuff on my face. "I wish I could be his friend forever," I sniffle.

"I know, honey," Mom says.

I don't think I'll ever forget those blue eyes.

But I do.

By the next day, I stop thinking about the baby in the cart.

I forget about him for a long, long time.

But it won't be forever.

From the moment I am able to put words together, I realise people like me. They can't help themselves. People like pretty kids, and I'm pretty. I'm told often too, even when I get older. Oh, they don't *use* the word pretty for me. Somehow to call a man pretty is a huge no-no. Everyone thinks men squirm when they're described in that word. Not me. I know I'm a pretty boy. I'm a masculine version of my mom. I have thick black hair and eyebrows and bluish-green eyes. The girls love my lips. Killer smile too.

As long as I can remember, I've believed myself photogenic enough to have a career in the spotlight—a movie star, a music star on MTV, or better still, a famous news anchor on CNN or ABC or something. I love to watch the news, even as a very small child. My heroes are Peter Jennings, Tom Brokaw, Wolf Blitzer. I also get to see the last few years of Cronkite's heroic reign.

In the third grade, I have several friends from church and school: Ray Battle, a big stocky boy a year older than me, Stacy Pendleton, a girl who's in kindergarten, and Benny Feldman, a tall, lanky fifth grader. After school and on Sunday afternoons, we chuck our clean clothes and dig forts out in Benny's backyard. Later, we make videos of ourselves doing commercials and newscasts. It's great practice. I'm always the leader, and I love the attention I get from Stacy, and from Ray's sister Yvette.

I spend childhood practising my smile, the one Uncle Price likes so much. When he and Aunt Sharon come to visit, he steals me away and we go to the movies or ball games, or to see the ocean. He even takes me to Marriott's Great America a couple of times, just us two.

I'm lucky to have him. Mom's worked in the meat department at Lucky's for many years, but she's had to take a year off because of carpal tunnel in her hands from wrapping meat eight hours a day. She gets disability now, and can never afford to take me places anymore. What little she gets has to go for bills and the payment on our bluish-grey wood panelled house on Truckee Street that we've lived in since she bought it after my first birthday. It's a smallish three bedroom house, built in the thirties or so. The front lawn is really small, not even two yards, separated in the centre by a red cement walk that doesn't match the three wooden stairs that go up to the smooth, glossy white concrete porch. The front porch is cooled all year round by the shade of an ancient live oak. Around each window, deep pink camellias bloom, and Mom parks her feisty old Ford Granada in the unpaved drive to the right of the house.

We're not as close as we used to be. She used to take me somewhere almost every weekend. Or, if we stayed home, we'd watch funny old shows together, like *I Love Lucy*, *The Three Stooges*, or *Bugs Bunny* cartoons. Now she's in pain all the time, both arms in braces. We live on frozen waffles. I butter for both of us and pour her coffee. I look after her quite a bit during this year. I don't get to play with my friends as often as I used to because Mom needs me around to help. It's a lonely life, and I blame her. She's always popping pain pills, so she's always drowsy and out of it. I have no-one to talk to.

I'm thrilled when Uncle and Aunt move up from Stockton so we can see each other more. He's glad to have a nephew, he always says. Aunt Sharon can't seem to get pregnant so they can have a beautiful boy of their own, he tells me, so he's awful glad I'm here. I'm happy they can't have kids. I have him all for me, and he tells me, all the time, that he loves me. His attention makes me feel special. He asks me to do things with him, but I'm afraid and say no. He just says, "Okay," and holds me close to him while we watch *Scooby-Doo* or *Tom and Jerry*. He's a good-looking guy, about six years older than my mom, tall, shares our almost-black hair and dark green eyes. He's not as cute as Christopher Reeve in *Superman*, but he's close.

I tell him I want to be special, famous, loved the world over. "You *are* special, Tammy. You're beautiful, smart—you've got it all. Don't forget that."

He takes pictures of me in all kinds of costumes: a football hero in big shoulder pads, a pirate with an eye patch and a sword, and an army soldier all painted with green and black camouflage. He tells me that when I'm a man I'm going to be a knockout, a lady killer. When he tucks me into bed he kisses me with his tongue in my mouth. I'm scared, but I like it too.

As I grow into the years just before teenhood, he lets me watch porn with him. Sometimes he holds me and makes me make out with him while people have sex on his TV. He unzips his fly. "Wanna touch?" he asks, and suddenly, yes, I do! I do everything he asks, and I love it. I love *him*.

Whenever we can, we sneak away, saying we're going to a show or to get pizza or to a ball game. We go to the Motel 6 off of freeway 80 in Sacramento. He never puts it in me, he just lets me touch it. Then he sucks mine. I think it's silly, him wanting to suck me. He looks ridiculous down there. I laugh sometimes, but he doesn't seem to notice. He asks me to put my mouth on him, and I'm scared. He keeps asking, and eventually, I do what he wants. I don't want to keep hurting his feelings. I want him to know how important he is to me. I don't want him to ever leave me.

Even after Mom is back to work and can afford to take me places again, I prefer the company of my Uncle. Mom's glad he's part of my life.

I'm not special to my dad. I don't know him. He didn't leave his wife when he slept with Mom. He's never even sent money to Mom after he got her pregnant. He doesn't acknowledge me, not even when he sees me in church. That's where he and my mom met. He's the Reverend Mark Sellers, pastor of the Southern Baptist church of Sommerville.

Mom feels an increased need to attend church because of her "illicit" affair with a married man, a "man of God" to boot. She's the only one who's ever given the slightest hint that she feels badly about what happened, and the only one for sure who's had to deal with the result of the relationship, that being me.

Though she never calls me a "bastard", I feel like it's the correct term for me. She tells me not to approach him, not to bother him, that he's a man of God, and that it wasn't his fault, it was hers. He's a prick to allow her to shoulder all the blame, and she's an idiot, blaming herself, while he just goes on with his life and his wife, pretending I don't exist, treating me like the invisible boy, because I'm the product of his adulterous urges. Leave it to Pastor Asshole to put himself before his own son, ignore my presence, never give a clue that would tarnish his "fine, upstanding Christian reputation".

I'd say, fuck him, but I can't. He's my dad.

The "thing" with Uncle Price lasts a year or so. When I'm almost eleven, he tells me Aunt Sharon is preg, and I know things are going to be different. I try to lure him to me by groping him and whispering in his ear. I tell him I love him and that I need a dad, that I want him to be my dad, not just my uncle. But he's so preoccupied with that stupid baby on the way that he pushes my hands away and says, "We can't do that anymore, Tam." I demand to know why, but he never explains. It's never occurred to me that what we've been doing is *wrong*. Uncle never says, "it's wrong", or "it's dirty". He just says, "We can't. I'm going to have a baby."

And I hate that baby. From the moment I first hear of her existence and far beyond the day she plops out of Aunt.

I hate the way she looks just like Uncle Price.

I hate that she has a dad and I don't.

23

I think of ways I can kill her and make it look like an accident or nature. One day I am *this* close to pinching her tiny nose shut, but then Aunt comes in and I pretend to be pinching her stupid fat pink cheeks. I smile and tell them how adorable Natalie is. Uncle says he's busier since the baby, and has no time to come visit us like he used to.

I hate her.

Early on I begin expressing my anger by being cruel to innocent bystanders. It will become a habit, blaming those who are blameless. I don't tell anyone what Uncle has done to me. Around town, I begin to notice him with his arm around other boys, boys who are around the age I was when I fell in love with him. Why does he have time to hang around with them if he's so fucking busy?! The jealousy in me burns and festers. How could he discard me and what we had together? He barely speaks to me when he and Aunt visit. The hatred born of his rejection begins to ooze foul green pus. I love him, I hate him, I want to *kill* him.

He told me he loved me!

My mom is a good, sweet, kind person, but she tries too hard with me. She has no idea how mad (in all known ways) I am. The more she tries—to get me to talk to her, spend time with her, like I used to, to get me to be a good boy, to get me to be more interested in Church, to get me to accept Jesus, be baptised and become a Christian—the more I rebel, fuelled by the rage Uncle Price left behind.

And the rage at my father, that sanctimonious prick who stands at the pulpit, Sunday after Sunday, preaching hellfire and damnation to "kids who don't live by the Word of God," all the while disregarding me like a piece of crap in the gutter.

I start to hate Mom too. I blame her for having to work and not being around enough. I blame her for being dumb enough to screw a married man. I blame her because he doesn't want to be my dad.

When she is home, she tries to establish a rapport with me. "Please talk to me, honey," she pleads. "We used to talk. What's bothering you? Please tell me." My side of the conversation is in single word sentences, one syllable replies.

In an attempt to show her love, she gets me a puppy. He's small, white and furry, part Pom and part Chihuahua, and I name him Cotton. I abuse him whenever Mom's at work, holding him down and grinding my elbow into his paw until he emits high-pitched screams of misery. The frightened look in his round black eyes makes me hate him *more*, so I beat him. He lays down and cowers whenever I go to pick him up, trying to prepare himself for my meanness.

I stick my fingers up his rear end like I've seen Uncle Price doing to Natalie not long after her first birthday. I don't think it, I don't plan it. I just do it. I feel like I'm in some kind of a trance. I'm not truly aware that I'm doing it, or that someone is watching me, until I hear Mom's voice, miraculously composed, "Tammy, don't do that."

I'm relieved when she gives Cotton away.

Mom begins to avoid me around the house. Seeing me doing revolting things to my dog has caused her to raise a wall around herself. I'm left lonely, alienated, misunderstood. I hate how she's afraid of me.

And I hate her more than ever before.

Having long since grown apart from the kids I did the newscasts with, I hang out with boys whose names I scarcely remember. The class clowns, we mouth off to the teachers and disrupt class any way we can, always seeking to make people laugh. The principal has had several conferences with Mom before seventh grade is half over. She grounds me, makes me get up on Saturday mornings to do yard work, drags me to service every Sunday.

But nothing works. After school, my friends and I sneak behind old buildings and smoke pot. We go to Chris's house to play video games until his mom comes home. Todd's dad likes guns, and though most of the good ones are locked in his safe, we have access to the BB guns, and we begin shooting at birds and cats. One day I shoot a robin and knock him off his feet, then I aim the BB directly at his chest. It doesn't even occur to me that what I'm doing is cruel, since the other kids do no different. I only know that it balms the sore inside of me.

I want to talk, really talk to these friends, about the

disturbing things in my head, but they're not interested in discussing anything except movies, music, video games, sports, weed, chicks and porn. I'm nowhere near as close to them as I was to Ray, Stacy and Benny.

I try to cry. I sit with my eyes wide open until they begin to dry, and hope tears will come to them. Nothing happens. I have to find other ways to grieve the loss of Uncle's love, the absence of my dad's.

During my thirteenth year, I start going to the library to check out books about famous killers like Charles Manson, Ted Bundy, the Boston Strangler, etc. When the librarian asks why a boy barely into his teens is so interested in serial killers, I tell them it's research, and half of me is telling the truth. It's preparation for my great future as a top newsman, perhaps a famous exposé reporter, a true-crime authority like Bill Kurtis.

The other half of me reads the grisly books with a keen absorption that spooks me. I begin to scribble my dark thoughts into "marble" pads, fantasies about doing away with Natalie, who is now going on three years old. A girly-girl already, she has a huge collection of Barbies, Kens, Skippers, and PJs.

My stories morph into a serial about a serial killer who murders young girls and chops up their bodies. The girls are of different hair and eye colour, all shapes and sizes, all pretty. Later, my victims are older men. The lurid particulars of my writings repulse me, but not enough to stop. I'm an angry boy. I steal Natalie's dolls and beat them and scalp them, slash them open, tear their plastic limbs off, and bury them in the backyard.

Mom is always working, and I'm a latchkey kid, so I go untreated.

Until Mom, upset by my refusal to relate to her, but still too traumatised by what she witnessed with Cotton to try to relate to me, urges Pastor Asshole to "talk to me". I go to his office at the church, believing he's called this meeting to inform me that he's finally going to acknowledge that I'm his offspring, that he's going to be the dad I so badly want and need. I give him my hope-filled attention, searching his sternly handsome countenance for any signs of myself in that coffee brown hair, or those narrow, somewhat severe brown eyes. I perk my ears,

26

keen to hear his plan to involve me in his life straight away.

Nope. He proceeds to chastise me about my choice of friends, my "dabblings with dope" (I have only smoked two or three joints thus far, and beer isn't a drug!), and the shameful matter of what happened with Cotton. He tells me about the evils of bestiality while I sit, shifting from annoyance to anger to shame to nausea. By the time Pastor has finished his sermon, I feel as tall as a microbe. After our little get-together in his office, he goes back to barely speaking to me.

The shame pierces me deeply, and I hate my mom all the more. Thinking Pastor's fixed everything all hunky dory, she tries to make small talk with me, tries to invite me out to movies on her days off.

I ignore her.

I pray to a God whose existence I question, *Please don't let me be evil. Please don't let me hurt any more dogs, or cats, or birds, or any other animals... and please don't let me hurt any people. Please make me a good person. I don't want Mom to be afraid of me. Please make me good. Please...*

When I begin high school at the age of fourteen, I should be a fledgling serial killer, but somehow, I defy the standard behavioural trajectory predicted by FBI profilers. Hormones begin flowing, and instead of wanting to kill pretty girls, I just want to fuck them. I lose interest in the compulsions of serial killers and in swiping Natalie's Barbie and Ken dolls. My desires turning away from death and destruction, transforming into a voracious appetite for sex.

I'll show that bastard that I'm better than those new boys of his.

I begin banging every chick that will let me within ten feet of her. I appreciate how abnormal my interests have run the past year or two, and perhaps being a teenaged horn-dog doesn't make me a "good" person, but when compared side by side with being fascinated by murder and blood, it's the lesser of the two evils.

I don't read those journals anymore. I'd like to throw them and their unspeakable contents into the bin, but I'm afraid someone will find and read them. I'd like to burn or shred them, but I don't have a shredder, and there's no place I can light a fire around here without drawing attention to myself. So I stuff them into my bookcase, behind a neglected set of orange Funk & Wagnall encyclopaedias.

I leave my gun-loving, bird-shooting friends behind, begin attending church willingly (I want to be a *good* person, remember), and reconnect with my old pals Ray and Benny. The robin I killed will haunt me for years after. Luckily, none of the cats I ever shot at have suffered. I was never close enough to get a good shot.

I'm so ashamed when I realise how awful I've been, how mean. Why did I desire to hurt other lives? I remember the Golden Rule from Sunday school: do unto others...

I'm changed.

I'm a good boy now.

But I've forgotten to thank God for answering the prayer I said some months ago.

I've forgotten that I had even *said* a prayer.

I don't know I'm a victim.

four:

jamie pearce
(aged thirteen to fourteen)

The neighbours across the road tell the police that they heard loud pops, but that they weren't sure if they were gunshots. It's the stench of putrefaction, of human flesh gently cooked by an unseasonable late April heat that prompts them to call. The cops break in and find my mom and daddy rotting. Every room is searched. The house is beyond filthy. Drug paraphernalia are everywhere. Dirt and hair are so thick on the floors that it sticks to their shoes. Mouldy food sits in pans on the cooker. More mould floats on the dishwater. The toilets are coated with shit and grime.

They use bolt cutters to get the locks off of my door and find me lying in purulent pools of faeces, urine and vomit. I can't answer any of their questions. "How long you been locked in here?"; "What's your name?"; "Were they your parents, or were you abducted?". I can't even tell them how long it's been since the shooting. Time has burned away noiselessly.

In the ER, I throw up my most recent meal, which has been sitting undigested for days in my gut: paint chips, wood chips, a scrap of bedsheet, all mixed with black, clotted blood so horribly foul that the police and the nurses and doctors all wrinkle their noses. I'm so ashamed I begin to cry.

I hear them talking about me as they shift my body from stretcher to bed, poke IVs into my arms and stick all manner of tubes up my nose, down my throat and up into my bladder. "There's no way," the doctors say. "He's dying. He weighs forty-three pounds."

I want to die. I need to die. At long last, the mercy of death, an end to this guilt, pain, hunger and endless desolation that has lasted the whole of my short life.

The two cops who had found me turn away. I can hear them crying. I keep drifting in and out, but whenever I'm in, I stare at the backs of the two cops. My mind is enshrouded with a thick narcotic fog, and I fight my way through it to form two questions: How could my parents do what they've done to me? How can total strangers care so much about me that they're crying? Something bursts through my will, my decision to let go and stop fighting. My heart is clogged with a wondrous pain. I know now that I have to live. If those two policemen can care enough about me to cry, there must be something to live for. I don't rationalise this as clearly as it appears on paper, but I know I need to survive. It's not necessarily my preference. It's just what I *have* to do.

They do their part, the docs and nurses, and I do mine. The feeding tube gives me strength. My kidneys have been ravaged by starvation and dehydration, but they're not totally destroyed, and once I am able to eat and drink on my own, they come alive, working overtime, flushing my body out. I've never had to pee so much in my life!

Three weeks after I am discovered half dead, I go to a less intensive floor at the hospital. A week after that I am given to social services. One of the policemen who saved me, Lloyd Tafford, becomes my foster dad. While I'm laid up, he prepares his home for me. It's a small country house a mile outside Sommerville going towards Sacramento, made almost entirely of bricks. He only has about eight years left to pay on it.

The day I go home with him, Channel 10 comes to cover my story, and everyone in town is there. The sun is out, the sky is a beautiful, pure blue, with cottony clouds. I smell flowers and freshly mowed lawn. I feel like I've just been born.

It's the first time I've ever been in front of a crowd. I'm scared at first, not used to so many eyes on me, wondering what they're thinking. They call me a hero and I'm embarrassed. "I'm not the hero," I tell them. "The police are the heroes. I'm not the one who saved somebody's life."

I'm so thankful to Lloyd for adopting me, for giving me a home.

But it's not easy getting used to a new home, or learning to trust a new parent. After all I've been through, I'm afraid. I can't tell him what I'm afraid of, only that I'm afraid. He soon learns that I'm afraid to let him, or anyone, touch me in any way. When Officer Bloom (Lloyd's partner on the force) comes over, or anyone from town stops by just to talk, I retreat to my new room and resist coming out. It takes a lot of coaxing. When anyone walks toward me to say hello, I become rigid as ice—I can't help it—my eyes filled with alarm and misgiving. I'm on guard even during sleep, my body curled into a tight ball. For the first few weeks it's awful, and Lloyd cries at least once a day, not just because his new son is terrified and unresponsive, but because he can't stop remembering the images from the first day he met me.

One night he begins to describe his recollections in detail. "You had big sores on your back from laying there so long. On your ankles where the chains dug into you. When I lifted you off the mattress you were so light—I almost threw up just from how light you were. You were barely there."

I wait for him to mention the infections all over my skin or the old scars in my anus, but he doesn't.

And then he hugs me, and I stiffen as usual. His big body shudders with sobs and something inside me softens. I put my arms around him and hug him back for the first time. His arms tighten, crushing me against him and the ice inside of me begins to drip away swiftly.

After that night, I crave his hugs. I think I *grow* on them. I gain weight and get taller, despite the doctors' fears that I'll be stunted because of the starvation and the kidney damage. By the time I'm fully grown, I'm nearly five-six.

⁂

In those first tranquil months with Lloyd Tafford, my permanent personality emerges. Lloyd is as much an influence on that as my biological parents. It's still there, that fear, but now I have Lloyd to balance me, and keep it from dominating every second of my life.

Lloyd's never been married, and my coming into his life must have awakened an instinct to love and nurture. He's a great, tall man with dark curly hair and a shy personality. He's a gentle man, not just a gentleman. He grew up in Van Buren, a small town in Arkansas. I've never been out of California, not since that long ago, blurry trip to Oregon. I love the way Lloyd talks. It's not an out and out twang or a deep-Southern drawl. It's very subtle. Only a person with a great ear for non-Californian accents would be able to detect all the unusual inflections, which I adopt as I grow up in his home. I'm glad to have an accent. I'm glad to be able to talk at all. When my birth parents stopped coming to my room, I had nobody to talk to, so I stopped speaking.

With Lloyd, I am introduced to a peaceful, nostalgic world. He loves old radio shows that I've never heard of, like *Fibber McGee & Molly*, *The Great Gildersleeve*, and *Jack Benny*. In winter, he likes to cover up with quilts while listening to these shows, or old music from the fifties. He loves really old movies starring Humphrey Bogart, Bob Hope, Cary Grant. In summer, he enjoys sitting outside on the back porch made of bricks, drinking lemonade and watching bees and hummingbirds sparring over the red liquid he puts into their feeders.

He cries easily, and after so many years of burying my most intense emotions deep inside, I cry a lot too, and the stupidest things set me off, like sad endings of old movies or the first sight I have of the Pacific Ocean. I fall immediately and absolutely in love with the broad, churning teal expanse, even the smells of sand and salt and seaweed. "Let's *move* to the ocean!" I beg him.

32

In fact, after smelling nothing but the rank odours of my own unwashed body—ancient sweat, pasty dead skin, stale urine and my own excrement—along with Daddy's semen—for so many years, I've come to love my sense of smell again. I never go into the bakery department of a grocery shop and take for granted the warm aroma of fresh bread.

All of my senses reawaken. When I see and smell my first rainfall outside Lloyd's front door, I run out and dance in it, loving the sound of the rain rattling the dry leaves, the sting of cold drops splattering on my skin. I trail my fingers over the bright green moss growing on the old, cracked bricks on the porch. I have a cold the next day.

My story slowly inches its way though town, from mouth to mouth. It's moved people to write letters of outrage and encouragement to me and Lloyd. On the street, people stare at me. I don't know if I see visages of fascination, curiosity or admiration. I know some of them want to talk to me, ask me how I emerged from hell alive, what went on in that room…

And I'm glad they don't.

Even though Lloyd and I are celebrities in Sommerville, we prefer to keep to ourselves. In fact, Lloyd is every bit the recluse and eccentric I am. Away from work, he likes to be at home. Our companions of preference are the stray alley cats we've adopted. We spoil them rotten.

I adore these kitties, which we call our "kids". Whenever one of them comes in with a runny nose or a goathead sticker embedded in the tender pink pad of a paw, I fuss over them with warm, wet washcloths and salt water soaks, and I decide to become a veterinarian.

We go to church at the Southern Baptist in town and that's where I discover how much I love to sing. It's the only time I come out of my shell and get in front of crowds. Once that last lyric is past my lips and I sit back down, I'm mute.

My timidity doesn't stop people, mostly older people, from stopping me on the street to ask me how Lloyd and I have been doing. Mrs. Cooke, the white-haired, coffee-skinned lady who runs the bakery on Main Street, calls me in and packs a dozen chocolate frosted éclairs into a pink box. Lloyd loves them, but with their creamy pudding centres, they remind me too much of Ding Dongs and Ho Hos. I politely nibble them to appease Lloyd, then I hide them in a napkin.

I enter school with only a week left of eighth grade, then I am placed into summer school to get caught up. I learn that kids my age are different from older people. I haven't seen a classroom since I was six or seven years old, and at thirteen, I have to learn the very basics of maths. I can't read or spell. I have trouble with dyslexia, always transposing numbers or writing my 'E's and '3's backwards. It's humiliating, and some of the kids are heartless. It's bad enough I'm very small for my age, and their taunting over my reading level makes me feel like a baby. Nothing shields me from the critical scrutiny of my peers. It's so bad some days that I beg Lloyd to let me stay home.

I meet Stacy Pendleton and her girlfriends a few days after I begin school, and soon the bunch of us are palling around and they're guarding me against the meanness of the others. They surround me like hens defending a little yellow chick, promptly dubbing me their "Baby" or "Babe".

Stacy's pretty, with almond shaped amber eyes and long brown hair that she takes to the salon for a spiral perm every few weeks, until too many chemicals have totally fried it and she has it cut into a cute, short pixie do.

Stacy becomes my best friend. She's so laid back, yet kind of wild and crazy, always the one to come up with a scheme. At first, we all ring doorbells and run away, we have food fights in the cafeteria and get sent to the principal's office, those kinds of things. Not long later, we discover we love music, especially the music that was new when we were babies. We listen to '80s new wave like Human League, Bananarama, Pat Benetar, the Police, U2 and the Smiths. We also like R&B music from the Isley Brothers, the Mary Jane Girls, Rick James, Prince, and Michael Jackson before "Thriller" was released. We practise singing songs from these bands, and we talk about becoming our own band one day.

The group of us dress alike, day after day. I'm not into frilly or flowery stuff and neither is Stacy, who is called a "tomboy" because of her disdain for pink party dresses and oversized hair bows. We just like to wear jeans and printed tees of our favourite movies or bands, even in church. We dye our hair crazy colours, Stacy's pixie cut in electric purple and my shoulder-length waves in dark magenta with bright yellow stripes. It's then that the pastor at the Baptist church politely tells me that I can't sing at the pulpit again until I dye it back to its natural colour. I'm stung, but I decide I'd rather sing new wave anyway.

I get my ears pierced and Stacy gets a nose ring. She gets an electric guitar and I get a karaoke machine. We begin a "goth" phase together, and get high by sniffing the black polish we paint our nails with before adding a topcoat of glitter. We like to get high, and we ask each other in whispers if it's wrong to inhale nail lacquer and take our brains to weird, wavering, colourful places. My new girlfriends begin smoking, and of course I'm invited to join them. The first sight I have of a lit cancer stick triggers images and sense memories, but before long, I become one of those awful people who actually *loves* to smoke.

Stacy's as lonely as I am. The thing is, we're having too much fun to realise it. Her parents are divorced, her mom having taken her older sister Michelle to live in Texas. Her dad is an agent at the Farmer's Insurance office in West Sac. Our experimentation with mind-expansion evolves into swallowing his Vicodin and drinking his beer after school. She gets pizza and ice cream out of the icebox for us to eat, and gets mad at me when I only have a few bites. She hates it when I go home, and wishes I could spend nights at her house, but her dad says no.

Pastor Sellers insists on a sit-down with Lloyd about me. I'm not invited, but Lloyd tells me everything. He tells me that Pastor is concerned about my "burgeoning sexuality", and Pastor says that now is the time to nip me in the bud about my pierced ears, my enjoyment of lip liners and mascara, my coloured hair, my penchant for black rubber bracelets, leather chokers, and other gothic jewellery, my non-existent interest in sports, having a girl as a best friend, et cetera and so on.

Lloyd is the best person on earth. He tells me, "Forget that windbag! Sitting around passing judgment on you, on everyone around him, while he ignores his own son!"

"Who's his son?" I ask.

"His name is Timmy," replies Lloyd. "My sister and his mama were friends, years ago. Big, good looking boy, on the football team, I think. He's still in school—you'll probably see him when you start high school. Don't tell anyone what I told you about the pastor. Timmy's mama told me about all that a few years ago, and I promised her I wouldn't tell anyone 'cause she's embarrassed he's married, you know. Just a bad mistake, she said. He ignores her and pretends that boy ain't his... I don't think a lot of folks in town know about the matter, so please don't say nothing... I don't want to get her upset at me.

"Anyway, forget Pastor Sellers. You are who you are. I'm never going to force you to be someone you're not. The Lord loves you as you are. And you're a good boy, Jamie."

We begin to miss church more often than not. Stacy and I find our outlet for singing at keggers. Stacy has to be there. I might be able to perform for a crowd, but *never* on my own. It's one thing to sing solo in front of older, kinder church people. It's something else entirely to try to sing in front of my peers. With each performance, our voices refine. People actually begin telling us how well we sing.

"Ray, where's Temmy been lately?" asks Stacy at a party one weekend.

"You know Temmy," a dark haired guy replies with a smile. "If he's got a girl with her legs open, that's high priority. He 'couldn't make it'. That's what I'll hear on Monday."

"Who's Temmy?" I ask. What a strange name!

"Who are you?" the guy asks me, raising his eyebrows at my hair and makeup.

"Ray, this is Jamie," Stacy introduces me.

"You'll meet Temmy sooner or later, I guarantee that," Ray snickers. "He'd have been here tonight. No parents. Lots of beer. Tons of chicks. Where there's girls, there's Temmy, but he had a date tonight, a guarantee, if I know my sister."

"Temmy's fucking *Yvette* now?!" Stacy chortles. "Oh my God, you're kidding!"

"Yup," Ray nods. "She finally snagged him. Won't be long till she's picking shitty wedding songs, God help us!"

After that night, Ray and his friend, an older guy named Benny, are part of our little clique, and it's not as fun. The girls take to whispering and giggling and acting silly when the guys are around. Besides, I think Ray and Benny are nosey and intrusive, always telling me about girls they know are single. I smoothly refuse their offers to introduce me. I just don't feel interested. Stacy's never been pushy like that.

Sometimes, I worry Stacy will start to like me in a romantic way. I hope not. I love her to pieces, but only as a friend. I feel so comfortable with her and I don't want to lose that. I've never had a best friend, and to lose her would end me.

Some mornings, Stacy comes over to my house an hour or so before school, and I borrow her makeup stuff. I use powder to conceal the light spatter of golden freckles over my nose. I use dark pink pencil to draw a line around my mouth, and then fill my lips in with shiny gloss. I *love* what Stacy's mascara does to my eyes. As I check myself in the bathroom mirror, Stacy hugs my shoulders from the side. "Look how pretty you are!" she beams.

I've gotten better with mirrors. As long as the mascara erases all traces of Mom's crazed, bloodshot eyes, as long as my fuchsia and neon yellow dyes have obliterated Daddy's honey blonde hair, I can look at myself in the mirror without feeling nauseated, without feeling the red rings of memory around my ankles begin to throb...

Once, Benny asks point blank if I'm gay, why I'm always tagging along with Stacy and always surrounded by her girlfriends and why I'm right in there painting my fingers and dyeing my hair. No other guy at middle school or at church wears makeup. No other guy at school or church has mostly

37

girls for friends either. Ray and Benny don't "get" me any better than other boys do. I don't wear makeup to seek attention. I wear makeup because it's always felt like the thing for me to do, and because I love makeup. Anyway, I know most of the boys ignore me, or they make remarks like, "I guess Jamie can *also* be a *girl's* name!". I'd be hurt if I didn't like being "one of Stacy's girls" so much.

Unfortunately, one of our girls, a pretty Mexican girl named Lydia Rocha, tells Stacy she likes me. Though I've always loved Lydia and had fun times with her, I have to avoid her for a few days, afraid she'll think I like her back in that same way. She's hurt of course, and stays away for a while. I'm relieved when later on, she tells everyone she has a crush on that guy "Temmy".

It's never occurred to me that I might be gay. I only know that unlike most of the other boys my age, thirteen going on fourteen, I've never kissed a girl or held hands or anything. But I've never been kissed or touched by a boy either. Instinctively, I know I keep to myself because I'm ruined. Lloyd's goodness can't remedy the damage done long before he came along.

Whenever Stacy gently hints or asks, I tell her I simply don't *know* what I am, gay, straight, bi. If the truth be told, I'm one of the A-Team. I don't feel attracted to *anyone*. I don't seek out that kind of companionship, I avoid it. As I get used to life outside that filthy bedroom, I realise that what me and Daddy did was wrong, and the mortification inside of me swells and throbs. I don't want to do that ever again. I hear kids at school talking about sex and how fun it is. I remember the sex I had with Daddy and it makes me nauseous. I don't ever want to be naked and do those disgusting things ever again.

I've told Stacy the barest version of what my birth parents did to me. Aside from Lloyd, Stacy is the only person who knows much at all about me. Of course, in the back of my mind is the fact that the Sommerville Police know things too, that they found things when they found me locked in my room. Channel 10 probably has some souvenirs as well.

There are others too, from long ago. I've always known there are others who know, people who liked the videos… I try not to think about it, how there are people on this planet who know the darkest, most wretched details about that room, those chains, that bed.

If I pick up the slightest indication that a girl is interested in me, I leave the situation immediately.

Fortunately, no guy has ever been interested, so I don't have to face the gay questions head on.

I have my *own* idea about when it's fun to be admired, and that's when I get up and sing on Thursday nights at The End, the only bar in town that lets kids in to sing karaoke. We've been going almost every week. The whole town seems to love it. Unless he has to work, Lloyd doesn't miss a chance to come see me sing, and he cries sometimes when we're up there. I'd be embarrassed, but I love him too much.

The only touches I accept are the warm, secure embraces from Lloyd and Stacy's friendly, energetic hugs.

To be frank, I've never kissed my foster dad, except maybe a peck or two over the past year. I feel bad about it—I don't know—I guess I'm just not a kissy person. I love hugging him, and I have let him kiss me, on the cheek or forehead a few times. I hope he knows I *do* love him. I tell him every now and again, but I still wonder if he *knows*.

At about the same time Stacy and I begin frequenting The End, we begin high school, and that's when everything suddenly changes, and I fall in love for the first and last time.

five:

tammy
(high school)

While I'm an underclassman, I learn that the seniors at
Sommerville High School know how to find the best parties in
Davis and Sac, and it's easy to charm my way into getting rides
from them. I bag my first piece of ass at fourteen. Her name is
Karla Grey, and she's a sophomore at UC Davis. She's short,
curvaceous, with straight honey blonde hair and a perpetually
grouchy expression. She's not interested in getting serious with
a high school freshman, and for all of a week, I carry a torch
before forgetting about her and hooking up with a twenty-four
year old redhead from Sac State.

As the first three years of high school unfurl, I find that the
days practising my smile in the mirror have been well spent. I
hardly study, but I manage a low A average, my best grades
being in English, Creative Writing, and Journalism. I'm no nerd,
and a 3.6 GPA will be enough to get me out of this pathetic
town.

I'm a reporter for the *Panther*, Sommerville High's school
paper all four years as well. At first I'm just a staff writer,
covering plays from the drama department, band and choir
performances for the music department, the efforts of SADD to

curb teen drinking and driving (yeah right!), club fundraisers, student body elections, and how-do-you-do-let's-get-to-know-you interviews of the foreign exchange students.

It's boring as fuck, but it's valuable experience for my future sitting alongside Wolf or Tom, and it's an outlet for my urge to write (even if it is stuff I find boring as fuck), and I get to travel to other schools all over the state (which means I get to hook up with all kinds of girls who aren't from Sommerville).

In my junior year, I'm promoted to head sports writer for the *Panther*. Let's face it, unless it's something I find important or at least interesting, like a crime against a student, or maybe vandalism against a teacher's car (heh!) I could care less. In this dull hamlet, sport is the most exciting thing I can write about.

I'm too busy trying to get into every girl's pants I can to bother with exhausting myself over piles of homework. Besides, I've gotta be sure to save my best for the game on Friday nights. I'm a fullback, number 19. It doesn't matter that I only score a touchdown every three or four weeks. What matters is I score with every chick I can. The combination of height, shoulder pads and mud is magnetic, and once I've been introduced to the pleasures of the flesh, I'm beyond hope. My groupies tell me I'm destined to be famous, and I'm already planning on moving to Los Angeles after graduation. I'm going to one of the *good* schools (no crappy community colleges for *me!*), getting my degree, and working for ABC or NBC News.

But I'm frightened of what was once inside of me. I hate that part of me that wrote stories of murder only a couple of years ago. I don't want to be a bad person. I want people to love me, not be afraid of me.

I don't know why I wrote that shit, why I beat poor little Cotton, why I've been so cruel. I hate to even think about it. I still wish I could get rid of those dust-coated diaries in my bookcase.

I turn seventeen in September of my senior year. One day,

one of the legion of sluts I regularly boink invites me to church. I'd rather have a root canal than see my old man, but the girl tells me she'll reward me afterward, so I consent. She's one of the girls I knew as a kid, Yvette Battle, Ray's sister. She's tall and brunette with black, beady eyes and a big, round rear end. She's really great in bed. The fact that she pretends to be such a good little God-fearing girl makes it hot. Every guy who's had her agrees to that. She suggestively whispers to me as my dad, the Pastor, lists all the prayer needs and requests.

"We need to pray for our sister, Evelyn Beehan, who's still battling breast cancer. And Frances Blackwell, who had her knees replaced. We should also remember Andy Welling, who is flying to Florida this week for his brother's funeral." The pastor goes down a long list. Then he asks, "And are there any unspoken requests this morning?" Several hands raise. "Alright then, take the hand of the person next to you as we pray."

Yvette's naughty words are in my left ear as I turn to my right to see whose hand I'm holding. It's a kid, small with wavy dark red hair, blonde at the tips. His head is lowered reverently. To his right is Stacy Pendleton, the girl I knew years ago. There's no mistaking that purple hair of hers. The principal's already threatened to suspend her, and she still hasn't dyed over it.

I start to recognise the boy as the one who's always been with Stacy the past month, as they've scurried all over the high school grounds, exploring their new territory. I glance down at him again.

Once, I think I've seen this little kid singing with Stacy at a kegger in Solano a month ago, only then it seemed like it was a brighter raspberry fuchsia with bright yellow at the ends.

The preacher asks us to stand, hands still joined, so we can all sing together. Yvette fondles my ass and starts whispering again. I plan to turn to her and whisper my reply, but instead I look to my right, and my eyes meet those of the boy holding my right hand.

They're blue. I've never seen eyes so blue.

Déjà vu. I feel like I've seen those eyes somewhere…

I can't remember where I could have seen him.

Enormous and set off by unplucked, yet graceful, naturally arched brows, his eyes nearly dominate his face. In that moment when our eyes meet, I quickly examine the rest of him.

I can't believe this kid's a freshman. He's probably only two or three years or so younger than me, but he's *tiny*. He looks way too small to be in high school. He's even shorter and smaller than Stacy, his skinny figure encased in a Depeche Mode t-shirt and black jeans. His little face is exotic and peculiar, with surprisingly high cheekbones, a pert little nose, and red lips, the kind you see on those old dolls in glass cases. He looks away, and Pastor begins droning an extended prayer. For a second, I wonder if Stacy's little friend is a girl, if I've mistaken him for a boy.

No, dumbass, I tell myself. He wouldn't be on the boys' side of the gym at P.E.

I can't stop myself from sneaking a glance at him every so often. His eyes are closed, his head is bowed towards the wine coloured carpeting, and I stare out of the corner of my eye at the long, dark fringe of his eyelashes.

The most subtle movement, a tiny contraction of his hand around mine, and my focus is fully stolen from Yvette in spite of her iniquitous attentions. I turn my head to the right, remembering the odd little flutter that happened inside me when his fingers curled just a little tighter around mine for that instant. Our eyes meet a second time as he looks up at me. The contact lasts for a few beats, but time is stretched like a rubber band. Those huge eyes open impossibly wider for a split second, and I see something I can't describe in words. I feel my stomach quiver again, and his eyes close, his fingernails gently dig into the palm of my hand…

…and I can barely breathe…

I've seen him. I know him. Where have I seen him before?!

When we're asked to sit back down in the padded mauve pews, everyone lets go of each other's hands. I can't fathom what's come over me. I've got the easiest piece of ass in town squeezing my thighs under the hymnal and instead of giving her my undivided attention, I'm…

What *am* I doing?

I have to ask myself that, because every so often, even as I scold myself fiercely, I feel my neck rotating away from Yvette, my eyes seeking his. I'm disappointed when he refuses to look my way again. After church, I search for him in the crowd, scanning for Stacy's violet hair or those big eyes.

But he's gone. Yvette has to drag me to her house. Both our moms will be gabbing in the fellowship hall for at least half an hour and then they'll have potluck. I can't believe my reluctant movements. Yvette's a guarantee when it comes to ass.

In her bed, my mind drifts away time and again. Angrily, I push the image away, the small, delicately beautiful visage, the bright, round, cobalt-blue eyes, the black bracelets encircling the slender wrist, the fingers around mine, squeezing…

It's absurd. As the hours pass, the little face fades from memory, and I can actually think about other things. It's a relief.

A few days later, I learn his name is Jamie Pearce. It's a small high school and from casual conversations, I quickly find out that he's an orphan and that one of the cops in town adopted him a year or so ago. As the weeks pass, I hear more whispers. I wonder whether to believe ninety-nine percent of them. He's never far from Stacy and Yvette's brother Ray. Sometimes he wears eye makeup. Principal's been all over him about it of course.

At the start of their freshman year, he and Stacy are both sopranos in the school choir. In late September, when the Panther sends one of the staff reporters along with the choir to cover a state competition in San Francisco, I find myself wishing I wasn't confined to the sports beat.

We're in a small town as well, and I begin to see the three of them, Ray, Stacy and Jamie, everywhere, including the Friday night home football games. One night, after we win against Rio Vista, I scoop Yvette up and plant a sloppy one on her. Feeling someone's eyes on me, I look over.

I'm magnetically drawn, *pulled*, into his eyes.

He's chewing on a rope of Red Vine liquorice.

A grocery trip with Mom long ago: a dark haired woman; a baby boy sitting in the cart ahead of us; Red Vines; the baby's

44

sweet voice and angelic blue peepers as he tried to talk to me,
reach for me...
I kissed his cheek.
He kissed my lips.
I taste the gooey sweetness.
It's him...

They're everywhere—working at the church rummage sale, riding in the van with the church youth when we all go out to eat, singing at the illicit weekend parties the seniors throw, singing at The End—they're everywhere.

And so am I. I'm not officially in the youth group of course, but Yvette insists I come along whenever and wherever they go, and since it usually results in sex afterward, I guess I don't mind.

When Ray begins going out with Stacy, Yvette starts acting like a first class bitch to Stacy and Jamie, always making comments about how her brother is too good for Stacy, and "Why do those little twerps have to tag along everywhere with us?"

One night we go to The End, where they have a karaoke contest every Thursday. Yvette, who prides herself on being one of the best voices in the church youth chorale, gets up and completely slaughters "The Rose" by Bette Midler. We sit in the back, howling our glee at how bad she is. "I could *fart* it better!" I proclaim, and everyone within hearing range of our table is bent over in such hilarity that their faces are bright red. I glance over at Stacy, Ray and Jamie as I laugh. Jamie's looking right at me, giggling helplessly in response to my comment. I feel my face involuntarily smiling back at him as I stare into his eyes for just seconds before he looks away. I'm elated, bewildered, my heart going ninety miles an hour.

Yvette is super-pissed at me when she makes her way off the stage and back to our table. She won't speak to me for the rest of the night.

Stacy and Jamie talk intensely for a few minutes. Jamie shakes his head vigorously and I hear Stacy nudging him, "Come on! It'll be awesome!" He finally stands up and follows her to the stage, hugging himself, tucking his chin into his chest, horror-stricken.

I squint through the stage lights as their song begins. It's one of my favourites, "The Warrior" by Scandal and Patty Smyth. I hardly ever hear it on the radio anymore and the cassette I had ages ago is long gone. They sing it as a duet, and I sit straight up in my chair, letting the melody, the lyrics, the rhythm flow through me. Their voices and attitudes are perfectly suited, along with their matching black shirts with long sleeves and their black jeans with rhinestones twinkling along the seams. That fear on Jamie's face when they first got on stage is gone. I *love* his voice! If it was a soprano before, it's not now. It's gotten deeper in the past couple of months. When he sings, he sounds like Billy Idol, or Morrissey, or Dave Gahan of Depeche Mode.

"His voice changed!" I say to Ray.

"Yeah," grunts Ray. "He finally sounds like he has a Y chromosome, so he's been moved to the boys' section." He sniggers, and I glare at him.

I love the energy in Jamie's slim, slight silhouette against the glare of the lights as he bounces in cadence with the music, the way his hair tumbles into his eyes. I'm so captivated that it's easy to ignore the rage I feel emanating off of Yvette like heat. The song ends and the crowd roars their approval. My eyes never leave Jamie as he and Stacy leave the stage and return to their table, bowing playfully and then sitting. Jamie feels not only my stare, but admiring eyes from all directions, and he tucks his knees under his chin.

I've been inspired by what Jamie and Stacy did. After a couple of weeks, I finally do it. I drag Ray and Benny up on stage and sing, "I Only Have Eyes For You". I wink in Yvette's direction throughout my performance, but it's not *her* I'm singing to.

Things begin to sour between me and Yvette when she begins to make snide comments about Stacy's hair, her clothes, her nose-ring, whatever. She also starts talking about Jamie because he wears the mascara sometimes, calling him "a little faggot". One night she says, "I'll prove it. I'll tell him I broke up with you and want to get with him." She returns later, boasting, "Yeah, he's a fag. He told me he wasn't interested. *Nobody* turns me down unless they're a fag."

After I've had enough, I sever ties with her as amicably as I can. She's not the kind who's without a boyfriend for long. She hooks up with Benny, who's almost twenty, and before we can blink, they're engaged. He's going into the marines in February, so they're set to get hitched in January. Yvette plans to continue high school as a married woman. I haven't bothered to ask whether or not that's allowed. If she can't return to campus, it'll be good riddance.

Even though Yvette won't have a thing to do with me now, I still hang around the church youth, sticking close to Ray and Benny. We go to some Mexican restaurant in Sactown in celebration of Yvette's upcoming nuptials (gag). In true form, she wants to hog all the attention. She starts babbling about baby names. I ask her if she's pregnant by any chance and she gives me a dirty look. "Of course not!" Benny looks more annoyed by the minute as she goes through a long list of atrocious names for boys. "And if our first is a girl, I'm gonna name her..."

"Bill!" I interrupt, and I'm surrounded by gales of mirth. Stacy and Jamie are about to choke on their chips and salsa.

I can't deny my delight whenever I see Jamie laugh or smile. He doesn't smile enough. I mean, he's always cutting up and grinning when he's with Stacy and them, but when he's alone and he doesn't know I'm watching him, he looks *sad*. I've never spoken directly to him, and I have to fight back the urge to walk up to him and ask...

The waitress comes to take our orders. I'm sitting in just the right seat for my new plan to make everyone laugh. "Yeah, let's see," I say, flipping nonchalantly through the menu. "I want a basket of chips. And some salsa, of course, and water to drink. And when I'm finished with that, I think I'll have… hmmm… some more of those great chips and salsa. Oh yeah, and you see that table over there?" I point. "Give 'em a round of waters, on me." The server is a good sport, shaking her head at me as I collect my aural reward before shrugging and ordering my usual carne asada with red rice.

On the day of the rehearsal for Yvette's wedding, I am tagging along every bit as much as Stacy and Jamie are. I'll bet it really sits well with Yvette when Ray asks Stacy, who in turn invites Jamie, to come to the church and watch the pre-production. I don't think anyone invites me. I just come. I know I'm going to enjoy myself if there's another episode of merriment that ends in Yvette being pissed beyond reason.

And there is. The sanctuary is adorned with lengths of wide, peach coloured silk ribbon, and reeks of peach roses and Yvette's Estee Slaughter perfume. The bride tries as usual to keep the focus on her and her oh-so-serious wedding business, but Stacy and Jamie (I've begun to realise that in their little capers, Stacy's usually the instigator and Jamie the reluctant-at-first-but-soon-enough-enthusiastic-as-hell follower) take possession of the mics and start lip-syncing to the song Yvette hand-picked as her "love-theme". "You Light Up My Life" by Debby Boone blasts from the speakers in the ribbon-festooned church, and Yvette's eyes are positively satanic as she observes the two serenading each other on their knees, emphatically mouthing the god-awful lyrics and laughing hysterically. Everyone is laughing, even Yvette's folks. Pastor Asshole clears his throat. "Ahem. And at this point, I'll have everyone join together in prayer." The preacher wants to practice the prayer, *now*, and waits, barely masking his impatience as he rolls back and forth in his shined black church shoes. Stacy and Jamie continue giggling, and clutching their microphones, and I just *have* to say something.

"Uhmmm, Stacy? Jamie? Will you join us in prayer?" I call, stifling a chortle, unable to keep myself from smirking at them. Pastor gives me a look.

48

For a moment, they gawk at me, thinking I'm scolding them and that I don't find them funny. But too many people are tittering. Even Benny is having a good time. I give Stacy and Jamie an approving wink, and they light up, both of them, like Christmas trees, loving that I am in on their joke. This wedding stuff is way too formal, everyone agrees, with the notable exceptions of Yvette and the old man.

When I tease him and Stacy about the Asshole wanting to get serious and pray, it's the first time I've spoken directly to Jamie. It's apparent I've opened a can of worms, when I try to sneak my millionth glance at him to find him smiling at me, his fine-featured face echoing my own joy as our eyes meet. I'm filled with both anticipation and panic as he walks in my direction, no smile, his movements ambiguous. He keeps a safe distance, his eyes refusing to meet mine again as he says softly, "You're funny."

His soft, lilting voice makes me hard. I swallow and reply with difficulty, "Oh yeah?"

"You always make us laugh." The cherry-hued petals of his mouth bloom full into a smile so gorgeous I have to bite back a moan. His eyes raise, and now *I* must look away. I'm sensing something that disturbs me so much that I grunt dismissively at him before abruptly walking over to Ray and Benny talking nearby. I don't even look back to see the effects of my sudden rudeness. I have to get away from him.

He likes me! I don't think it in words, I just feel it. My heart throbs, my cock throbs, and pleasure flash-floods warmly throughout my body. I find refuge with Ray and Benny, eager to get my mind on something else… anything…

That night I dream about him, and I wake up floating on cloud nine and simultaneously filled with anxiety and disgust in myself.

What's *wrong* with me?! Why am I acting this way, feeling this way? Why am I constantly thinking about him? Why do I always look for him in the milling crowds at school? Why does his sad little smile make me ache inside? Why do I perpetually wish he'd look at me so I can get lost in those eyes?

From that day, I'm a mess, uneasy and thrilled whenever I'm

within a few hundred feet of him, fucking *confused*, not understanding what's happening, not *wanting* what's happening (I'm not gay!), yet viscerally loving every second.

Around Valentine's Day I find a card clamped under one of my windscreen wipers. It says:

I wish I could tell you, I wish I could <u>show</u> you how I feel about you.

Other than the *XXXOOO*, it's not signed.
I hope it's from him. I can't believe myself.
Or what I do next.
I buy a bag of those little pastel candy hearts. I handpick two or three, put them in an envelope and shove them between the vents of his locker at school, praying to God nobody catches me. If anyone sees me doing this, I'll end up having to leave town before I'm ready to.

The ongoing turmoil manifests itself as moodiness. I begin reacting to Jamie's every smile, his every attempt to connect, with irate growls and icy scowls, and I watch, in covert horror, as his joy melts away, substituted by a dejection that is wrenching.

One day while I'm practising with the soccer team, someone kicks the ball and it lands right by him as he's walking home. My entire body reacts joyfully to the very sight of him. Though nobody can see it, I'm embarrassed, and it makes me so angry, at him, for existing! When he tries to pick up the ball for me, I scream so viciously at him that he flinches, stumbles backward, almost falls, and the hurt sparkling in his eyes mangles me. I never knew I could be so evil. I turn my back on the urge to put my arms around him and crush him against me…

…and I leave him standing there. I feel my soul rejecting my actions the way a body rejects a defective heart. That evening I skip dinner and go to bed early, but I don't sleep. I cry silently under my blankets in the dark. I want to wail, get this agony out of me, but if I cry too loudly, Mom will hear me. The pain sits there.

I'm miserable, but I go on doing what I'm "supposed" to do, fucking every easy girl from the home and away teams I can possibly put my dick into, bragging about my conquests in the locker room, doing everything I can to prove to myself that I'm a "normal" guy, straight, randy, meat-eating and beer-drinking, and all about pussy.

Anyway, so what? Just because I frequently catch him watching me (with those spectacular blue eyes), just because my smile (along with my huge boner) is involuntary whenever I see his smile, it doesn't *mean* anything. I'm reading too much into this! Maybe he's just *friendly*, for God's sake!

But, just in case, I never fail to enforce the sculpture—a derisive frown from the clay of my smile—so that if he *does* like me in that certain way, he'll get the message. He'll give the idea up, and he'll turn away (leaving me with a distressing pain in my centre after I've seen the resultant grief).

There's nothing here. He needs to know, and I have to be strong. I'm not gay and there's no way this can be...

And yet, whenever he's absent from school, or not there when the church youth get together for something, I'm not just dismayed, I'm desolate, unable to enjoy anything or anyone, incapable of prohibiting myself from hoping he's just late arriving on scene. After a day or more of not seeing him, a mere glimpse of him, even from a distance, is like water for a man lost in the Sahara.

six:

jamie
(high school)

It all starts in September, right after high school begins, on a Sunday at church. It's such a small thing. He simply holds my hand while we have prayer… and I've been obsessed ever since.

Stacy's the first and only one I've told, and it takes me a long, long time, at least a few weeks after school starts, to work up the courage. We've been passing notes back and forth, writing about the massive crush she's developed on Ray Battle. He got held back in sixth grade so he and his sister Yvette are both seniors. She's a snob but Ray's pretty cool. We three hang out a lot, mostly with the youth at the Baptist church, many of whom attend the high school with us. I don't go to church as often as I used to, but lately I've been willing to attend again. It's where I can see Tammy Mattheis when we're not in school.

Before I tell Stacy that I'm in love, I make her swear. Not to laugh at me. Not to think I'm a freak. Not to tell another living soul, not Lydia, or Sylvie, or Patti or Deeanna, not Ray, or that other dude Benny—not even Lloyd, as long as she lives. She promises, and when I tell her, she's so great. She doesn't say, "So you *are* gay!" She just hugs me and says, "Oh, my God, Jamie! He's so *hot*!"

He's at least two or three years my senior, stands at least six feet one inches tall, his fatless, flawless body weighing in at one-eighty or one-eighty-five. He stalks the campus like he owns it. He dresses in t-shirts fitted to flatter, jeans that hug his superb rear-end, Nike shoes, and his letterman jacket draped over those ample shoulders.

But it's not just the stuff that's so obvious about him, the beauty and confidence that is immediate and on the surface. There is something in his *eyes*, a real and solid presence of mind. He's very smart, with a self-possession that unnerves me. Believe me when I say, that is what really makes him irresistible to me. If he was the typical jock airhead, a big, dumb muscle, he wouldn't make me swoon as I do. I'm not one of his dozen or so bimbos. None of the other jocks interest me. Not a one of them can compete.

My heart pounds mercilessly in my chest and a hot blush stains the white skin of my throat and face when I see him, hear his voice, hear his name, think about him or even *talk* about him. "Oh my God," I sigh and hug her back, burying my scarlet face against her neck. "He is!"

My secret brings us closer. Our notes are now about Ray *and* Tammy. We've always heard that Mr. Monroe takes notes and reads them aloud to class when he catches people passing them. One day he takes a note from a girl and reads every private, embarrassing word to everyone. After that, Stacy and I are extremely cautious, and our grade point averages climb a notch or two.

We go to the Friday night football games to watch the guys we're in love with collide noisily in tackles and get mud splattered all over their beautiful blue, black and white uniforms. I've never wanted to play football in my life, and at my size, I doubt anyone would allow me on the team, but watching Tammy Mattheis throwing that ball, jogging lazily across the turf, running swiftly to crash against other bodies, does something to my insides.

I'm fourteen at this time, and in spite of what I'd experienced at the hands of my biological parents, I'm something of an innocent. I'm not ignorant, just ingenuous. Just because I've been penetrated and fucked, it doesn't mean I know anything about the exhilaration that comes over me whenever I look at this towering, dark haired icon whose hand held mine for the duration of a prayer.

These are *feelings* I'm having. Feelings that are *new*. Feelings that are *real*. I see the distinction between what I experienced with my parents and my feelings for Tammy.

I'm shy—far too shy to approach Tammy Mattheis and talk to him. My introversion is an enduring consequence of the life I lived before Lloyd changed everything with those bolt cutters. I've had to spend a lot of my energy pushing away memories of the abuse I suffered, and it's exhausting. Miss Halliday, the psychologist Lloyd sends me to, tries to help as much as she can. She's very kind and open-minded, and the way she lets her yellow hair hang down on her shoulders instead of wearing it in a severe bun puts me at ease. Lloyd's debriefed her on all the incest and abuse, but because I can't stand to talk about it, and because she doesn't force me to, I don't think the counselling's done me much good.

I'm frightened when I wake up with an erection. Being told in Sex-Ed class that "morning wood" is a "natural and normal occurrence in adolescent boys" makes absolutely no difference. Because I see my dad's when I see mine. And I don't love him anymore, I hate him. I'm ashamed. Because I feel dirty. Because it feels so *good*. All these ingredients boil together in a witch's brew of disarray, foreboding and degradation. I can't bear to open up to Miss Halliday about the darkest details of my childhood, and her not being the pushy type is either a blessing to my mangled emotions or a defeat to my complete recovery and understanding.

Miss Halliday asks, "Do you think your parents committed suicide because they felt guilty about what they did to you?"

As I sit in a chair in her office, I only shrug at her, digging my index nail into the glossy, softened, splintered wood of the arm.

I wish I knew.

I'm diagnosed with anxiety and depression, and Miss Halliday prescribes Zoloft, which makes me feel everything less intensely, which is great for me, until Stacy remarks that it's making me into a zombie. After the first bottle is gone, I pretend to Miss Halliday and Lloyd that I'm getting it refilled, but I don't think I need it.

🦟

In September, she's ready to give up our weekly sessions and see me once every other month, but even with this new schedule, her hopes of getting me to trust her and volunteer my childhood skeletons are in vain. I just can't bear to let those memories out. I have to keep them in check, securely subdued in my mind, lest they assert themselves in all their hideous, pornographic detail. I can't talk about them to anyone, not even dear Lloyd. Close as we are, this is one topic that is too demoralising to raise even with him. I can't even talk about it with Stacy.

It's worse when Pastor Sellers talks to the adolescent portion of his congregation about how, now that our bodies are changing, we must take extra steps to avoid the sins of the flesh. "Better to cut your hand off if it causes you to sin," he says, "Or poke your eye out if it causes you to lust."

I'm already liable. My experiences with sexuality make me ashamed, and my inexperience with intimacy makes me withdrawn and lacking in that sophistication that most of the kids my age already have, but I have enough knowledge deep down inside to feel guilty about these new feelings. All I *know* are my feelings. There are no words in my brain when I look at Tammy, at his tall, strong body, the chiselled features of his godlike face, the dark stubble over his lips, jaw and chin, the eyes the colour of the ocean I love so much. There are only these wonderful, sinful emotions that surge through me and leave me weak and breathless. The more Pastor talks about them, the more guilt-ridden I feel.

So I admire him from afar. I stare at him at school, at church, on the football field, everywhere I can possibly see him. I'm happier and sadder and more ashamed than I've ever been in my life. I'm so determined to see him play football every single Friday night, whether it's home or away, that I'll suffer anything. One night it's below freezing. I put on three pairs of pants, three pairs of bulky socks, and four shirts underneath a heavily padded jacket, and let's not forget two thick pairs of mittens, and I'm still shivering.

"It's no wonder," Stacy remarks. "You're thin as a spindle! You need to gain some weight!" We buy hot dogs and hot chocolate at the concession stand, but I'm still frigid when they're sitting in my belly. I feel even colder when the game ends and I see Yvette running up to Tammy and kissing him on the mouth. His muscular arms go around her, lift her off the ground, and swing her in a circle. That night in my bed, I weep, wishing, and not *caring* how wrong it is, that I was the one Tammy had treated so right. My daydreams are of Tammy talking to me, holding my hand like he did in church, kissing me, touching me, loving me. My innocence dissipates rapidly during these horrible, beautiful months of my first year in high school. My usual nightmares go on sabbatical, and I'm waking up from dreams of Tammy leaning down, whispering to me, his lips close to mine, and I'm wet and my heart is only beginning to drop out of warp speed. I know what I'm feeling now. I know *exactly* what I'm feeling, and it feels too agonisingly good for me to care what the Pastor has to say about it. I'm a boy in love with a man.

I've never been in love... I've only been fucked.

I want to be loved. And I want Tammy to love me.

In October, the church has a rummage sale to raise funds to improve the building. As always, if there's a chance that Tammy will be there, even if it's with that slut Yvette, I'm there. They put Stacy and me over at the pots and pans and kitchenware table. We spend most of the day giggling at Yvette. She's been given the position of "supervisor", which means she's to stand in the middle of the yard and make sure nobody's running off without paying. She stands stock still, her jeans so

56

tight around her big butt it looks like she's about to bust out of them, hands on hips, really swanky, just staring like a statue. The look on her face says she's doing all of us a favour by being there. Meanwhile, Tammy's supposed to walk around asking anyone if they need help, so he's walking, he's circling, over and over, like a tiger in a cage. He's not even asking anyone how they're doing, he's just pacing, circling, really fast, not looking at anything but the grass he's quickly mashing down. The whole thing is so comical that we can't stop laughing. Yvette standing there like a wax statue, in her old (she's probably had them since eighth grade) Jordache jeans, and Tammy pacing in a big circle at top speed.

After a while, they abandon their posts and come walking up to us with one of the other girls from school. My heart begins its routine maniacal thumping as Tammy nods at us, his customary salutation to nobody in particular.

Their friend walks right up to me. "You're sure pretty," she says, leaning into me with a huge smile. I nearly choke swallowing the poorly-chewed liquorice I've been gnashing before managing, "Oh, thank you," in a shaky voice, my lacquered eyes averting up and down, back and forth, seeking a safe place to land.

The girl straightens and regards me closely. "You know, you're wasting your time selling pots and pans. You ought to move to L.A. and be a Calvin Klein model. Don't you think so, Yvette? Don't you think he's pretty?"

Lard-Ash gives me a saccharine smile. "Sure," she says in her trademark blasé manner, "But shouldn't he have to be *taller* to be a model? He's kind of puny too."

I'm ready to crawl under a rock when the girl nudges Tammy. "Don't you think he's pretty, Tam?" My stomach somersaults painfully as Tammy's handsome face creases into a scornful glare, and he snaps, "How in the *hell* would I know?! I'm a guy!"

Their friend cuts her eyes up and insists, "Well, I think you're adorable."

My eyes are now fastened to the pots and pans in the box in front of me. I'm paralysed. I can sense Stacy grinning at me. I

57

silently warn her to stop it.

When they walk away, Stacy squeals, "Tammy was looking at you!"

"Oh, please," I snort.

"He was smiling at you, kind of."

"He was pissed!"

"Yeah, he looked like he wanted to haul off and smack Yvette! I think he *likes* you!"

I give a dismal laugh. "Get real."

"I was watching him, Jamie! He had this goofy little smile on his face, and his eyes were on you the whole time!"

"You're full of shit. He was probably smiling at Yvette's nasty-ass crack!"

Ignoring the probable double meaning of what I've just said, Stacy argues, "Why?! Why do you think it's so impossible? You're beautiful!"

"No, I'm not."

"You really have no idea. You're gorgeous. Even that girl thinks so!"

"She was making fun of me!"

"*Listen* to you!"

"Just stop!"

"I think he likes you, Babe." She's resolute.

"Whatever." I look up from the box of pots just in time to see Tammy looking over his shoulder at me as Lard-Ash pulls him by his arm to her car. I ignore my rising panic and force myself to keep my eyes on him, scanning his divine face for any hint. I think I see something, but I can't trust my own eyes.

That evening, I try not to dwell on Yvette's mocking words. I try not to analyse what I saw in Tammy's eyes when they met mine before he got into the car and rode away.

I know all about that "beauty is in the eye of the beholder" crap. I don't want to hear about it. I wouldn't believe him if he did come up to me and tell me he loves me, that I'm beautiful. All I see is ugliness when I look in the mirror. All I see is Mom and Daddy.

Another new year. We go to The End each Thursday, and one night Tammy gets up with Ray and Benny Feldman to sing

"I Only Have Eyes For You". His deep, gravelly voice (Ohmygod!) leaves me melting with desire and dissolving into anguish. He's singing to Lard-Ash, and I despise her, sitting there winking and blowing kisses at him.

Eventually, they break up, but that's no consolation. He already has another bimbette at his beck and call. I'll never have him. I have to face it. And I try to tell myself to forget about him. I really try.

But it's in vain. I'm in love, and knowing he's infinitely off limits to me doesn't stop me from desperately wanting him.

The approaching pink and red romance of Valentine's Day makes my feelings for him intensify. I'm going to explode if I don't do something, so I buy him a card. It takes up all my strength as I carefully pour my heart out to him. I want to sign it, but I'm not stupid. Nothing will come of this. He'll believe it's from one of his female fans and I'll scratch my itch. Nobody will be harmed. I excuse myself from last period to go to the restroom, and I leave it on the windshield of his car.

Two days later, I find a beat-up white envelope in my locker. No note, no card, just three conversation hearts.

You're sweet.

Love me.

My love.

They're probably from Lydia. Poor thing.

But I keep them.

The next months are painful as I begin to realise that soon he will be graduating and I won't be seeing him around school next year. I try to savour every moment I can, but dashes of bitterness begin to taint. One day I hear a couple of girls talking about him, describing how he's slept with every easy girl in school and is now working on those from surrounding schools. Of course, I *knew* all along, deep down, but hearing it from those girls… I wait until I get home to cry.

And the hits keep coming. One morning Stacy confides in

me that she and Ray have had sex. It hits me hard, and I flee to the restroom and have a bizarre panic/crying attack.

I've been left alone in a dark forest.

All my friends, all the people who claim to care about me are leaving me behind.

I'm so afraid and so angry! Damn, I hate them! I hate them all!

So now she's a woman and I'm still just the undersized dweeb in love with someone he can't have, now or ever. In the locker room I overhear Ray regaling his jock buddies about "finally" getting my best friend into bed. "She was ready, and she was willing!" I won't talk to her for at least two days. I feel so left out.

I'm not a goody-goody. I'm not angry at Stacy for losing her V because I think she should have waited for the marriage bed. I'm jealous, lonely, resentful, and wishing Tammy would deflower my ass.

The kicker, and yes, that's a pun, comes when I'm walking home one day after school and a soccer ball bounces near me. I go to pick it up and I hear a familiar voice roar, "Don't touch that ball!" I'm already bent halfway down and my fingers touch it when Tammy runs up to me. "I said, don't touch it! Are you *deaf*?!" I'm too stunned to react as he grabs it from under my floating fingers and jogs back to where he and the team are practising. I continue walking home, and as soon as I'm safely away from school grounds, I no longer try to stifle my sobs of despair. Stacy is wrong. He doesn't like me at all. He *hates* me, and I have no idea what I've done to provoke such rancour.

Obviously, that's *still* not enough. Even though she's now married and no longer in school, Lard-Ash begins to spread venomous rumours around town that I'm gay. How do I know? Because kids at both school and church are walking up to me, the ones who have never liked me taunting, the ones I get along with simply informing, "Yvette says you're a queer." And then one day, I'm walking home as usual when three sophomores jump me. I'm out of school for three days waiting for the welts and bruises to fade a little.

Stacy notices the subtle change in me after that. "Don't let them get to you, Baby."

"Everyone hates me."

"You can't let them get to you."

Then Ray tells me that Tammy is moving to L.A. after graduation, to attend broadcasting school, and my torment is complete. I've been thinking, *well, at least I'll see him around town.* But no. He's going to L.A. Might as well be going to the other side of the galaxy. He'll find a new harem to service him. Stacy and Ray will probably be getting married soon.

And I'm just going to stay the same, the same little loser that nobody loves.

It isn't a full two weeks after the first attack when I'm beaten up again, by the same three guys. They call me a faggot and pound me unconscious and leave me laying on the sidewalk, my homework scattered all around me like smaller victims.

I dream. I hallucinate. A voice says, "Come on, Jamie." My body is swooped into the air. I hear a door slam. The world around me is rumbling.

"Everyone hates me," I murmur.

The voice is familiar. "Don't worry about those assholes."

"Why does everyone hate me? What have I done? Even Tammy hates me."

For a moment, I think the voice talking to me has left me, then I hear it say, very quietly, "That's not true."

"He hates me! He yelled at me when I went to pick up the ball. I wasn't going to steal it! I was going give it back to him, but he screamed at me. He's mean! He's hateful! I don't understand what I've done to make him hate me!"

I feel a hand touching my hair, my face. "He doesn't hate you, he's just a prick sometimes." Then, "I'm sorry. I shouldn't have yelled at you. I was just..."

I shake my head violently, and even with my eyes closed, my head spins and aches. "He hates me! Nobody loves me! Nobody will ever love me..." My world blackens.

When I finally come to, I'm in the ER at Davis Hospital. I'm surrounded by bright, glaring white. An IV drips into me. I'm cold. I hate the plastic, medicinal smell all around me. My right arm is broken. For a while, they think my jaw is fractured, but the x-rays say it's just bruised. Stacy is here and she has the most idiotic grin as she says, "Tammy brought you here!"

She's so happy. The pain in my jaw is becoming unbearable.

"He chased those fuckers away and *brought* you here!"

I shrug and turn my face away from her. All I want is for everyone to leave me alone.

"He said he's been following you home since you got beaten up last time! He was worried about you! He told Lloyd not to let you walk home alone again!" Stacy is so excited it's sickening.

I look up to see my foster dad smiling at me.

I see it in his eyes.

He knows! He knows I'm in love! He knows I'm in love with Tammy!

He nods. Winks.

How did I get such a great dad? Why did God give Lloyd to me?

I manage a weak smile, willing to reassure him, but I'm too exhausted and beaten in body to keep it up for more than a few seconds.

"Here, let me sign your cast," Stacy says, gingerly adjusting my arm and using her teeth to pop the lid off a dark blue marker. Lloyd writes on the cast too.

I'm in the hospital for two days, and several friends from church and school have come by.

Back home, I finally muster enough interest to read all the autographs on the graffiti-decked shell holding my mending bones together:

> *Get well, Baby. Don't let them win. Don't let them have that power. People who hate you obviously don't know you. I know you and love you. Your bestest friend in the world, Stacy*

> *You've been here before, and I know you'll be okay. Love, Lloyd.*

I've never called him "Dad". I feel like an asshole for not

calling him that. It's just that I don't want to call anyone with a *good* heart "Dad" or "Daddy".

> *Hi Baby, hope you feel better soon! Love Lydia*
> *Miss you, Take care, Deanna*
>
> *Heal up, Ray.*
>
> *Baby, get well soon. Sylvie*
>
> *Babe, I hate those assholes and I hope they get what they deserve. Hurry back, Patti.*

Benny, home on a three-day furlough, simply signs his name.

And on the underside, where the cast covers my elbow, in blue, wavy chicken scratch, as tiny as the felt tip had allowed, and palpably bashful:

> *You're wrong. Everyone does not hate you.*

I read it again. And again. I nearly tear my rotator cuff reading it over and over.

I wrack my brain until it hurts, but I can't remember anyone writing in that spot, and it's not signed.

Twisting my arm painfully, I ask Stacy, "Who wrote this?!"

"Tam did, while you were asleep."

I shake my head. "No. He didn't."

"I watched him, Babe."

"Why didn't you wake me up?!" I'm riotous.

She just shrugs. Smiles. "He didn't want to bother you. He sat beside you and wrote where he could reach."

He's been shadowing me.

He's been worried about me.

He chased those guys away.

He drove me to the hospital.

He cares about me.

And it scares me.

63

I'd almost rather go on believing he doesn't know I'm alive.

After my insults from the second beating heal, there are only a few more weeks before school is out. Now everyone sees the difference, and Stacy gently tells me it's not a change for the better.

But it's my last line of defence. Now I'm just as curt to Tammy as he has been to me whenever we come into contact in any way. Whenever he and Ray and any of the other jocks walk up to us to ask us if we want to go to The End or to the mall or to a movie, I always mutter, "Look, Stacy, here comes Tammy and his nerd herd." I refuse to acknowledge him, turning my face away at every opportunity.

I'm decent. I thank him for helping me when I was jumped by those three shitheads (who were *expelled* by the way).

But I'm careful. I have to be. The way he's treated me (especially screaming at me over that stupid soccer ball) has made it arduous for me to dare to open myself to any more hurt. Better to just enjoy what little I can get.

I'm still in love with him.

I still love the very sight of him.

And I know he cares a little…

At this juncture though, I've had enough of the mean looks and the Jekyll and Hyde mood swings. I can't let him hurt me anymore. I won't. Passive weapons I had stowed away are taken from their holsters, dusted off, and put to use again.

But there's something else. I'm shamed. I'm horrified that Tammy has seen me like that, beaten and bloodied and humiliated. I've been free from my childhood dungeon for a year, and now, I feel like I'm being thrown back in, the locks engaged with echoing clicks and snaps. I'm irreversibly damaged, and the jagged pieces are precariously hanging together. I'm on the verge of losing hope. The beatings I've recently suffered are threatening to set loose those feelings that pound and claw against my chest, screaming to escape, to be recognised by their host—feelings that I am hated, hated by everybody, hated by my parents, hated by God, hated by all decent, godly society, that I should never have been born. It's easy to forget that Lloyd and Stacy would give their lives for me. I only know that I have to protect myself. I can't have any more hurt, any more rejection.

I must remember the lessons I learned. I must remember the value of control...

In moments of unguarded softness, when I look at Tammy, I cannot believe my eyes when they detect an emerald nanosecond of tenderness before he looks away. I protect myself by looking into mirrors, reminding myself of my eternal ugliness, and by treating him coolly.

But no matter what icy methods I employ, I'm always, without failure, startled over and over again by what I see shimmering in his dark teal eyes.

Can it be?

No. No way! I might be a little flaming pervert, but Tammy's straight. I should know by now who he likes to sleep with. I can't have him, and I have got to stop torturing myself. He's going to L.A. and he's going to be a famous news anchor. Women will be all over him. That's that.

"You don't fool me for a minute," Stacy says with stern sweetness.

seven:

tammy
(approaching the end
of high school)

Their fists pummel him into a bloody pulp as they call him, "Flaming faggot", "Pervert", "Pussy-boy". I scramble out of my car and charge at the three pukes, but they're already on the run. He yelps when I shake his shoulder, and gently as I can, I gather him up and put him in my car.

I've been following Jamie since the first time they jumped him. He makes his way home on foot, walking the mile from the high school, down a stretch of paved road, past the town limits, to his house. I follow, my car slowly crawling a few hundred yards behind, keeping enough distance to monitor him without making my presence known.

I've caught those sonsabitches red handed, and they're going to pay.

I keep one eye on traffic and one eye on Jamie. God, he's so little. Fucking cowards beat the holy shit out of him. I hate seeing him like this.

He stirs. "What's...?"

"It's okay. I'm taking you to the hospital."

Slurred words squeeze their way through his swollen lips. "Why does everyone hate me? What have I done? Even Tammy hates me. Why did he scream at me? I wasn't going to steal that ball... I don't understand what I've done to make him hate me!"

Remorse assails me as tears and blood begin to ooze out of his nose. I find an old napkin from Burger King or someplace and dab at the mess carefully.

"Nobody loves me." The way his breath hitches in his chest makes my eyes sting. "Nobody will ever love me."

"I don't hate you, Jamie. I'm a prick. I'm sorry. I didn't mean to yell at you."

But he doesn't hear me. He's passed out. I smooth my hand over his forehead, cheek and chin, and he recoils. I think his jaw's busted.

I stay for two hours. His jaw isn't broken, but his arm is.

When I get home, I shut myself in my room and cry.

It's not just that he's small for his age. He's different, and it makes him an outcast, a target. Until Queen Bitch spread that shit around town about him, he's been overlooked. He'd probably be invisible if not for Stacy and Ray and the girls.

I want to be his friend...

I'm "popular". I'm constantly surrounded by people—football teammates, fawning girls, the journalism staff—but I have no real friends. Ray and Benny are the closest thing, but I can't say that I'm "friends" with either of them.

I don't have friends. I have laughs in the locker room. I have groupies, each hoping they're next on my list of conquests. I have colleagues that I discuss the latest campus news with.

That's all.

I haven't known how lonely I am.

I want Jamie to be my friend. And I want to be his.

I've always wanted to be his friend.

I could never hate him.

But I've been a prick to him.

Because I'm scared.

I'm fighting a losing battle with my attraction to him, and I don't *want* to fight anymore.

If he likes me and I like him, why shouldn't we see where

this leads? Why should we care what the world thinks?

But, I *do* care. I *am* afraid of what people will think.

There isn't a person on earth besides my mom who truly cares about my happiness in life. Yeah, she's flubbed up and made me mad at her, but all her actions have had the best intentions. Nobody else gives a shit whether I'm happy or not.

But they're sure going to have something to say if I let them see I love Jamie. The Asshole, Queen Bitch, Ray, Benny, the guys at school, the girls… they'd crucify me if I dared to reveal my crush on the petite freshman with the bright red and yellow hair and the spectral blue eyes.

I'm worse than the ones who openly hate him, because I'm a poltroon. I'm afraid to face the truth, afraid to stand up and tell the world.

That I want Jamie.

The Panther plans an article about Jamie's bashing. I recommend to our advisor, Mrs. Collins, that the piece should mention that the beating was motivated by false rumours spread about the town, that it's a hate crime, and that the victim should not be named, because he has already been bashed twice, and to name him would put him in danger of being attacked yet again.

She disagrees, "We don't *know* it's a hate crime."

"He was beaten up once before this! It *is* a hate crime!"

She shakes her grey head stubbornly. "I'm not going to publish an article based on your *opinion*, Tam. We're mentioning you as a hero, because you drove the boy to the ER We will keep him anonymous for his protection, but we're not going to call it a gay-bashing when we don't even know if the boy is gay, or if those rumours even were the cause!"

I argue with her for half an hour, but the entire journalism staff ends up overruling me. They're yellow down the back.

Just like me.

After the latest battering, Jamie's not the same. When he's released from the hospital, his right arm encased in hard plaster, he approaches me, guardedly says, "Thank you for getting me to the hospital."

"Are you alright?" I ask.

He nods. "Yeah."

"Sure?"

He shrugs.

"I'm glad they didn't mention Jamie's name in the paper," Stacy says.

"I told them they shouldn't, for his own safety," I reply.

Jamie speaks up then, "Who cares?! Everyone *knows* it's me!"

I feel so bad for him, and I feel stupid.

A short time later, Ray begins driving Stacy and Jamie, negating my need to follow him.

Weeks go by, and whenever I look his way, expecting to see him gazing at me, smiling at me, and then averting his eyes, he's looking elsewhere.

Enough dirty looks and grouchy snarls have worked. I've finally gotten through. He can't have me.

So why do I feel so fucking wretched?

After all, I can't stay here. I've gotta go, and follow my dream... there's no real opportunity here like there is in Los Angeles, and I've been planning to leave right after graduation forever.

It's best this way. I can't have any attachments here. Besides, we'll never make it. Nobody around here will abide it. Everyone we know would be opposed, except maybe Mr. Tafford and Stacy.

I'd like to think my mom would be supportive about it.

But I don't know. *No. Probably not...*

There's no way for Jamie and me, not in this town...

Not in this life...

Best to just leave it alone...

That afternoon in my room after the beating is just the start. I find myself in tears at odd moments as my senior year draws to a close. I'm sad, lonely—I don't bother asking anybody to the prom. I turn down three or four invitations from generic tarts I care nothing about.

I keep hoping, in spite of myself, that his definitive sweetness will resurface, that he'll smile and make my insides tighten and melt the way I secretly love.

But he doesn't. He's cold. Aloof. Subdued. And the sadness I've always sensed in him is amplified.

At The End, a few nights before graduation, I spy him sitting at a table with Stacy. He doesn't sing that night. He's doesn't even talk. He's just sitting there, in self-imposed exile, and it chews at me. My eyes catch Stacy's and I see a concern there that mirrors my own. I pull her aside. "Is he alright?"

She observes me steadily before replying, "He will be."

"Get him up there and sing something. Maybe it'll help."

Still looking at me strangely, she shrugs, then goes over to their table. Jamie only shakes his head listlessly. "He doesn't want to."

Frustration leaps inside of me. "It might cheer him up."

"Why are *you* so worried?" she challenges, and just a hint of a grin twitches across her face.

I think she's on to me.

I leave The End as hastily as I can.

eight:

jamie
(graduation night)

On the last night of school, my resolve not to let Tammy into my heart goes sailing out the window. Ray invites just the few of us to party and swim in his parents' pool. He invites Stacy and me, strictly to piss off Lard-Ash, who brings her furloughed husband and makes out with him in front of everyone. Stacy wears her blue bikini. I wear a t-shirt and tan cut-offs, even though I don't intend to swim.

There's a lot of food, thanks to Ray's mom, who's bought bags and bags of chips, along with dips, candy, and a great big graduation cake for Ray, Tammy, and Yvette (even though Lard-Ash didn't get to officially graduate and is still at least two months from getting her GED). I look around, wishing they had red liquorice among all the snacks and candies. Ray's dad loves to barbeque, so he fires the old thing up and cooks hot dogs, hamburgers, chicken and steaks. The evening is mild, balmy, a little muggy. The aroma of savoury meat makes our stomachs rumble.

It's the perfect evening on the brink of summer. I'm so pleased to be here that I can almost try to forget that soon Tammy will be leaving Sommerville behind him.

He helps Benny smuggle alcohol in, and we drink beer and wine coolers and sign each other's yearbooks. When Ray and Stacy are done signing Tammy's, I take it, making sure he's turned away, and write:

Dear Tammy, thank you for being my friend, Jamie Pearce.

I wish he'd ask to sign mine.

There's no girlfriend in sight tonight. I watch how Tammy's wet red cut-off tweed shorts cling to his penis, beautiful and semi-erect from the cold, bouncing, in spectacular slow motion, as he springs off the diving board. A hot flash engulfs me.

Abruptly, Ray and Benny grab me by my hands and feet and throw me in. As the water closes over me, I hear Stacy scream, "You assholes! He can't swim!"

Someone grabs me from below and pulls me back up to the surface. It's Tammy. As I hold onto him, I blow the hot, burning water out of my sinuses.

"You okay?" he asks.

"No!" I sputter, perturbed and electrified by the fact that he's *holding* me, that his arms are around me, that my cheek is brushing his chest, that his arms are under my knees.

That he's holding me, in his arms…

"You asswipes!" I scream at Ray and Benny, who are already scampering back over to the chips and dips.

"I'll teach you to swim," Tammy smiles, bouncing me playfully.

Every sound around us is suddenly muted, except for the water, splashing softly. His smile—Oh my God—incredible, compelling, I'm powerless… My heart begins to tremble and skip as I feel my lips stretch wide in response. The palpitations tickle my ribs as we stare at each other, our smiles unchanging, but our eyes transforming. I see it in his, I feel it in mine. Our smiles follow the course of our eyes. Tammy gazes down at me, his eyes and lips gentle, soft, dreamy. He's in a trance—it's the same look I've caught in his eyes so many times lately. It's here, now…

From my periphery, I can see Stacy grinning at me like the

devil.

My eyes are locked with his, and this moment expands into a small forever.

Then Tammy blinks, looks flustered, says, "Come on!" in an overly loud, edgy yowl, and pulls me under with him. The moment is over.

Within fifteen minutes, I know how to swim. We dive down and touch bottom, and on the way up, he grabs my hands, pulls me to him and takes me back up.

After a bit, Yvette and Benny call him over, and I'm forgotten. Stacy and I sit at the pool's edge, talking with our legs in the water.

I feel fingers tickling my feet.

Tammy surfaces, grins at me, his green eyes twinkling, then he goes under again. As soon as I'm back to talking to Stacy, his fingers trickle over the soles of my feet, making my legs twitch and my heart quicken.

Stacy squeezes my hand and nods at me. "Go talk to him."

I don't trust life enough to believe he's really enjoying all of this, teaching me to swim, vying for my attention, playing with me, talking to me, teasing me, touching me. I mean, I can't *fathom* this. I'm afraid that what I've always wanted is what is happening to me tonight. He's *flirting* with me. The hours pass, and he's *staying* with me.

I imagine he's just lonely because he left his girlfriend at home, whoever she is this month. He's bored. Why else would he be wasting time talking to *me*?

He tells me this crazy story about having met me. *Me*! In a grocery store when I was two and he was four. "I know you," he smiles. "I've known you for years." His deep baritone turns me into jelly. "Do you remember?"

"N-no," I stammer apologetically.

"I know you," he murmurs. "I do…"

Lord, what is he *doing* to me?!

We splash each other between swimming lessons, and we talk about his going to L.A.

"So you're going to be famous," I pout. "The next Barbara Walters."

"Noooo," he corrects me. "The next Walter Cronkite."

We climb out of the water for a while, and I bring my yearbook to him, feeling much more comfortable with asking, now that we've talked quite a lot. "Tammy?"

"Yeah?"

"Would you sign my yearbook?" I ask, bracing myself for one of his unforeseen mood swings.

"I did already."

"You did?!" I start trying to flip through the pages.

"No!" He grabs it and tries to wrest it from my fingers. "Don't *read* it!"

"Why?"

"Read it later," he says, with the most amazing smile I've ever seen. He's blushing!

We tug of war gently. "I wanna see what you wrote!"

"No, read it later, please!" He won't let go.

"Oh, alright!"

"Will you sign mine?" His cheeks are dark red, his hair is beginning to dry, forming little spikes across his forehead.

"I did… a while ago," I confess, biting my lips.

He gazes at me. "You did?"

"Are you mad?" I dare to ask.

His smile makes my temperature go up several more degrees. "Why would I be?"

"I didn't ask you first." I'm feeling more daring, more flirtatious.

"I'm gonna read it!"

"No!" I cry, grabbing him.

He stares at my fingers digging into the skin of his forearms, then looks so deeply into me that I almost swoon.

"You have pretty eyes," he whispers.

"Shut up!" I whisper shakily.

Back in the pool, I'm so grateful that Stacy has the radio up so loud. His smile doesn't change, not one tiny muscle of it. I read his lips, *I want to be alone with you…*

My heart gallops ahead of the rest of me, straight into him. The water can't cool my joy and desire, and I bite my mouth until it's bleeding. *I want to be with you, too*, I inform him

74

telepathically.

He blinks and asks, "Did you spell my name right?"

"T-A-M-M-Y. I know. Ray told me you hate it when people spell or pronounce it wrong!" I snicker.

"That's right," he nods precisely.

"So why is it pronounced different than it's spelled?" I challenge.

He responds to my cheek with a warning smile. "Because I'm *not* a girl."

No *shit*.

"Why do they call you 'Baby'?" he asks. Ohhh boy. I'm so embarrassed. "Because I'm… small… They used to keep the bullies off me. I'm their Baby, they say." I turn away, feeling flames wanting to leap from under the skin of my face.

"Can I call you 'Baby'?'"

"No!" I laugh anxiously.

"Please? Make up a name for me, if you want…"

"I don't know what to call you!" I burst out laughing. "I like your name anyway. Tammy. It's pretty. It's different. Tammy…"

He stares at me, obviously recognising the quandary I'm having thinking out loud and adoring him at the same time. "You like it?"

I give a small, terrified nod.

"You think it's pretty?"

"Uh huh."

"Thank you," he whispers. It's the voice he's used to wilt the petals of dozens of girls and women. I'm not wilting though— far from it. I'm sprung up like a weed. My heart's beating so loud I'm sure the whole of Sommerville can hear it.

"Let's play shark."

"What's that?" I ask suspiciously.

"You swim and I chase you. If I can catch you, you're the shark."

"Why don't you save yourself the time and just call it 'tag'?" I sneer.

He gives me a droll smile, then shouts, "Go!"

I torpedo under, heading for the bottom, but he catches me,

grabbing my feet, tickling them, and then wrapping his arms around me from behind, spinning me around to face him. We're in our own liquid world.

When we break the top of the water, he smiles, I smile...

His smile crumples...

"I've gotta go," he mutters, and leaves me in the pool. He says his hasty goodbyes to Ray and them, clutching his soggy clothes against his body.

Stacy watches me as my eyes following him all the way out the iron gate. She carefully steps into the water and wades over to where I am beginning to cry, my joy waterlogged, drowned, by his rejection. She puts her arms around me from the side. "Maybe he had to get home. Maybe he's got a curfew."

"Yeah, right! That'll be the day."

"He loves you. It's all over his face every time he *looks* at you."

"Do you think he took it wrong when I told him to shut up?"

"Of course not! You were teasing each other! You were flirting with each other! It was *adorable*!"

"One minute he acts like he likes me, the next it's like I *repulse* him!"

"No, Baby, he loves you. I can see it." She nods toward the other three parties in our vicinity. "He just can't let *them* see it."

"Who cares what they think?!" I hiss, loud enough to draw stares.

As we slosh out of the pool and towel dry ourselves, Stacy sighs. "You have to understand, Jamie. It's not the kind of world we live in. Civilisation has come far, but it has a way to go yet. I want to see you with him more than anybody. I'm sorry."

"He hates me," I say as I pull on a long-sleeved blue and white shirt. "I'll be out by your car." I don't even bother saying goodbye to anyone.

She shakes her head. "You're full of shit and you know it. He *so* loves you!"

I'll let Tammy tell you what happens in Ray's drive a short time later. I haven't told Stacy about it. When Stacy comes out to the car and finds us together, I'm still in shock as I stammer,

"Tammy was telling me this funny story about how he met me in a grocery store when we were little. I'm sure he's just goofing."

"I'm not, I tell you!" Tammy insists.

"You never know, Jamie!" grins Stacy.

"Later," he smiles, and walks to his car.

As she drives me home, she pokes and winks at me. "Told you he loves you!"

"What do you mean?" I bluster guiltily.

"He couldn't even go home without talking to you again!"

That night, I dream that I'm back at Ray's house, with Tammy. He's holding my hands underwater, and we're staring at each other. He pulls me close to him. His lips touch mine. "I love you," he says. I don't notice how strange it is that his voice is crystal clear under the water. I feel his lips. I *taste* them, like I tasted them when...

I touch him, feel the crisp hairs growing on his chest...

I merge slowly into wakefulness. I usually cannot sleep in total quiet, or darkness, but my room is pitch black, save for the faint, silvery glow of the half moon through my window blinds. I reach over to turn on my digital clock radio, which reads, 1:57am, wondering who's turned it off. Lloyd wouldn't. Did I forget to turn it on when I went to bed? I can't seem to get my thumb and forefinger around the little knob.

A light tapping distracts me. It's coming from my window. I hear a voice floating over to me from where the window has been raised just a bit to let in some cool night air. "Jamie!"

Ohmygod!

I leap out of bed and trip my way to the window. "What are you doing here?" I ask as I open and raise the blinds.

He only says, "Come out."

"It's two in the morning!"

He stands there, smiling at me. "Open your window. Please? Come out."

"If Lloyd catches me, I'm grounded!" I whisper loudly, raising the glass.

He just stands there, below me, waiting, his chest heaving.

I undo the wire latch and release the screen and climb up into the square making the window, dangling my legs out. I'm in an old white t-shirt and my pyjama bottoms. In the distance, I hear a dog bark. Tammy reaches for me, pulls me out of my room. My heart scampers as his lips search for mine in the half-light. I dig my fingers into his hair and pull him closer. Neither of us says a word. We just kiss, the humid pre-summer air growing more warm and moist around us, as our kisses and moans increase in volume. More dogs begin to bark. "Fucking dog ears!" Tammy curses, and I laugh as he snatches my mouth with his, deep, hungry moans vibrating from his throat.

Close by, a human voice shouts, "I don't hear anything!"

"Shit!" snaps Tammy. From about fifty yards away, a vehicle horn blares, and we're forced, from the heaven we've been sharing outside my bedroom window, back into reality. "Go to bed, nosey assholes!"

"Tammy," I sigh ruefully.

"I know. I'd better go, before those dogs wake the entire town." He helps me back into my window. I bend over and we kiss again, again, again... "Do you want to come inside?"

The longing in his eyes makes my stomach plummet into my loins. "What about Lloyd?"

I sigh again, "I know."

One more long kiss, and we finally let go.

He waits for me to close and lock up, and I watch him go back to his car and drive away.

I get under my sheets, my entire body humming with happiness and desire. I wish Lloyd had been working tonight! I would have invited Tammy right into my bed!

I can't believe this is happening! To me! How many people at school are in love with someone who doesn't even know they're alive?

I can't get over it!

I jolt awake, wet and shivering. Had I been asleep just now? Was the entire thing outside my window a dream?

My room is dark, the radio is off. The time is 3:04am.

It felt so real.

My hair is soaked with perspiration. I smell chlorine.

I'm stupid enough to believe I'll see him a few more times before he moves away, that I'll share a few more incredible evenings with him, more conversations, more touches, more kisses.

Maybe he'll stay! Maybe he'll decide to stay here and go to school, so he and I can see each other, go places together...

I want to be with you, I whisper, willing my plea to reach all the way across town. *Stay with me. Stay. Stay home...*

But he doesn't. He leaves the very next day and I cry in my room, for five hours, like a heartsick little schoolgirl. Now I'm glad I didn't mention the kiss to Stacy. For him to just leave, just like that, after everything that happened, after we talked for hours, after he touched me the way he did, after we kissed...

He didn't even say *goodbye.*

He's been playing with my mind.

It meant nothing to him.

I'm too vulnerable for games. He's disarmed me, and I'm more in love than I ever thought possible—madly, deeply, terribly in love.

Yvette put him up to these pranks. She's the biggest bitch in town. and I'm the pawn in a heartless scheme. No doubt, from day one Lard-Ash has probably known that I'm completely in love with Tammy. She's probably seen the want in my eyes every time I've looked his way, clear back to when he was going out with her. That's why she came to me, trying to see if I'd go out with her, and when I rejected her, she began calling me a faggot.

They've probably been in cahoots for the past nine months, since that historic day in church. They've been planning and preparing for the theft of my heart, guffawing together as they survey my unrelieved hunger, my stupefaction, my dejection, as he yo-yos between being genial and spiteful.

It's all been a prank. Like everyone I'm stupid enough to love, Tammy has only been out to amuse himself, to toy with me, before leaving town and recommencing his important life.

And yet, can I hate him? Can I regret experiencing my very

first kisses with him? No.

No matter how cruel he is, I'll always love him.

It's all I can do not to splatter tears and snot all over the clean white pages of my yearbook as I weep over pictures of him, the impeccable senior portrait of him, unsmiling and dangerously beautiful, in a black jacket and shirt unbuttoned to reveal the dark hairs on his chest, the glorious action shots of him playing football, soccer and baseball, a group photo of him and his jocks hamming it up. As I thumb through my autograph pages, I come across something that seizes my breath in my throat:

Don't change. There's only one Jamie in this world. Your friend, Tam Mattheis

I'm inconsolable.

Stacy tries to help, pointing out boys for me to crush on. Boys.

Ray, who doesn't seem to know I've been pining after his best friend for the past year, keeps suggesting "shorties" who would love me.

I hope they'll get a life and leave me alone so I can punish myself in peace.

If he cares about me, why did he go?!

I return to Miss Halliday, and she renews my Zoloft, gently scolding me that I should never stop taking something without checking in with her first.

I begin smoking more heavily, bumming more and more cigarettes off of Stacy and Patti, and putting each one out on the big scar on my left ankle.

nine:

tammy
(graduation night/college)

After graduation, we all go to Ray's and swim and sign yearbooks. I wait for Jamie to turn away from his and grab it.

I want him to sign mine too, but I don't know how to ask. In his, I take everything inside of me and compress it into a couple of simple sentences, erasing at least five times before I think I've got it right.

I spend the entire evening with him. We talk more than we ever have. Stacy cranks the radio and everyone argues about what music we'll listen to. Ray and Benny want AC/DC, Ozzy, Metallica, etc. Queen Bitch wants the "soft rock" station. Stacy finds a classic rock station playing Heart, The Pretenders, The Police. Yvette sulks as the rest of us nod in consensus.

This unexpectedly charmed night with the elfin boy I secretly ache for starts when Ray and Benny toss Jamie into the pool. After I ream their asses about grabbing him by his bad arm, I teach Jamie to swim. When I first take him under with me, he resists, kicking back up to the surface and spitting water. "I can't hold my breath!"

"Yes, you can!" I encourage him. "Just take a breath. Don't pooch your cheeks out, silly!" I chortle.

He lets me hold his hands as I guide him, and I rejoice in any excuse to touch him. We play "shark", under the water. We eat chips and mango salsa that Ray's mom made.

And we talk and talk and talk. Jamie asks me, "So you want to be on TV? The next Cronkite?" His voice has a diminutive drawl I haven't detected before, like he's from Texas or something. I *love* listening to him.

"That's the plan."

"I like your stories. You're a good writer."

"You like sports, do you?" I ask coyly.

"Not really," he blushes. "But I like reading your stories."

"You don't like sports?! Then you don't know what I'm writing about do you?"

"Well, I've learned a little, watching you play. It's… very… interesting…"

"And what have you learned?" I tease.

He shrugs. "I don't know, but I like watching."

"You're weird!"

"Shut up!"

"What do *you* want to be?"

"Veterinarian," he says.

"Ah hah! Going to take care of dogs and cats and horses and cows, eh?"

"I don't want to take care of horses and cows, or lizards or birds or anything like that. Just cats… maybe dogs."

Cotton. I try not to remember him, but there he is. I croak, "That's cool."

"Are you alright?" he asks.

I must be green under the gills. "Just thinking about a little pooch I had a long time ago."

"I love cats," says Jamie. "I love talking to them. I love the way they purr. It's so soothing when I'm nervous or upset."

"Talking to them? How do you talk to a cat, Dr. Doolittle?"

"Very softly, in a baby-talk way," Jamie explains, his face pinkening. "It sounds ridiculous, but they love it. They just purr and drool all over me!"

"Give me a sample."

"Nooo," he shakes his head briskly.

"Come on! Please?"

"No way!"

"Please?"

His cheeks bloom. "Tweet didda idda bidda kidda." His voice is thin, keening, like Mel Blanc doing Tweety Pie. "You toe tweet. You toe tweet!"

I'm tickled. "You're weird!"

"If I'm so weird, go find someone else to talk to!"

The hours pass. We talk and talk. We tease each other. The smile I've missed reappears tonight, and I'm in heaven.

"Is that your real hair colour?" I ask him, yanking gently on a freshly dyed cranberry coloured lock whose tip is so yellow it looks like it's been dipped in mustard.

He rolls his eyes. "Does it *look* real to you, genius?"

"Well, then, what *is* your real colour?"

"Dark blonde… boring!"

"Ah, so you're a blonde! So, when you dye your hair red, is that, like, artificial intelligence?"

He snorts glibly. "Well, dyeing my hair can't be too effective. I'm talking to *you* aren't I?"

"Shut up, Doctor Doolittle!"

"Shut up, Walter Cronkite!"

We trade insults, laugh, yell at each other. It gets quiet for a minute, and I begin to fidget. "Well? Say something!"

"*You* say something!"

"I don't know what to say!"

"Funny… you usually *never* run out of things to say!" After more awkward stillness, he murmurs, "I wish I had some liquorice. Or a cigarette."

"You shouldn't smoke."

"Okay, Surgeon General Koop!"

"Why do you smoke?"

"'Cause I'm a nervous person."

I ask softly, "Do I make you nervous?"

He tries to glare at me. Instead I see his heart in his eyes.

He does like me.

Before thinking, I say, "I've known you a long time, you know."

"What?!" he snickers.

"You and I met a long time ago," I tell him. "In a supermarket. You were with your mom. I think it was your mom…"

He looks away.

"You were two," I stammer. "I was four. I remember your eyes…"

"You're undeniably weird."

"No. It's true."

"You're lying!" he giggles. His smile makes me glow inside.

"I'm serious."

He doesn't believe me.

But as we sit at the pool's edge and time wriggles through my fingers, as the sun oozes out of sight, as golden-red light settles over everything, he smiles, endlessly, his eyes far away as he pretends to be acutely interested in the yellow pool raft floating at the far end of the pool. He smiles, biting his soft, pouty lower lip, swirling his feet through the water, sending ripples of imperfection across the glassy surface, ripples of pleasure through every cell of my body.

The moments tick by, and I'm afraid of what I'm feeling tonight, what I've been feeling since the beginning of the year. I'm paying all of my attention to Jamie. And I'm not being very discreet about it. Now and then, I look up and around, expecting to see Ray, Stacy, Benny or Yvette gawking at my conspicuous behaviour. I'm ignoring most everyone except Jamie Pearce.

But Ray is busy salivating over Stacy's tits and the newlyweds are sucking face behind one of the jasmine bushes over by the rot-iron gate.

Tick-tock, tick-tock, tick-tock. Time passes faster than I want it to. We go back in the water again and again, our bodies slicing through the depths, our hands walking over the grainy blue of the bottom, keeping each other in close proximity. When we resurface, he's so close that his arms go around my shoulders…

His eyes paralyse me.

And he makes no effort to take his arms down.

He's so close. Too close…

I want to kiss him.

He's trembling. I'm trembling.

Does he know how close I am?

I see three terrifying words in his eyes as he stares up at me.

I'm afraid of the fact that I've fallen in love with him. I don't *want* to go to L.A.

A few minutes after I've grabbed my clothes and fled Ray's barbeque, I'm sitting in my car, crying and despising myself for running. As I struggle to shove my damp body into my dry clothes behind my steering wheel, I see the front porch sensor throw a glow over Ray's front yard and drive, and Jamie's little silhouette walks over to where Stacy's car is parked. He rocks on his feet, facing away from me, peering into the dark glass windows.

I should have driven away ten minutes ago!

He's a magnet and I'm a piece of iron. I close my car door silently, sneak up to him, grab him from behind, my hand muffling his cry of fright. "You really can't remember the day we met?" I murmur into his ear.

"In-in-in th-the st-st-store?"

"Yes."

"No… I can't… I-I-I'm sorry…"

I turn him around in my arms, lift him to sit on the hood of Stacy's car, settle my hands over his shoulders. I can see him trembling in the sparse light, his eyes dewy, his nose red.

"Have you been crying?" I ask.

He shakes his head, his mouth quivering invitingly. Can he see I've been crying? Tearfully he whispers, "I have a crush on you."

"Really?"

"Yes."

"Big crush?"

"Very big, yes…"

"You love me?"

"Yes," he nods.

It bursts quietly from my heart, like a bullet. "I love you too." My arms press him closer to me. "I kissed your cheek," I murmur, and he moans softly as I brush my lips over the creamy pink curve, surprised I'm not tasting the candy coating of liquorice there. "And you kissed my mouth. Kiss me…"

He's about to rattle himself right off of Stacy's car.

"Please, kiss me."

"I don't know how," he says, his lips trembling, smiling, grimacing in joyous angst.

"You don't have to know how," I plead. "Just kiss me."

He touches his mouth to mine, and instantly, fireworks of every conceivable colour explode within me. I can't stay passive for more than a second. My mouth grabs his, and I probe him impatiently, his taste, his texture, his softness, as I suck and pull at his lips with my own. If he's new at kissing, it doesn't take him long to learn how to kiss me back. We converse without words, my deep sighs of bliss mingling with his soft, high cries of shock and delight. I'm already on the verge of popping my cork. I pull away and our lips part with a moist, luscious sound. "Do you remember now?" I gasp.

"I don't know," Jamie cries, quaking vividly. "I don't know!"

"Jamie," I whisper.

"Tammy…" He reaches for me, trying to pull me back.

"Would you…?" I gulp, disbelieving the diffidence that suddenly steals my nerve.

We hear Stacy calling out, "Bye!"

It's too late to dash back to my car. Jamie makes a high sound of exclamation as Stacy approaches. "Hey, Tam! I thought you'd gone home!"

"We were just talking," I lie, my hands in my pockets pushing my pants away from my body, my cock is like throbbing concrete. "My car wouldn't start for some reason… I saw Jamie and thought I'd come talk to him… the car's okay now…"

"Crap!" Stacy gripes. "Left my dad's favourite container!" She scurries back to Ray's backyard to retrieve the plastic dish she brought the Chinese chicken salad in.

Still seated on Stacy's hood, Jamie smiles down at me, reaches for me…

Like he did in the grocery store…

86

I go to him, take his hand in mine. "Jamie…"

"Tammy…"

All too soon, Stacy's back. "Okay, I got it! My dad would never let me hear the end of it if I left his salad dish behind!"

I sigh.

Jamie sighs with a little smile.

"Later," I nod to him, and they drive away.

Once they're out of sight, I drag my feet back to my own car.

I'm supposed to leave tomorrow.

I didn't tell him that.

Maybe I should.

Maybe I should call him.

I really don't even *want* to go now.

I could apply to UC Davis instead!

Then I could stay.

I want to stay, forever.

But…

This is too small a town.

I love him.

He loves me.

We could be together.

But…

He's been beaten up, twice.

We're the only two of our kind in this shitty little town.

I don't want him to be attacked again.

Because of me…

Is it reasonable, feasible, to expect to be able to have a life with Jamie? In *this* town? With these people who don't understand? Who will *never* understand, no matter how we try to explain?

I don't want to leave. I want to be with him. I love him.

My heart bleeds as my mind leaps back and forth between impetuousness and practicality.

No…

I *have* to go. I have to forget Jamie and this pipe dream that has virtually countermanded my plans and ambitions.

In kissing him, in telling him that I love him, I've given him hope.

I've been unfair to him, letting him hope.

It's going to hurt.

In my bed during the wee hours following, I have the most erotic dream of my young life. We're in Ray's pool. I'm tickling Jamie's feet. We hold hands as we dive, touch the rough bottom of the pool, and then kick our way back up.

Suddenly, I'm in my bed. My room is dark. My door silently opens, and there he is. "I'm just going to shower," he says quietly to somebody. He's wrapped in a white towel. He lets it fall to the floor. The heavy shadows and sparse lighting play over his exotic facial features and his petite, slim body, his graceful neck, his narrow shoulders, the development of muscles along his arms, his hairless chest, the delicate ridge of his spine, his taut belly, the perfect, subtle curve of his ass, his slender thighs. His smooth porcelain skin gleams as he turns slowly to face me. "Tammy," he says breathlessly. His voice sends my pulse into a mad frenzy. He lets me see all of him.

"Jamie," I call out softly in answer.

He pushes his hands through his hair. His eyes are half-closed, his lips parted. "What are *you* doing here?" he whispers.

I have the most intense, throbbing erection I have ever had in my life. "It's my bedroom," I say helplessly as he takes a step closer.

"Then what am *I* doing here?" He smiles at me. Closer, closer, closer he comes to me, and now he's pulling back my blankets and getting into bed with me. His cool, damp thigh touches my feverish one. His chest presses into mine. My hands cup peaches, round and ripe. "Hmmm? What am I doing here?" His lips graze mine softly, again, and again…

I wake up coming, my entire body glowing.

But my bed is cold. My arms are empty…

My clock says it's one forty-five. I take a leak, flush and lay back down.

I argue with myself about driving over to Jamie's.

I want to see him.

I need to see him.

I want to go knock on his window.

I want him to let me into his room.
But if his dad is home… he mentioned that last night.
I don't want to get him into trouble.
I shouldn't be creeping around outside anyone's window at this time of night anyway!
He's asleep. I shouldn't disturb him.

At noon, I leave. I don't say goodbye to anyone except my mom, to whom I impart a solemn goodbye kiss. "I'll miss you," I tell her. "I'm sorry about the way things have been with us."

She shakes her head, "Don't worry about all that anymore."

I want to tell her how sorry I am that I've always blamed her for what happened with Uncle Price.

But she still doesn't know what he did.

I want to tell her how sorry I am about the thing with Cotton.

But I can't. I can't even think about Uncle Price, or about that sad, scared little dog whose life I probably destroyed, without getting sick.

I jump into my car and drive, as fast as is legal, to my new life in L.A. I'm going to start school immediately so I can get out sooner, so I can be famous sooner.

I wish I could have stayed home for a while…

If I had known all of this was going to happen… but I'm already registered and classes begin in just a few days. I've been planning on this since clear back in my junior year.

At least they *sound* like good excuses.

I should have said goodbye to him…

Perhaps it's better I didn't. As it is, I'm choking on a lump in my throat and stifling the most exasperating sighs of regret as I merge onto the freeway. I'm on my way. New town, new school, new friends, new fucks, new everything.

I should be keyed up, stoked, but instead tears are blurring my vision.

A few days later, settled into my dorm, I find his writing in my yearbook.

I *am* his friend.

I'm worried about him.

✤

I begin the summer semester at UCLA, financed by a couple of grants I earned with my low A average. I major in Mass Communications in preparation for my shining future on CNN. I take courses in writing and public speaking, along with current events classes in polisci, sociology and psychology, focusing on the mind of the criminal sociopath. Within two weeks of enrolling in the psych course, I'm happy to report that my prior fascination with true crimes and serial killers has vanished completely, replaced by such an abhorrence that I don't even want to do the requisite reading or video watching assignments. I decide to concentrate on sports journalism, but I find that my years of writing sports for the *Panther* have left me bored with that as well. I decide not to worry about what I want to specialise in. I have four years to figure that out. As time passes, I am baffled to find that everyday local and nationwide news is what gets my attention now. I join the college rag, and write the same kinds of articles I used to find dull—campus issues, the latest club happenings, pieces about minor crimes on school grounds, etc.

In my first semester, I get field experience as a DJ at the college radio station, giving traffic and weather reports, which are mind-numbing.

I get other experience that remedies the tedium. The parties are unbelievable. At first it's the dorm-room keggers at UCLA. Gradually, I make my way up through sports bars and nightclubs, until I'm invited to posh vacation houses on seaside cliffs, owned by the oblivious parents of those spoiled, pretty, vain, over-privileged college girls, the kind who believe that because they're pretty, they don't need anything else. They're not here for an education, they're here to party. I bang every hot chick I can seduce into bed with the promise that they're about to fuck someone who's going to be famous.

I'm a control freak as much with my sex life as with watching my calorie intake and making sure I put in at least five

90

days a week at the gym. I've learned to pace myself, never getting too drunk to fuck or too high to retain control of my mind. I pick a girl I like and move in deliberately. I choose the kind of girls that have sexuality wafting off of them like steam. I never bother to memorise faces.

Once I have one singled out, I use everything I have to get her. I give her a false name, staring into her eyes while making pleasant conversation, steadily moving closer to her, swaying my body to whatever crappy slow-dance song is on. I use my fingers to lightly touch the undersides of her arms, my eyes locking to hers. I feel her begin to tremble after a few moments and I know I have her. My system never fails. I make sure the sex is always hot, so that at the end of the night, my victim is exhausted, happy and looking ahead to much more.

It's so fun that it becomes an addiction. I can't get enough of luring gorgeous women into bed and giving them the time of their lives. I tell them that I live in the dorm and there's no privacy, so we have to go to her place.

I love the attention, the acclaim spilling from their lipstick-stained mouths the morning after, but when they ask for my phone number, I give them a phony. I make them believe they've got me, then disappear. If I accidently run into one of them at a party or a club, I just tell them that they must have dialled wrong, or that I had to change my cell number due to crank calls.

My addiction to seduction becomes so that I sometimes have five girls at once, all believing that I belong to them. Some places I learn I have to avoid because I have had too many marks. I'm not looking for love and marriage. All I want is the brief pleasure of their company.

No, that isn't all I want.

I want their souls too. I'm not obsessed with violence and physical death like when I was a boy, but I feel the same rage. I'm angry again, and like before, I know what's kindling the fire of my meanness. I don't wish to torture with fire or knives or even elbows, but I use the weapons of my looks, my charisma, and my cunning. I'm unhappy. I've been denied the love I want, and now someone has to pay, lots of someones. I was mad when

Uncle Price denied me his love. Now I'm angry at myself, because I've denied myself Jamie's love, and at the world, for making me do it. I can't punish myself; I don't know how to. So I punish others.

It doesn't concretely occur to me for several years that in having sex with dozens of women I feel nothing for, I am condemning myself to a joyless existence.

I *am* punishing myself.

I'm too ashamed to try to call him. I stay busy with my classes, my writing, my parties, and my innumerable sex partners.

When I gaze into their eyes, I want to draw them out to me, capture them, hold them fast, take what I want, and then let go. They only know I have them when it's too late for them to do anything to prevent it. They try to go back to their lives, but they realise they are missing their souls. They can't find me to make me give back their soul or agree to a commitment, and it's a heady feeling, having this kind of power.

The bodies begin to pile at my feet and I'm at my happiest when I'm back in my dorm, laying on my bed, relishing the imagined bewilderment on their face as they dial the fake cell number I've given them and receive either a recording saying, "We're sorry, the number you have dialled is no longer in service" or a Mexican lady's greeting, "Bueno?".

The fun I'm having stealing and discarding the souls of unsuspecting co-eds isn't enough to stop my fingers from dialling Ray's number every couple of weeks to ask how he, Stacy and Jamie are doing. It's easy to slip Jamie into the conversation since he *is* Stacy's close friend and Stacy *is* the girl Ray's dating. I always get the same monotonous answer, "They're fine." The only time I get more than this two word reassurance is when Ray complains that Stacy invites Jamie out with them on every date. "Long as she puts out after, I let it slide," Ray grunts.

About a year after I move to L.A. Ray informs me that he and Stacy have broken up. Now whenever I inquire about Stacy and Jamie, he mumbles, "Don't know, don't care." He says he no longer goes to The End. "Don't wanna run into her."

"What happened that you two broke up?"

"Fucked around on her," he says carelessly. "She got boring after a while."

I can't talk. I'm fucking around more than anyone. "Can I have Stacy's number?"

"Why?" Ray asks sharply.

Why is he being jealous when he just dropped her? "I just want to call her and say hi... say hi to Jamie too. Do you happen to have Jamie's number?"

"Nope," Ray replies indifferently.

I call 411 and get the number listed under Lloyd Tafford. I let it ring once before I hang up in a panic. The next evening, I dial again.

"Hello?"

My heart is lurching in my throat. "Is Jamie there?"

"No, I'm sorry. He's working right now. May I ask who's calling?"

"Is this Mr. Tafford?"

"Why, yes. Who's this?" He has a slightly twangy accent, like he's from Texas or somewhere over there. Jamie sounds like him sometimes.

"I don't know if you'll remember me. My name is Tam. I went to school with Jamie last year."

"Well, hello, Tam! Sure I remember you! How are you?" He really is a sweet guy.

"I'm alright."

"I'm sorry you missed Jamie. He's working, taking care of an old couple here in town. Let me get your number and I'll have him to call you as soon as he gets home. You're down south, right? Going to school?"

I stutter, "Oh, no, Mr. Tafford. I don't..."

"Yeah, give me your number. I'm going to have him to call you. He was just talking about you the other day!"

"Oh." So I give Mr. Tafford my number.

"And let me give you the number over at the Stolpers' house just in case. Jamie's a little shy, you know. He might fight me about giving you a call."

"I shouldn't bother him over there…"

"Aw, he'd love to hear from you, Tam. He always thought an awful lot of you. You've been really nice to him."

Not always, I say to myself.

"If I remember right," Mr. Tafford drawls, "You're the one who drove him to the emergency after those boys beat him up real bad."

"Yeah."

"Well, I know he'd love to hear from you."

After we hang up, I dial the number of the house Jamie's working in, but I lose my nerve after two rings.

I wait four or five days, hoping he'll call me. But he doesn't. I try his home phone again, but there's no answer after six or seven rings.

Weeks pass. I can't get the guts together again.

I need to concentrate on school anyway.

Great excuses.

I left him without saying anything. I just left him.

As if that last night had meant nothing to me.

He probably hates me now.

I couldn't blame him if he does.

And I'm too ashamed to call him and tell him.

I'm sorry I left, I'm sorry I didn't say goodbye, I'm sorry I'm such a wet noodle.

In a moment of carelessness, I acquire the unwanted girlfriend. Her name is Nancy Simpson. My negligence comes from one too many shots of to-kill-ya, and I not only tell her my real name, I give her my real number. At first it's like having my teeth pulled without nitrous, answering my phone. But after a few dates she actually begins to grow on me. She's brunette, smart, pleasant, pretty, very unlike my usual airheads of preference. I try to ignore the nagging awareness that I'm really not as into her as I wish I was. But I stick it out. I meet her parents and everything. Before I know it, we're talking about getting married.

The second the "m" word crosses her lips, I'm scared shitless and promptly begin to cheat on her. I have no spine. I put a rock on her finger, lease an apartment in Glendale, and call my mom to announce my engagement. She's tickled of course.

The façade lasts as long as it can. How did I let this happen?! I don't want to get married, ever, to anybody! I finally confess all to Nancy, and the breakup is shockingly graceful in spite of the tears and the profanities she hurls at me for screwing around on her.

A year passes, maybe two. One day I'm walking through an alley and I see a kitten caught in the tangled strands of a cast-off toy tennis racket. He's making choking sounds as the nylon tightens painfully around his throat. I bend down, in tears as I try to figure out how to help him. I remember my pocket knife that I've had since I was about ten, the same knife I used as a teenager to chop the hair and heads off of Barbie dolls stolen from my cousin Natalie. I slice the strangling wires from around the kitten's neck and begin to bawl shamelessly as I clutch him close to me, listening to him draw his first relieved breaths.

His name is Bootsy, for he's black with white boots on all four paws. He hates canned cat food and goes through a large bag of dry each month. The day I save him, an onslaught of remorse over long-forgotten wrongs begins to tumble onto me, guilt over beating and molesting my puppy, guilt over killing birds and scaring cats with BBs. I remember the despicable thoughts and desires I journalised in those notebooks.

Why didn't I throw them away? Burn them?!

Better yet, what kind of a person shoots at defenceless animals? What kind of monster writes stories about butchering girls? I can't believe myself. The only consolation I have is that I've never actually done anything beyond shooting BBs at birds and cats.

Bootsy opens the door for my atonement. I volunteer at the animal shelter down the road, cleaning cages, walking dogs, helping socialise semi-feral cats, and I begin what will become a very long process of forgiving myself.

Ray moves to Reno and I lose touch with him completely. I'm twenty-two when I graduate UCLA and go to work full time at their station. I begin doing the AM campus news and eventually I find myself replacing a DJ who is fired over a money dispute, and becoming the host of an awesome late night show, four nights a week, three hours a night, playing long-lost hits from those archetypal '80s groups that have huge fan followings, but somehow are *never* on the radio: the Specials, the Runaways, the Smiths, the Cure, Joy Division, the Boomtown Rats, English Beat, the Pixies, the Violent Femmes, Modern English, the Cult, the Clash, the Ramones, the Human League, Squeeze, Lene Lovich, Gary Numan, Elvis Costello, Adam Ant, and Kate Bush. You'd think by now they'd be categorised as "classic" rock, like Blondie, the Talking Heads, U2, R.E.M., the Pretenders, Heart and the Police.

Over a year, the show becomes popular enough that it's purchased by the network and broadcast on their University of California affiliate stations all over the state.

With this new job, I get a substantial raise. I use my new clout to plug the animal shelter every day, giving the names and descriptions of adorable, deserving cats and dogs who are waiting to be adopted. The shelter says it's getting great results.

It isn't the illustrious career I fantasised about in high school and when I first came here. I'm not a famous anchor for CNN. I'm not winning primetime Emmys or Pulitzers or Nobels. But I'm happy anyway. I'm doing things I love to do.

Well... I'm almost happy.

ten:

jamie
(high school and after)

It's easy to convince yourself of anything when you're in as much pain as I've been in. Little by little, I get used to life without him. During the summer between my freshman and sophomore year, I accompany Stacy on almost every date she goes on with Ray. To say I feel like a third wheel is an understatement. I want to scream when they make out in front of me. I feel stupid when we're in a restaurant and the chair next to mine is vacant. A void forms between Ray and I. To be honest, he's been distant since his sister started spreading the gay rumours about me. He acts like he can't stand me.

When he dumps Stacy the summer after our sophomore year, it's a relief to me, I'm sad to disclose. I give her my shoulder to cry on, hoping she'll find a better guy, but I also pray with all my might that she'll stop insisting that I come with her on dates because she feels sorry for me. Truly, I'd feel less left out if I stayed home.

We keep going to The End to sing, and the whole town comes to expect a weekly performance. They even give us a band name, Old Reliable. Because we can always be relied upon to sing something they'll love.

My grades hover at a steady low B average. My dyslexia improves, and I pass English, algebra and biology. There's no chance I'll ever get into calculus or physics, but I'm thrilled to be able to read and solve moderate math problems and name the organs in the human body, and I decide I want to be a doctor for people, instead of a vet.

"What about becoming a nurse?" suggests Lloyd.

"A nurse?!"

"What's wrong with being a nurse?"

"I'm a boy!" I laugh.

"So? Lots of men are becoming nurses now. It's a great career, very respectable, very responsible."

"I don't know…"

"Some of the nurses who cared for you when you were so sick were men." Lloyd does not enjoy talking about the day we met, so I know he's serious about this. "You'd make an excellent nurse, Jamie."

For my first experience in preparation for my new career, I take a part-time position taking care of an elderly couple in town, Mr. and Mrs. Stolper. It doesn't pay much, but the experience will look good on a résumé. I want to help people. I want to earn my place on this chunk of dirt. Maybe, just maybe, I can get out of my own head by focusing on the problems of others.

My philanthropic ideals will be smacked silly by reality soon enough.

He's ninety-three and pretty sharp mentally, a real go-getter, while she's eighty-nine and sorrowfully senile. I work for them after school until 9pm, and two weekends a month, cooking, cleaning, doing errands, etc.

One night I get a call from Lloyd. He tells me Tammy called a couple of days before, asking about me. "Give him a call, son," says Lloyd.

Ever since the pastor at the church told Lloyd that I'm suspected of being gay, Lloyd has been a champion for my accepting and loving myself for who I am. That's who Lloyd is.

98

He loves me no matter who I might be. He's my hero. He's the angel who came to me and lifted me up out of a deathbed. I don't know why God spared me. I don't know why I didn't die behind those locked doors. I love Lloyd so much that I remember to thank God for him in my prayers every single night.

"He'd *love* to hear from you," Lloyd encourages me, but I can't concede it. All this time later, he's calling? It's probably another prank, someone who's noticed things between us somehow, in school, in church, in town, doesn't matter, and they're hoping to torment me because they have nothing better to do. Tammy's *busy*. He doesn't have time to bother with calling me. He *has* a life. *I'm* the one who needs to get one.

I try to forget it, but I can't. I want to hear his voice, but I can't bring myself to call him.

I keep remembering that awful day when he screamed at me for touching the soccer ball.

He hates me.

Months go by. One night, I can stand it no more and I dial the number Tammy gave to Lloyd.

It's been disconnected.

It's time to let him go.

After graduation, the Stolpers ask me to become a full-time live-in, and I leap at the opportunity. It doesn't take long for my altruism to be t-boned by an annoyance at their everyday habits that worsen with each passing day. After six months, I come to the sad realisation that I'm a human being, not a saint, and a human being can take only so much.

They're semi-rich, but you'd never know it the way they live. They own a small chain of home improvement stores in and around Sacramento and Stockton. They have one hundred and seventy thousand dollars (I've seen their bank book). Mr. Stolper's as anal as you could ever imagine someone being. He wants breakfast on the table at seven sharp, lunch at noon and dinner at five. If I'm one minute late or early, he gets really ruffled. But he admits he loves my cooking. When I met him he weighed about a hundred and fifteen. He weighs one-thirty-four now. They're so tight-fisted that it's a wonder. He won't buy anything unless it's dirt cheap. Even their coffee is awful. I like boiled coffee. It satisfies. But all they have is instant.

And I can't sleep well. It's really noisy with traffic and the ambulance goes constantly through here, we're right close to downtown you know. Across the street there's an apartment building and in one of them there's a bunch of drunkards. Their kids are out playing till twelve or one o'clock every night, kicking a ball while the folks are inside with the blinds pulled, drinking I imagine. The kids scream and yell until I'm so nervous I think *I'm* going to scream. Eventually they go home and I'm able to sleep, but it seems the alarm is going off a minute after I close my eyes.

Sometimes their daughter Doris helps me with whatever she can. Mrs. Stolper smells musty, like an old, wet dog, even after we bathe her. I'm always so glad when Doris brings her four-door car to take us out shopping or to the doctor because I can get in the backseat and not have to sit up in front by the old stinking thing. Ugh, they live like tramps, and all that money. If you saw their cooking utensils, you'd puke.

I miss Lloyd's company, and his health is not as good as it used to be. I'm tempted to ask them to let me go back to part time, but Doris acts like that will kill her.

Christmas arrives and they don't give me a gift or a card. After all the things I go through to have his breakfast on the table and eating at seven, and his lunch at twelve and his dinner at five, not one thing do they give me, not one thing. I shoot my mouth off politely to Doris, telling her that I'm thinking I might not be the right person for this job. Besides I should probably be in college. That evening the old lady comes up to me and says, "Here, this is for your Christmas." I open the card. They've given me five dollars. I say, "Aw, no. I don't want that."

She shoves it into my hand again. "Yeah, we want you to have it." So I guess Doris told them I'm not going to stay, so they're trying to butter me. But it's too late now, Muvvins. The

100

little pee-on's done got his mind made up. I don't have to live this way, nose to the grindstone day in and day out, unable get a decent night's sleep and staying tensed and nervous wondering what I'm going to put together for them at mealtimes. I feel a twinge of guilt when I walk away, but hey, he'll find someone to replace me, maybe someone who cooks even better than me. He's gonna have a time finding one who'll work as hard as I do though, because he isn't going to put out the ducats.

After I quit, I complete my prerequisite courses and enrol in the two-year associate nursing programme at Sacramento Community College. I figure there is better than decent money to be made taking care of people who can't care for themselves, and there are much more generous people than the Stolpers. No sense in being a 24/7 slave when I can just punch in, pull an eight hour shift and punch back out for better money and more dignified treatment.

It's tough, nursing school. It's like boot camp with some of the instructors. It takes almost two years and I feel like dropping out more than once, but I get through by telling myself that quitting everything I don't find easy isn't going to get me anywhere.

Stacy is at the same school, enrolled in the Respiratory Therapy program. I graduate when I'm twenty-one, and Stacy and I go to work at Saint Paul's in West Sac. I don't have my own car, so we arrange to have the same shifts most of the time and I ride with her. When she's off, I borrow Lloyd's car.

They've got a strict dress code for nurses at St. Paul's, either all white (really, who came up with that?! Why should anyone have to wear white where you can get blood, shit, piss, puke or all of the above splattered on you at any time?!) or solid, dark colours. Stacy and I dress alike even here, preferring dark navy blue, forest green, maroon or dark turquoise/teal.

I think my cortisol level shoots through the roof my first year. The nurse to patient ratio on the cardiac telemetry/med surg overflow floor is one to sixteen. From the first moment, I am terrified of losing any patient put into my care. Each time I enter a patient's room, I dread finding him/her laying there, turning blue, because I couldn't be there every minute of my shift, even though I know that's impossible when I have sixteen patients in my charge. I know how our healthcare system operates, and I know how doctors, administrators and HMO bureaucrats are. When something goes wrong, it's the nurse who is hung out to dry.

Before my first year is over, I am asked to become a charge nurse, which means even more responsibility, and more stress. I head off the otherwise guaranteed weight gain with a strict diet of one small meal a day. Lloyd worries about my thinness, naturally, but when I tell him I need to be slim and quick and light on my feet in order to meet the demands of my work, he backs off.

I usually work graveyard shift, and every morning when I come home, I tell Lloyd stories that are either horrific or hilarious.

Like the one about a sixty year old lady with terminal cancer who is catastrophically overdosed with tincture of opium. A Nurse named Rita misreads the dosage instructions. The small bottle says, "Six drops every two to four hours for severe pain". Rita gives the woman six *dropper-fulls*. Within a few minutes, the woman's pulse rate is down to twenty, and her respirations are down to three a minute. They cannot revive her, and when I hear about it upon my return from a couple of days off, I say to my supervisor, "I'm just glad it happened on my night off. I don't know if I could have stood it."

I know I sound like an asshole, but I mean what I say. This woman was dying, but if I were her family I would sue. They were cheated of their opportunity to say goodbye the way they were supposed to.

I tell Lloyd about one incident that leaves a particularly foul taste in my mouth. A fifty-nine year old man who has had bypass surgery is transferred from ICU to our less critical telemetry floor. During the evening, his tele alarm begins to signal that he is skipping heartbeats. The pattern looks funny every twenty or thirty beats or so, and I tell his nurse to keep a sharp eye. He goes back into normal sinus rhythm for a while, but abruptly the tele alarms chime that he's in full-on v-tach. I

102

run to his room and he's just lying there, supine, his eyes fixed upward. I punch the code button and scream, "Code blue! He's symptomatic in here!"

No-one seems to act all that concerned, so I scream again, "Get the crash cart! He's coding!" I tilt his head back and yell at him but there's no response. I start pumping his chest with my fingers laced together. Finally people are arriving. "Come on, you guys, get with it. Get the back board and the paddles!" The doctor arrives, just sort of strolling, you know? I can't believe this bunch! They're just standing there, staring vacuously. "Come on! Help me! He's a full code!"

Things finally begin moving, and before all is said and done, they've shocked the shit out of him, literally. They've opened his chest and pried apart his sternum, and they've worked him over for almost a full hour. But he's gone. He lays there afterward, a huge hole in his chest, with an unsightly indentation in the flesh surrounding. I feel nauseated for days following. It happened the Friday before Easter. I still call it Bad Friday.

Not all the tales are grim. I tell Lloyd about the Turd-pedo, or the Turd-tanic episode. It happens on a day when I have to wear all white for once, because I've neglected to do my laundry on my prior days off. Oh well, I think to myself, so I have to wear white today. What could happen? I bring a big pasta salad in to work because we're having a potluck for someone's birthday or something. I get report from the departing nurse about a pitifully demented old man who hasn't shit in four or five days, in spite of their efforts with stool softener, milk of magnesia, and laxative suppositories. They forget to mention that the poor impacted old coot has also been given an enema, and very recently. So, when I take one of the aides in to check to see if he's had a nice poop yet, we roll him onto his back. He cuts a deafening fart and an enormous black turd shoots out of him and thuds against the wall. When we try to flush it, it won't go down, and we nearly fall down laughing, "Well, I guess he's had his poop!"

We roll him over again, his butt towards me, and before I can do anything about it, he farts again, and loose black shit

103

sprays the front of my pristine, white smock. I laugh, because why cry when you can laugh? I can't go home to change—too far away. I'd like to borrow a light blue top from the surgery department, but there are none available, so I put a hospital gown over my soiled self and try to partake of the potluck, but the stench is so overpowering that my appetite is nix. Lloyd is in stitches at the sight of me when I get home that night.

"Oh, Lord," he cackles. "Your stories are a million times better than my police beat!"

In spite of the nonstop non-boredom of working in a hospital setting, I've been fairly ambiguous about the wisdom of my career choice. That is, until a recent day when I take care of a fourteen year old girl whose father has been raping her for three years. We don't know that at first. She is initially admitted as a suicide attempt. She's taken twenty Tylenol. We have to give her that awful Mucomyst, which smells like rotten eggs. The red flags go up when we find that she has PID, Pelvic Inflammatory Disease.

We do all we can for her. We call CPS, social services and of course, the police, who interview her in her room.

I take a Mylar balloon left over from a gift given to a patient who went home earlier and I write on a blank card, "I know what you're going through. My dad hurt me too. Please don't give up." I don't sign it. I wait until the others are doing rounds, and I leave the gifts in the girl's room while she's asleep. When she wakes, she stares at the balloon and reads the card. She doesn't smile, but I don't expect her to. I'm not sure the Head Sister would approve of a nurse giving gifts to a patient, but as long as I don't call attention to myself, what's the harm of letting someone know you care?

She reminds me of me.

She is the reason I am now one hundred per cent sure I went into the right field.

Stacy's had a few boyfriends since that flake Ray, and she

still begs me to go with her on her dates. I'm glad to have to work some of those nights. My other excuses have been: "I've got a bad headache", "Lloyd's not feeling good", or "I'm on call at work".

We've been employed by St. Paul's for about three years the night I feel generous enough to go to The End with her and this new guy she likes but isn't sure about.

While Stacy's in the restroom and her date is hitting on another girl nearby, I am approached by a guy from UC Davis. He's cute, wears glasses, seems nice enough, but I'm not interested. I try to be, and I talk to him for about fifteen or twenty minutes. He suggests my going home with him, and I tell him I have to use the john. Instead I snatch Stacy's keys from her in passing and go hide in her car.

When I tell her that her new stud is a philandering swine, she begins acting weirdly. Suddenly everything I say is outrageously funny or nauseatingly endearing or fiendishly clever. Her hugs last longer. Her kisses linger on my cheeks. She tries to hold my hand longer than is comfortable for me. One evening she coos, "Oh, Jamie, if only I could melt that ice around your heart!"

I'm taken aback, and I try to laugh it off without cruelty. She beams at me through shiny hazel eyes.

Oh dear. I'm forced to tell her that although I love her to death, I don't love her like *that*, that I wish I could, and that if I could, I'd marry her in a heartbeat and have a litter of children with her and treat her like the queen that she truly is. She's the best friend anyone could hope for. She's stood beside me through everything, always there for me. I wish I was a girl. I wish I was anything that would make it possible for me to be her best friend without her falling in love with me. Then I realise that being a girl wouldn't necessarily make the difference. By the time I'm done telling her the tragic truth, we're both crying. She preserves herself by separating from me for a few weeks, then she returns. "I can't be mad at you," she says, and we blubber even harder as we hug our reconciliation.

"I guess it's because of who you are, Baby," Stacy says softly. "It's easy to love you because you're beautiful, inside and out."

I pull away from her, shaking my head.

"Whether you believe it or not," she nods firmly. "I don't understand anyone who's ever hurt you, who'd ever *want* to hurt you. I don't understand Tammy. How could he just leave? How could he *resist* you? He must be nuts! I *know* he loved you."

"Stacy," I plead, "Please *don't*."

She stops.

🦋

During my mid to late twenties, my opinions of myself and my particular station in life are amended every three or four months. I begin my self-exploration by adopting a peculiar half-hearted pride in my status as an asexual. I try to believe that being a virgin (a word I detest) at my age makes me unique, a rarity, a novelty. Sometimes the girls at work ask me point blank, "Jamie, are you a virgin?" And I blurt, "Of course not!" I'm too flabbergasted to rebuff them any better than that. "You just look so innocent," one of my Filipina friends gushes at me. "You're so pretty. You look like a little angel!"

I laugh at her, "Honestly, Marilyn!"

When I get sick of the "I'm rare and special" bullshit, I believe it's repression, an inability to express myself sexually. It's that damage left in the wake of my childhood abuse.

And it's not just the violence of my birth parents. The pastor has had a hand in this too. Though I've never had sex (willingly) and I'm technically an "A", I'm closer to gay than I'll ever be to straight, and it's been hammered into me at church that being gay is wrong, so I feel like I don't *deserve* to be loved. That I am an *abomination*. Self-hatred flows as smooth and natural as my own blood. I believe that in order to be "good", I must quell my feelings, deny myself.

That is, until I become drained, and then fed up with myself. I consider the unspeakable thrashing I took at the hands of those "good, Christian boys", and I become incensed with the self-righteous bigots I hear at the pulpit, on the radio, on television,

106

in the White House. They *hate* gay people. I feel hatred in their words, in their actions. They don't just preach against the gay community, the gay lifestyle, and laws providing gay equality, they *hate* gay people. And their inimitable hatred seems to say it's okay for people to do what was done to me in high school. I was viciously attacked for "being gay" even though I've never done anything sexual with anyone (willingly). I was beaten because of what I look like. I'm small, I like to wear eyeliner and dye my hair and I like to wear stud earrings in my ears sometimes. But I'm a male so that isn't allowed by "decent" Christian society, apparently not even the being small part. Pastor Sellers at the Baptist church has confirmed his abhorrence of me on more than one occasion over the years, and it's left a pretty bad taste in Lloyd's mouth.

When Matthew Shepard is abducted, beaten and left to die in Wyoming, I keep my eyes fastened to the television, praying that he will survive.

He doesn't.

Was that God's will? Is God that hateful?

Our attendance at church has dwindled, but Lloyd and I still read the bible. My favourite scripture is from Philippians, *He who hath begun a good work in you will perform it until the day of Jesus Christ.* I've come to rely on it so much when I feel bad about myself. About my smoking, burning myself with cigarettes, hating my dead parents...

...and hating myself. That's a sin too. I don't think God wants me to hate myself any more than he wants others hating me because of who I am (or who they suspect I am) or how I look.

It's not right that I should have to repress myself. Some of us men are just naturally smaller and daintier than the others, with personalities that people call "fey", "femmie", "sissy", and several other terms, some of them derogatory, to describe us as "effeminate". I like to cook (I especially like to make pies), and I've planted bright pink roses in our front yard.

I guess that makes me a pussy. Whatever.

Even after the rationale I've employed, I grapple with the fear that God is going to "get" me for being gay, or at least

107

"believing" I'm gay. And Pastor Sellers' outspokenness against homosexuality has indeed frightened me, even made me feel that to question God Almighty is to invite a bolt of lightning or a chunk of flaming brimstone down to strike me dead.

Lloyd and I continue to withdraw from church, repelled by the idea of going among people who hate me. Most of them are people I have very little in common with anyway. I've become weary of them. They never really talk about God, or Jesus, or their happiness as Christians anyway. They're boring. If they're not boasting about their kids' achievements, or yammering on about So-And-So's ugly shoes, they're running each other down behind each other's backs, having their perpetual "Who's the Best Christian?" contests.

I don't think I'm being arrogant when I say Lloyd, Stacy and I are evolved. We love God as much as those folks do, and we don't have to assemble with them in order to prove it.

I have to fess up. I may or not be gay, but I'm no different from anyone else. I long to fall in love, be married, have a family. I dream of living near the ocean, in a cottage, with kids, with cats…

…with Tammy. Always with Tammy. With the words she spoke on Graduation Night, Stacy has impregnated my mind with hope. Wouldn't it be perfect if it were true, that Tammy *does* love me the way I've always loved him? That he *wasn't* playing with my heart, toying with my affection, that unforgettable evening at Ray's house?

Around July Fourth one year, Ray comes back to town to visit his folks (he'd recently left Sommerville for the frills and glamour of Reno) and invites us to another barbeque. I love the scents and sights and sounds of summertime, of sizzling meat, sun-heated chlorine, happy chatter, blooming flowers. Ray's mom makes a really cool Jell-O dessert in red, white and blue, the white part being gelatinised evaporated milk. Stacy and I have a wonderful day with them, mainly because Yvette and Benny don't get to come. It's almost like old times.

The only thing missing is Tammy.

So everything is missing.

Ray tells us about stumbling onto Tammy on late night college radio. Even though Tammy's show is only on University of California stations, Ray found the Davis channel in Reno, and staticky as it was, he recognised Tammy's voice.

It's on from 9pm until midnight Monday through Thursday, and I become his most faithful listener. Every single evening he's on, I'm right there, in my room, my earphones sealing away the outer world. Lloyd wonders why I'm not out there watching movies with him. "Only from nine to midnight, Lloyd." He understands as soon as I tell him whose show I'm so interested in.

"Well come on in *here* and put it on!" Lloyd laughs. "I'd like to hear it too!"

Tammy: his voice still makes me melt, and with this new radio show, I'm newly in love.

"He sure is a sweet boy," Lloyd says softly when Tammy talks about dogs and cats at an animal shelter who need forever homes.

"I know," I half lie.

Time hasn't eroded it away. Every night, we listen. In the winter, we eat cookies and drink hot chocolate, snuggled cosily under our beat-up old quilt. In the summer, we take the radio out to the back porch and crank the volume as we sip on lemonade or iced tea.

And his voice just isn't enough to satisfy me. I punish and delight myself by keeping his magnificent face fresh in the shrine of my mind by looking at pictures of him in the yearbook every few nights. I keep my hopeless hope alive by remembering how he laughed and smiled whenever something funny happened to us, by remembering those wistful looks he gave me, by remembering the way he helped me after those guys beat the tar out of me.

He never mentions where he's from or his life before he became a radio host.

I'll never learn.

I refuse to learn.

I still want him, and if I can't have him, I don't want *anyone*.

I've long since stopped worrying about seeing my parents in my mirrored reflections. Being a nurse gives me little leisure time, and after I initially chopped my hair off to get rid of the bright red dye so that I would be hired, I let my hair grow back, long, golden, ignored. I continue wearing mascara, until I learn that my exertions on the job only cause it to leak onto my cheeks and make me look like I've got two new raccoon shiners.

I navigate the following years using a brave front. Every day I try to find a reason to be happy, and it's increasingly difficult. On September 11th, 2001, I feel like the world is ending. Every time they show the videos of those skyscrapers crumbling into flaming piles of rubble, I cry so hard my eyes hurt. I begin calling in sick at work. I feel drained. All I want is to sleep.

A few weeks after September 11th, Miss Halliday decides to increase my dosage of Zoloft. I end up with bad headaches. She switches me to Effexor, but that stuff scares me, because if I run out and don't take a dose within twelve hours, I have these seizures, like electric shocks, up and down my arms and into my neck and head. Next, we try Lexapro, but it makes me nauseous. Celexa and Paxil do absolutely nothing. Finally, she tries Prozac, which she had been avoiding because it has a tendency to cause patients to lose their appetite for food. "You're already so thin," she says dubiously, "but we'll go ahead and try it."

Of course, it works.

In 2004, a big tsunami devastates the countries in the Indian Ocean. Less than a year later, Katrina wipes out the Gulf Coast. I want so badly to travel over to these places, help these people, but Lloyd isn't feeling very well anymore, and I'm afraid to leave him.

I go out of my way to make people laugh, to make them cheer when Stacy and I sing. I fill my time with taking care of Lloyd, our cats, and my patients in the hospital. I exist in the

110

now, but I *live* for what I dread is an impossible future. The longer Tammy stays gone, the older I get, the more I realise that love is simply not in the cards for me. But I refuse to admit to anyone how lonely I am, how I stubbornly dream that Tammy will come home someday.

I go on, masking my perpetual heartache with a valiant façade of acceptance.

eleven:

tammy
(up until now)

The years zip by too fast for comfort.

On September 11th, 2001, America falls under attack by terrorists. I keep seeing a couple, holding hands, jumping to their deaths from one of the Twin Towers.

What if that happened to me? What if I died and everyone I love never knew just how much I cared about them?

Like tiny fish, time slips through my fingers. I put great importance into my youth and beauty for so many years, and youth is escaping me. Bootsy, who had a long life with me, is gone. On September 8th of this year, I turn thirty-four. I've finally begun to silently admit to myself that I've never been attracted to any of the women I've hooked up with, but at least I'm no longer out to seduce and destroy them. I simply tell them that I'm single and not looking. My one night stands are kinder and gentler.

I'd believe I'm gay, but honestly, none of the *men* I've flirted with have caused any sparks either. The guys I originally intend to be casual sex partners become friends instead, "breeze friends", I call them, the kind of friends that you hang out with once or twice tops and then willingly lose in the wind. I've been tested for HIV every few months and I'm always neg. After all the women, and five men, I'm still healthy. After my fifth encounter with a male that doesn't result in any satisfying connection, I become celibate. Yeah, me! Celibate! I know it sounds about as likely as me living on Jupiter. I determine not to go to bed with anyone else, male or female, unless I feel the smallest glow of an emotional ember.

And I never do. I meet them, and I always go home alone.

I'm not sure when it happened, but I'm no longer infected with virulent rage at my Uncle Price. He's senile, Mom says. He's a loser, why bother with him? My only regret is not reporting him when I saw him messing with Natalie and those young boys around town. I guess I was young and in denial, but I still feel like shit.

I'm writing again, supplementing my income with articles for the animal shelter's monthly newsletter, about animal cruelty, which has just recently gained my passionate attention. Unlike the days of old, in which I shot at cats with BB guns for sport, I am disgusted and repulsed by the blatant atrocities committed by humans against animals. Videos depicting wanton cruelty that I do not wish to describe are widely known as "crush" videos. I inadvertently watched one online a year ago, sent by some "friend" who opened his email with, "You need to watch this!". To this day, I know not whether this acquaintance was trying to alert me to the seriousness of the issue, or trying to get off on repulsing someone with visual violence. I only watched about thirty seconds or so of it, but the video made me physically ill and heartsick, and so fucking angry I wanted to find the human perpetrators of this sick "entertainment" and kill them dead. I don't think I was able to get those grotesque images and sounds out of my mind for at least three weeks. I refuse to watch another one of them. I have no need to be emotionally tattered in order to voice my vehement opposition to these videos. I write out a prayer for the animals who are victimised, and for their abusers/murderers. The editor of the newsletter likes it and decides to publish it:

Do you believe in God and that all creatures belong to Him or Her? Then pray with me. It doesn't matter what God you believe in. If you love God and hate violence against God's creatures, pray.

Dear God in Heaven, Dear Great Spirit from Whom all things come,

Bless those innocent creatures who are being tortured, maimed and killed for the entertainment of sick, perverted human beings. Deliver them from the pain and horror they are facing, for they are Your creatures, and if they were of no importance to You, You would never have created them. Deliver them from the evil people who are hurting them, even if that deliverance must come in a merciful death. And punish those people who are hurting these innocent beings. They must be punished. If they can't be punished through our earthly justice system, then bless them with remorse, regret and reform. Make them see the evil of their deeds, make them see the hatred in their hearts, and make them truly repentant for what they've done. Make them stop doing those horrible things. Make them so sorry that they absolutely cannot stand the thought of what they've done. Bless Your creatures, and deliver them to peace and painlessness. Rescue them, deliver them, whether it's by the actions of good human beings or by the mercy of death. Amen.

The prayer gets a huge response from people who show up in droves to adopt cats and dogs the following weekend. We screen each potential adoptive family as thoroughly as we can, praying under our breaths that my prayer/article has not drawn out any deranged abusers looking for their next victims. But it's fifty dollars for each cat adoption, not including shots if the cat needs them, and eighty dollars for each canine, and I wonder if abusers would really fork out that kind of money, just to kill the animal.

My naiveté annoys me: who am I kidding? How ignorant I am to hide hopefully behind the absurd and prejudicial assumption that people with money don't abuse animals! The recent headlines about professional athletes who fill their idle time with the brutal thrills of dog fighting pop into my brain...

So I pray that our adoptees go to loving, caring, happy homes. I've come to realise I'm powerless in this evil world, but that God answers prayer.

I also write pieces about the serious problem of abandonment, a box of kittens left on a roadside in the heat of August, pit bull puppies who are found running crazily in the middle of downtown traffic.

In addition, I begin helping a cat sanctuary in Glendale with their monthly magazine. It is called the Purrfect Peace Cat Sanctuary. They're cageless and "no kill", which I love. I've fostered a few cats from them myself. "Wheatie" is a pale yellow cat who is terminally ill with the feline leukaemia virus, which is basically AIDS for cats. When I lose my friend, I pen an article to resurrect awareness of the FLV.

Another of my fosters is a beautiful chocolate brown long hair with a creamy white chest. His name is "Wonka". I'm told he was raised in a mobile home full of hearing impaired people, so he's used to loud noises, not that I make any. Also he's been in so many foster homes in the four years since he came to live at Purrfect Peace, he's poised and mellow, around other felines, around kids, and even around dogs. He's easy-going and affable, but he doesn't take shit either. In one of his many foster homes, a jealous little schnauzer charged him once, and Wonka cuffed the dog right across the face. After that, there was a grudging respect between them.

Another cat I've fostered is a shaggy black boy who jumps right into my arms from the floor. He reminds everyone of a black bear cub, so he's called, "Teddy".

I'd adopt Wonka and Teddy forever, but I don't have anyone who could sit them if I want or need to leave town for more than a day or so. I give them special mention on my show, hoping they will find the homes they deserve. If they don't, I'm going to find a way to give them my home forever.

I've changed. My heart is tenderised. Nothing I do now will ever erase the repulsion I feel about my hateful past though. Animals have souls, contrary to popular belief. You can see their souls when you look into their eyes. When I gaze into the grieving eyes of a kitten who's been starving or the big, lonely eyes of a dog who's been abandoned, I have to steel myself against the urge to cry. And consequently, I often find myself overwrought and having to take a break from the sadness of this world of big lonely eyes and adorable whiskery faces, because I'll burn out if I don't. Either that, or the endless despair of millions of homeless animals will drive me insane.

To this day, I stare at the only pictures I have of Jamie Pearce, the small black and white portrait in the freshmen section of my yearbook, the group picture of the choir, of Jamie standing next to Stacy.

I wonder how he's doing, where he is, what he's up to. He's probably long gone from Sommerville, married, maybe even a father, though I can't honestly picture it. I'm pretty sure he's gay. He's doubtlessly with a guy, a guy who's nicer, better looking, more successful and more deserving of him than I've *ever* been.

I will myself to pick up the phone and call him, ask how he's doing.

Tell him I think about him every day.

Ha! I think about him constantly.

He visits me in the night. Every night. In my dreams. He kisses me. He touches me. He holds me close. And I'm not lonely.

Until I wake up and see.

He's not here.

I left him without an explanation or even a goodbye.

My shame won't let me call him.

I've made a few visits to Mom and home in the past sixteen years, each lasting a weekend or a day or two, and our fractured relationship is on the mend.

But I haven't seen Jamie or Stacy around town anywhere, not once. I go to The End, and I ask the regulars.

"Oh no! They're still here! Old Reliable!" And they laugh heartily.

"Old Reliable?"

"Yeah," one jolly, pickled local grins. "Whenever those two can, they get up there and wow us! They oughta have a record deal!"

I go to church with Mom, hoping to catch sight of them there, but the only people I see from school are Yvette and Benny and their three kids. I wish Jamie was sitting here, and that the pastor would request prayer.

When I ask Benny if he ever sees Stacy or Jamie around, he replies, "Now and then, but they keep to themselves. Don't come to church much anymore. They're backslid."

Though things have vastly improved since my high school and early college days, my life as a whole has been as empty and meaningless as the dozens of fastidiously plotted encounters I have had with blameless women.

I never should have left home. I ran away from home. I miss everyone and everything familiar.

I ran away from Jamie when I ran away from home.

It's sixteen years since I've seen him. I fucked up royally, but I'd love to see him again.

Blue eyed baby.
Red liquorice.
The beatific scent of his skin.
The smell of sweet, sticky red fructose.
The way he kissed me in the checkout line.
The way he kissed me in Ray's drive.
After all this time, there's no such thing as time.
I'd love to...

Around the 9th or 10th of December, Mom calls. She's fallen and hurt herself and is in the hospital.

twelve:

jamie
(up until now)

Lloyd dies right after my thirty-first birthday in April.

I've just come home from a double shift and he's sitting at the kitchen table, where he always sits, eating cream of wheat for breakfast. He's only sixty-six.

The night before his death, he doesn't sleep well. Misty, the mama cat we've recently adopted, has gone missing a day or so before, and he's been up all night, worrying about her and giving her week-old kittens milk from a dropper. We give no thought to the idea that if they die, there will be four less kittens in the world to feed and worry with. We're cat lovers. Every time we see a cat, even if it's not one of ours, we try to talk to it, approach it, pet it. At one point we have twelve cats living on our premises. Over the years, they come and go. They wander away, they die. The neighbours dub Lloyd the "CatMan", because he never hesitates to take in any stray that needs his help. He leaves food outside and cardboard boxes all over the front porch, hoping cold kitties will seek shelter in winter. It's a universal belief that cat lovers are eccentric by nature, and we are, Lloyd and I. We watch TV, eat, talk and even sleep in our living room, surrounded by cats. I love this life. With each passing year, I've become increasingly accustomed to things being the way they are, and I feel safe and warm in Lloyd's cocoon.

But his once olive complexion has faded to a dusky grey. He's been retired from the force for about four years now, and the doctor has diagnosed him with dangerously high blood pressure and diabetes. He is supposed to take the pills the doc ordered him, but Lloyd's a very adamant anti-pill guy. I have to browbeat him just to get him to swallow Tylenol for everyday aches. I try to convince him that it's extremely important, mandatory, that he take those blood pressure pills, exactly as prescribed. But he's in denial, saying he's not as sick as the doctor thinks. He takes a pill whenever he feels bad, even though I keep insisting that he needs to take one daily for them to be effective.

I come in from my double shift and find him smiling pleasantly. "Misty's back," he says. "She's in there feeding the kids." He stands up. "I'm making a doctor appointment as soon as they open." It's about a quarter to eight. "Not feeling good." A tremor of trepidation dances through me as he heads toward the bathroom. In slow motion, he falls, facedown, to the kitchen floor. Grabbing the portable house phone, I kneel beside him, dial 9-1-1, search frantically for a pulse.

I apply my CPR skills, but it's different when it's your own dad lying there rather than a stranger. The five minutes it takes the ambulance to arrive feels like a year. Lloyd's eyes fix toward the ceiling. His face contorts gruesomely, and I can hear his teeth grinding. The paramedics take over and work him over for half an hour until finally, one of them says, "No, I can't raise a pulse." I ride along in the ambulance. They don't flash the lights or use the siren.

At the graveside service, Stacy sits beside me and holds my sweating hand as I wrinkle my nose at the potent scent of the white roses surrounding the pretty white urn, made of milk glass, sitting up by the microphone. Pastor Sellers recites a few nice words about Lloyd, his life, his role in the community, the goodness of heart required for him to take in an orphan. Pastor looks bored, keeps glancing at his watch.

Lots of people show up for the memorial, Officer Pete Bloom, Lloyd's old partner, Stacy, Lydia and my friends from school, Ray's mom and dad, Mrs. Cooke, the lady from the bakery, and people I've seen at The End, most of whom I know by face rather than by name. They come up and shake my hand, offering kind words that don't help.

I recall a bible verse about the dead knowing nothing. I want it to be true. I don't want Lloyd to see me as I quietly fall apart. I drive his ashes to Fort Bragg, on the coast, where he and I used to go on spontaneous road trips when we were both younger:

He comes home from work on Friday nights and says, "Let's go!" And we throw a few things together and get in the car and take off. By the time we get there, it's always night time. We go to the Motel 6 or the Travelodge, order from a local pizza place, and just veg out, watching The Silence of the Lambs *or* The Fugitive *or whatever's on TNT or USA. In the morning, the cold, clammy coastal fog like a cape over our backs, we comb the Glass Beach, gathering round pieces of seafoam, baby blue, rose and peach-coloured glass, leftover from smashed beer and pop bottles, whittled over years by the sand and the pounding waves. I have several jars full of beautiful, smooth glass beads.*

Now, I let Lloyd's ashes fly into the wind and they distribute gently over the rocks and sand. When I return to our home, I bury myself in the quilt his grandmother made, the king sized one we always shared in front of the TV, pale yellow with colourful stripes. I cry on the little shoulders of our cats, Misty and Sam. I listen to cassettes and CDs of Lloyd's old radio comedies. At night, I listen to Tammy play his '80s rock songs and sometimes I forget. I turn my head, and say, "Remember that song, Lloyd?"
And he's not there.
I refuse to answer the front door to people wanting to lend their comfort and support. They leave food and flowers on the steps outside.

Pete Bloom, who is pushing seventy, his sandy blonde hair replaced by silver grey, asks me if I'd like to move in with him, the wife, and their two young grandchildren, whose parents are deadbeat dopers in San Diego. "Of course, you'd have to give your kitties away," Pete says. "Maggie's allergic."

I appreciate him, and I tell him how sweet his offer is, and that I'm okay. I promise to let him know if I need anything. I'm far too used to Lloyd's enduring quiet to deal with the noise and vigour of small children, and I'm not about to give up our kids. I meet with Lloyd's probate attorney and learn that the house is now in my name. I begin planning extra work shifts so I can make the annual property tax and insurance payments.

I have to do something, so I get online and begin building a website in memory of Lloyd. I write about his life, how he saved mine, how he loved cats and cared for them, and I provide links to the Humane Society and the ASPCA websites.

Eventually, I let Stacy in, and I face her with red-rimmed eyes, telling her that I'm going to save money, sell the house, and move to Fort Bragg. "Forever," I ramble, manic because I haven't slept. "This valley's too hot... there's too much pain in this house... too much pain in this town... want to start fresh somewhere else... it's not the same without him... I love the ocean... I've always wanted to live there..."

Stacy's stunned, but she's not judgmental. She could say, "His ashes won't care whether you're there or not," but she doesn't.

I want Lloyd back. I want him walking around dumping food into the cats' dishes. I want him fiddling with old VCR movies. I want him hugging me so hard I can't breathe. I want him telling me the police beat before anyone else reads it in the paper. I want to hear him laughing at my funny work stories.

And I can't have what I want.

I can never have what I want.

My fragile mental state worsens in the weeks and months following Lloyd's death. I feel unsafe in this house, always imagining someone breaking in and attacking me. I can't sleep. I don't want to sleep. I start taking more double shifts, and after we clock out, I stay out all night at The End, with Stacy and whatever boyfriend she's with, filling my empty stomach, lungs and spirit with vodka, tobacco smoke, and spirited music. At first, Stacy's thrilled. She always likes it when I'm with her on "dates" regardless of what the guy thinks. Jamie's going to be fine, she thinks. Grabbing life by the tail and holding on.

As she observes my mourning more closely though, she begins to see—and worry. I can't eat. I don't want to eat. My refrigerator is empty except for sodas, bottles of water, a few old eggs, leftover canned cat food, and a jar of dill pickles. I don't know how it works. It just does. I'm tired of crying every time I realise Lloyd is gone, forever. Staying empty soothes me somehow. I'm in control. It's taken a while to become accustomed to chronic hunger, to become able to discount the ongoing, persistent quiet shrieks issuing from my stomach. I smoke more now than I ever did, painfully aware that Lloyd is no longer telling me that I'm going to croak from cancer or emphysema.

As my body melts, Misty's kittens grow old enough for new homes. I give two away and keep two, an orange tabby stripe boy I name "Tigger", and the sweetest, most beautiful orange and white kitty who ever lived. His face is mostly white, like the little monkey in *Outbreak*, and he has dark, sad little button eyes. I name him, "Ginger".

The days begin to shorten and the air begins to cool, and the increase in humidity makes my right arm ache. In early-mid December, on an overcast evening about eight months after Lloyd's passing, I spot Tammy Mattheis in one of the aisles at Safeway. I'm terrified and filled with ardour all over again. That long dormant desire flares back to life as I huddle against a cereal display and watch him in the checkout line.

The song "Déjà Vu" by Dionne Warwick plays on the speakers up above.

I suddenly get a cloying whiff of red liquorice…

Dressed in a nondescript solid dark green pullover shirt and dark jeans, he's divinity personified. To say the years have been good to him is absurd. The passage of time has made him rougher-looking, a little worn, and therefore a trillion times sexier and more magnetic than he was in high school—his neatly cropped dark hair, straight, strong nose, obscenely full lips, deep, dark green eyes... I didn't think perfection could be perfected, and I feed feverishly from my hiding place as he takes his grocery bags and exits.

I feel him seizing my life again...

I've just gotten used to Lloyd being dead. I've just become complacent in my solitary, ordered existence. I've just come to the decision that I don't *need* love. I've been without it all these years, and I've survived.

And now he's back. Should I cry... or cry?

book two:

miracle

Split

You felt safe
I know
In that little space
Laced with love.
Your cocoon
You called it
Warm
Warm.
I cried with you
When it split.
Oh, safe
Cannot compare with sky.
I like you so much better
As a butterfly.

~Carol Lynn Pearson~

thirteen:

tammy
(early-mid december)

It's been raining a lot this month. At a church fellowship in West Sac, Mom has slipped on the wet sidewalk in front of the church and landed hard and painful on her rear. They call the ambulance and by the time I'm in town, she's been at Saint Paul's Hospital, flat on her back in a skinny cot, for two days.

She's off to a bad start there. Her orthopaedic surgeon, Dr. Mumy, thinks at first that her hip is broken. So she gets x-rays and they come back saying her hips are fine. So they yank her up out of bed and make her walk down the hallways, several times a day. All this time, she's crying, in excruciating pain, *begging* them to let her lay back down. She insists she can't even get up to the toilet, that she'd rather have to lie on a cold silver bedpan. I hear one of the nurses call her "lazy" and I'm ready to bring the house down on all of them.

Mom says, "No, they're not all jerks. There's one nurse here that I love. He's so sweet."

"Sweet doesn't mean he knows what he's doing," I grumble.

"No, he's wonderful. He's very careful, and he knows what he's doing. When he gets here I want you to meet him. He's the only one who seems to know anything. They don't listen to him of course. I hate it when he's not here."

A few minutes later, she points outside her door. "He's here! Thank God!"

I can't look or get up. I'm frozen when I hear a disturbingly familiar voice saying, "Well, I've tried to tell Dr. Mumy that it's probably her pelvis, but they've been harping on and on about her hip and 'We can't find anything wrong with her hip!' She's in so much pain, and you guys are still making her get up and walk, and nobody's really *checked* to see if she has a fractured pelvis!"

I hear the female nurse who called Mom "lazy" say, "Well, that's up to the *doctor*. I'm only following orders!"

I stand up and peer out the door to the nurses' station, feeling an unmistakable current rippling through me as I inspect the shock of wavy, golden hair above the dark blue scrub shirt and the small, slender physique wearing it.

I can't believe it.

I've got to get out of here. Now. My hands shake and sweat as I stammer, "I've gotta go, Mom. See you tomorrow."

"Honey, wait! I want you to meet my nurse!"

"Tomorrow!" I bluster as I dash out of the room. Out of the corner of my eye I see him, facing away from me, getting his report from the nurse who's going off duty. I all but trip over my own feet in my effort to flee.

As I sit in the dark of Mom's living room, I wonder why I can't face him.

Why I ran just now.

The same reason I ran before.

My feelings for Jamie are as perplexing and intense as they were the last time I saw him. I didn't even see his face tonight. I didn't have to.

It's as if no years have passed at all.

I still love him.

And I still don't know how to handle it.

I don't sleep worth a shit, and I return the next morning at around five, thinking I can avoid him, but there he is. He's pulling a double shift. Oh my God...

Mom gives me the latest news. During the past evening,

132

Jamie's managed to persuade Dr. Mumy to order another round of pelvic x-rays and Jamie's been right all along. There are two large cracks in the pelvis and her tailbone is broken. She's on strict bed rest, like she should have been in the first place. She'll be in the hospital for at least another couple weeks, and she'll be unable to leave her bed for anything. She's mad as hell. "Those old biddies!" she gripes. "Too busy looking down their noses at me to listen to a thing I have to say! Jamie's the only one who pays any attention to what's going on with me!"

I'm sitting across the room in a beige vinyl chair, nodding, only half listening, feeling him coming toward Mom's room, willing him not to.

But he disobeys me. When our eyes meet, I'm the first to look away. I'm engulfed in fire. Perspiration streams down my back. A fine tremor shakes my body. I pray he's too busy to notice.

Mom chirps, "Jamie, this is my son, Thames."

I cringe at the silly name she gave me. "Tam," I correct her.

"Hi," he whispers in a tremulous voice. "I remember you."

I can't look at him. *Oh, my God, you divine little thing, you. If only you knew how I've never forgotten* you...

"Hi," I whimper, closing my eyes, burning alive.

My eyes are on the floor, but I swear I'm watching him as he assesses Mom from head to toe. I can see him using his stethoscope to listen to her lungs and heart.

Mom asks, "Are you alright this morning, hon?"

He checks her pulse. "Sure," he half-whispers. "A little tired, but I'll be off in a while. Need something for pain?"

My eyes lurch away from my wilful grip to look up at him, and I feel my breath catch. He's still small and slim in build, *too* thin in fact, and it makes his eyes seem bigger and bluer. There's a difference in his face, the tiniest tracing of crow's feet around his eyes, but it's of no consequence, not with a face like that. He's a man now, and he's beautiful, more beautiful than I remember, more beautiful than anything I've ever seen in my life. There's nothing about him I don't love. I even love the way he looks in his dark blue scrubs. (A nurse, I sigh...) For the first time ever, I'm seeing his hair in its natural colour, like dark wheat. I love it. As he bends close to Mom, I see a few dark blonde little wisps of hair on his upper chest…

"No, honey, I'm fine."

Beneath a day's growth of beard, his skin is like porcelain. Maturity has filled out his jaw and chin, making his cheekbones appear even more exotic under the dark shadows of his long lashes. His pink lips turn down in a gentle, sensual pout as he moves quietly around Mom's bed. The combination of male and female traits in his face is intoxicating. Even his *nose* is pretty. As he examines Mom's feet, he smiles, "Good pedal pulses," and I silently combust in my chair. I keep my eyes fixed on the gold linoleum squares under my feet, and I hear him say, "Okay, you let me know."

"Thank you, sweetie. So glad you were on last night."

I feel him pause beside me.

I can't look up. I *can't*…

"You look like your mom," he says in the soft, breathless way I remember.

The air around me begins to swelter. I try to smile, but it's a grimace of pain. "Yeah," I choke.

He leaves, creating a breeze that mercifully cools the back of my neck.

He spoke to me!

I must look a sight, because Mom asks, "Honey? Do you know him?"

I'm smothering. "Went to high school with him."

"He's wonderful, isn't he?"

Every time I hear a footstep outside Mom's room, I startle to full attention, my entire body rising off the chair. But Jamie does not come back.

I'm flustered. I'm tired. I need to go home, I need to wind down.

Mom interrupts my thoughts. "Tammy, can you tell Jamie I'm starting to have some pain now?"

It's six-thirty. My feet feel like they weigh a ton as I make my way to the nurses' desk. He sits in front of the open spot on the clear glass shield, writing in a big green chart. I clear my throat. He looks up, and his weary eyes barely graze mine before they're back on the papers before him. "Hi," he stammers.

"I'm gonna go home for a while. My mom says she might need a pain pill now."

His eyes flicker up at me. "Okay, I'll make sure she gets one."

"You've been working since last night, huh?"

He smiles, "Yeah. I'm sooo tired."

"I can imagine. You don't have to work again tonight, do you?"

He grins wanly. "Have to be back at three."

I exclaim, "I'll bet you sleep like a log when you get home! Before your head hits the pillows!" I imagine him, dead exhausted, not even undressing, collapsing onto his bed in his sweaty uniform.

He bequeaths me the gifts of his eyes, another smile. "Luckily, I only have to do eight hours tonight.

I can't hold eye contact. I focus on a torn spot in the fabric binding the green chart he's holding. "Well, get some rest."

"Will do."

"Okay… goodnight… I mean, goodbye…"

His voice is silken. "Bye, Tammy."

I feel his eyes on me as I incinerate all the way down the hall and into the elevator, and I finally, silently respond to what my mom said about him.

Yeah, he's wonderful, more than wonderful. And he's still here. He's here, and he's all I've ever wanted.

fourteen:

jamie
(early-mid december)

It's a typical Thursday night. I've just come off another monster double shift, day into swing, but instead of going home, I'm at The End. I'm already in Tipsyland and making a fast detour to Drunk Off My Ass. Guilt gently prods at me. I've been feeding the "kids" and making sure they have water and their litter pan is clean, but otherwise I've been neglecting them. I miss them, I wish I was at home with them. I wish Lloyd was there so we could all get under that huge quilt and watch an old black and white Cary Grant movie.

As I puff on my cigarette, Stacy begins her usual chastisement. "Why don't I order us some buffalo wings and ranch? You look like any minute you're going to dry up and blow away."

I roll my eyes irascibly and spew a thick cloud of smoke. "Told you, I'm not hungry."

"You never eat!"

"Why eat when I can drink? And smoke?"

Stacy frowns at me like a worried mother. I had a mother who didn't worry about me one bit. I don't need Stacy to be my mother now.

"I know it's because of Lloyd," she says gently.

It's only been eight months. I didn't know there was a law that says I have to get over a death in "X" amount of months. I don't say any of this to Stacy. I just hold it in, like I hold everything else in.

"You've lost so much weight, you're as thin as a spindle." Her usual lecture. She stubs out her smoke and digs out a five to get us another couple of midori sours. "How much weight *have* you lost exactly?"

The look I give her says I don't want to discuss it, but she doesn't take the hint.

"Fine. I weigh one-thirty-eight."

"You're lying to me," she frowns. "I weigh one-twenty-five and I *know* I weigh more than you do! Besides you said one-thirty-eight when I asked you almost a year ago! I didn't believe you *then!*"

I let the cucumber flavour of my midori sour sit on my tongue for a moment and then swallow. "I can't be mad at you because I know you love me."

"I'm glad of that," agrees Stacy.

"But you're not my mother."

"Maybe not, but I'm worried about you. You work too hard, you don't sleep, you don't eat, you're all alone and won't let anyone in…"

"I'm fine, Stacy."

"No, you're not. Don't tell me you're fine."

It's one of those rare times when I'm ready to tell her to fuck off and mind her own business, that by now, she knows who I am, and why I am, and if she doesn't like me this way, she needs to find a new best friend.

She intrudes on those thoughts. "I know you have your reasons. I know, Jamie. But you're my best friend and I worry about you. It can't be helped."

"Think we're too drunk to sing?"

She brightens. "You wanna?"

"Yeah. I know just what song I want to sing tonight."

We sing "How Soon Is Now" by the Smiths. She doesn't know it, but it's my response to Stacy pestering me about my life. I'm alone. Sure, Tammy's back in town. So what? He won't be here long. He'll only be here long enough to disrupt my peaceful existence, to throw my order into chaos. Then he'll be gone, back to his perfect life.

I try to hate him. I *want* to hate him. For coming home. For being so perfect, so sweet. For making me fall in love with him all over again.

"*I remember you,*" I said to him the other morning. What I wanted to say was, "*Why did you have to come home* now, *you asshole*?!"

But I don't hate him. How can I hate him, how can I even be mad at him, when he's so beautiful? So wonderful?

I'll *never* hate him. I'll go on worshipping him long after he's back in L.A.

"I loved your song."

He's standing in front of us.

Immediately, I'm sober as a judge. "Thank you." I'm unable to speak above a whisper. While I grab another Wave menthol and light up with shaking hands, Stacy leaps up to hug him. "Hey! When did you get back in town?"

He looks at me expectantly.

As I focus on the orange-red tip of my cigarette, I explain, "His mom's in the hospital. She fell and broke her pelvis. Dr. Mumy," I sneer the name, "Thought she'd broken her hip. When he couldn't see anything wrong with the hip he had her up walking all over the halls. He's such an ass."

Stacy laughs, "Sit down, Tammy."

He smiles hugely. "You guys are still singing!"

"Almost every week, unless one or both of us has to work."

"You both work at St. Paul's?"

"I'm a respiratory therapist," Stacy says.

"But you guys stayed in town?"

"Nothing wrong with Sommerville," Stacy shrugs.

Tammy blushes. "No, I mean… I've been back home to visit Mom several times and I never saw you guys. I looked, at church, around town, here…"

"Oh, yeah?" grins Stacy, and elbows me.

Tammy's face turns even redder. "Shut up."

138

"Unless we're working, we're here," Stacy says.

He smiles at me full force. I feel something clutch tightly inside of me. I take another long drag and turn my face away, so I can blow the smoke somewhere other than towards him.

"What are you doing now, Tam?" asks Stacy.

I read her mind. We're going to pretend we know nothing about his radio show.

"I work at my college radio station. I host a show, *College Rock Lives!*"

"Sounds cool," she replies, her voice laced with innocence.

He shrugs. "It's nothing. We play rare stuff that the other stations don't play, like the Smiths! I love them. And R.E.M., the Pixies, all kinds of great stuff."

"We could use a station like that around here," Stacy says, her eyes wide and unknowing. "I hardly listen to radio anymore. It sucks from one end of the dial to the other."

"No, not the Jammin' Oldies station!" I protest.

"Oh yeah. All me and Jamie have ever listened to is New Wave and Jammin' Oldies," Stacy laughs. "We can't get into all this new stuff. I don't even know who Lady Gaga and Katy Perry are! Who *are* they?"

"We're really getting old now!" I add.

"Actually, there's an affiliate station in Davis where you can hear my show." Tammy's trying to be modest, but I can tell he loves his job. "We're also in San Francisco, Berkeley, San Diego, and Santa Cruz."

"Ah," Stacy smiles. "So you're kinda famous up and down the state, eh?"

"Nooooo," he rolls his eyes.

"How long you been doing it?"

"About twelve years."

"Shit! Why don't we ever hear about these things!" Stacy curses a little too gaily. "Are you on every night?"

"Four nights a week," Tammy replies. "They're probably playing a show from a few months ago since I've been home."

Home is *here* for him.

"I would have thought Ray had told you about my show," Tammy says dejectedly. I want to tell him we're pulling his leg, but I can't seem to talk right now.

All the alcohol I've been consuming on an empty stomach must have evaporated the moment he came to our table. It's getting an F for effort. I'm shaking so hard my teeth are clicking loudly in my ears. I can barely look at him. My insides won't stop their ruthless lurching.

"I can't stay," Tammy says. "I'm heading back to the hospital for a while. I just wanted to say thank you, Jamie."

I gulp, finally meeting his eyes, but only for a millisecond. "For what?"

"For convincing that stupid damn doctor to see that her pelvis was fractured." He reaches across the table and shakes Stacy's hand. "Gotta go." Then he turns to me. "Thank you, Jamie."

Whenever I hear my name cross his lips, it's all I can do to maintain my sanity. Now, I put my cigarette in the ashtray and give him my tobacco-stinking hand. His fingers wrap warmly around mine. My heart skips, stumbles, like a man falling down an embankment. My eyes fix on his big, warm fingers…

Tammy says something to Stacy, and I blink. He's still holding my hand. I have no idea how many seconds have passed since he started shaking it. I feel him piercing into me with his eyes. I see Stacy smiling wickedly at me from the side. I feel like I'm about to die. He's not letting go of my hand. He's gently squeezing it…

"Okay, goodnight." I'm pleading with him to let me go. He's killing me.

He's not letting go. The sooner I get it over with, the sooner he'll let go, then I can function normally again. I shove my eyes up to meet his. It's torture, but I hold the contact.

He slowly smiles. Time congeals.

Joy floods me, overwhelming, overflowing, spilling out of me, cascading out of me. Our eyes lock. Nobody else is in this room right now. Nobody else lives in this entire world.

Finally, he releases me. The loss of contact wakes me. I look at the ashtray. All that's left of my cigarette is a long grey ash. Embarrassed, I let it fall among the six or seven other butts and grab a new one.

"Bye, you guys," Tammy says, backing away slowly, his eyes on me.

"Bye," Stacy and I say in unison. He finally turns and strides toward the glowing green exit, looking back over his shoulder, still smiling at me, driving me insane even from that distance.

"Jamie!"

Please, God, don't start.

"Oh. My. God!"

Still trying to ignore her.

fifteen:

tammy
(mid-december)

They sing the classic Smiths song flawlessly. The sadness in Jamie's voice makes the air around me warm, moist.

I can't stop thinking about him.. The re-acquaintance I've made with his face keeps it sharply drawn the next couple of days and nights. That graceful, androgynous face, that luminous smile that sets my heart pounding in time with my throbbing cock.

I've never felt so euphoric. Not a one of those one-nighters could ever compare to this. I'm happy. I'm genuinely happy. I'm not planning stylish seductions. I'm not inventing counterfeit names and numbers. I'm not about to give this feeling up. When his face begins to fade, it's time to see him. I need to see him, and I can't wait for the feeling to explode inside of me again.

As long as she's in the hospital Mom's the perfect pretext. I tear up the stairwell to the third floor because the elevator takes too long to arrive.

There's no sign of him at the station, and I'm like a kid who didn't get what he wanted for Christmas.

Besides, whenever he's not on, Mom gets substandard care.

I stop a guy who has "RN" on his badge like Jamie. "Is Jamie working today?"

"Jamie Pearce or Jamie Fillmore?"

"Pearce."

"He and Stacy went to lunch," the nurse says. "They should be back at four, or look in the smoking section outside the cafeteria."

I don't even stop to check on Mom before I stampede in the direction the nurse indicates. I can't bridle myself. Something bigger than me is spurring me.

He and Stacy sit smoking at a cement table, in the shade of a droopy willow, twenty yards away, as I enter the courtyard. They're both dressed in blue uniforms. He's wearing a long-sleeved white shirt under his smock. His long tawny hair is out of its on-duty tail and flows wildly around his shoulders.

I stand, surrounded by tables, my eyes glued to his face, his lips, as he draws off his ever present cigarette. I suddenly feel exposed, and I'm prepared to do an about-face, but Stacy sees me. Too late. She waves me over vigorously as I hold my breath and try to be casual as I stroll up to their table.

Feeling more idiotic with each passing second, I greet them with a guttural, sea lion yelp, "Hey!"

Jamie's intently scrutinising the glowing tip of his cigarette as usual. I wish he didn't smoke. He looks annoyed, like I've spoiled a really fun private lunch. I feel my heart start to founder as I stutter awkwardly, "I know you guys are working. I just stopped by to see my Mom..." I'm rapidly losing my nerve. This is just not *like* me.

"Well, don't just stand there, sit down!" chirps Stacy. She glances at Jamie and gives me a sly wink. She's an ally.

"How are you guys?"

Jamie still seems irritated. "Fine."

"We were just talking about Jamie's latest adventure up on three south," says Stacy. "When he came on duty this morning, he found one of his patients had been in a diabetic coma all night. The night nurse was too busy sleeping to check the guy's sugar."

"Stacy," Jamie chides her in a sing-song voice, "Patient

privacy."

"Oh, Tam doesn't know him! Anyway, Jamie checks the guy's sugar and it's five hundred and forty-eight!"

"Is that bad?" I ask.

"Hell, yeah!"

"I knew something was wrong the minute I went into his room," says Jamie. "'Cause he was breathing funny, and his room smelled fruity."

"Fruity?" I parrot.

"His body was trying to get rid of excess sugar because Dumbshit didn't give him his insulin. We sent him up to ICU. They have him on an insulin drip now."

It's all Greek to me, so I say nothing. I'd rather listen to him talk anyway. He can talk about his job anytime. He can talk about anything, anytime. I love how he talks a little twangy like Mr. Tafford.

"Is she in trouble?" Stacy asks.

Jamie scowls. "They wrote her ass up, but they won't fire her, even though she always sleeps on the job. They've asked her to switch to days, but she won't—too much work, you know." Suddenly, he brightens and grins decadently. "It hasn't been *all* bad today. I'm also taking care of a guy who popped two Viagra last night. He's still pitching a tent!"

Stacy and I bust up laughing. "Are you shitting me?" I ask.

"Nope. He's trying to be discreet about his… condition, but every time I pass by his room, I look in the little window and there it is!"

"Shut up!" I howl.

"Yeah. I think his girlfriend wanted a three day orgasm or something!"

The three of us snicker, and I begin snorting like that bimbette Chrissie Snow on *Three's Company*, and that makes us laugh even harder.

"Is your lunch almost over?" I ask, when the hullabaloo abates a little, even though I already know. Jamie nods.

"I want to see you guys sing again. Can I have your number, Jamie?" God! I'm supposed to be *used* to asking for numbers. I asked for dozens during my virile college years. I'm supposed

144

to be used to taking charge and making the moves. My voice still sounds like a barking seal as I quickly deploy another innocuous addendum. "Then I can call you and find out what night you guys are going to sing."

"My number?" he asks. His voice is like warm honey.

"Yeah," I manage to croak, my hands rattling as I dig into my pockets for a scrap of paper. He borrows a pen from Stacy. His hands are as unsteady as mine as he scribbles down the numbers. As he hands it to me, I deliberately wrap my fingers around his. A current races up my legs and into my belly. A smile completely ungoverned by me spreads across my face. He stares up at me, and now I know. There's no doubt in my mind. It was true then, and it's true now.

"Didn't mean to interrupt your lunch." *Oh, yes I did*, I think devilishly.

His eyes are back on his cig, but he's still smiling, and quivering. "It's okay," he says so low I can hardly hear him.

Still trying to be cool and detached, I nod, "So I'll see you in there, I guess." I get about ten yards when Stacy runs up to me and grasps my arm. "He's very shy."

"Yeah."

"No, I mean it. He's very, very shy."

I smile. "Got it."

She's not smiling. "He's been through a lot, Tammy. You have to be careful with him."

I kick a few clods of dirt with my toe. "I understand, Stace."

"No, I *mean* it. He's been through some shit, a long time ago, before any of us ever met him. You don't know. *I* don't even know. I sometimes wonder if Mr. Tafford knew everything that went on."

I search her face. "I... heard things like... his folks beat him..."

"Yeah, but that wasn't all. There's more. I can feel it. I know not to ask."

I watch him stare at his cigarette. He's still smiling, lost in a tiny world of black ash and red glow.

What is he thinking about?

"He loves you, Tammy," she says softly. "He really loves

145

you. He always has."

"I know." I've always known.

I've had his phone number for years.

Maybe I just love touching him.

"But he can turn off his feelings faster than anyone I've ever known."

"Yeah," I nod. I've seen him do it.

"Please, if you're going to… just please, be good to him. Don't hurt him."

A breeze sighs across the back of my neck. The blue sky is disappearing swiftly, giving way to grey overcast, an approaching storm. A single raindrop lands on my nose.

His protean face silently works on what's just happened.

I'd never… I shake my head silently at her. *Not ever.*

sixteen:

jamie
(mid-december)

What a circus it's been! I don't think anything's been right since Peggy Mattheis came here with her fractured pelvis. I mean, *nobody* around here can get anything right! You name it, it's been the shambles. Even at mealtimes. We give out a menu and the patients circle what they prefer, chicken, pork, fish or beef. Well, Peggy says she can't digest pork and she doesn't like fish. So what does she end up with? Pork or fish, every time.

Tammy's as glad to see me clock in as his mom is. On one of my nights off, Peg rolls over too far in her bed (some dingbat aide left the rails down) and starts sliding to the floor. She uses her call button and some flake answers, "Can I help you?" really snotty like.

"Yes," Peg moans. "I've rolled over in bed and I'm about to fall out!"

"Okay, Ma'am, someone will be right there." So Peg waits and waits. She grabs the call light again. "Can I help you?"

"Yes, please. Someone needs to come help me get back in bed. I'm weak and in pain and about to fall down on the floor!"

"Alrighty, Ma'am. We'll send someone right down."

She uses the call button five or six times, and nobody ever does come, at least nobody from the nursing staff. She finally sees a housekeeper or somebody pass by the door and she cries, "Excuse me, sir, can you help me? I know you're not supposed to touch the patients, but can you *please* help me get back into bed?" When I hear about it the next day, I'm fit to be tied, and Tammy's ready to take her home against medical advice.

Then, around December 15th or 16th or so, Peg develops a dry cough. They do chest x-rays and tell her it's pneumonia. I'm off that day, so what happens? Some nurse walks in with Levaquin. For some reason, the allergy sticker has vanished off the front of the chart. The nurse argues with Tammy, "It's not in her chart!"

"Trust me," Tammy says. "She's allergic to that stuff! I'm her son, I would know! Get your head out of your ass!"

After a good fifteen minutes of arguing with Tammy, the nurse finally calls the MD and gets the Levaquin changed to something else.

Some of the disasters that occur are quite entertaining. Like the Fan Episode, as we call it. Tammy's Uncle Price and Aunt Sharon come to visit, and right away, Sharon starts raving about "that good looking Dr. Mumy". I don't wonder. Her husband used to be kind of nice looking, Tammy says, but now he's old and has unruly grey hair and a long, wild beard like someone from the bible. Sharon is dressed to impress, in this really tacky bright blue sequined top and screaming fuchsia lipstick. She has me, Tammy and even Peggy chortling with hands over our mouths as she goes on and on about how cute she thinks Dr. Mumy is.

Anyway, the Fan Episode. See, Peggy's sick of laying in bed day after day and they keep it so blasted hot in that place that she feels like she's suffocating. So Tammy goes to K-Mart or Wal-Mart and buys a nice, small oscillating fan and brings it in. Peggy loves that cool air blowing right into her face. We're all standing around feeling cold and she's feeling great.

I come in to check on Peggy. She's dozing. Tammy's sitting in his usual chair. Aunt Sharon sits on the other side of the bed,

148

and she starts rattling off about, "Well, I think if Sis would get out of this bed and get walking, she'd feel a lot better."

"Uh, no," Tammy says, rolling his eyes. "Her pelvis is fractured, which means she can't walk anywhere until it's *healed* completely."

She snaps, "Well, who are *you*? You don't have no credentials!"

Tammy shrugs and fixes his eyes on the TV. Meanwhile, Uncle Price is just leaning up against the wall, staring at nothing in particular. Sharon starts in again, "Yep, I'll bet if Sis got up and got moving around, she'd feel better."

"That's not what the nurses say," sighs Tammy. "They say that with a fractured pelvis, it's best *not* to move."

He might as well be talking to the TV. "Don't you think so, Price?" asks Sharon.

Uncle Price says slowly, thoughtfully, "That's... a nice... fan."

Tammy and I snort.

"Maybe someone should *ask* Dr. Mumy," Sharon says forcefully.

"Dr. Mumsy?! He's a quack!" Tammy sneers. "Jamie's the one who had to convince him to take more x-rays so they'd see how bad her pelvis is!"

"Hmph!" Aunt Sharon regards me through narrowed eyes. How could *anyone* badmouth or challenge Dr. Mumy? "I think maybe Price should go talk to him. I'm sure he'd know better than a *nurse*. Price, why don't you go find that Dr. Mumy?"

"You just want to see him because you're hot for him," Tammy laughs.

"And you're a smart ass!" blusters Sharon. "You should've had your ass paddled a lot more growing up."

"What... kinda... fan... is that?" Uncle Price says. He hasn't heard one word of this discussion. He's not interested in anything but Peggy's fan. We watch him as he shuffles over to the fan, and he starts touching it, *rubbing* it. Meanwhile, Peggy's out of it, just drifting in and out of sleep, and the whole time, Sharon's just rattling, "Well, I think if Sis would just get up and get moving, she'd really get to feeling better..."

Price moseys out of the room, to go to the restroom of something, and in twenty minutes, he's back with a bunch of nurses and orderlies and housekeepers. "And I want you all to see this *fan*!" he bellows, jolting Peggy out of her half-sleep.

Tammy and I run out into the hallway and just split our guts.

"Is he crazy?" I giggle.

Tammy stops laughing, looks at me, frowns. "No."

Terrified I've offended him, I stammer, "Oh... no... I..."

"He's *gone*," Tammy giggles. "Hasta-fucking-luego!"

As we crack up, Tammy leans into me and grasps both my wrists. His head bumps into my chest as he laughs. I smell his sweat and shampoo. I inhale deeply.

He steps back. "Sorry."

I look down at my shoelaces. "Well, I have to go do some rounds."

"Alright," he whispers. "Come back when you're done."

Unless I'm doing rounds or answering call lights, I'm sitting with them during my shift. I even take my charts into their room. I can't concentrate very well though. Every so often, I look up and find him looking at me. We watch TV late into the night while Peg sleeps. When she's awake, the three of us talk quietly, and I feel like I've always known them. I dare to feel like I have a new family. So much for deciding to be a loner. It's almost as if Tammy never left town, as if sixteen years was no more than a moment... almost...

Even after my shift ends, I linger, wanting to spend every possible moment close to them. Tammy laughs at me. "Are you ever going home?"

"Pretty soon," I yawn.

"You're lonely," he winks.

"Shut up." I stick my tongue out at him. "I have my cats."

"I'm getting pretty tired. I'm going to go home for a while."

I follow him out like a lost puppy, and we walk quietly together until I reach Lloyd's car.

"How come you haven't called me?"

He stumbles over his answer. "Oh. I'm never sure if you're asleep. I don't want to wake you... you work hard, you know? When do you work again?"

"Tonight. Probably another double."

He reaches down and cups my chin. "See what I mean? You work too hard." He smiles, then continues across the lot to his car.

I never thought it possible to be more in love with him than I was in high school, more in love than I was just a few days ago. With every passing moment, I tumble deeper. He's a master. A spider. And I'm a fly. Everything he does magically pulls me in to where he's waiting.

That evening, the fan is gone. We search the entire floor, but it's disappeared. Tammy's pissed and so am I. Who on earth would steal a fan from some poor bedbound lady?

We report it to the big old nurse manager I've worked with for the past two years. She's a big-boned, sour-pussed, grey-haired old biddy who was a day shift charge nurse over in the OB wing before being promoted to a night super. Her name is Paulina Holstein. I call her The Heifer, Tammy calls her Nurse Ratchet. He can't stomach her. (She's the one who called Peggy "lazy" when she couldn't get out of bed.)

She comes in and drawls, "*What* fan?"

"It's a fan I bought for my mom. I brought it in few days ago."

"Hmmm," says Paulina Holstein. "You shouldn't have been *allowed* to bring it in. We have a policy. No outside electrical appliances. *Jamie* should have told you about it." She gives me a dirty look.

"I didn't think a brand new fan was that big a deal," I reply. "His mom was feeling smothered. She needed it."

"Humph!" Paulina scowls. "Don't you think maybe a fan would make her pneumonia *worse*? Since she can't *get up* and walk herself to the bathroom? I'd think a fan would be the *last* thing she'd need."

Tammy has a great retort. "She *wanted* the fan, I *got* her the fan. You people keep this place too hot! I think *that's* what would make her worse!"

I can *see* the smoke billowing from Paulina's ears. "Well, I'm really sorry about your fan, but we can't take any responsibility if someone came in and stole it." Her white oxfords (she prides herself on being a nurse from the "old school") squeak loudly and her huge rump wags in her starchy white skirt as she leaves the room.

Tammy nudges me gently. "You in trouble?"

"Naw," I say. "I've been here ten years. She doesn't bother me."

"Kind of a bitch though, huh?"

"She's been that way from the first day I got here. I've only had to deal directly with her for a couple of years, praise God."

"Ten years? How come *you're* not the manager?"

"Ugh! No thanks. Don't want the headaches. Being a charge nurse is stressful enough. Besides, this is a Catholic hospital. They don't promote guys like *me*, if you get my drift."

"Oh," Tammy frowns.

Paulina returns with a fan. It's really dirty and dusty and right away we both say, "That's not her fan."

"Well, I *know* it's not her fan. It's the fan from our prayer room. She can borrow it for tonight, but we'll want it back."

"Well, thank you most kind," Tammy says, emulating her patronising tone without a glitch. "We'll still be on the lookout for ours."

The Heifer flashes him a phony smile and goes her way.

For a while we wonder if Uncle Price took it, since he found it so irresistibly fascinating. Tammy's about to question him when the fan reappears out of the blue, right back at Peg's bedside. Later, a housekeeper tells Tammy, "Oh, I'm sorry. I thought it belonged to the hospital and I took it. Someone needed it in the prayer room for a death or something."

The Cool-Aid Episode occurs a couple of days after the Fan Episode. Peg has been feeling really dehydrated. The nurses encourage her to drink water, but the water at our hospital is heavily chlorinated, terrible. Anyway, Tammy says Peg's never been one to drink plain water, glass after glass, so he mixes up some orange Cool-Aid and what he has available to carry it in is a two litre soda bottle. Peg has had a couple of glasses of it and is feeling better.

A few hours later, the Cool-Aid's gone.

The Heifer comes waddling in. "I see you found your fan," she says snidely.

"Yes, well, there's another little problem," I inform her. "The Cool-Aid's missing."

"The Kewl-Aid?" she cries.

"Yes!" and Tammy describes how he mixed up the orange drink and brought it in. He also adds a tidbit about the hospital water's chlorine content.

Uh oh! That's a no-no. Paulina turns on her heels and marches out the door without another word. Less than five minutes later, she returns with the Head Sister and some other nunny nurses. "Don't you think someone just carried it out on the tray?" asks Head Sister, sickening honey pouring from her mouth.

Tammy shakes his head, "No, I doubt it. It was a bottle about this big…" He explains it to them that he brought it in from home for Peg to drink because she was dehydrated, and there's no reason a nurse or anyone else should have taken it. The nurses look at him like he's crazy.

A short time after, in come Sharon and Ol' Price. The old buzzard says he poured the Cool-Aid out and threw the bottle away. It was in his way, he says.

After that, the nurses have Tammy's number. They're so mean to him. Both he and I try to apologise but it does no good. "You don't bother *me*," Paulina Holstein says with her phony grin. "I've been here for twenty years. You don't *get to me*." She must have heard me talking about my ten years here the other day. She's a real hateful thing.

Disaster drops in on Peggy every time I have a day or so off. The latest snafu has me praying furtively that they'll release her ASAP. I'm with Tammy. She'd be safer at home. I mean it.

seventeen:

tammy
(approaching christmas)

Mom is no sooner over the worst of her pneumonia when something scary happens on Christmas Eve eve. When I come into her room a few days after the Cool-Aid incident, I'm met with Jamie, returning after two days off, running worriedly around the room, unplugging Mom's machines, tucking her IV tubes carefully around her. Mom smiles at me, but she looks scared too. "What's wrong?" I demand, knowing it's not something stupid, like with the fan or the Cool-Aid.

"I just came on. I'm sending your mom upstairs," he says anxiously.

"Why?"

He whispers, "Don't worry, Tammy. It might be nothing. I just want to be sure."

I can tell he's lying. "Uh-uh, tell me what's wrong," I say harshly.

He murmurs, "She might have a blood clot in her leg." He pulls her blankets back. Her left leg is swollen huge, red and tight. It's hot to the touch. "I can't feel a pedal pulse in that foot. I told them to watch for this, but she's been like this all day, she says! She's been telling the nurses, but they didn't listen! She told them that her leg's been hurting really bad!"

I barely keep my temper in check as Jamie wheels her to the elevator. "What'll they do about it?" I ask.

"The doctor's ordered a CT scan, and a heparin drip if there's a clot, to dissolve it. They'll watch her closely. It's very serious."

"Yeah, no shit," I mutter. "Fucking *incompetents* working here!"

Jamie tells me that when he phoned Dr. Mumsy about Mom's leg, Mumsy yelled at him and almost hung up on him. "He just mad because he's on call today and doesn't want to be."

"Not our fucking problem," I hiss. "And Nurse Ratchet better be watching her back for a while, that's for sure!" I'm so loud, Jamie practically shoves me with one hand while he's steering Mom's bed with the other.

Once she's in ICU, they watch her like a hawk, but that's only because each nurse has a maximum of two patients each. They do a CAT scan on her leg, and sure enough, there is a clot. If Jamie hadn't caught it when he did, it might have broken loose and gone into her heart and killed her.

When I cool off, I go looking for him. He's on his break, outside smoking. And crying. I've never been good with Jamie crying. He looks so thin I want to drag him to the cafeteria and make him eat something fattening. "You okay?" I ask softly. It's cold, a low fog clings to the earth, that humid cold that seeps into your bones and makes them hurt.

"Yeah... just worried about your mom." His breath makes a mist.

I kneel close to him. His body contracts into a little knot of tension. "She'll be okay," I say, trying to smile.

"I'm so sorry, Tammy," he sniffles.

I don't understand why *he's* apologising. He's the one who helped her. He's the one who saved her. "You don't think I'm mad at *you*, do you?"

"No."

But I'm not convinced "Don't worry about Mom," I say, and he flinches when I touch him. "They'll keep an eye on her." My voice shakes. *How can he think I'm going to* hit *him*?! I recall that long ago day when I yelled at him about the ball. I still haven't gotten over it. What the hell was *wrong* with me? I'm such a fucking *prick*.

"Hey," I say softly. "What is it?"

He shrugs.

"Why'd you flinch from me? Did I hurt you?"

"No. I just have funny reflexes."

"You have that… what's it called… fibromyalgia?"

He laughs, sadly. "No."

"Jamie."

"Hmmm?"

"I'd never hit you. You know that, right?"

"I know. I flinch all the time. It's a reflex thing…"

"I just lost my temper up there," I explain guiltily. "I'm feeling better now. And I'm sure they'll take care of her in ICU."

"They better, or I'll raise hell." His blue eyes are glistening.

"She'll be fine," I insist, patting him sheepishly.

"She's not on my floor now."

"But she's on the right floor now, you said so."

"I know, but now we won't get to watch TV all night." He looks so forlorn I have to suppress a smile. His eyes raise slowly. "Tammy?"

"Hmmm?"

"How long are you going to be here? Till New Year's?"

I gaze at him steadily until he loses the contest. "I'm going to stay."

His body jumps. "What about your job?"

"I can transfer to the UC Davis station and do my show. I've been wanting to move back home for a few years," I tell him. "Besides, Mom needs me."

He nods with a little smile.

I smile back, willing him to hold eye contact, to show me what's inside of him. But he won't.

"Jamie?"

"Yeah?"

"I've missed you."

156

His eyes close, his body jumps a little again.

"Every time I came home to visit Mom for a day or so, I'd look for you. I couldn't find you. I even looked in the church..."

"We don't go much anymore." His dry lips part. "I mean, *I* don't..."

"I'm sorry about Lloyd, Jamie..."

He nods.

"I looked for you at The End."

"We must have been at work that night."

"You still sing duets with Stace, huh?"

"I won't sing without her."

"Are you with her?" I ask, dreading the answer. They're Siamese twins, always have been. I'm sure Jamie is gay, but I wouldn't be surprised if they became a couple anyway, because that's karma. I should have accepted his love when I had the chance.

"No, Tammy," he says then. "She's my best friend, and I love her. I'd give my life for her. But we aren't like that."

"Are you with anybody?" I ask in my usual headlong way.

He gulps. "No... I don't go out..."

"Why?"

"I don't know."

"Jamie... I'd... I'd like to... I'd..." I falter, lean closer to him. "I've thought about you constantly, since..."

In a melancholic whisper, "I've thought about you too. And I miss you..."

"I've come home because I want to be with you... I always have."

"Tammy... I... I... don't know..."

"Please, Jamie. Please, let's try. Let's go out to dinner or something. I want to get to know you again."

"You do?"

I nod.

Jamie's mouth half smiles. He's still not looking at me. I don't know what kind of smile it is. "I have to go back," he stammers, and jerkily tries to stand up.

I hold him down by gripping his forearms. "Please, please, give me another chance." I close the chasm between us, touch

157

my lips to the corner of his mouth, feel him tremble. A soft sigh escapes him, spills over my lips. I shiver.

"I'll never be mean to you, I'll never hurt you, ever again…"

He says nothing.

"I love you, Jamie. I've always loved you."

"Please," he sobs. "I have to go back now."

I let him up, preparing for him to react to my declaration by walking away from me.

He steps away, walks toward the building, turns back, faces me. "Are you staying for a while tonight?"

"Yeah," I choke on my relief. "I'm gonna go up and sit with her for a while, then I'm going to call it a night."

He waits for me and we walk back in together.

While we're in the elevator, I take his hand. I hear and feel the change in his breathing, but he doesn't pull away, and I don't turn him loose until we reach his floor and the doors open. He practically leaps away from me. "Bye." We regard each other pensively until the elevator doors separate us.

It's not till I get to the house that I realise that I didn't even thank him for saving my mother's life. All I did was throw a tantrum.

I'm the reason he was crying.

I can't sleep.

I have to make it up to him.

The next afternoon, I show up at his front door. His home is out in the country just northeast of town. It's mostly a brick house, like the ones you'd see in Oklahoma or Kansas. The front porch is cement with a green metal porch swing. A small topiary of neatly pruned green bushes with small, glossy leaves encircles the front yard. Pink roses embellish the small flowerbeds along the base of the house.

I relish the look in his eyes when he sees me. "Hi."

"Can I come in?"

His sigh shudders out of him. "Yeah."

The living room is small and homey, with a hardwood floor, little braided area rugs, two big overstuffed beige recliners, a big dark blue couch and an oak coffee table. On each piece of

158

furniture a cat dozes. "So, you're a cat lover too!" I exclaim.

"You like *cats*?" Jamie's eyes widen to thrice their normal size.

"I love cats. I've been volunteering at a cat shelter down south."

"I never had a cat when I was a kid," Jamie says. "Lloyd adopted these guys." His eyes fix on the hardwood floor.

"What are their names?" I ask, and he introduces me to "Misty", a pretty long haired female with silver and gold fur, a salmon coloured nose, and light gold eyes, a male orange tabby named "Tigger", a solid black male named "Sam", and a beautiful orange and white long haired male named "Ginger".

As I hold Ginger and scratch his head, I say, "I came to ask if you want to come to the Christmas party at The End with me."

Again, his huge, sapphire eyes widen until I see the whites all around the irises. He quickly shakes his head. "Oh, no, thank you, Tammy. I'd better not."

"Why?" I implore softly. "You have plans? Where are you going? Can I come with you?" The questions fly out of me before I can catch them.

"No. I... I'm just going to stay home tonight."

"Why?"

He stammers, "It's... it's my... first... first Christmas without L-Lloyd... and I'm feeling... I'm..." He gives up and shrugs.

I let Ginger off my lap and stand. "Jamie, I need to apologise to you."

He backs away a step and murmurs, "What?"

"I didn't even thank you last night."

"For what?"

"You saved my Mom's life."

He stumbles over his dismissive laugh.

"*You* found the blood clot. Jamie. She could have died if you hadn't been there." I step forward.

He retreats instantly. "It's just my job. I pay for liability insurance too, you know." His smile contorts into an alarmed grimace as I step forth again, and before he can take another step back, I kneel down. Of their own accord, my arms go around him, my face nestles into the crook of his neck. "Thank you, Jamie. Thank you for saving her."

Now he's shivering so violently that I'm shaking myself like a building next to one that's being detonated. I press him against me. The mild, musky scent of his skin sends a hot flood into my dick. "Come on," I murmur. "Come to the party with me."

"Oh, n-no, Tammy. Y-you g-go ahead and go. I-I-I'll only r-ruin it-t. I d-don't think-k I'll be m-much f-fun."

"It won't be any fun unless *you're* there."

"I'm depressed. I'm…"

"That's why you need to get out."

"I'll ruin it for everybody."

I shake my head slowly, rolling my forehead against his. "That's impossible."

"Please, Tammy… I…"

"Look at me."

He won't.

"You can't spend Christmas all by yourself," I scold softly.

His eyes are clouding over with something I don't like.

"Jamie, look at me."

His lips barely move. "I can't."

"Yes, you can. Come on, look at me."

The shaking has stopped. His eyes are lifeless, his body like a mannequin.

"No," I plead. "Don't turn off your feelings, Baby, please."

No response.

"Please, look at me, Jamie."

"I'm scared," he says, and lets out the breath he's been holding.

"Don't be," I whisper. He's not faking this. "Look at me."

An agonised wail, "I can't!"

"Come on," I insist. "Come on, look at me." Patiently, gently, I coax him. "Come on. Come on, Jamie." Slowly, agonisingly, his eyes lift, and when they touch mine, we both gasp as the current, so familiar and still so mysterious, twists and curls and entwines itself around us, inside us, between us, drawing us closer… closer. He can't hide from me now. My

160

eyes refuse to leave his. He stares into me, his eyes caressing me, adoring me. The desire in those eyes, the guileless lust, the innocent, ravenous hunger, reaches in, robs me of breath.

I stand on tiptoe to give him my kiss.

He leans over the safety rail on the shopping cart, and I receive his...

My arms are like boas around his slender form, crushing him closer, closer. For an eternal moment, we're motionless, his lips so close I can taste his warm breath. Then he's kissing me, his lips latching fiercely to mine, releasing, latching on again, releasing. He struggles to free himself, sobbing, "I'm sorry!"

"I'm not!" My arms tighten around him again. "I'm not," I repeat and fasten my mouth to his. The sweet, almost-forgotten taste of him drives me crazy as our lips meet and part in a frenzy of firm, moist kisses. The soft yearning sounds escaping his throat reach all the way into my core, and I almost come.

I release him, we labour for our breaths, and I say, "You're coming with me to that Christmas party."

He nods.

"Yeah, I *know* you are," I growl, kissing him softly on the place where his shoulder joins his neck. I take his hand, refuse to let go, all but dragging him out to my car, opening the passenger door for him, smiling inwardly at the look on his face. I love this. I've never had anything close to this. And I want this. I want to treat him like a prince. He deserves nothing less.

As soon as I'm belted into the driver's seat, I seize his hand again. His eyes fly up to meet mine, his lips part in a gaping smile.

It's here. It's been here since that day in church over a decade and a half ago, since that day in line at a supermarket thirty years ago.

It's always been here.

Where else would it be?

Where else had it ever been?

eighteen:

jamie
(approaching christmas)

"We're going to eat first," Tammy says, one hand on the wheel and the other holding mine prisoner. "Where to?"

I'm still in shock. "W-Wherever you w-want." I don't tell him I hate eating in front of people. I'll get something inexpensive, like a salad, and I'll hide most of it in a napkin and flush it when I get a chance. It isn't because I'm watching my weight. It isn't because I think Tammy will think I'm a pig if I eat something that actually has flavour. It's because I need to be calm. I need to keep my head. I need to maintain jurisdiction, because right now I'm so scared I'm ready to shit my pants.

He smells the same. He tastes the same...

He picks a nice Sizzler-esque restaurant with a huge bar of potatoes, salads, breads, pastas and desserts. My stomach doesn't know whether to cramp with hunger or churn with nausea. I love food as much as anyone. I could shovel these goodies down and rupture my stomach like any glutton.

But I like to stay empty. I like to stay strong.

I hope he's not planning to pay for both of us. It was his idea to have dinner, but if I can just pay for my own meal, I can order a nice simple green salad.

162

"What do you want," he asks as we get in line.

"I'm just gonna get a salad," I say, digging into my wallet.

"Put that away. I'm buying."

"Oh, no, Tammy," I protest. "Don't do that."

"Put it away," he says, eyes narrowing.

"You shouldn't. I'm not very hungry…"

"Bull. You're starved. I saw the way you looked at that food."

"But…"

"Nope," he says firmly. "Tonight you're eating. You can go back on your pointless diet tomorrow."

"I'm not on a diet!"

"You sure as hell don't need to be. You're too skinny!"

I'm obviously taking too long to decide, so he orders the entire smorgasbord for both of us: salads, muffins, pastas, potatoes and desserts. To add to my suffering, he also orders a small steak for each of us. As we approach the pasta bar, he says, "Oh, macaroni and cheese. My favourite."

It's not my favourite anymore.

I'll eat just enough to keep from offending him. I'll take whatever I can hide and flush it. I'm going to throw up after I eat anyway. I don't even have to force myself. It just comes up whenever I eat more than a few bites.

I spend more time watching him eat than eating myself. He digs in with knife and fork, snatching huge bites of steak and potato and chewing. His Adam's apple bobs up and down as he swallows his soda. He catches me staring at him. I avert my eyes.

"Eat!" he orders. So I take small bites of the seafood salad and the steak. My stomach clenches its rebellion. After a while, I excuse myself, most of my food tucked into a wadded napkin. After my visit to the lavatory I'm wonderfully evacuated, weak…

…calm.

When we get to The End, Tammy lets go of my hand. "Only for a while?" he asks. I agree.

Then I wonder, is he mad at me for not eating much of the

food he paid for?

Stacy's there, along with Lydia and some of the kids we hung out with in church and school. It's a reunion in fact. Ray Battle is home for Christmas too, and sitting at our table. I guess he and Stacy are friends again because they're being quite chummy after all these years. Even Lard-Ash Battle-Feldman and her husband Benny are sitting at a table nearby. I freeze when her dagger eyes meet mine.

As soon as Tammy finds Ray and they start schmoozing about the good old days, Stacy pulls me aside. "What's going on?!" she squeals her eyes dancing back and forth between me and Tammy. "Did you guys come together?"

"Uh… he… uh… brought me… to thank me," I stammer, thanking God she can't see my blush because of the Christmas lights over our table.

She grins wickedly. "For what?"

"Oh… uh… I helped his mom yesterday. She was really sick. I put her in ICU."

"Hmmmm," she winks. "So… tell me everything."

"Oh, Stacy, really! We just went out to eat!"

"Ohmygod, I'm so excited for you!" she gushes.

"Please stop!"

Tammy's trying to recruit Ray and Benny to go up and sing karaoke with him. But they decline, shaking their heads good-naturedly at him as they guzzle their beers.

He crooks his index finger, "You."

I cower down in my chair, shaking my head so hard it's about to fly off my neck. He comes to me, and whispers clearly and crisply in my ear, "Get your ass up."

I glance at Yvette and the look she gives me sends a bolt of fear up my spine.

I entreat Stacy to join us, and Tammy sings "Blue Christmas," in flawless imitation of Elvis. Stacy and I sing the "Ooh-ooh-woo-ooh" backup part. Cheers, candy canes, and mistletoe shower us when we're finished. While he's chuckling with Ray and Benny, Tammy shoves a sprig of mistletoe into his pocket, and his eyes flash darkly.

Your eyes touch me… physically…

164

As I leave the bar to visit the restroom, Tammy watches my every move and my knees nearly fail me. As I wash and dry my hands, I feel him coming...

I find the back exit. I open the door, relieved by the fresh air on my face. I rest against the cold bricks and wait, knowing he's going to find me. My heart thumps wildly in my ears.

The back door bursts open and he charges me. "Trying to get away?"

"No!" I squeal as he dangles the mistletoe over me for a second before throwing it into the shadows. He seizes me by the shoulders and slams me against the wall, kissing me savagely, deliciously. I'm frightened and excited by his roughness as his tongue slips into my mouth for the first time, and I cling to him like a limpet, making ridiculous mewling noises as his mouth rips away from mine, moves over my neck and ears, whispering, kissing, softly biting, while his arms crush me into him.

"Ohmygod." He's hugging me, his face against my neck, squeezing me full against him. "I missed you so much," he groans.

I'd answer him, "You just saw me five minutes ago," but he's cutting off my air with his crushing embrace. It feels so good. I don't realise he can until he constricts around me even harder. My legs wrap around his hips as I press him closer, trying to absorb into him.

He loosens his hold on me, tries to set me down. "Again!" I beg. "Do it again!" He smiles wickedly, his arms roping around me, smashing me against his solid warmth. An incoherent verbal stream trickles out of my mouth, and I slide my fingers into his dark hair, pull his face down to mine. I let myself go, kissing him, releasing the love I've been storing, not only the sixteen year old love I've had for him, but the love I've had inside of me for thirty-one years, the love I've always wanted to give to somebody. It's like a caged pride of lions, liberated, roaring forth, invading him, saturating him. He shivers and crushes me even closer.

The stubble on his face scrapes my mouth as he ravages my lips with his. I wonder if anyone can see us here in the dark alley behind The End, how we're all over each other.

Tammy pulls away. "We have to stop, Jamie."

"I don't want to," I gasp, reaching for him.

"We have to go back."

"I don't want to."

"Come home with me tonight," he whispers, and I tremble anew. God, I know what this means. I can't conceal my concern. "What is it?" he asks, nuzzling me. His hand slides up my arm, covers my hand. The skin of my palm is so sensitive to every tickle of his fingers. "I'm nervous," I gasp.

"You don't want to?"

I do, oh God, I do. But...

"Jamie, I want you to come home with me. Don't be nervous."

I'm not nervous. I'm fucking *terrified*.

"You don't have to do or be anything. I just want to spend time with you," he pleads so sweetly.

"Okay," I say with a tremendous shiver.

We go back inside and I make a bee line for Stacy. "He wants me to go home with him tonight!"

"Yes!"

"No!"

"Jamie–"

"What if he wants to have sex?" I practically scream my panic.

She stares at me incredulously. "Are you *kidding*?!"

"What am I going to do?! What am I going to do?!"

She braces me. "Calm down. You don't know that's what he wants."

"Are *you* kidding?!"

"Baby," she says gently. "What are you afraid of? It's Tammy."

I *am* afraid. And Stacy can't help me.

I'm riding with a stranger. That's why I'm afraid. I'm alone, with a guy I've always loved, but in truth, a guy I don't really know. I'm afraid, and it's all I can do not to lose my shit. Somehow, holding his hand tightly is helping me to stay calm. Whenever he takes it away to make turns, I'm ready to disintegrate.

The worst is, I have no idea what to expect. The fact that I've agreed to go home with him assuredly has him assuming we'll have sex.

How do I tell him? That I'm afraid? That I have issues? That I've never had sex, with anyone (willingly)? That, aside from him, I've never let anyone touch or kiss me except for Lloyd and Stacy?

That he's my first? That he's my *only* in all my thirty-one years?

That he's the only one I want to do this with?!

How do I tell him? And will he laugh? Will he think I'm a freak? Worse, will he get angry if I find that I *can't*? Will he call me a cock-tease? Will he *force* me?!

I don't know him. Not like I'd like to think I do.

That's the hard, cold truth. He's taller, heavier and stronger. He could rape me as soon as he gets me into his house.

I begin to shrink into myself. The scars on my ankles begin to sting.

I hear my biological father's voice:

Come on, Pretty. Open for Daddy.

My eyes are dry and tearless, and I blink repeatedly, trying to moisten them. We pass the road to my house, and I want to leap from the car and run home, all the way, to my house, to my kids, to the mundane safety and blessed routine that lives behind those wonderful locks and deadbolts.

Please, God, I pray silently. *Please help me. Please don't let Tammy be a bad guy. Please let it be that he loves me as much as I love him. I think he loves me, but I don't know for sure. I didn't plan this, God. I didn't plan anything. He came home and it's happening. I want this. I want him. I love him. Please, don't be mad. Please help me. Please...*

I need Him to help me to trust, to not be afraid.

I need Tammy to be for real.

God, I'll die if he isn't.

nineteen:

tammy
(christmas eve)

He's all I want. He's all I've ever wanted. I have spent the better part of my life prowling around clubs and parties when I should have been here, with him. We should have been together. Because this is meant to be. I'll never be happy without him. His is the only face I can see when I close my eyes.

I still sense what I've always sensed about him. He's vulnerable. Some asshole burned him bad. I've got to be careful. I won't force him. What I'm hoping is to make him *willing*. I can't take much more. I'm ready to go crazy.

It's quiet as I drive. We don't try to talk just to prevent awkward silence. We don't need to. I feel this invisible thing in the car with us. We're so keenly aware of each other. His hand seeks mine, takes it, wraps snugly around it, and it's almost more erotic that when we made out a while ago.

I try to distract myself with traffic and road signs, but nothing works. I remember how he pulled me to him and kissed me so fiercely. Before today, I don't remember ever really kissing anyone, where the kisses are completely fulfilling in and of themselves, not just an appetiser. All by themselves, they are terrifyingly real and maddeningly sexy.

I remember Ray's drive, almost twenty years ago—that was real too—oh God, it was so real...

He says he likes Mom's house, but the skittish look in his eyes tells me he's not here, with the carpet, furniture, TV or the faint scent of cinnamon from the Christmas Airwick freshener she sprays around this time of year. Even when I introduce him to Tillie, Mom's ancient tortoise-shell/Persian, he just nods fretfully, ready to faint, pale as a ghost, his chin tucked down into his neck.

I've got to try to put him at ease. If he's been burned, it's going to be hard for him to trust me. I have to earn it.

I can't believe how much I've changed since I saw him last. I don't recognise myself. I'm so glad.

I turn on my computer and show him the articles I've written for the newsletter at the Glendale Animal Shelter and Purrfect Peace Cat Sanctuary. "You're such a great writer," he says. "I wish I could write stories." Then he takes me to the website he made for Mr. Tafford, and I'm moved by what he's created. He *has* written a story, a beautiful tribute to his dad.

"It's awesome, Jamie." He turns to me and smiles. The ice chips are flying.

I turn on the TV and VCR. "What do you want to watch?"

"I don't care," he says, anxious again.

"I'm not into primetime TV, are you?"

"No, I like movies better."

"What kind? Action movies? Sci-fi? Horror?"

"No, no horror for me!" He's trying to laugh, but I see something else. "I can't even watch *Indiana Jones*. I hate any movies that have people being burned."

I'm about to ask about this when he says, "What I really love are old movies—the kind with Cary Grant, John Wayne, Bob Hope—that stuff."

I'm delighted. I put on my most recent favourite movie, *Bringing Up Baby*.

"I had you figured for the type who loves blockbusters," says Jamie, reading the VHS cover. He's still nervous. Tillie jumps silently onto the couch with us. Within three minutes, Jamie is her new best bud. She sits on his lap, purring and kneading.

"I can't believe how much of a cat lover you are," Jamie says. "You just don't look the type. You always seemed more like a dog person."

If I ever told Jamie how I used to treat poor little Cotton, what would he think of me?

"Remember that night we were talking about me being the next Dr. Doolittle?"

"Yeah, what happened?"

"It took less time and money to become a nurse."

"I never knew how much I loved cats until I met Bootsy," I smile. "I'm going to open my own cat shelter one day."

He lights up. "Yeah?"

"Uh huh. I can't seem to think of a cool name though, like Purrfect Peace."

"I think Lloyd would have opened his own shelter one day if he had been healthier. He was always taking in stray cats."

I ask, "Where did you take him… his ashes?"

"Fort Bragg."

"I've never heard of it."

"It's up past San Francisco, on the coast."

"I love the ocean! I wish I could *live* there."

Jamie gasps, "Me too! I'm trying to save some money so I can move there. It's all I've ever wanted!"

I smile at his enthusiasm until he flushes. "Maybe we could start a cat sanctuary, on the coast."

He searches my eyes, wonders if I'm serious. "I've always wanted a little house, like a little cottage or a farmhouse, on a hill, about five or ten minutes walk from the water. The cats can run all over the property."

"No cages," I say.

"Exactly!"

"We could name it after Lloyd."

"Yeah?"

"Of course."

He looks away, his chest heaving. "I miss him."

"I know, Baby."

"He was so good to me. What am I going to do without

170

him?" He blinks, splattering tears.

"Hey! You're doing okay."

He speaks rapidly, his breath hitching, "No... not really, Tammy. I thought I was, but... I want someone to love me. I can be alone, but I don't *want* to, not anymore."

"You're not alone. I'm here."

His wet eyeballs waver back and forth in their sockets. He looks deep into me. "I love you, Tammy. I've always loved you. I need you so much."

An instant later, he turns away. He's dropped his guard, opened his heart...

"I love you too, Jamie, I do."

"You love me." It's not a question.

"You know I do."

"Why did you leave?"

I choke on my effort to answer him.

"You hated me," he says plainly.

"I *never* hated you."

"Then why?"

"Because I was a coward," I sigh. "I ran away because I loved you and couldn't deal with it. I was afraid. I was confused. But I'm not anymore. I know who I am now. I know I'm sixteen years late, but I love you."

"Tammy?"

"Hmmm?"

"Hug me, please, tight, like you did earlier."

God, finally! My arms encircle him. His go around my shoulders. I squeeze him like a python. "More... more," he cries. It's like he wants me to crush the life out of him. The tighter I hold him, the more he loves it. "Yes... yes..." I feel his lips on my neck. The heat of his breath against my ear shatters what's left of my control. We make out for long moments, his tongue tentatively touching mine, until I'm forced to gasp, "Jamie, we have to stop now... if you don't want this to go any further tonight."

He pulls away. I can't believe he's being so hesitant. I'm so hard I'm about to pop. "Jamie..."

"I've never had sex."

I blink stupidly at him, trying to wrap my brain around what he's just said.

"Liar," I tease.

"I'm not lying."

"You're too gorgeous to be a virgin."

He turns away. "I hate that word."

I stroke his chin, feeling the first pokes of day old stubble. "Why?"

"I don't know…"

"There has to be a reason."

He shrugs. "I just haven't. I've tried, for years, to come up with a reason, and I can't. I've just never been interested in anyone but you. You're the only one I've ever kissed."

I'm the only asshole who's ever burned him.

"God… Jamie…"

"I know… I'm a freakshow."

I lean into him, and he shies from me.

"Are you afraid of me?" I ask softly.

"A little."

I love him… everything about him… He's so shy, and it's so sexy it's driving me fucking *bananas*.

twenty:

jamie
(christmas eve)

I want to trust him, because I *want* this to happen, but I'm so afraid. What if this is, after all, a cruel joke? "You won't hurt me?" I ask him as we make our way to his bedroom. I can't help it. I don't think I've ever been this afraid.

He's taken my shirts off. I feel him tracing the scars on my shoulder blades. My body tenses under his fingers. I don't want him to ask about them, the ugly scars on my back, the little round burns on my buttocks and thighs.

He does not. "It will probably hurt, Jamie. I'll be as careful as I can. But we don't have to do *that...* tonight. Let's just see what happens."

The sight of his bed, a big, broad king that nearly takes up his whole room, adds to my terror. He takes all of his clothes off except his underwear. I don't look. I always imagined this moment, believing I'd be ogling his goodies, oohing and ahhing, drooling over his body like a rabid wolf.

But this isn't a daydream. This is reality, and I'm forced to acknowledge the fact that inside his shorts is a penis that he hopes to penetrate me with. I pray I won't faint as he takes my jeans off. We're both in our tighty whities (actually, his are dark green) when he peels back the black and red checkerboard flannel spread and the rest of the covers. "Come on. It's okay."

Once the blankets are over me, my fear is thousand fold as he pats the sheets beside him. "Come closer." I obey, and he gathers me against him. "Want a bear hug?"

"Yes," I plead, and he crushes me close, his skin branding me, the hair on his chest tickling me. His strong, sexy smell fills my nose. My heart slams wildly against his. I can feel his woody and I know he can feel mine. It shrank when I got scared, but when Tammy hugs me like this, my entire body responds by reaching for him...

"Let's take off our underwear," he whispers. The ice begins to refreeze but I force my frostbitten fingers to work, make myself pull my whities off and kick them away. He pulls me up against him, and our nakedness touches everywhere. The alien hotness makes me tingle and shudder with fear and pleasure. I had no idea that his naked body against mine would feel so terrifyingly good. The double shock of his hands on my ass and his tongue in my mouth makes me lurch and cry. I don't know where to put my own hands, so I just leave them around his neck.

Tammy's not shy at all. His hands are everywhere, scorching me, yet I'm shivering like a baby bird in a blizzard. His thumb finds the soft pink of my nipple and brushes it. Instantly it hardens.

I brace myself for the question, "What's this?" when he finds the mark left behind by the feeding tube that saved me.

But he doesn't ask. He strokes my body until he reaches my belly, where he slowly rubs in a hard, circular caress that has me crying softly against his mouth. My insides begin to burn and clench. "You're so beautiful," he whispers, as his hand closes around my erection and the fingers of his other hand probe up between my buttocks. I flinch. "It's okay," he soothes. "Open your legs. Open..."

Open for Daddy.

He gently slips two fingers into me. I'm too lost in what he's doing to think straight. Then he finds a place inside of me so sensitive that I jerk and let out a keening yelp. His other hand

174

yanks on me softly as I mindlessly thrust against him, my fingers digging into the bunched muscles of his shoulders.

"There you go, Jamie." I hear strange music, as I move my hips faster and faster. His fingers flicker and tickle that ultrasensitive spot deep inside my body, a match striking, white heat flaring, alive, again and again. Our eyes are opened, our kisses are closed-mouthed, noisy, hard, suck and release... suck and release. It's sexier than any French kiss in history, and more formidable, because he's seeing as deeply into me as his fingers are twisting, and the look in his eyes is scary, sexy. He knows he has me, and I can't stop him from taking me, from toying with me, from possessing me.

Nor do I want to. Our kisses go on and on, until his mouth, and the skin around it, begins to blush lustily.

The matches keep striking and I'm igniting, catching fire. I begin to make those preposterous whimpering sounds again. My ears start to ring. My heart beats so fast and so hard it's about to burst out of my chest.

You're nasty, Jamie.

I push her away. How can this be *wrong*? Faster and faster I dance to the symphony roaring in my ears, until suddenly I'm enveloped in brilliant, blissful heat, an incredible warmth surrounding me, radiating from the top of my head to the tips of my toes. The heat begins to leave me in hard spasms of indescribable delight. "What's happening to me?" I cry out loudly, my voice muffled by the deafening music.

"Let it out, Jamie. Let your love go..."

I'm dying. I'm leaving my body and yet here I am. I feel every single thing my body is doing. It's so completely overwhelming that love flows from my eyes as well. I sob helplessly as Tammy strokes and fists the last spurts of warm fluid out of me.

My heart thuds softly, calmly now. The world is still spinning. It's a while before I can speak. "What... what happened to me?"

Tammy kisses me softly on the forehead. "You creamed, Jamie. You came..."

"I came?"

He studies me carefully. "Have you had wet dreams?

I think back to my teenage dreams of him. A few times I woke up sticky and moist, but I can't remember ever having that warmth spreading through my body, or those intense throbs and spasms. I can still feel little aftershocks rippling through me. Tammy's eyes delve into mine, and inside me blossoms a warm desire—to do to him as he's done to me. "I want to touch you, Tammy."

He sucks in his breath. "You don't have to."

My body tingles. "I want to."

He takes my timid hand and puts it on him, shows me how to touch him. His smile, tender, wicked, sends another little earthquake rumbling through me.

It's big, thick, solid...

Like Daddy's.

...twitching, the tip like a shining, dark, ripe plum. It throbs warmly against my fingers as I watch him make faces. His hips begin to thrust toward me, and instinctively I begin to increase my speed. His body is singing the same incredible song mine just sang, and watching him lost in pleasure makes me begin to sing all over again. My hips undulate, my tummy clenches, melts. His hand folds around me, and we watch each other as the gorgeous music intensifies, reaches a shattering plateau.

I close my eyes against unwelcome visions... *I'm not letting them ruin this!*

"Come on, Tammy," I murmur to him.

He lets out a deep groan. Another unwanted image looms and I shove it aside in anger. *This is love! This is my miracle and nobody is taking it away from me!* Tammy's semen splashes against my hand and belly.

It's lingering, trying to ruin this beautiful moment. I thrust against him.

"You're hard again," he rasps.

"Yeah," I whisper.

"I am too. Already," he laughs softly. "Rub against me. It's okay... rub against me."

We rub together, stiff and sticky. It feels so good. The orchestra begins to play again, rising, swelling...

176

Then he cries, "Jamie, let me inside of you, please? Please let me inside."

I freeze.

"Please? Let me…"

"It's going to hurt."

"Yes, and it might bleed. I'll be very, very careful, I promise."

"It'll get on your sheets!"

"Don't worry about that," he pants. "Please, Jamie?"

This is the most monumental, most important, most terrifying night of my life. I'm so in love, so ready for him to take everything he wants from me. Even if he wants to break me open, take my heart, leave me cold and deserted, and crying endlessly for him, even if he *is* the most heartless, cold-blooded snake alive, I love him, I want him.

I want this.

I nod. Tammy reaches under my thighs and lifts until my legs are wrapped around his neck and shoulders. I don't take note of much, I'm too frightened. I think I see the letters "KY", then his fingers are smearing something cold and gooey into me. He presses inside slowly, carefully, and I'm unable to keep my body from clamping down in an effort to protect itself.

And that makes it hurt worse.

I *want* the pain. I want it to be just like it is with everyone else. Tammy's lips are on mine, his tongue in my mouth like a needle injecting me with joy.

He's inside of me. He's making love to me. He's hurting me. He's making me cry…

…and I love it. Even before he begins to thrust deeper and deeper and the pain begins to transform into pleasure, I love it.

It's really happening.

It's really happening to me.

And Tammy is here.

twenty-one:

tammy
(christmas eve/present)

I watch his eyes, how they widen in fear and then fall half-closed, dazed in rapture. I watch how when the light hits his eyes just so, it transforms the deep sapphire blue of them into an iridescent prism. I watch his lips crumple in pain and then curl in an agape smile of bliss. He claws me with his nails, climbs up above me like a man using another man to keep from drowning. I can't stop watching him. His face is beautiful even when it's distorted. His arm muscles quiver like the muscles surrounding me as I reach deeper inside of him, seeking something from him, from myself. We move together fluidly. I thrust towards him, he thrusts towards me, faster, deeper, faster, deeper. He squeals as I strike his prostate, and when he comes, I watch him. Then I come, and he watches me.

We doze for a while. I need to piss. I nudge him. "I gotta go to the bathroom, Jamie."

"Noooooo," he moans, and snuggles closer to me. He begins to brush his lips against mine, just barely touching, teasing.

"What are you doing?" I ask.

"Playing with you," he murmurs. His lips whisper against mine. I've never felt anything so soft. Then he lightly licks me.

"Oh!" My cock, still inside of him, is back to life, thrumming madly. His butterfly kisses meld into one long, soft kiss, and God, it's sexy. Our tongues reach out and greet each other.

I can't believe this sweetness. We begin again, sexing, thrusting, reaching for each other, seeking, finding, speaking with tongues, without words, and it feels so clean, so pure, so perfect. Our hands clasp, our mouths fuse, our eyes lock. We're united, completely. I'm still not used to this bittersweet ache in my centre.

He closes around me like a velvet fist and we explode together so powerfully, so violently, that we yell into each other's mouths. It goes on and on, and I can tell by Jamie's catching, sobbing cries that his orgasm is as hard and slow and as agonisingly glorious as mine. On and on it goes—so long that I begin to worry that we'll never stop coming, that we'll be suspended in ecstasy, forever. And that wouldn't be a bad thing, except that there'd be nothing left to wish for.

And I want more. I *want* to want more.

At last we descend from heaven, like two angels, hand in hand.

We look at each other; we've both felt it. It scares me, what we've felt. It scares him too. I see it…

"Baby, I've got to go pee," I plead. The look on his face kills me. "We have to sooner or later," I say softly. His eyes well up. "We'll do it again, you little greedy thing, you. Don't tense up," I warn, and we count, "One, two, three," and I pull out, his muscles clenching around me the whole way. My dick is smeared with his warm, dark blood and my own jizz. I peel off the rubber, notice that it's torn because it's twice used.

"I bled!"

"Don't worry about it," I say.

He refuses to let me go as we cross the house to the bathroom, his lips all over my face and neck as I lift the toilet seat.

"My own personal leech," I murmur against his lips.

He laughs softly, releasing me only to aim his dick.

We pee, our streams splashing and mixing. "You don't

regret this, do you?" I ask teasingly.

His long lashes sweep up. I love the dead-seriousness in those eyes. "No, Tammy. I could never regret this."

I crank on the shower, wait for the water to heat up, then I lift him into my arms. He weighs next to nothing. We bathe the cum, sweat and blood off ourselves in the warm cascade. We wash each other's hair and make out while he gives me a soapy hand job. His eyes are inquisitive, fervent, thoughtful, as he watches his hand stroking up and down.

We go back to bed, pull the covers up snug around our chins. "Something's bothering you, Jamie. Please, tell me."

He bites his lower lip. I love it when he does that. He's thinking. His eyes water. "It's something that I had for thirty-one years, and now, it's just…"

"What?"

He rolls his eyes, believing himself ludicrous. "My virginity." More tears seep from under his eyelids.

I snuggle closer. I smell shampoo, soap, his individual musk. "It's gone," he whispers.

I only had mine until I was fourteen, not even that long if I count the thing with Uncle Price. I want to understand, but I can't. "What is virginity anyway?" I ask. "It's a state of mind. A half hour ago you didn't know about that part of your life. Now you do. It's not like you're a girl. You didn't have a cherry that I *literally* popped."

"Excuse me," Jamie says correctively. "I *bled*."

I smile at him.

"And I wanted that. I wanted it to hurt, I wanted to bleed, I wanted to be scared. I wanted everything to be like it is with everyone else. And it was perfect."

"So, what's…"

"Where is my virginity?"

I don't have to think hard to come up with the answer. "It's with me," I say. "I have it."

He thinks about it for a moment. "What do *I* have?"

He means it.

"You have *me*," I tell him.

And I mean it.

180

I'm disturbed by what looks like doubt in his eyes.
He doesn't trust me. He doesn't fully trust me.
It hurts.

The small, soft hearth of him warms me, makes me drowsy, but I fight it.

It feels incomplete, this night. Something is bugging him, and I'm frustrated. I'm interested. I want so badly to understand him.

But I have to be patient.

For now I'll just hold him and silently love the dark fringe of his eyelashes resting against his flushed cheeks, thirst for his full, soft lips against mine. I imagine my cock between them, fucking this gorgeous mouth.

I want everything from him. Everything I can possibly get, and I want to give him all of me.

Be patient, I soothe myself. *Take it slow. He'll open up. Give him time.*

I can't stand this space between us. I try to reassure myself that if I just give him time, he'll know I care about him. He'll know I'll never leave him again. And he'll feel secure enough to share himself with me, his *whole* self.

There's a lot he's not telling me.

The sun begins to peek through the mini-blinds above my bed. It's Christmas Day. Jamie's thick, dark lashes sparkle like they're dusted with gold. He's so incomparably beautiful, lithe, delicate. His dark, honey-coloured hair splays across the pillow. His bewitching androgynous beauty arouses me, draws me.

I lean over him and kiss the large maroon scars over his shoulder blades. He moans and cries softly, still half asleep. I roll him over on his back and examine the big, red lumpy scar around his right ankle before gently kissing it.

"What happened here?" I ask, nodding at his left ankle. It looks like something's bitten him. The sore is raw and puckered and seeping a small amount of clear fluid.

He shakes his head, his eyelids heavy. "Don't ask."

I manipulate him like play-doh. He whimpers as I play with his supple body, as I kiss and bite his tender nipples, his soft tummy, the uncharted silk of his inner thighs. My hunger is out of control, my lips loudly kissing him where his thigh melds into his ass. I dip my head and rim him, gently at first, teasingly, then I thrust my tongue deep. He sobs, twisting his fingers in my hair. His pretty, weeping sex pats against my cheek softly, shyly, as if to say, "Here I am." The smell of it, of *him*, makes my nostrils flare. I'm a wolf on the scent of something good. My own cock pounds, demanding to be satisfied. But I'm a gentle predator. My intention is to love him, to suck and lick him, to kiss and tease him, until he cries in ecstasy and we're both drenched in his warm, sweet, sticky spunk.

And then I want him to do the same to me.

I go to take him in my mouth.

"No!" he screams, and clamps his legs around my head.

"Jamie?" His knees are smashing my ears.

"NO! DON'T!"

"I want to suck you!" There is no euphemism, no refined substitute, that sounds anything other than preposterous. My mouth descends again…

"No! Please, don't!"

"What's the matter?"

"You can't! I can't!" He pushes me away, curls up like a woodlouse, crying frantically, his hands over his eyes.

"Man, this is so fucked up, Jamie!" I sit up and blink away my own tears.

"Tammy, please don't be mad, please!" He leaps up, throws his arms around me, kisses me all over.

"Don't you trust me?"

"It's nothing to do with *you*," he mutters. "It makes me feel dirty."

"I'm not trying to make you feel dirty. I want to make you feel *good*."

"No! I don't want it!"

I don't understand this. I don't understand *him*. "Okay, okay, Jamie!"

He's still crying, kissing, screaming, "I can't do *that*! I won't do *that*!"

"Oh, Jamie," I sigh.

"I'm sorry," he sobs. "I'm ruining it!"

We lay down, face to face. "We don't have to do that, then, Baby. We don't *ever* have to do anything that makes you uncomfortable."

"I hate myself."

"No, Jamie. Don't…"

"I'm ruined. And I'm ruining this too."

God, I wish you'd talk to me. Tell me everything.

Instead, he kisses me hard, desperate to make amends. He climbs on top of me, straddles me, Frenches me until we're both gasping. He kisses his way down my body, nibbling me, tonguing me, teasing me… I'm on fire. Then he takes me into his mouth.

"Jamie! You don't *have* to do that, I said!"

But his mouth is so hot and wet on me that when he lets go of me to say, "I want to," I almost die. His vermillion lips close over me again. I'll say this for him, he's unpredictable, but I'm not about to start bitching now, not when he's working on me so wonderfully—the rough velvet of his tongue dragging up and down my cock, the warm nectar of his saliva coating and lubing me, the pillowy perfection of his lips gently whispering over my flesh. God, even the sounds he's making, moist sucking noises, soft little moans that vibrate against my skin—sounds that tell me he's enjoying this every bit as much as I am. Everything he's doing is so fucking good, so expert, that I find it very hard to believe that I'm his first lover.

Why wouldn't he let me go down on him? Why did he suddenly want to suck me? How did this shy little boy swiftly become the sweetest, dirtiest (I dare not ever describe him that way aloud), wildest lover I could ever have wished for?

"You didn't have to do that," I pant a few minutes later.

"I wanted to," he murmurs.

"I thought it made you feel dirty."

"Only if it's done to me. I'd rather do it to *you*."

I'm confused, intrigued. "Why, Jamie?"

He's quiet for so long that I think he's fallen asleep. Then he smiles up at me. "Merry Christmas, Daddy," he says softly. He spits into his hand and massages the mixture of saliva and semen onto my cock.

"Daddy?" I repeat. He's an inventor. He's come up with an affectionately kinky nickname for me.

He lays back on the bed, opens his legs, tilts his ass up, beckoning me.

It would be perfect. It nearly is.

I lower myself onto him, lose myself inside of him...

But something about this moment gives me pause. He's wearing an odd, uncharacteristic smile and an unnervingly vacant glint in his eyes.

Something's wrong. *Something's* wrong.

twenty-two:

jamie
(christmas present)

She fondles herself as she watches. "You're such a dirty boy, Jamie."

I'm a disgusting, dirty boy. I hate myself. I love to do it. I feel dirty but I like feeling dirty. She beats me with the big, thick belt when I'm done making Daddy shoot his wad. The cigarette makes a vivid sizzling noise when it contacts the sweat on my back.

I don't cry because of the pain.

I cry because I'm happy.

I cry because my dream has come true. Tammy is here. With me.

I cry because I'm afraid. Now I've given him my body. I'm his, and I know, deep down in a place I don't consciously acknowledge, that if he breaks my heart, I'll die.

If I fuck this up and lose him, it's all over.

He squeezes KY onto his fingers and lubes me. I implore him, "I want you inside of me." And he carefully enters me, sighing in contentment as my walls hug him. He lovingly yanks on me with one hand while his other firmly rubs my tummy, pressing my pubic bone against my bladder. Between his gentle

185

tugs, hard caresses and deep thrusts I'm in pleasure and pain, heaven and hell. He pulls me up and kisses me hungrily, my smile in his mouth. We make love face to face, with me sitting in his lap, his cock deep inside of me. I can feel him throbbing, his heart beating through his cock…

Please, God, I pray. *Please let this be for real. Let it be as real as it feels. He has me. I'll never belong to anyone else.*

I have to work today. At about seven o'clock, he drops me at my house. I apologise again and again about the dark maroon stains on his sheets. "Stop worrying about that!"

I open my door and he says, "Whoa! Where do you think you're going?"

I stare at him dimly until he says, "No kiss?"

I don't worry who might see us. I'm too busy being glad that he *wants* a kiss. He says he'll call me tonight.

"I'm off at four-thirty. Are you coming over later?"

"I gotta go visit Mom. It's Christmas. I should spend it with her."

He's done with me. He's probably already scoping someone new.

He drives away, and I go inside to feed my emotionally neglected kids. They crunch through their food and rub and purr against my legs.

I don't want to eat. My response to being returned to my home, newly devirginised, after a night of unbelievable sex with the love of my life, is to cry uncontrollably while the kids snuggle against me fretfully.

His throbbing hardness in my mouth, the way he buried his fingers in my hair and gently pulled—no rough shoving, no forcing himself into my throat the way Daddy always did—just softly tugging, massaging, whispering, indelibly sighing, "Oh, Baby… Baby… Baby…"

My heart grabs. My eyes flood.

He's so sweet. He's just so sweet…

And I'm being an ass. He's not done with me just because he's visiting his mother tonight.

I go out on the porch and light a cigarette. The smoke fills my lungs and as always, it soothes me like food never can. I press the red hot tip into the blistered skin of my left ankle, the screaming pain an outlandish solace.

Stacy picks me up for work a short time later. "Merry Christmas!"

"Yeah, right," I snort. "Christmas spent answering call bells, fighting with doctors…"

But I'm smiling, and I can't stop.

"What's new?" she demands, a greedy twinkle in her eye. "Haven't heard a peep from you since you went home with your boyfriend!"

I bite my smile.

"You didn't!"

I shrug.

"Oh, God! Are you alright?"

"Uh huh," I say. "A little sore."

"You're in such a zone, I guess I didn't even have to ask. You're glowing, doll!"

"Oh, really!"

"I'm so happy for you, Baby. Was it good? Is he good?"

My face is lobster red. "I have nobody to compare him to!"

"Was he good to *you*? That's what I'm asking."

"Yes," I smile. "He was good. It was good. It was perfect."

She studies me intently. "Did you tell him? That he's your first?"

I nod.

She has more questions, maybe advice. Instead, she says, "He'd better be good to you or I'll beat his ass!"

"He's a good guy, Stacy. He's been very, very good to me."

I tell her that he's been better to me than I've been to him, that I went apeshit on him. I don't tell her how I saw my dad's face, his cock, heard his voice crooning to me over Tammy's. I don't tell her how my stupid dead parents showed up for what should have been the happiest night of my life.

I mean, I *am* happy. I love him so much. I'm so happy that this is happening. But it should have been perfect. It almost was.

Stacy probably knows that my parents did more than just beat me. She understands how much I need for her *not* to ask about the details.

187

I can never thank God enough for her.

"Some of the things Tammy wanted to do in bed… scared me. I yelled. I've got issues."

"I don't think he meant to scare you, honey. He probably thought you'd like it."

I wince. "I wish."

"If he's an ass, you'll know soon enough. But if he loves you, Jamie, he'll respect your feelings and *never* push or force you to do anything you don't want to do. This is all new for you. It's going to take some adjustment."

But I'm not being truthful. Nothing scared me. Everything scared me. I felt dirty in a way I liked. In a way I hated.

Like with Daddy.

And I don't like to think about Daddy. Ever.

It's like I became two different Jamies last night.

I called him *Daddy.*

Why?!

"I won't be able to stand it if he's just using me," I say brokenly.

Stacy sighs. "Well, honey, sad as it is, we all meet jerks and get our hearts broken sometimes. Just know, if he hurts you, I'll kick his ass and then I'll be here when you need me."

He can't. He can't! I won't be able to bear it if I'm just another one of his booty calls.

Stacy sees me crying, "Man, I remember this. I remember Ray. Oh, I was so in love. I cried so easily, worried so much. He treated me so good. And so bad. Welcome to the world of sex and love." She laughs and sniffles. "I'm thrilled for you, Baby, and worried too."

"Ray broke your heart."

"Yeah, he was an asshole. But I survived it, Jamie. And if Tam turns out to be a dick, you'll survive too."

I shake my head.

"Yes you will. You're a survivor. And you know it."

I don't argue. I just keep praying that Tammy will never break my heart. I can feel it. It's already too late for me to turn back. In one evening, he's altered my life forever. He's so much a part of me now that if he tears himself away, I'll bleed to death.

I'm distracted at work, by happy memories of this new life; by recent, yet distant snapshots of the secure, solitary life I had before Tammy Mattheis had to go and return to town and make me fall in love with him all over again…

…and by hated, unbidden visions of a life that I lived before a kindly man named Lloyd Tafford adopted me, repressed memories that I'd never before had to deal with during waking hours.

I was afraid this would happen.

When the phone rings that evening, I pounce on it like the fool I am for him. My heart thunders in my ears. "How's your Mom?"

"She's right here, asleep. She's better. They're talking about letting her go back to your floor soon."

Not having to look into his eyes is not making it any easier to talk to him. "I want to see you again," he breathes in a soft, singsong voice.

All I can muster is a giddy, "Yes."

"Last night was… God…" He chuckles. "You wore me out."

"I did?" The living room is beginning to spin around me.

"Yes, sir, you did."

I flail my hand for a chair to sit in. "Tammy?"

"Hmmm?"

"Why do you like me?"

After a long silence, he says, "That's a strange thing for you to ask."

"Yeah, I guess so."

"Why do you like *me*?"

What do I say and not sound like an idiot? "Because… I… think you're really sweet."

"Sweet?" I'm an idiot after all. "And you're good looking," I add hastily.

"Oh yeah?" Now he's pleased.

"And…" I'm trembling. I forget that he can't see me right

now. I relive everything from yesterday, last night, early this morning. He's so good, so experienced, and I *love* it. I'm so afraid of him, and I love it. He's forcing me to abandon who I've been all these years without him. He's making me relinquish the fortitude that has sustained me, the refusal to be vulnerable, to let anyone into my heart, to be humiliated by love.

I know humiliation. I was not the pristine virgin I wanted to be for him last night. I probably lost my virginity at a younger age than he did. The damnable, miserable shame of it is, it was my own parents, the two people who were supposed to love and protect me, who violated me, raped me, made me into pornographic entertainment for their friends.

One by one, Tammy's making me drop the weapons I've been wielding. Every smile, every word, every touch, every kiss is collapsing the wall of armour around me and introducing me to a part of life that for years I believed I'd never get to experience, because I believed that my parents had destroyed that part of me.

I'm wrong, and I'm happy. I've never been so happy. I've never been so afraid. I've been in a coma, and Tammy has awakened me. He has reached inside of me and awakened my sexuality.

"And?"

I blush hotly. "And you're sexy," I whisper.

I love it when he whispers back, "Yeah?"

"Yeah. You're *so* sexy." My mind's eye roves over his thick, dark hair and eyebrows, the incredibly long, pretty black lashes framing his kind, intelligent teal eyes, his olive skin under dark stubble, his handsome nose, his perfect chin, his generous lips, his strong neck and his Adam's apple, his wide shoulders, his muscled arms, the just-right amount of hair over his broad chest, the dark pink of his nipples, his belly button, his hipbones, his lovely hind-end, the dark diamond of his pubic hair, his beautiful, long, veined sex, the round red swell of his scrotum, his long, muscular legs, his wonderful hands and feet.

A breath rasps out of him. "You're not being shy at all right now!"

190

"I would be if you were here."

"Why? We've... already... uh..."

"Because you're so sexy I can't stand it," I gasp. "I feel like I'm going to die every time I look at you."

"God, you're driving me so crazy. I wish I was there. Right now..."

"Why do you like me? Your turn."

He doesn't even hesitate. "Because you're the sweetest, sexiest, most beautiful little boy I've ever seen in my life."

The house is melting. "More," I whisper.

"I love your eyes, your face, your voice, your hair, your sweet, sweet body. I've never seen anything like you. I've loved you, I've wanted you, as long as I can remember. I want to live inside of you. I want to crush you against me and just feel you breathing. I want you so close there's nothing between us."

I'm tingling, fluttering. "When you're not inside me, I feel a draft. I feel cold."

"Yes," he moans. "I'm coming over, in just a while, and getting into your warm bed."

"I'll be waiting for you."

"I'm going to fuck you senseless. Be prepared."

I'm afraid of him, deliciously afraid. We hang up, and I dash into my room and burrow under my bedcovers. I can't wait. I masturbate as I remember the wondrous things our bodies did together, the things he's going to do to me tonight. He's left me in a chronic state of sexual arousal. I'm already hooked on him.

Early in my life, I'd been forced to have sex while being love-starved. I've been starved for sexual love, but Tammy's is the only love I would ever have accepted, and now, I've not only accepted, I've taken, selfishly, greedily, ravenously, of the pleasure he's given. Just thinking of his hands all over me makes me touch myself. Just thinking of the way he kisses me, hard, sucking, nipping, causes tiny orgasms to quiver through me.

twenty-three:

tammy
(december 26)

As I pretend to sleep, Jamie stares at me through adoring eyes that are dark and round, the pupils dilated. I watch him through the slits of my eyes as he touches my hair, nuzzles me, smells my skin, leaves feather-soft kisses over my neck, chest, shoulders, ears and even my eyelids. He bathes my face with kisses before releasing a gorgeous whimper and latching onto my mouth hungrily, sweetly. He tastes like the chocolate pudding pie he made for us a few hours ago.

"I love you," he whispers over and over. "I love you. I'll never stop loving you. My love… my love." He uses his fingers to lightly stroke and tickle the back of my neck. Everything he's doing to me excites me and relaxes me simultaneously. It's impossible to remain unresponsive.

"What are you doing?" I pretend to murmur sleepily, when in reality, I'm so turned on I can barely control myself.

"I just love kissing you."

He takes my love and gives his to me.

It feels so good.

"Let's make out until we come," he moans, his mouth brushing mine, his tongue teasing. We grind against each other through our underwear. I stop counting the kisses.

At last he sighs and curls his body up beside mine, hugs my shoulders, kisses my cheek, and dozes off, his lovely mouth curved into a contented smile.

※

In the morning, Jamie ignores his cell phone alarm signalling him to get up for a day shift at St. Paul's. When I blow a raspberry against the back of his neck he sighs, "Lord, I'm tired."

"Don't tell me I wore you out. We only did it four times!"

He sits up and moans, "I'm dizzy."

He looks pale, his face lightly sheened with perspiration.

"You have a fever?" I ask, feeling his face. Cold, clammy.

My concern grows as he struggles to put on his socks and shoes. He keeps dozing while sitting up.

"You should call them and tell them you're not coming."

"No, I told them I'd do a double today. We're really short-staffed this time of year." His slender shoulders slump. "Why am I so *tired*?"

"I'll go easier on you tonight," I tease, and kneel down to help him get his shoes on. "You really shouldn't go in if you're this tired. You might be coming down with something."

"I'll be alright. I just can't seem to get myself going."

"Because you've been pulling too many doubles. You work too hard, Jamie. You don't get enough rest."

He rolls his eyes. "Stacy's been talking to you, I see. I told them I'd be in today. I can't back out now. I've gotta be there in less than two hours."

"It ought to be illegal for them to make you work that many doubles in a week!" I frown.

"They don't make me, they *let* me. I'm trying to save money to move to the coast, remember?"

"Well," I say firmly. "It ought to be illegal to *let* you then."

Stacy arrives to pick up Jamie for work. That is, Ray has driven her here.

Oh boy, how are we going to explain this?

When Jamie teases Stace and asks about Ray being her chauffeur, she turns red and says, "I spent the night at his place last night. He's going to drive us in and pick us up later."

Good. They can leave without Ray finding out I spent the night here.

But when I wrap my arms around Jamie to give him a discreet goodbye kiss, it feels like he's melting in my arms. His body sags limply, his eyes half closed.

"Stacy! Something's wrong!"

"Shit!" Stacy hisses as Jamie's body becomes a dead weight, sliding to the floor. "I'll bet his blood sugar's dropped!"

"All I did was kiss him!" My arms are under Jamie's, supporting him in a half-sitting position on the floor.

Stacy runs to Jamie's refrigerator. "Of course! No fucking orange juice! Does he have anything around here with sugar in it?"

"I doubt it," I sigh. "I brought Chinese food for dinner last night and he barely touched it. We had chocolate pie for dessert, but he only had a bite or two, then I ate the rest of it," I add guiltily.

"Come on," Stacy says. "He needs to go to the hospital." We carry him out to Ray's car and speed off toward Sacramento.

"Stop at McDonald's," Stacy orders Ray. "We've got to get him some OJ and sugar." When we get the juice and sugar packets, Stacy tears them open and stirs them in. "Come on, Jamie," she yells, leaning into the backseat and prying his mouth open with the cup. "Drink!"

But he won't swallow. The juice spills over his chin and onto his blue scrub top.

"Come on, Jamie!" She tries again, but he's incoherent. She slaps his face. "Jamie!"

Ray's doing at least eighty on the interstate. "Guy charged a dollar fifty for the juice," he complains. What an asshole. I mean Ray, not the guy from McDonald's.

When we finally get to the ER at St. Paul's, Stacy and Jamie are recognised by the nurse working there and she immediately takes Jamie behind a vinyl curtain to check his blood sugar. We follow and watch the nurse poke his thumb with a little needle thing. "Twenty-nine," she says, hurrying away and returning quickly with an armful of stuff. She squirts something into Jamie's mouth as another nurse arrives with a big IV bag and tubes. Blood runs down his arm and all over the sheets as the nurse starts the IV and pushes a syringe full of something into him.

"I didn't know Jamie was diabetic," Ray says.

"He's not," says Stacy. "He just doesn't eat, then he exhausts himself working double shifts. Tammy says he didn't eat more than a bite or two of dinner last night."

"Last *night*?" echoes Ray.

"I had Christmas dinner with him," I say.

"I keep telling him." Stacy shrugs her shoulders like she gives up.

Striving to ignore Ray's stare, I ask, "Why doesn't he eat?"

She replies, "I don't know. He's been bad ever since Lloyd died. It's been hard on him. He's trying to get over it, but... this thing with his blood sugar... it's happened before."

Ray steps out to have a smoke. It's been on my mind, and I seize the opportunity. "Stace, you know Jamie really well, don't you? I mean, you're his best friend."

She nods.

"Was he really a virgin until..."

"Yes," she says.

"Are you sure?"

"Yes, Tammy. I'm sure."

"Why?"

"Because, you're the only one he's ever loved." Her gaze is level.

"I don't deserve him."

"But you have him, and you'll have him forever if you want him." Her voice lowers, intensifies. "Just remember what I said. Don't hurt him. If you're good to him, you'll deserve him."

"I'd never hurt him. I love him. I love him so much it scares me."

"I know, Tammy. I've always known. You belong to each other."

I watch Jamie's eyes slowly peeling open. The nurse says his

195

blood sugar has risen to eighty. He drifts in and out of sleep, his back to me. "I've got such a headache," he complains to Stacy, who gives him a drink of what's left of the orange juice. "I keep telling you, you need to eat, dammit!"

"I eat," Jamie slurs.

"Yeah, a bite of food, once a day… maybe!"

"How are you feeling?" I ask, strolling up to his bed, acting like I've been out of the room for a minute.

He answers by smiling up at me so prettily that there's no hiding this from Ray any longer.

Hell… I don't even care. I'm gay. Ray can accept it or fuck off.

"Looks like you're taking today off, like it or not," I nod at Jamie, sitting beside him.

"You win," he whispers as his bed sinks under my weight.

I tilt his chin up with two fingers. "Give me a kiss," I growl.

He's still pretty dazed, but he's alert enough to be nervous about Ray. "Don't worry about him," I say. Doctors, nurses and other hospital personnel are milling around as well. "Don't worry about any of them."

"But I work here," he says anxiously.

I lean forward and kiss him softly, in spite of his attempt to resist.

"Whoa, whoa, whoa!" is Ray's remonstration. "You guys are *gay*?"

I straighten and regard him for a moment. "Yeah."

"When did this happen?" Ray stuffs his hands into his pockets.

I suddenly realise I've never prepped myself for this. "It just… happened," I stammer.

"God, no *wonder* Jamie was never interested in any of the *girls* I tried to introduce him to!" The objection on Ray's face doesn't miss me.

"I wasn't interested in guys either," Jamie says. At least one of us knows something to say! "I wasn't interested in anyone… just Tammy." He smiles up at me. My heart squeezes.

Ray looks so uncomfortable I almost feel sorry for him. "Well… I don't know what to say…"

"You don't have to say anything, Ray," I tell him.

Stacy beams, "I swear, from the time we were in high school, I could see those cartoon hearts coming out of them every time they looked at each other!"

Ray only frowns. "Since *high school*?"

I'm sick of him already. "Yeah. Since high school."

Jamie is released after several hours. Stacy has to stay and work, so the rest of us return home in Ray's car, in almost total silence. Jamie sleeps in the backseat while I sweat on the passenger side. I think I've just lost my first "friend" due to my choice to be true to myself and to Jamie.

After we're dropped at my house, I carry Jamie inside. Ray offers no help, and I don't ask.

I lay Jamie on the couch and wrap him in my chequered comforter.

Then I do something I never do. I cook. I peel a bunch of potatoes and onions, I chop up a clove of garlic, and I cut up a chunk of the ham Mom bought for Christmas dinner the day before she fell and hurt herself. Might as well not let it go to waste. She doesn't even like ham. She only got it for Uncle Price, who still eats here at holidays like nothing ever happened. Since Mom is most decidedly out of commission this year, he won't be partaking of this particular ham.

"Here," I nudge Jamie awake with a big steaming bowl.

"What's this?" he smiles through sleepy eyes.

"Potato soup. Made it just for you. Eat!"

And for once, he eats, or rather, drinks every drop, every wedge of potato, every bit of savoury pink ham. It isn't long before his eyes are even droopier. "What'd you put in this stuff?" he asks. "I'm soooo sleepy."

"Potatoes, onions, garlic, warm milk, butter, salt, pepper, and ham."

"It was so good."

"I'm glad. Is your headache gone yet?"

"Yes, thank you."

"Now, what do you want to watch?"

"Something old. Funny."

I put in a video of *The Jack Benny Program*. "How's this?" I ask, sitting him up and snuggling under the comforter with him.

"Perfect," he murmurs and turns himself around to face me. He takes my face in his hands and kisses me once, twice, three, four times.

"No. No fooling around tonight," I say sternly. "Tonight you need to rest. Go to sleep!"

He pouts, then resigns himself to watching the TV. "Man, Jack's so cheap he makes the Stolpers look generous!"

I laugh, remembering Jamie's stories of how he slaved for the infamously rich couple who dressed like hobos.

He goes to sleep with his head tucked under my chin.

His chest swells against mine with each quiet breath. His warmth enfolds me even when I'm not inside of him. I am his. I've always been. I've been with a lot of people sexually. I've been with a lot of women and a few men too, but it means nothing. None of it. I love Jamie. We belong to each other. I never want this to end.

I doze off listening to Jack arguing with Rochester Van Jones.

twenty-four:

jamie
(december 26 and 27)

Tammy's oath of celibacy for one evening doesn't last more than two hours. Before dawn, we've done it at least five or six times. He's insatiable, but I love it. I love him so much. When we're not fucking, we talk and talk and talk, about everything.

I tell him all the stories I've told Lloyd. The sad, scary ones leave Tammy aghast. The funnier ones have him choking with laughter, especially the "Turd-pedo Episode".

We cackle until we're in tears. "I love making you laugh," I say. It feels so good to laugh with him, to be this comfortable with him, to make small discoveries. He snorts between laughs like a pig!

"I guess I can still make you laugh as well," he chortles.

The conversation takes a left turn then.

He asks, "Why, Jamie? Why me?"

"At first it was just because you were so gorgeous." His eyebrows raise. "You're *still* gorgeous! But in high school, it was a crush. I couldn't stop looking at you. I loved everything about you. I loved watching you play football. I just *loved* you.

"Then, the day those guys beat me up, and you helped me—I knew I *really* loved you. Because I knew you cared about me—

enough to follow me home."

He tries to deny it. "I was just in the neighbourhood."

"Stacy told me, Tammy. You were *following* me."

He sighs. "She can't keep a secret to save her."

"Why me, Tammy?"

It takes him a long time to gather his thoughts. "There's something about you, Baby. You're beautiful, but it isn't just that. There's something in your eyes. It's like... they *called* to me. That day... in church... there was something so familiar about you. I *knew* you. I couldn't put my finger on it. It just... it felt like we knew each other... and when you held my hand... it was like... a miracle."

I gasp, "Yes."

"Then one day, I remembered," continues Tammy. "I remembered meeting this beautiful little boy in a grocery store when I was only four years old. He was so pretty, like a little angel. It was you. I *know* it was."

How I wish I could remember too!

He stares at me endlessly. "Your eyes... they're so happy sometimes, so sad other times. Whenever you were sad I wanted to talk to you.

"That last night that I was here... I loved it. It was one of the best nights of my life," Tammy murmurs. "I think I knew, really knew, that I loved you, that night. I never forgot you."

"I never forgot you either."

"I looked at pictures of you in the yearbook, night after night—the ones of you in choir."

"Those *dorky* pictures?!"

"You were never a dork!"

"My razzleberry hair!" I blush.

"I *loved* it."

"On Valentine's Day I got you a card. I left it on your car."

"That was *you*?!"

I nod.

"I *wanted* it to be you," he says in a tremulous voice. "I wanted to ask you. I wanted to so badly, but I couldn't."

"Why?"

"I was shy."

200

"Shy?!" I laugh. "You're not shy, Tammy Mattheis!"

"Yes, I am!"

"Now I've heard it all," I sputter helplessly.

"I put an envelope with those candy hearts in your locker."

My eyes are stinging, leaking. "I didn't think it could have been you. I wanted it to be, but I just knew it couldn't be."

"Why?"

"Because I figured you hated me. I wanted you so much but I knew you were straight. I couldn't believe you could possibly like me, not like that."

"I never, ever hated you."

"You acted like you hated me. You yelled at me about that ball," I sniffle. "You made me cry." Why does that incident with the soccer ball still bother me so much? I guess it's because that was the cruellest he'd ever been to me.

"I'm sorry, Jamie. I yelled at you because I liked you. I know I was an asshole. I'm sorry."

"Well, just so you know, you broke my heart."

"I *never* hated you. I loved you. I know I treated you like shit. I didn't mean to make you cry. Honestly…"

He kisses me.

"I kept those conversation hearts," I whisper. "I still have them."

"I still have your card."

He offers another confession on my altar. "That night, in the pool… I wanted to kiss you, right in front of them."

"I wanted you to," I breathe against his cheek. "But I understood why you couldn't."

"I should have just planted one on you," scowls Tammy. "Why did I give a shit *what* they thought?!"

"You made it up to me very shortly after," I sigh. "Our first kiss…"

"No, our first kiss was in the grocery store," he insists.

"You're really sure that baby was me."

"I know it was you, dammit! I cried in the car all the way home, telling Mom how I wished I could be friends with you forever. I already loved you. I've loved you almost all our lives!" He shudders and hides himself against my neck.

I pray that one day I'll remember it. God, how I'd *love* to remember that.

"You were eating Red Vine liquorice," he says.

The scent of it fills my nose.

"After you were beaten up, you changed," says Tammy. "I was so worried about you. I should have stayed. I could have been here, with you, all these years. I know we would have made it. I *know* it. But I ran away. I'm a coward. I loved you and I didn't know how to deal with it!"

"Don't worry about it anymore, Tammy. We're here *now*. That's all I care about."

"I'm a coward. I couldn't deal with it. I didn't want to deal with it. So many years, wasted."

"You're *not* a coward!" I say vehemently. "People like us are persecuted, beaten up, killed. Maybe you knew that, and that's why."

"It just proves I'm a coward," Tammy mutters. "I want to kiss you, hold your hand in public. It's ridiculous how we have to hide, how Ray treated us when he found out."

"Sometimes," I offer timidly, "Not always, but sometimes... I wish I was a girl."

"Why?" he asks, and I see something like panic in his face.

"Because, I've always been picked on. I'm small. There's nothing I can do about it. I've been beaten up so many times... I just think life would be easier for both of us if I was a girl."

"Would you want *me* to be a girl?" he asks. His mouth twitches as he tries not to smile.

"No!" I almost shout. "No!"

He lets his smile spill. "I don't want you to be a girl. You're a boy—a man—I love you, I've always loved you, just the way you are. You're perfect."

"I'm not perfect," I mutter.

"You are to me," he whispers. "You're a *man*, Jamie. I love what you are."

I shiver inside. "But... what if one day I decide I want to become a woman?"

"Uh..."

My heart begins to falter.

202

"If you really wanted to," he whispers, "I'll have to get used to the idea. But... if it would make you happy..."

"But I want *you* to be happy too."

Tammy is quiet for a long, long time. I allow him to think. "I would still love you."

"Are you sure?"

"You would still be Jamie. Maybe your body would be different, but your brain..."

"I'm not saying I'll do it, but it might make things easier for us. People... might tolerate us..."

"Why should we worry about whether people can tolerate us?" he asks with a small grin.

I shrug.

He sighs, "I hate the way we're treated, just because we're both men."

"We live in a small, hick town," I soothe. "It's just the way it is. That's why I want to move to the coast. I'm sick of this place!"

"Yeah."

"I don't know why being near the ocean would make our lives peaceful, but somehow I know it would."

"God, Jamie," Tammy whispers, running his knuckles over my cheek. "This is almost too perfect."

I feel a frown pinching my forehead. "What if something goes wrong?!"

"No, don't say that," he shakes his head. "We've been punished enough, both of us."

I hold his head between my hands, look into his eyes. I delve as deeply as I can go, and it shakes him up bad.

"What?" He tries to wiggle free of me.

"I can see your soul."

His breathing quickens. "My soul."

"Your soul."

"Is it good or bad?" Suddenly his eyes flood.

"It's good, Tammy," I whisper, kissing his mouth again and again. "It's very, very good. Strong."

He shakes his head. "*You're* the one who's strong. I'm not strong at all."

"Yes, you are," I argue. "You're very strong. I see it in you. You're smart, you're strong, and you have a good soul. I feel it, Tammy."

"I've done things," he sobs. "I've done horrible things! I'm an evil, horrible person!"

He tells me, about the anger, the rejection, the jealousy, the hate he felt, for his dad and his uncle and himself, after his uncle molested him.

"Your uncle fucked with you?"

"Yeah," he says softly, incapable of meeting my eyes. "When I was about eleven or so."

"What did he do?" I ask before thinking.

There's no reply, and I say, "Forget it. It's none of my business."

"No, I want to tell you. It's just… I'm ashamed."

If only he knew how I understand.

"He made me love him. He told me I was beautiful. He told me he loved me! He told me that what we were doing was beautiful and right, because we loved each other. He told me I was special! Then he just… threw me away… like I was nothing!"

I never would have guessed.

"I was so angry. I did things…" Tammy tells me about stealing his cousin's Barbies and mutilating them. He tells me about how he and his friends shot birds. He tells me how he used to be cruel to his puppy. He tells me that for a while, he was obsessed with death, serial murderers, and writing violent stories in diaries.

Gooseflesh rises along my arms.

"When I put my fingers inside of you…" Tammy divulges haltingly, "I… remembered Cotton. I sort of molested him… when I was young… I put my fingers in him." He swallows audibly. "I saw Uncle Price do it to Natalie… put his fingers in her vagina, when he was changing her diapers. I don't know why I did that to Cotton. It was sick… I get sick every time I remember it. I'm so ashamed. I almost… couldn't do what I did to you… I almost had to stop… but I reminded myself… I wasn't hurting you…" But his voice is laced, tangled, with

204

humiliation.

He stops, nestles against me, waiting.

I'm afraid.

Afraid of Tammy, afraid of these revelations from deep within him, afraid of what could yet lurk there.

My faith in him wavers.

I'm fourteen again.

He's only playing with me. He doesn't love me.

I should excuse myself and go, now. Out of his life. To preserve my own.

Is he evil? Does he want to hurt me? Has he been planning to hurt me all this time?

"I liked it when Uncle Price touched me down there!" he cries. "I was in love with him. It was *wrong*! He *knew* it was wrong!"

I blink. No. Hell, no. I'm looking into his eyes, his soul. I'm seeing the very opposite of evil. I mustn't be afraid.

He's opened himself.

To me.

I have to stop believing that Tammy hates me simply *because I love him.*

He needs me to help him. I have to rise above my perpetual distrust of the human species and help him.

He doesn't want to hurt me. He loves me.

He went away for sixteen years. He left me without saying goodbye. He did *hurt me.*

He just explained why, Jamie, I scold myself. *He's tried to explain his struggles. He's opened his heart and revealed things that anyone with an ugly soul would never dare unveil.*

He trusts me.

And I, for one, understand lifelong guilt, the revolting flashbacks, the disparaging voice of the Accuser, the spoilage of irreplaceable moments and the tainting of treasured memories. The sins committed against the powerless by the lecherous, the leftover ruination that turned me into an amoebic recluse who believed I was content with my life and my self.

The same kind of shame turned Tammy into a confused, restless seeker of comfort and self-acceptance, who found only more self-hate.

I understand.

And it's high time to show him I trust him. He's the only human being I'll ever love like this, and if I can't trust him, I might as well live in a sea cave. He wouldn't have revealed these staggering secrets if he didn't trust me.

"You haven't hurt anyone, have you." I say it, I don't ask it.

"No, Jamie, I swear. Except Cotton, the birds, the cats. I don't know why I did it."

"You were a boy," I tell him. "You were hurting. You were crying for help."

He sobs, "Yes!"

I hold him close to me, and he cries and cries. "You have a conscience, Tammy. Evil people don't have a conscience. Evil people do evil things and they don't feel sorry afterward. They never feel sorry."

The difference between the saved and the damned, I think to myself. *Was Hitler sorry? Did a glimmer of remorse ever cross his eyes? Was Saddam sorry? Is Bin Laden sorry? What about Bundy, Gacy, Dahmer? Were any of them sorry for the things they did? Will they be in heaven?*

"I can't believe I wrote those stories! I can't *understand* myself!"

"Feeling guilt isn't pleasant, I assure you," I say, holding his face in my hands. "But I'd rather feel bad about something I did wrong than go through life not feeling any guilt or remorse. You felt it. You *still* feel it. You let it change you, make you a better person. That's why I know your soul is good. That's why I know you'd never hurt anyone now."

"I don't understand! Why? Why did I do those things?! Sometimes, I just want to *kill* myself! Because I hate what I did! I *hate* it!"

"Kids do weird things. They don't understand how cruel they're being. You were a *child*, angry and hurt, and that was how you expressed it. You're an adult now. You feel bad about those things. Your uncle never apologised to you. I wonder if he's ever repented. I hope so, for his sake."

"He's senile," Tammy sniffles. "He doesn't even know

where he is half the time."

"I'd rather be you than him, not feeling any guilt. All the kids he's hurt!"

"I didn't report him! I should have!"

"You were a child. You didn't know *how* to report him. You didn't even know what he was doing was wrong." I sigh. "No wonder you're so torn up."

He weeps, in soundless misery. It's not fake.

"It's going to be okay, Tammy."

"I don't want you to be afraid of me now, Baby. I told you all this, and now I'm so afraid you're afraid of me."

"I'm not afraid of you, Tammy," I decide. "You're a good person. And you have to forgive yourself. We all do bad things. We all make mistakes. Have you ever asked God to forgive you for those things you feel so bad about?"

Barely above a hoarse whisper, he speaks. "I don't know if I believe in God, Jamie."

"You should, Tammy. How can you have hope without God?"

He shrugs.

"I have to believe in God. I can't, I won't, listen to people who say that people who believe in God are too weak or lazy or stupid to rely on themselves." I pull his face to mine. "We *are* weak, and delicate, and mortal. If I didn't believe in God, I wouldn't be alive today. I went through some things, Tammy. I'll tell you about it. I'll tell you everything, someday, very soon."

"How can you believe in God, when you went through so much?"

"If I hadn't prayed, Lloyd wouldn't have found me." Of course, I leave out that I had prayed to die, not to be found.

"Maybe it was God's will that Uncle Price messed with me," Tammy explores. "Maybe He's trying to teach me something."

"No, Tammy. It wasn't God's will. It's never God's will for innocent children to be violated, or beaten up, or worse…" A hot shiver rattles my entire frame. "A God that cruel I refuse to believe in."

"Then why does He allow terrible things to happen?" asks

Tammy. "Why? I thought nothing could happen unless He allows it."

"I don't know," I admit quietly. "But it's something I intend to ask him one day… I think it's the least He can do… answer a few questions that are nagging me…"

"Me too." Then, "What happened, Jamie?"

"Not tonight."

"Tell me," he pleads. "I want to know you. I care about you."

"I know, and I will… soon. I promise… It's going to be very hard for me, but I owe it to you. I'll tell you. Just not tonight, please?"

He nods. "Okay."

I love him so much. He's not prodding me, pressuring me. He's tied with Stacy as my best friend.

"I will say this. I don't believe in hell." I shake my head resolutely. "Or maybe I do, but I've already been there."

His arms tighten around me.

"Anyway, can you believe in your own soul if you can't believe in God?" I whisper. "Our bodies die. Our souls live forever. We don't just vanish into nothing when we die."

He doesn't look at me when he asks, "Do you believe Lloyd's soul is okay?"

"Absolutely."

"In heaven?"

"Not yet. He's asleep," I say. "He's asleep and knows nothing. That's in the bible. His ashes are at the coast, and his soul is with God, but he's asleep. He's waiting."

"Waiting? For what?"

"For God to wake him up."

"You took him to the coast."

"Yes, and when I die, I want to be scattered there too, right where he is."

"You want to be cremated?"

"Sure," I reply.

"Ugh! I could never be burned. How can you stand the thought of it? I thought you hated fires and burning."

"In movies," I clarify, "When someone's being burned

alive..." I shudder. "I can't stand that. Like in *The Temple of Doom*. They tore that guy's heart out and put him in that lava pit. The way that actor *screamed*... it was so horrible... it gave me nightmares for years. Lloyd was so upset with himself for letting me watch that." I take a deep breath. "When you're dead, you feel no pain. That's not you anymore. It's just the body, Tammy. It's just organic material."

"But doesn't the bible also say that our bodies are supposed to be glorified or something when Jesus comes? I heard Pastor say that once. How can a body be glorified if it's been burned up?"

"Well, God can do anything. He can piece anyone back together. What if we died in a car accident? Got burned beyond recognition? Don't you think He'll still know it's us?"

"Yeah, I suppose He would." Tammy shudders. "I don't want to talk about this anymore, Baby. It's too..."

"I know," I whisper. "Let's not talk about it anymore."

I try to assuage him. "If you ask God to forgive you for the things you've done wrong, He will. And you have to forgive yourself too, Tammy."

I should talk. I still haven't forgiven myself for the things I've done.

I dread the day when I try to explain it all to him...

twenty-five:

tammy
(december 28)

Mom is released from the hospital the night of December 28th, and after I take her back to the house and settle her in the living room with her favourite John Wayne film and a bowl of potato soup with the bits of ham fished out, I head over to Jamie's.

I have a belated Christmas gift for him.

I sit on one of the dining chairs and pull him into my lap. When he opens the small square package, his eyes are shining, his lips are quivering.

It's an angel made of pewter, and a silver chain.

"I didn't know if you'd want the angel as a necklace or a keychain," I say, and then I add quietly. "Thank you for taking care of my mother, Jamie."

He's in hot water now, and he knows it. "Now, now, I h-had no ch-choice. I-I g-gotta pay that m-malpractice insurance p-premium-m every year, y-you kn-kn-know?" His eyes glimmer wetly. He's as gorgeously agitated and vulnerable as he was the afternoon of the Christmas party.

I'm not having it. "You're my angel." I mouth the words silently, and watch Jamie's eyes as his defences crumble.

"Tammy," he whispers. We kiss each other tenderly as he wraps his arms around my shoulders, grasping the little angel and the chain in one hand. Our mouths meet and separate softly, and my ears tingle at his endless cries of pleasure.

"Just kissing you," I moan between kisses. "Just kissing you, holding you and kissing you, and not even going any further... it's magic."

"Yes," he gasps against my lips. "Yes."

It's magic. We make out for what seems like hours, right there in that dining chair with him in my lap, my gift still clutched in his fist, until I can no longer neglect the forceful pulsing behind my fly. "I want you," I breathe, rubbing my stubble against his lips. "Tell me you want me."

He answers with a frantic sob, "I want you. I want you..."

Our lips never part as we feverishly remove each other's clothes. We don't even make it to his bedroom. In the hallway, I press his back into the wall, hearing him cry out as the cold plaster shocks his hot skin. I hoist his legs up and around me, my fingers digging into his buttocks, his fingers digging into mine, trying to push me deeper into him.

We fuck wildly, our noisy exclamations startling the cats and sending them darting under Jamie's bed. "Poor things," we chortle through our moans and kisses.

When we climax, it lasts even longer than that incredible time on Christmas morning.

"Are you still coming?" I laugh when my spasms finally ease off enough for me to speak.

Jamie nods with a rapturous whimper, "When is it going to *stop*?!"

"I think my dick is numb!"

"My ass is numb!"

I laugh. He laughs. We both laugh softly.

Then we're both crying.

Then Jamie is smiling, really smiling. I've never seen such a beautiful smile.

It's inside of us both. "Do you feel it?"

He gasps, "Yes."

"We're one," I cry, my lips crushing his. "We're not two

people anymore. We're one now."

"I feel it," Jamie nods, his eyes closed, his smile glorious.

"This is what people want, Baby," I whisper as our eyes touch again. "This is what everyone wants, everyone on earth, this feeling we're having right now, you and I…"

"Yes, I feel it."

"God, how I love you." I've never felt it or meant it more than I do at this moment.

I do. I love him. He surrounds me and warms me inside whether we're fucking or not.

We had a long, good talk the other day. I told him my darkest deeds, the shames that haunt me constantly.

And he didn't jump out of the bed and run from me.

He stayed and talked to me.

He told me God loves me.

And I cried, because all my life I've been lonely. I've been looking for someone to talk to, someone to really talk to me.

He doesn't judge me. He's not afraid of me.

That's the bonus.

"I love you too, Tammy. I love you so much." He reaches up and drops his little angel and the chain around his neck, and beams at it.

He loves me…

twenty-six:

jamie
(december 28)

Tonight I'm on heat. My mouth waters as I look him up and down, my eyes moving slowly, deliberately over his body. He towers over me, strong, perfectly proportioned, with an imperious poise that belies the deep, hidden sweetness I know. He wears nothing except for a plain silver chain similar to the one he's just given to me for Christmas, unadorned and masculine—absolutely perfect. I move close to him, take his hands in my own. "You're so sexy," I whisper, putting his hands on my ass. Then I slip my arms up around his neck, pull him in for a hot kiss. My eyes fasten to his erection and stay there until he's driven to exclaim his embarrassment. "Hey! I'm up here!"

"Mmmmm, you're down *here* too," I moan softly, my hand wrapping around him.

He throws me onto the bed and we devour each other, rolling over and over like mud wrestlers, our hands everywhere, our tongues down each other's throats. "I want your sweet ass," he says, squeezing me. He spreads my legs wide, eats me, his tongue lashing deep and hot into my hole. I melt like lava, crying for mercy. "Please, oh God, please. Tammy…

213

Tammy…"

He lets me up and I try to crawl away, but he leaps behind me, grabs me around the waist, rubs his hard length against me. "You want it doggy style?" he gasps.

"No," I whimper, unexpectedly ravenous for something forbidden, resting my elbows and chest against the bed and lifting my ass. "Kitty style! Do it!"

"Kitty style! What's *that*?"

"Bite me. Hold me down, bite the back of my neck."

He lowers his face, nibbles me politely.

"Harder. Bite harder… like you're a big, mean tomcat and I'm your hot little pussy." I purr and trill, rubbing my head against his. "Please fuck me. Fuck me Daddy. Fuck my hole. Fuck me like a beast."

He groans, "I don't want to hurt you."

"Hurt me! Bite me!" I squeal desperately.

He indulges me, thrusting furiously, biting me and growling at me dangerously, sending shockwaves of delight shooting through me.

"God this is hot. This is so hot," he pants.

"Spank me!" I scream.

"Jamie…"

"Spank me, *please*! Spank me *hard*!"

He taps me gently on the ass. "Harder!" I insist. "*Harder*!"

Slap! his hand says against my pale skin. *Slap!*

While the fingers of his left hand tangle into the sheets, his right hand lands hard and solid on me. The stinging impact of his hand, the hard, wet clamp of his teeth into the nape of my neck, the force of his thrusts, the friction of his cock as it scrapes against my G-spot. Oh, God. I spray all over the bed, screaming out my pleasure with embarrassing loudness and sending our poor, traumatised kids scurrying out from under my bed into another room.

With Tammy wheezing above me, I slowly recover, and as the throbbing bliss begins to ebb, it should be replaced by relaxation and a feeling of contentment. But it's not. This time, my smiling face slowly metamorphoses into a grimace of the most profound shame, and I begin to cry, immediately rousing

214

Tammy's concern.

"What is it? Jamie? What's wrong?!" He leaps off of me and kneels beside me. "Baby? What's wrong?!"

I'm in a ball, my hands covering my eyes. "I can't *believe* myself! I'm so dirty! I'm so disgusting!"

"Jamie!"

"I'm a disgusting, dirty freak!" I sob.

"You are not!" Tammy's crying now.

I can't help it. I can't stop. I'm hysterical, hopeless, saturated with self-hate. I sob and sob and Tammy does too.

"Jamie, *please*! Talk to me! What did I do? Did I do it wrong?"

"No!" I bawl. "You didn't do anything wrong. I'm sorry! I'm fucked up! I'm perverted! I'm sick!"

"Why are you saying this, Baby? *Why*?"

"Making you do that! Making you fuck me like we're a couple of animals! Making you bite me, spank me... I'm disgusting!"

"Hey! Come here."

I unfurl myself and throw my arms around him. "I'm sorry! I'm so sorry!"

"Jamie." He sounds like his heart is about to break. "You didn't do anything wrong. Please listen to me."

My sobs hitch and hiccup in my throat, I'm crying that hard. I hide my face against his neck. My tears roll down his chest, through the wiry hairs, salt rivers in a black forest.

"Listen, Jamie."

I nod because I can't speak.

"What we did just now... it was fun. I liked it."

I shake my head. "It was dirty. I'm sick..." I would throw up all over him but there's nothing to throw up.

"No, you're *not*."

My gag reflex spasms hard. My sobs haven't subsided yet. Tammy's fingers caress my scalp. He's sitting Indian style with me in his lap. "Someone's really hurt you, Jamie. Someone's fucked you up... badly."

"That's what I mean!" I cry out against his throat. "I'm ruined! I'm a freak! I'm a pervert!"

"No, that's not what I'm saying!" Tammy sighs loudly. "I'm saying someone has really made you ashamed of yourself. Someone's hurt you so bad, Jamie. Please talk to me. Please tell me what they did to you."

"I can't."

"Please?"

"Tammy… don't…"

I see her, looming over me with her lit cigarette. "You're a dirty, nasty boy, Jamie. You're so bad. What are we going to do with such a nasty, naughty boy?" A piece of hot ash lands on my thigh. It burns for a nanosecond, not nearly as hotly or as horribly as the end of her cigarette.

I'm screaming, "Please, no! Please don't! Don't do it, please! I'll be good! I'll be good!"

"Jamie!"

I feel the hot glow. "Please, Mommy! Please don't do it! Please don't do it!"

"Jamie!" Tammy shouts. "Jamie!"

I dissolve into a sobbing, soggy mess as Tammy frantically tries to extricate me from the memories I'm trapped in.

They're like quicksand.

twenty-seven:

tammy
(december 28 and 29)

This anguished, screeching, coiled wreck has replaced the wild, inventive tempter I was fucking only a few minutes ago. I can't understand it. It kills me.

He screams, "Please don't do it, Mommy! Please don't!"

He's clearly having a panic attack or something. His screams sound as if they're tearing his vocal cords apart.

I hold him. "Jamie, it's Tam. I'm here. I'm here. Your mom isn't here. She's not here. Come back. Come back to me... It's okay... It's okay..."

Slowly, he comes back. But he huddles against me and cries, calling himself a freak, a pervert, a disgusting, sickening, dirty pig.

"Jamie," I say softly. "Please, talk to me. Tell me what they did to you. They hurt you so bad. I know it. Someone hurt you so bad. Was it your mother? Did she hurt you?"

He won't answer. After a long, long time, he lifts his head. "I'm sorry," he sniffles, his eyes and nose bright red and running.

"You have nothing to be sorry about. I just wish you would tell me what's going on."

He shakes his head. "It's too horrible to talk about."

"Don't you think I'd understand, Jamie?"

He sobs, "It's just too horrible…"

"Jamie," I say gingerly. "What we did… I liked it. I thought it was hot. It was fun."

His shame is killing him visibly.

"Sometimes… trying new things makes it even more fun," I whisper. "It was like a game. We were playing a game, that's all. Lots of people play different ways when they have sex. It makes it fun."

"It felt dirty," Jamie says.

"Why?"

"Because… it felt so… good…"

"It was good."

"I feel so dirty."

"What's wrong with feeling good, Jamie?"

"I don't know. I really have issues."

I nod. "Yes, sir, you really do have issues."

"I'm stupid, I know…"

"That's not what I said! No, you're not stupid!"

"It was fun," he admits finally. "But it made me feel dirty."

"It made me feel dirty too," I moan, "But in a good way."

He shudders. "It was gross."

"No. It wasn't gross. It was a really fun way to play. Sex is new to you, Baby. Why not play? Try new things with me. Don't be afraid of me."

I don't believe he was a virgin now. I think he's had a lover, and that his experience with that person has left him a mess. They used him and after they got their rocks off, whoever they are, they called him names. Maybe they abused him in other ways too…

They made him so ashamed of himself that now he can't even have fun.

I don't want to make him even more a mess by voicing my opinion. If he wants me to believe he was a virgin that first night with me, I won't derail that. And I'm not sure what his *mother* has to do with all this, but she must have done something awful to him for him to have screamed bloody

218

murder the way he did. I want him to talk to me, tell me about it.

But I can't push him. I can only wait.

"Discover yourself, Jamie," I whisper against his hair as he clings to me. "Play with me, and discover yourself. You're not dirty. You're not disgusting. You're beautiful. You're mine. I don't ever want you to feel ashamed of yourself. I love you. God created sex. How can sex be dirty if God created it?"

"I thought you didn't believe in God," Jamie says, raising his head and smearing tears over his face.

"If I did, I certainly wouldn't believe He made anything *dirty*."

"Pastor used to say that God made sex only for people to procreate, that it's a sin to do it... for fun..."

"Pastor Asshole?!" I roar, the very mention of His Holiness raising my hackles. "He is so full of *bullshit*! He's a fucking hypocrite!"

"And that it's a sin for two men to love each other."

"He's my dad, you know..."

His eyes widen. "Your dad is Pastor Sellers?"

"Yeah. He had an affair with my mom. She got pregnant. He didn't leave his wife, but Mom never asked him to. All she ever asked him for was help raising me. But he didn't give her a nickel, never wanted to see me, to get to know me, nothing. He pretends it never happened. He ignores me."

There. My pain is out. And now, maybe he'll soften, open, like a rose.

"Tammy..." He holds me.

"I can't stand him," I mumble.

"But it still hurts, doesn't it?" He's reading my mind again.

"Yeah, it hurts. He is why I'm not a big fan of going to church." I sigh heavily. "You and I... we spent sixteen years alone, apart, unhappy, lonely. We punished ourselves when all we wanted was to be together. I used to swallow that crap, Jamie. I used to believe it was *wrong* to love you. *That's* why I left! *That's* why I went away and left you here alone. Because I was *ashamed*. I tried to like women. I *tried*. But all I wanted was *you*. I didn't even want other *men*! Only you. And if that's so wrong in God's eyes—if you and I are supposed to go through life without love, if we're supposed to be condemned to a miserable, lonely life—well, maybe I *don't* believe in Him."

Jamie is quiet, gathering his thoughts. "You said I should try and discover myself."

"Yes, Jamie."

"What if I don't like what I discover?"

"Why do you say that, Jamie?" I am practically beseeching him…

He says nothing. His eyes are glazed in misery.

"Jamie, we're adults, both of us, and we care about each other. Nothing we've done so far has hurt either of us, right? Have I ever hurt you?"

"Only the first time, and I wanted it to hurt."

"Because you wanted punishment?" I ask very carefully.

"No, just because I wanted my first time to be scary—and painful—like everyone else's. And because I wanted to be sure you *cared* that it hurt me."

"I did."

"I know," he nods.

"I'd never hurt you intentionally. I'd never play with you and then turn around and abuse you or call you names afterward."

Jamie's eyes leap up and search mine furtively.

I think perhaps I've gotten through to him.

When I get home the next day to check on Mom, she hands me a package, a large orange envelope with my name scrawled in curvy handwriting. When I tear it open, it's a VHS tape with no label. There's no return address on the envelope. So I take the tape to the VCR in my bedroom.

Soon as I press the play button, Jamie's face appears. He's very young, I'd guess only about seven or eight. There's no mistaking those enormous blue eyes or that preternatural doll face. For a moment, I believe Jamie has sent me an old home video of him as a surprise. How delightful! To see a video of my boyfriend as a child, maybe having a birthday party or something!

220

Then I begin to notice the wrongs. The camera is capturing him from the waist up, and he's not wearing a shirt. He's smiling, looking directly into the camera that is trained on him.

But his eyes are not sparkling, his smile is not happy.

It's not real.

A woman's voice sings out, "Jamie just *loves* big, creamy Ding Dongs, don't you, Jamie?" The voice is medium-deep, raspy, like she's had a long history of smoking. There is a mocking tone to it.

"Yeah," Jamie says in a small, frightened voice, struggling to keep his smile from crumbling. His eyes glitter with tears.

"Take a bite, *Jamie*," the woman says.

His name in her voice... there is a malicious quality that can't be mistaken. Jamie nibbles on the chocolate snack cake in his hand as the camera zooms out.

"Take a *real* bite!" the woman snaps. Jamie flinches, and pushes the entire cake into his mouth, tries not to choke.

He's so thin.

"That's the way!"

The camera zooms out further, and it's then that I see Jamie is completely nude, sitting on a bed. The wall behind him is painted putrid yellow. Big chips have been stripped away, revealing a loud, bizarre shade of turquoise.

I see the now familiar red around his ankles, the bruises, old ones in green, new ones in purplish-black.

I see the welts, the burns...

A man comes into the picture and sits on the bed with Jamie. The man has dark blonde hair. I can't make out the colour of his eyes.

He's naked too.

I need to turn this off, now.

But I can't.

Jamie's naked, in a bed, with a grown man.

I have to see what happens.

Why? You'd think I'd realise that this video is over twenty years old, and that it isn't the real Jamie in that video. It's only an image.

He's not in that room with that man and woman anymore.

Instead, I think, *Jamie's in trouble. Someone is doing things to him. I have to see what happens. I can't leave him like this.*

God, how sorry I end up being after watching it.

The man leans close to Jamie and says, "Gimme kisses."

Jamie frowns and shakes his head vigorously. "No, Daddy, please. I don't want to do the show."

"Come on, Pretty," the man begs. "Show Daddy how much you love him. You *do* love Daddy, right? *Daddy loves you.*"

Guilt stabs the boy's eyes. "I know," he says, unable to look at the camera, unable to look at the man calling himself "Daddy." His eyes fix downward, clouded over, miasmas of terror.

I've seen his eyes do that...

"Smile!" the woman screams shrilly, and Jamie's body jumps. "And do what you're told!"

Jamie smiles. I see the fear.

My heart begins to crack and crumble. He reaches up and lightly kisses the man on the mouth.

The woman's voice is low with malice. "Smile right, Jamie, or you'll be *really* sorry..."

The little boy begins to cry. Little pieces of my heart are splashing into my stomach acid.

I need to turn it off. Now.

Jamie tries to smile right for the woman. His mouth trembles as he tries to stretch it to the left and to the right. It's not quite right, because the woman shrills again, "Where's my lighter?"

"No!" screams Jamie. "Please!"

"Then you smile *right*!" is her growling injunction. "I *mean* it, you little fuck!"

The boy turns back to the adult man, and slowly, Jamie's terrified, unreal smile transforms... his lips...

It's the same smile I've seen countless times in the past several days.

The only thing missing... is in his eyes...

He's doing what he has to do.

He's acting.

He drapes his bony arms around the man's big shoulders, his small pink lips smiling.

222

Like a pro...

"That's more like it," the woman laughs lewdly. "Very hot, very hot... yeah... good... good... oh, yeah... keep going... what a *nasty* boy you are, Jamie!"

It's a metamorphosis before my eyes, and I can feel the breakfast I had at Jamie's this morning, the toast with apricot jam, lurching up my oesophagus. *Turn this off. Turn it off. You can't do anything about it. You can't help him. You can't save him.*

But I watch...

The man's low grunts churn my gut. I burp sourly.

Over and over I have to *remind* myself that the boy is being forced to do this, that he does not like what's happening to him, *that he is less than ten years old.*

Because he's such a good actor. He's been well trained. The threats he's being given by the woman have facilitated his ability to convince anyone watching that he *loves* what the man is doing.

I hate myself as I watch this video. I watch as the boy uses slow, tentative, economic movements, the palpable fear of "doing it wrong" coming straight through to me from the TV screen. He doesn't say a word, doesn't make a sound. I hear the woman's gruff, vulgar commentary as she hands the camera to the man.

Now I see what she looks like. Her hair is almost black.

Jamie has her eyes.

No he doesn't. Her eyes are watery, bloodshot... glaring, wet blue ice...

It's the rude bitch in the grocery store.

I suspected she had something to do with why he's so frightened and ashamed.

"Please, Mommy! I'll be good! I'll be good!"

I figured she'd been a religious drill sergeant, guarding her son's purity and turning him into a neurotic tangle that I'd have to comb through.

How far off I have been... how fucking far off...

I had no idea it was anything remotely like this.

Undigested food crawls into my mouth as I watch the

223

woman use the thick, black flashlight. When Jamie cries in pain, she screams at him to shut up, pulls the flashlight out of him, hits him in the head with it. Blood begins to dye the white pillowcase.

She lights a cigarette. "Come on," she says, and the video camera wobbles and jumps sickeningly. "Hold him."

Jamie begins to scream. "No! No! Please!"

"You're a bad boy," the woman says happily. "You gotta be punished."

The man uses one hand to pin Jamie's scrawny shoulders to the mattress while he continues filming with the other. He kicks and thrashes hysterically. "Please, Mommy! Please! Please don't hurt me!" His screams drown what's left of my heart. My stomach eats it away. I see the woman's lit cigarette slowly descend, down, down, down...

"Please don't do it, Mommy!"

The camera zooms in as the cigarette hisses against Jamie's skin. Grey smoke wisps away from the blackened hole left behind. His wrenching screams split my soul into two huge red shreds and they collapse beside me.

I burp back the vomit and eject the video. I run to the bathroom. The contents of my stomach violently project into the toilet.

I feel weak as I make my way back to my room. Whether there are more videos or not, I won't watch another second.

I feel convicted. I feel like I've victimised him every bit as much as the man and woman did, just by watching.

He told me that he'd been through some things. I never would have believed it was this bad. I'd heard his parents had mistreated him, beat him up.

I hear Stacy saying, *"He's been though a lot—more than any of us knows—and I know not to ask..."*

I remember the way he smiled, the way he kissed the man.

The way he was so utterly convincing.

I recall the threats his mom made to get him to do those things.

My mind's eye sees the way the red-hot tip of the cigarette sizzled against his pallid backside. I smell cooked skin. I hear

224

his screams tearing the membranes of his throat out. My rent soul shudders in memory.

I'm so angry I could kill them.

If they weren't already dead.

I'm on a seesaw of emotions. No, a mechanical bull. It's flipping me, tossing me, up, down. I'm falling off, into a sobbing heap in the dirt.

He was a child, a baby, and they desecrated him. They took everything pure and sacred about their own child, and raped it.

They hated him. There's no other possible way to explain…

…the repugnance, the evil, of what they did.

He did nothing wrong. I have to keep reminding myself. He was a child. He had no power.

He didn't judge me when I opened up to him. I can't judge him now.

No matter how it hurts.

He was so believable, with Daddy.

I have to forgive him…

…but he didn't do anything to forgive!

My mind argues with itself.

Because it hurts. So much.

Why did I *watch* that fucking thing?!

I feel like a pervert, a degenerate, my Uncle Price. It doesn't matter that there's no way in hell I was aroused or titillated.

I watched. That's all I had to do.

And now realisation avalanches onto me.

It is a video depicting two adults defiling the body, and crushing the spirit of a beautiful, innocent child.

It is a crush video.

twenty-eight:

jamie
(december 29)

I haven't heard from him since early this morning, and that's not like him. Sure, we had a bit of a thing last night. I had a meltdown after I asked him to do me kitty-style, but we had a long, good talk about it, and he's convinced me that we did nothing wrong. I didn't hurt him, he didn't hurt me. We're both adults. It was completely consensual, and in all honesty, we both enjoyed it. We loved it. It was fun, and like he said, it was dirty, but in a good way.

I'm tired of feeling *dirty* about sex. I'm tired of feeling dirty every time I have an erection or an orgasm. I'm tired of the after-effects of what my parents did to me.

They made me do things I didn't want to do, then they *punished* me.

Guilt. Guilt. Guilt. Guilt. Guilt.

My middle name is Guilt.

I'm fucking *tired* of it!

I called him "Daddy" again. Why did I do that? Fuck!

Nausea and guilt are one and the same.

He hasn't called. He hasn't come by. I've called twice, and there's no answer. I've left messages on the machine. I wonder if his mom has had some kind of setback, if they released her too early and she's back in the hospital with another clot or something.

I call St. Paul's. She has not been admitted and she's not in the ER.

I have a feeling something terrible has happened.

Maybe he's had a chance to think about it.

Maybe he does think I'm a sicko.

Maybe I've lost him.

More Guilt. Guilt. Guilt. Guilt.

Late afternoon becomes evening, and still, nothing. I call over there again, leave a third message. Where *is* he?!

By nine-thirty, I'm weeping in front of my TV with my kids surrounding me. They know when I'm sad. Misty drapes herself around my head like one of those neck pillows. Sam tucks himself under my left arm. Tigger snuggles under my right. Ginger sits on my lap and kneads my chest.

At least I have *them*. *They* don't get angry and stop talking to me for no good reason!

A knock at my front door has me knocking the kids off of me as I scramble up to answer it.

But it's not Tammy, it's Stacy.

"Ray stood me up. Wanna go sing?"

"I don't feel like it."

Her shoulders slump. "Why?"

I have no idea how to talk to her about this. And somehow, just telling her that Tammy and I are having a "thing" isn't gonna cut it.

She guesses correctly, "Are you and Tam having problems?"

"I'm not sure."

"Well, what happened?"

"I don't know."

"You don't *know*? Well, call him and find out, for pity's sake!"

A big tear rolls down my face. "I *have* called him. I've left messages. He hasn't called me back. I haven't heard from him since this morning."

"Did you guys have a fight?"

It didn't feel like a fight. It felt like a problem, followed by a discussion, followed by what I thought was the resolution. It felt very similar to when Tammy was feeling bad about his childhood, and I was able to comfort him. Tammy comforted me today. Why would he suddenly...

"No," I answer.

She smiles. "Oh, maybe he had to take his mom somewhere or something."

"Maybe." I hope it's something that simple.

But usually, he calls me at least once a day, just to say, "Hi."

"Come on," Stacy prods me gently. "Let's go out. You need to get out. If he comes by, he'll know where to look for you."

I scold myself for being such a simp. My whole existence has become so wrapped up in him and how happy he makes me feel that I don't seem to have an independent bone in my body anymore.

"I'm on call tonight."

"So? You can still go out. Get your ass up," Stacy says with more force. "You still have a life. I know you're in love, but don't stop being yourself, for goodness sakes!"

The End is decorated for New Year's with brightly coloured balloons and foil streamers. The only songs I have in my heart are melancholy love songs from the Jammin' Oldies station. From the catalogue, we select an early '80s R&B ballad we're both familiar with, entitled, "I Call Your Name" by a band called Switch. It's a pleasant surprise for the crowd, who is used to us doing up-tempo New Wave.

"Here they are again," the emcee announces. "Old Reliable. We're still not sure they even like us calling them that!"

Laughter, cheers and whistles fly up from the audience.

"Jamie's in love," coos Stacy, and I take a swing at her. The mob goes crazy as we sing our hearts out. The song's mood can only be described as mutually sad and joyful, and the way it's structured, it soars into the air subtly... you'd have to hear it to know what I'm saying. It's every feeling I've ever had for Tammy Mattheis, and my voice, though deeper than Bobby DeBarge's falsetto, effortlessly carries each morosely

228

effervescent note.

I'm still me. I'm still a star, here at The End. I can still sing and make people happy.

The song ends. We bow. The crowd applauds.

Then I see him, sitting at a table in the back, alone.

He's here.

He's smiling at me.

My life begins to move again.

I leap off the stage and run to him, jump into his arms. I have absolutely no concern for the shock I give the assembly when I kiss him passionately, frantically, barely letting him up for air. When we finally part, he gently sets me down, and I glance all around me. Stacy's still up on stage, clapping and smiling. A few faces look surprised. Maybe a few are frowning their denunciation. I don't care. I'm so relieved he's here. I'm so relieved he's not angry with me. I begin to see more smiles. The cheers begin to increase in volume. "Woohoo!" Stacy hollers, and the rest follow suit.

The people of Sommerville see the expression on my face as I run into Tammy's embrace.

It's something they've never seen before.

As the attention begins to shift to the next singer taking the mic, I ask him, "Where have you been all day? I called your house. I was worried maybe something happened to your mom!" I hug him again, feel his big arms roping around me. He's trembling.

"What's the matter?" I ask, gazing into his eyes.

They're... I don't know... sad? Angry?

Something is wrong. I know it now.

I glance to my right. Lard-Ash Battle-Feldman is standing there with her husband. Benny is only gazing nebulously, but Yvette is giving me one of those looks that makes my blood run ice cold. I turn away from her scorn and examine Tammy's eyes again.

"Tammy? What's wrong?" I plead, smoothing my hand up over his hair, loving the way it clings and curls around my fingers.

"We need to talk," he says in a wavering voice. His eyes are a sombre dark evergreen.

Stacy nudges me with her cell. "It's the hospital. They couldn't get you on your cell, so they called mine," she scowls. "They want you to come in at eleven."

"Shit. Why did I agree to be on call tonight?!" I turn to Tammy. "Sorry. I have to go home and get ready."

"I'm coming with you," he says. "We really have to talk."

Yvette walks up and taps Tammy. "Can I have a word with you?" She ignores me. "It's important."

"It can wait," snaps Tammy. "It can wait *forever*, whatever it is!"

"Noooo," Yvette shakes her head, still disregarding me entirely. "It really cannot."

So Tammy sighs sharply and accompanies her over to another table. Nearby, Ray and Benny sip at their beers, neither of them looking our way.

I turn to Stacy, who is wearing the same perplexed, insulted look as I imagine I am. "What's that shit?" she asks, indicating Lard-Ash with her chin.

My heart is pumping ice water. "I have no clue."

She hollers, "Hey Ray! I guess you forgot me!"

But he doesn't raise and come over to us. He only mumbles vacantly, "Uhhh… yeah? Oh, shit, Stace… Sorry."

"Fucker," Stacy mutters under her breath.

"I think something's wrong. I think Tammy wants to break up."

"What?! What are you talking about?! You and he practically made out in front of everyone just now!"

"He's acting funny," I insist. "I think he's done."

"You're jumping the gun, Jamie. Maybe he just needs to talk to you about something."

"No! Something's *wrong*! I see it. I know him."

He's leaning into Yvette. They're talking intimately. She reaches over and brushes her hand across his arm, smiles into his eyes. He shakes his head at her.

But he's not resisting her advances.

I look back at Stacy. Now she's not so sure.

twenty-nine:

tammy
(december 29)

How beautifully he sings, I think as I hold him against me and inhale his scent. I think about how most of this throng of people are cheering, how they love his singing. I think about how happy they are for him when Stacy spills the beans.

These people love him, most of them.

But there are some who hate him. Why else would they have sent it to me, that video containing the most despotic and violent atrocities I have ever seen. It is not a well-meaning person who sent it. It is someone who wants to hurt Jamie, to expose his horrifying secret, to open his wounds all over again, expose him to new ridicule and hatred.

And when Yvette Feldman heralds her presence at The End by requesting a one-on-one with me out of the blue, after how many years of not even speaking to each other, you'd think I'd have sense enough to guess.

"What is it?" I ask in exasperation. "I'm busy!"

"Did you get your package?" she asks sweetly, a cruel smile curling her lips.

Nausea and disgust burn through me all over again, the corrosive contents of my stomach ready to leap from my mouth.

"You bitch!" I hiss under my breath.

Her eyes widen. "What's the matter, Tam? Don't like seeing your little boyfriend fucking other men?"

"Where did you get that tape?!" I grab her arm and my nails pinch into her sleeve.

"Let me go or I'll tell Ray and Benny," she growls. "Let's just say I have a friend at the police department, and I was able to convince him to give me the tape. It's no secret that Jamie was a little whore before he was adopted by that bleeding heart cop!"

"You're a fucking cunt from *hell*!" I shriek.

"Oh, just deal with it, Tam," she sneers. "You're in love with a queer who's been fucking old men since he was barely out of diapers! How can you stand to *touch* him? Who knows what *diseases* he's got?"

"Fuck you!" I spit. "Did you even *bother* to watch the whole thing?"

"I didn't *have* to," she groans. "I watched just enough to get sick to my stomach. I was right about him, little faggot!"

"If you didn't watch the whole thing, you have no fucking idea what you're talking about. You have no fucking idea! They coerced him! They raped him! They tortured him!" I'm crying.

"Didn't look like he was being forced from what I saw," Yvette grins odiously. "Looked to me like he *liked* sucking that guy's cock!"

I force back another caustic dry heave. "You didn't watch it to the end! And obviously, you couldn't discern from the beginning that he didn't want to do those things. Did you miss the part where his mother threatened him and yelled at him?"

"His *mother*? Well, no wonder he's such a mess!"

"She made him do those things!"

"Oh, come on, Tam! Are you serious?!"

"Yes, I am!" I scream at her. "Jamie was a child! No older than seven or eight! You really think he *wanted* to do those things?! They burned him, Yvette, you stupid fucking *moron*!"

But there's no dealing with an unobservant and self-righteous bigot. You can try to reason with them, you can try to explain, but when they're dead set on hating someone, your

232

endeavours are useless.

"Tam," Yvette says softly. "Are you *really* going to let that dirty faggot drag you into hell with him? He's corrupting you. You know full well what the bible says about people like him. And about what you and he are doing now. I'd hate to see you lost…"

"You know what, Yvette? Fuck you! You're not a Christian! You're an evil bitch and I hope you rot in hell!"

With that, I turn tail and run. "Come on," I mutter, taking Jamie's hand. "Let's get the fuck out of here!"

"Bye, Stacy," Jamie says over his shoulder as I pull him out to the car.

I've got to get him and myself as far away from that sick bitch as possible.

He's not in that video now. *He's in the car, with me. He's safe, alive, in good health.*

He's got a good heart. He takes care of sick people for a living. He loves cats. He loves to sing. He created a website for Mr. Tafford, whom he loved.

I keep remembering the way he kissed the man in the video. The way he called the man "Daddy". *Was it his daddy? Or was it a stranger? Did Jamie really fuck scores of grown men?*

Did he love it?

Like she says?

No! I silently rebuke myself. *What the fuck is the matter with you, Tam? You watched that fucking video! You saw what happened!*

I hate myself for not turning that VCR off, for watching on and on…

My gag reflex starts in again.

The woman screams at him about what to do, every minute detail, even how to eat a Ding Dong. She terrorises him, "Where's my lighter?" She makes ribald comments, derisive statements, about everything she forces the boy to do. She transforms from instigator to accuser. She punishes him, tortures him with a lit cigarette after he obeys every order she gives him. He shrieks in agony as the hot ash burns deeply into his buttock…

The man called "Daddy" seems less hateful than the woman, but he is every bit as evil... no... more, because he is pretending to love Jamie, pretending to care. I can hear Daddy now, "If you suck me real nice, like I showed you, I'll bring you hot dogs and mac and cheese! I know you're pretty hungry, right?"

Jamie's skinny... he's fucking emaciated.

I see the hate in those two adults for that helpless, undersized boy. The unadulterated, ceaseless hatred.

They're monsters.

Yvette is a monster.

"Tammy? What's the matter?" Jamie reaches up, brushes the tears off my cheeks as the car bumps into his drive.

I jump out of the car and run to his front door. "Hurry," I gulp as the vomit climbs vehemently up my chest. He opens his front door quickly and I dash into his bathroom. It's only saliva and stomach acid, because I haven't eaten.

I raise my heavy head to look around, thinking of nothing, but unable to shake the horrid visuals. I try to contemplate the banana yellow of the wall or the whisker-coated razor sitting on his sink, or the lone bottle of Cool Water by Davidoff that I've watched Jamie spray over the puerile arch of his neck.

Jamie enters the bathroom, pulling on a white shirt and a dark scrub shirt. "Do you have the flu?"

I shake my head. "Jamie, we have to talk."

He looks at me. "Okay, then, let's talk."

I step away from the toilet and face him, then change my mind, about-facing, feeling more retches building within me.

"Is it about Yvette?" he asks. "I saw her talking to you." His voice takes on an edge. His eyes narrow. "I saw her hitting on you, in fact, so I guess you're through with me."

I taste puke. "No. Jamie. That's not it…"

"You think I'm stupid? I know what you're doing!" he shouts. "You don't return my fucking calls all day long, you come up to me, all sad-eyed and serious, and 'We really need to talk!' Just spit it out, Tammy! You want to break up so you can get back with Yvette!"

"Jamie!"

234

In a bitter, sing-song voice, Jamie scoffs, "Just be kind about it! Don't let Benny know! Don't flaunt yourselves!"

"Jamie!"

"How could I have trusted you?!"

"Jamie, calm down, please! It's not that at all!"

"Then what the fuck is it, Tammy?! What's crawled up your ass all of a sudden?! You've ignored me all day long! I called the hospitals, thinking your mom had gone back in or something!"

"No," I mumble. "Mom's fine."

"Just tell me what's going on already!" snaps Jamie. "It's after ten and I need to get ready for work!"

I struggle to figure out how to do this, and sigh, realising there's no way I can do this without harming him. "I don't know if I should tell you."

He expels an annoyed breath. "Why?"

"Because it will hurt you."

Regarding me through apprehensive blue eyes, he says, "I don't like Yvette. I never have. She's disgusting, vulgar. I can't stand her... and she scares me. Sometimes she gives me these looks... she's evil."

"Yeah, fucking-A, she's evil," I scowl. "I don't like her either, Jamie. Believe me, the last thing you'll ever need to worry about is me fucking around on you with *her*."

"What about other women? What about other men?" His eyes dagger into me.

"I haven't been cheating, Jamie. This isn't about anything like that."

Another sigh hisses through his teeth. "Tammy, what *is* it?!"

"I just wish you'd told me yourself."

"Told you *what*?" His eyes widen.

"I wish you'd have opened up to me."

"About *what*?!"

"About why you feel so... dirty about everything."

His slim shoulders wilt. "So you *do* think it was a fight."

"What?"

"I thought it was only a discussion." Jamie shakes his head. "I'm sorry about the meltdown, Tammy. You're right. It was a

235

game. It was role-playing. It was fun, and like you said, if it was dirty, it was dirty in a fun way. I'm just not used to that kind of thing. You're right, it's all new to me, that's all."

You are used to it, I think to him. *And that's why you feel so ashamed and dirty.*

I go to him and try to hug him, saying, "I wish you'd open up to me, tell me what happened to you."

He shoves me. "You're pushing me, Tammy! I told you I'm fucked up! I told you I have issues! Do you *listen*?!"

"I do listen, Jamie. What did they do to you?"

"What do you mean, *they*?" His dark blue eyes are snapping.

"Someone hurt you terribly, didn't they?"

"Yeah, they did, Tammy! Why do you want details? Do you think I'm fucking *lying* to you?!"

"I don't know, Jamie… You won't let me in. I don't even *know* you."

Immediately, the aghast dejection shimmering in Jamie's eyes makes me regret everything that's just crossed my lips.

There had to have been a better approach.

He stands in stunned silence for a few moments. Then he murmurs, "I won't let you in? I won't let you in? After everything we've shared… I let you inside of me! I never let people inside of me! After sixteen years…" His eyes empty of feeling, become dull blue stones, the way I hate. "You don't know me. After all I've shared with you. You don't *know* me?"

"You let me inside of you *physically*," I say, and I realise now, this is the *only* way I can say it. "But not completely. You haven't shared everything with me. I thought we were completely united, but I think I was wrong."

Now he's crying. "What's the rush, Tammy?" he sobs. "I'm *trying*! I'm really trying! Why can't you understand that I need *time*?! Did it ever occur to you that I love you so much that if I tell you these horrible things about me and I lose you, I'll die of a broken heart?! Did it ever occur to you that I've been trying to figure out a way to tell you that won't make you either be sick to your stomach or hate me?! Or *both*?!" His voice rises in pitch until he's screaming and crying wretchedly.

I feel weak. I wobble toward the bathroom door.

"Alright, go then!" Jamie screeches. "Go and don't come back! Ever!"

I turn back to him. "Jamie…"

"No! I'd rather be alone. I can't deal with this. I'd rather go back to what I was, a hermit, a recluse, safe behind closed doors, snuggled up with my kids, in my nice warm quilt, my cocoon. I wasn't meant for this… sex, love, heartache, bullshit…"

"Baby…"

"No, please. Just go." He walks over to the toilet, pulls a length of tissue off the roll, runs it under a trickle of tepid tap water, and wipes his face.

"Baby. I saw the video. I saw you. I saw them. I saw what they did to you."

thirty:

jamie
(december 29)

"Wh-wh-what?" My eyes are like saucers. Now it's my turn to stumble as I stare in hollow incredulity at Tammy's disclosure.

His eyes overflow. "I saw them molest you... FUCK!" a high wail floats from his mouth. "I saw them *rape* you. I saw everything, Jamie."

"What do you mean, you *saw* it?!" I roar, making my throat scratchy.

"A video... you were about eight years old... a little boy..."

My breath begins to leave me in shallow, terrified pants. "Where did you *get* it?!"

He can't look at me now. "Yvette. She got it from someone down at the police station. I don't know. They let her have it. They..."

"She sent you a video?!" My stomach is whisking. "You had her send you a video?!"

"No, Jamie! I didn't!" The pain in Tammy's eyes stabs me. "I didn't *have* her send it to me. She has a friend at the police station, and she got her hands on this awful video, and she mailed it to me. I watched it. This morning..."

"How do you know it was Yvette?" I'm hyperventilating and retching simultaneously.

"That's why she pulled me aside at the bar tonight, Jamie. To tell me she sent it to me."

"Why did you *watch* it?!" I shriek.

"It had no label. I didn't know what it was, until it started playing..."

"What did she have to say about it?"

"Never mind, Jamie..."

"What did she say?!" I snap.

He sighs crossly. "What do you care?!"

"I want to know!"

"She said it was disgusting."

"What else?!"

"Jamie..."

"What else?!"

"She... thinks you... liked it." He adds hastily, "She didn't watch the whole thing."

"Oh fuck." I'm dizzy, and I fall to my knees, my heart haemorrhaging. "Why did she send it to you?! Why?!"

"Because she's a fucking evil bitch!" Tammy screams, sinking down, trying to touch me. "She was quite pleased with herself. She was *gloating*! She's a fucking cunt!"

"Get off!" I roll into a ball on the floor. I'm destroyed. After all the years of trying, God has finally killed me. He's finally stamped me out. He's wanted to do it for thirty-one years, and now, mission accomplished.

Tammy scoots away on his knees, crying, his face in his hands. "I'm sorry, Jamie!"

"You watched it... you didn't turn it off, did you?" I sob bitterly. "You watched the whole thing!"

He nods, his face hidden, like a child caught red-handed.

"And now, you think I'm a whore, just like everyone else! They filmed themselves fucking me, burning me with cigarettes, so their sick friends could get off on it! But I'm a whore! Right?!"

"You're a *victim*, Jamie!"

I ignore him. "Did *you* get off on it too?" I know I'm being

239

evil, I know I'm being hateful, but I'm so ashamed. I'm so ashamed, I can't escape it. I can't get away from my past. I can't get away from the horror, the scandal of it... no matter what I do, where I go..."

"How can you even *think* that?" Tammy roar-sobs. "Maybe I should ask you the same thing! Is she right? Did you *like* fucking 'Daddy'?"

"You motherfucker!" I slap Tammy's face as hard as I can. He recoils, his hand covering his rapidly reddening cheek.

Why are we hurting each other? Why are we stabbing each other with blades of accusation, with vindictive indictments?

Because it hurts.

And this is *exactly* what Yvette wanted.

Regret tumbles out of his mouth like marbles out of a cloth bag. "Oh, God, Jamie. I can't believe I said that to you. I didn't mean it. I didn't mean it... I swear."

"Oh, yes you did!" I screech at him. "You meant it, every fucking word! You think I *liked* it! And you think I had it coming, what they did next! You think I deserved that! Don't you?!" I'm out of control, raging full throttle.

"No, Jamie! I didn't mean it!"

"Yeah, you did!"

"It hurt, Jamie. It hurt to see you... doing that!"

"I didn't *want* to!"

"I know. I watched it! I saw what they did to you..."

"Don't you believe Yvette, your best good friend?" I sneer. "*She* thinks I loved it!"

"She didn't watch all of it. But I watched the whole thing!"

"Why?! Why would you *watch* that?! How could you?"

"Because I needed to know. I knew if I watched all of it, I'd see the whole story. I know you were forced! I *know*!"

"Yeah. You needed to know, because you don't *know* me. I didn't 'let you in', right?" I laugh bitterly. "How could you watch them do that to me? I feel like you raped me yourself, just by watching that sick shit!"

Tammy gulps loudly. "It made me sick. I've been sick all day. I wish I hadn't watched it. I can't get those horrible images out of my head now... those screams. I did *not* get off on it! I

240

wanted to save you. I wanted to help you. I had to keep reminding myself that that video is over twenty years old, and that you're here. With me. And that you're okay."

"I'm *not* okay, Tammy," I mutter. "Believe me when I say, I'm not okay. Welcome to my world. I carry those memories with me every minute of my life. My dead fucking parents live forever. The first thirteen years of my life are the ones I carry around constantly. I can't escape, I can't forget, and I guess Yvette is going to make sure everyone around here knows all about it. She wants to annihilate me. She's been out to destroy me for years. I have no idea why she hates me so much, but then, I never found out why my own parents hated me, so…" I trail off, my shoulders sagging in squashed subjugation.

"Jamie…" Tammy reaches for me. I easily evade him by leaning to my left.

"And now she's done it. She's finally done it. I guess God *does* hate me."

Tammy's voice raises a few decibels. "What do you mean?"

"I've tried, all my life, to believe God doesn't hate me. I tried to believe Lloyd when he said God loves me as I am. But when everyone else around me, the pastor, the kids at church, the kids at school, the Christian radio stations, says God hates homos, it's pretty hard to believe otherwise."

"Jamie. Please?"

Again, I'm sullied in front of Tammy. I can't take it anymore. I've tried to overcome the shame, the guilt, the torture, the self-loathing… all these years. But now I give up. God hates me. He won't let me live it down, what my parents did. I can't move forward and put that shit behind me, because Yvette has to dig it up, like the dog she is. They're raping me again.

"I can't do this anymore. I give up. I just want to die."

"No, Jamie! You don't mean that…"

"I mean it, Tammy. I'm tired. I'm tired of living with this guilt. I can't even have sex with you without remembering what they did to me. What they did gets into everything, taints it, ruins it. I can't enjoy my life. I should never have gotten with you, because I knew, deep in my heart, something would ruin it.

241

I should have stayed alone. At least I was able to get through my day without constantly reliving the torture…"

I can feel his pain, but my own is too great to cosset him right now.

"And I can't even go back to being alone. Not now. You've made your mark on me, Tammy. I'll never again be able to live alone and semi-happy, able to push my mind past how it feels to be totally and pathetically in love with someone. I'll never again be able to almost ignore how bad it hurts that I can't have a normal life, ever." I plaster my hands over my eyes and cry and cry. "Why did you have to come home? I was doing okay, really I was…"

I'm breaking his heart, I know, but I can't…

Without taking my hands away from my face, I whisper, "I'm sorry, Tammy. I can't do this anymore. I can't. It'll only hurt us to stay in this thing. Let's just say goodbye now. It will be better just to say goodbye now…" My nostrils are clogged with snot. After suffering all day long from that paralysing fear that Tammy was through with me, that he wanted to dump me for whatever reason, I'm doing it to him.

He steps forward and takes my arm gently. "You can't do this, Jamie. You can't." His voice is nasal.

"Let me go, Tammy."

"No, you have to listen to me. You can't give up."

The pain is crushing me, all of the pain, from all directions. "I want to die. I just want it to end! I want this shit to *stop*!"

"Please, Jamie…"

He's begging me.

Don't do that, Tammy. Don't add to my pain.

"Let me go, Tam!" I jerk my arm free and reach back, ready to slap him again. For a moment, Tammy stares, his already soaking eyes puddling with new tears.

I've called him, "Tam".

I never do that.

The bruise on his cheek is beginning to glow a deeper, more livid red, as if I really have slapped him again. He steps close to me again, tries to put his arms around me.

"No!" I shriek. "Leave me alone!"

242

"No," he replies.

My arms flail wildly. "They raped me! They raped me! THEY RAPED ME!"

"I know, Baby, I know. Shhhh..."

"THEY RUINED ME, TAMMY!" I scream shrilly. "THEY RUINED ME! I CAN NEVER HAVE A NORMAL LIFE NOW! JUST GO! GET OUT OF HERE AND SAVE YOURSELF THE HEARTACHE! YOU CAN'T HELP ME! NOBODY CAN HELP ME!"

"Stop it," Tammy says calmly, locking his arms around my upper body.

"I'm just so sorry about this," I whimper. "All of it."

"If you're talking about us being together," he says with an edge on his voice, "I'm not. I've never been sorry. Because it's all I've ever wanted, all our lives."

"I can't do it anymore, Tammy. I can't... and I don't want to."

"Yes, you *can* do this, Jamie. You can do this—we can do this. We were happy. We were so happy..."

"We *were*," I clarify. "And now..."

Tammy sobs feverishly. "Jamie, if it will make any difference, I apologise. I love you. I never meant to hurt you. You're right. Just watching it... I shouldn't have. I should have turned it off."

I'm too lethargic to respond.

"But... I kept forgetting it was a video, that it wasn't the real you anymore. It was almost like I... didn't want to leave you... alone... with them... hurting you."

And abruptly, I understand. It comes to me through the layer of ice—the slightest bit of appreciation. Tammy's eyes are overflowing. Mine are dry now, gritty. I feel dead inside. "I'll tell you everything," I say quietly, limply, utterly depleted.

"No. You don't have to. I know now," he says.

"You know what you *saw*," I say determinedly. "And now you're going to listen to *my* side of it."

"Jamie..."

"No! You're going to listen to what I have to say about it!" I declare in a controlled voice that astonishes me. "It's only fair you hear *my* side of it. You've heard what Lard-Ash Feldman has to say, even though she knows fucking *nothing*! You watched my parents call me names while they stuck things in me, while they burned my ass with cigarettes, while they used me and tossed me like I was a piece of *shit*! Now you're going to listen to *me*!" My voice is shrill and gravelly, raw from screaming.

Tammy gives me a tiny nod of surrender.

book three:

unspoken request

thirty-one:

tammy
(december 29)

"They started beating me when I was about three," Jamie says in an eerie matter of fact manner, and I instinctively know he's employing his survival skills. He'll have to, if he's going to be able to tell me this without going insane. He gently frees himself from my embrace and puts needed distance between us. I let him, because he won't be able to do this with my arms around him. He has to be alone. There can be no vulnerability.

"It's the earliest memory I have. They managed to duck the authorities whenever a teacher called in the signs of abuse." He swallows. "They began to lock me in my room right after first grade began. They removed me from school and locked me in my room."

My eyes close. I had heard about Jamie being locked in a room, about how the Sommerville Police found him, but how many years?

"They let me out every so often, to shower and stretch my legs. One night, Daddy came into the shower with me and made me blow him. I tried to escape out the window. They caught me and beat me bloody, then they chained me to my bed, by my ankles."

I'm sick. I'm so sick.

Jamie just sits there, not a trace of anything on his face or in his eyes, like he's simply telling a story. He hasn't put his socks or his work shoes on yet, and I see his ankles beneath the hem of his scrub pants. Both of them have rings of scar tissue around them, an angry, glossy, lumpy deep red. The left still looks a degree worse, as though he has recently been re-injured there.

"They gave me a bucket by my bed to piss and shit in," Jamie continues. He walks slowly back over to the bathtub, curls his hands around the towel rack hanging there. "They fed me whenever they felt like it. When I was about seven or eight, they began to come into my room and make the videos, which they sold to their friends, their friends' friends, et cetera. They fed me less and less often. I couldn't leave my bed because I became too weak. The videos changed then. Though it was a lot more fun to film me trying to fight them off, they said, some of their friends really liked watching me lay there too weak to move while they fucked and beat me, too weak to even participate."

I don't understand why he's not crying, or going crazy, and I have to remind myself, his catatonia is a survival thing.

He grips the silver bar and pulls. "I stopped screaming. I learned to stop myself from screaming when Mom put her cigs out on me. I learned how to go away in my mind, to leave that room, to turn off my fear, to ignore the hurting... When I did that, they stopped making the videos. They stopped, because, if I don't scream, what fun is that?"

I dry heave. When the lurching of my stomach eases off, I interrupt him in a rough whisper, "Did their friends rape you too, Jamie? Did you have to have sex with their friends?"

"No, just my dad," he replies in sterile, sullen monotone, pulling the towel bar, slowly dislodging it from where it's fastened to the wall. "Aside from you, the only other person I've been with is my dad." His eyes change, become wild and angry. "I'm sorry! I didn't *want* to be fucked by my own father!"

"I know that, Jamie, I know..."

Brown pieces of wall and bits of white plaster begin to crumble from where he's pulling. "Say what you really think, Tammy!" He spits the words out like bitter seeds. "Just say it!

252

Say what my parents' friends said! Say what you *all* think! I looked like I *wanted* it! I looked like I *loved* it, right? Right?! I made out with Daddy like I was a little *slut* for his big cock, right?!"

"No, Jamie. They made you do it, I know…" *Why won't you believe me?*

"I was no different than *you* were, Tammy! He told me he *loved* me. He told me he'd never let anything happen to me, that he'd take care of me, and I believed him!" His emotional reserve is deteriorating before my eyes. "He kissed me, he touched me, he made me feel loved. I went for days, weeks, without human touch, and when he gave it to me… I'm *human*, Tammy! He made me feel like he cared about me. Is that so horrible? To need someone to touch me?!"

One end of the towel bar comes free, leaving behind a gaping hole. More plaster rains into the white fibreglass basin. The other end remains bolted securely to the wall.

His voice rises to a fever pitch. "Am I such a horrible person?!"

"No," I sob. "No."

"Mommy," Jamie sneers the word, "Was the truly brutal one. Daddy just liked to fuck me. And I would do anything for him, anything he wanted, just so he'd keep touching me, kissing me, loving me. When he didn't come to my room for days, or weeks, I'd cry for him to come…" Jamie's barely holding himself on the edge, teetering on the cliff. "I loved him. I loved *both* of them. I only wanted to *please* them. I only wanted them to love me too!"

"Your dad manipulated you," I tell him. "Every bit as much as your mom did. I think that makes him more evil. I watched him. He made me puke, acting all sweet, making you believe he loved you! He didn't love you, he used you!"

"You think I don't *know* that now?!" he screams at me. "You think I'm still so stupid?! He wouldn't even let me *eat* until I blew him! I was *hungry*! I was so hungry, Tammy!" His wails bounce from the bathroom walls. Plaster continues to avalanche down into a snowy porcelain valley.

"I know… I know…" My heart hurts for the child that's still

trapped. It *hurts*…

"The reason I can't bear to let you suck me," Jamie mutters between dry retches, his white knuckles gripping the edge of the bathtub, "Is because it would make me feel like I'm my own father, like I'm turning into him. I don't want to feel that, ever! Ever! Because I HATE HIM! DO YOU UNDERSTAND ME? I *HATE* HIM!"

"Jamie, I understand… I know…"

"If I blow you, I'm still me. If I let you blow me, I feel like Daddy, forcing a child…" Vomit spills from Jamie's mouth, tumbles down the front of his shirt, into the tub, mixing with the rubble.

Holding the freed end of the towel rack, Jamie begins to twist the metal off from where it's still affixed to the wall above his bathtub. "The police said Daddy shot Mom and then turned the gun on himself," Jamie says, deadness in his eyes, puke and saliva copiously dripping in long strings from his chin. His hands and arms work in a circular motion. Twist, twist, twist…

It's quarter past ten. He twists, twists, twists. The towel rack separates, a portion stays embedded in the wall. The twisting has created a long, thin, warped edge, sharp as a needle, a razor, a crooked ice pick. Jamie touches his index finger to it. "The cops ought to have let me die in that room. I'm ruined. I'm a maggot. I'm a dirty, disgusting piece of filth."

"Why do you blame yourself, Jamie?!" I sob, past the point of hysteria. "Why do you hate yourself when you did nothing wrong?!"

"There's no hope for me." His voice is as hollow and metallic as the towel rod he holds in his death grip. "You thought I was so pure, so sweet. I told you I was a virgin. I *lied* to you. I wanted to be a virgin, but the truth is, I'm *garbage*."

"Stop it!" I yell.

"Go, Tammy. Just go home."

"No. I'm not going anywhere."

"You gonna watch me kill myself?" He positions the spindle-like point of the towel bar against the delicate, transparent skin of his wrist.

"I'm not going to let you kill yourself!" I step carefully

towards him.

"I want to die. I don't want to live like this anymore."

"What about Stacy? What about your friends? What about your cats? What about ME?!"

His serene fatalism is a clean, cold blade, shredding my innards. "Stacy will have to deal with it. I'll leave instructions for the kids. You... You'll live over it, I'm sure. As for friends, what fucking friends? Everyone hates me."

"You know what? I'm sick of hearing that shit!" I shout at him. "If everyone hated you, you wouldn't have had Lloyd, Stacy or me! And my mom! She loves you, you know that?! If everyone hates you so much, why do they cheer whenever you're up there singing?"

He shrugs. "They're just people in town. They don't *know* me, and if they did, they'd hate me."

"They just saw you kiss me, with tongue! And they cheered... most of them."

"Whatever," he rolls his eyes. "They're strangers."

"'Cause you won't let anyone in, Jamie!"

"Because I can't trust people, Tammy!" he retorts. "I can't trust people not to pretend to care, only to stomp on me as soon as my guard is down!"

"And you think I'm one of them! You think I couldn't give two shits about you, don't you?!"

He shrugs indifferently. I can't button my mouth now. "You selfish, heartless... You're cruel... I can't believe how cruel you are!"

"I might as well be dead, Tammy. I feel dead. They ruined me, forever. They killed me. I just didn't realise it, until now."

"They did not kill you! You're a survivor! And you know it!"

His eyes interrupt their lifeless stare with a small blink.

"What we have, Jamie, it's beautiful. It's real. It's always been real..."

"I was happy alone," he whispers.

"You're lying to yourself!" I hiss. "You weren't happy! You were *miserable*! Just like me! Miserable, alone, hiding, afraid. Fucking afraid... just like me!"

"Please, Tammy," he says dispassionately. "Just let me go. Let me die…"

I feel the entire world being crushed by a giant, invisible, insidious evil. "I guess you *are* fucked up. Go ahead, then! Do it!"

"Leave," he commands in a small voice.

I lunge at him and grab the towel bar. We struggle for a few seconds, and I pry it from his clammy fingers and fling it. It clatters metallically into the tub. I take him in my arms and hold him. He resists, thrashing and screaming. My voice is a pained howl. "I'm not letting you go. I'll never let you go."

He yields, his body becomes pliant, and he sobs into the front of my shirt. "Now you know why I don't trust anybody, why I'm so afraid and ashamed, why I only feel safe when I'm alone, behind locked doors. I don't know who I can trust. I don't know who's for real, who's going to hurt me next…" He frees a torrent as I hold him against me.

"You punish yourself for everything *they* did, Jamie. You lock yourself away, like they locked you in your room…" His body congeals again. "You deny yourself food, because they starved you."

He begins to squirm. "Tammy, please!" He sinks to the floor, his body rolling up like a woodlouse.

"And you burn yourself, like they burned you."

"Stop!"

"Look at this!" I shout, reaching down and lifting his left ankle. "Look what you do to yourself!"

I can feel his heart fracturing. I can feel *his* shame. He wears it like a badge, a scarlet letter. His pain is exposed, open, a wound, a large, swollen, blistered sore. "I don't know why I do it," he sobs. "I went to school, became a nurse. I had a foster dad who loved me, but I keep doing it. It hurts, but I can't *stop!*"

"You think you're a bad person. You think you deserve what they did to you. You think you deserve to be lonely. You think you don't *deserve* any happiness. You're in *prison*, Jamie! You're still locked in that room with those monsters! You have to break out!"

"Tammy, stop!"

"You can't punish *them*, and there's nobody else to punish, so you punish *yourself*!"

"Please!"

"It's all you know. You have to break out! You have to let yourself trust again! Don't push me away. Let me love you. Let me care!"

He wants to sink down, all the way down, and I won't let him. I reach down and pull him back up.

Even through the starchy cotton of his vomit-encrusted scrub top and the soft layer of the white shirt he wears underneath, my fingers trace over the big, thick scars over his shoulder blades. "What are these from, Jamie?"

His breath hiccups. "They're bedsores. From lying in bed, from starving, from my bones poking out…"

I thought my heart was already broken.

thirty-two:

jamie
(december 29)

A gut-wrenching sob squeezes from his throat, "Jamie…"

And his arms constrict around me, crushing me, smashing me against him.

Here it is, the feeling I had when Lloyd hugged me that night, so long ago when he spoke of his horror at finding me starved, tortured, beaten, lying in my own waste, in a death bed, condemned to die for no reason other than my parents hated me and wanted to kill me as surely as they'd killed themselves.

Tammy soaks me as he holds me so tight that I'm likely to smother. But I love it. My arms slide up around his neck. I feel my heart slowly beginning to gather itself back together.

I'm safe. I'm loved. I'm home.

I belong… here.

"I know why you call me 'Daddy'," he cries. "You're trying to deal with feeling dirty. But you don't know how. So you go back to that place where you can pretend you *like* feeling dirty, and then you punish yourself. It's all you know. You can't help it. You're still trying to survive. You're a survivor."

My heart and lungs discordant, I wince at the familiar compliment. How does he do it? How does he understand me, inside and out?

I don't understand why God is so good to me, giving me these people. Every time I think God hates me, every time I think God wants me to go away and die, He gives me someone to help me, to care, to love.

"Tammy, I never meant to imply that I don't like making love with you. I like it... I love it... I don't mean to make you think that I feel like you're raping me every time we do it. I didn't mean to call you that. It just... came out. It's like... I became a little boy again, just to deal with feeling so dirty, because every time I feel pleasure, it feels dirty."

"I know, Jamie, I understand."

"In so many ways, you're dealing with a little boy, you know?"

"Yeah," Tammy says quietly. "I know."

"How can you forgive me for all this?" I sniffle. "How can you love me after this? How can you *look* at me?"

"There's nothing to forgive, Baby," he whispers.

"I lied to you, told you I'd never had sex. I used you as a surrogate 'Daddy' to try to deal... I said horrible things to you. I'm so hateful. I said you probably got off on the video. I accused you of cheating on me with Yvette."

Now I really have something to be ashamed of.

"You *were* a virgin, Jamie. You lose your virginity when you make love for the first time, as a consenting adult, with somebody you care about. When you were little, you did what you had to do to survive. I know you love me. I know you know the difference between me and your father. I know what you feel for me is *real*, otherwise you would have latched on to any guy who paid attention to you."

That's right.

He continues. "As for the thing with Yvette, I know she's a slut, and she is a mean, spiteful bitch, and not to be trusted, but I need you to trust *me*. I don't like her, and I'll never sleep with her. I love you. I'll never stop loving you. And I forgive you, for wanting to kill yourself. God, do you know what it would *do* to me if you killed yourself?!"

"I'm sorry, Tammy," I whisper, my head hanging down.

259

"And I'm sorry I slapped you. I will never, ever hit you again."

"I'm sorry too, Jamie. Asking you if you liked doing those things. I knew you didn't. I was being hateful too, because I was hurt, but I know good and well you didn't *like* any of it."

"I know you know."

"I swear to you, I didn't ask that bitch to send me the video."

"I know."

"I didn't know it existed. I'm sorry I watched it. It upset me so much. I don't want to think about it anymore. And I don't want you to either. It's over. It happened, and neither of us can do anything about it. If I could, Jamie, I would have jumped into that video and saved you. I'd have killed those fuckers…"

He inhales and exhales slowly, his chest expanding against mine. "And I'm sorry I forced you to tell me about all this before you were ready to."

My arms tighten around him. I squeeze him with all my strength. I've got to let him *know*. "It's okay, Tammy, it's okay now. I'm glad I told you. Maybe you *had* to force me. Maybe I never could have otherwise."

"I don't want you to die," he whispers raggedly.

"I'm not going to."

"Are you sure?" he asks.

"I don't want to die."

"Are you *sure*?" he repeats, his breath quickening.

"I want to live. I'm going back to Miss Halliday."

"I need a good counsellor myself," he admits.

"I'm sorry, Tammy."

"We're going to be okay now, aren't we." He isn't asking.

"Yes." I bury my nose in his chest, nuzzle his throat, my eyes closed, like a newborn kitten seeking the scent of mother's milk.

"I love the way you smell," I sigh.

"I'm not wearing cologne."

"I don't care. I just love your smell… your skin… your hair."

"What about my breath?"

"That too."

"So it doesn't stink?"

260

"No." I clap my hand over my mouth. "Does mine?"

"No."

"I just puked," I say through my hand.

"I puked too. You smell fine."

"I'm getting puke all over you. My top…"

"You never stink, even after you smoke, which I wish you wouldn't do."

"I'll quit."

"I won't nag you about it. It's just you have such a good voice. I don't want you to get throat cancer."

"I know."

"I want you to be around, so I can grow old with you."

I stare at the seam in his collar. "You want to grow old with me?"

"After all the years I wasted, you think I'm going to let you go now? You're not going anywhere! You're *stuck* with me!"

"My very own leech," I murmur, inhaling his scent again.

"Damn right," he says fervently.

Reluctantly, I pull away from him. "I'm sorry, Tammy. I need to get going. I'm going to be late…"

"Take me with you," he says, and I laugh, "Really, what are you going to do all night besides be bored out of your mind? Your mom's home now!"

"Talk to you," he says softly.

I stand on tiptoe and kiss him.

"Really, Jamie. Let me come with you. I don't want to be away from you. I…" He falters, then he straightens his posture, and with more conviction, he says, "I think I should come with you."

"Tammy, I'm going to be fine, I promise. I won't do anything to hurt myself. Everything's okay now. I feel better. We're going to be okay. I love you. I mean it. I do. Don't be scared. I would never hurt myself, because I know it would hurt you. I won't do that to you."

He bear-hugs me again. "I love you."

He's trembling.

"I love you, Tammy. I'll love you always, all my life."

He resists as I gently push him out my front door. "Jamie,

I'm worried... please?"

"Nooo, go on home and get some rest. Eat something!"

"Jamie, it's no trouble. I can drive you. I can hang out in the lounge, take a nap in there if I get sleepy."

"You're too sweet."

"Baby, I'm *scared*!"

I push the door ajar and examine him. He really is afraid.

Unsettled by what I'm seeing, I sigh, "Tammy, I'm going to be okay. Please believe me. I'm not going to hurt you. I swear..."

"It's not that. I have a bad feeling..." A tear slips from his left eye.

"About what?"

"I don't know, but..."

"Tammy, everything's okay now. You go on home and I'll see you in the morning. I've got to feed the kids, and..."

"I'll help you!" he offers, like a helpful little boy.

"Go," I laugh, "Or I'll never make it to work."

He finally slinks away, like a puppy with his tail between his legs. He looks so crestfallen, I almost call him back inside, because really, I'd love for him to stay.

But then we'd start talking again, or kissing, or fucking, and then I'd really be late. No. I need to get my ass in gear and go. I pull off my odoriferous scrub top and throw on a new one. I pour the kids' food, give them each a goodbye pet, grab the kitchen garbage.

My cell chimes from my pocket. "Are you on your way yet?"

"No, I just fed the kids. I got to take out some trash, then I'll get going."

"I'm worried. I can't put my finger on it, but..."

"Tammy, please," I entreat. "Don't think about that video. Put it out of your mind."

"If only," he says solemnly.

"I'm okay. I have you, and I know I'm going to be okay."

"Are you really sure I can't come to work with you?" he asks.

"Tammy, I'd feel like shit if you spent a miserable night

trying to sleep in one of those lousy Geri-chairs. No, please, try to stop worrying and get some sleep. I'll be home around eight-ish."

"Will you at least give me a call when you get there? Let me know you made it?"

"Of course. I'll call you, sweetie."

"Better yet, call in sick," he says. I'd think he was being playful, but I hear his fear coming through the line.

"I can't, sweet. I'd love to stay home with you, all night long, but I can't. I promised them I could work, so I have to go... they're going to be pissed as it is when I show up late."

"So? Let me. They can't fire you. You're the only nurse they have that knows what he's doing!"

"You're silly. Tammy?"

"Hmmm..."

"I've never pretended with you. I did things to deal with feeling dirty, but it was because of my parents."

"I know that, Baby," he says. I know, we'd just been over this, but it's still sitting there, on my chest. I have to be sure he *knows*...

"I *love* having sex with you. You *have* to believe me. I don't know how you *can* believe me, but I've *always* loved you. I *always* wanted to be with you. If they hadn't made me feel so... I would never have had all these issues. I'm not afraid of *you*. I'm not repulsed by *you*. You're the most beautiful man I've ever seen in my life. I want to be with you all the time, forever, for the rest of my life! I love being near you, I love being close to you..."

I hear him crying.

"I'm just so afraid you're going to decide... that this isn't... that it won't..."

Now I'm crying.

"Uh! No, Baby. You're stuck with me. I mean it."

"Good," I sniffle. "I don't ever want to be able to rid myself of you."

"You won't," Tammy says wetly.

"You said people lose their V when they make love for the first time with someone they really care about, right? So maybe

263

that means *you* were a virgin too, that first night with me… in a way, you know…"

"Maybe it does," he agrees. "We pretended, Jamie, to get through things we didn't want to do, to survive, to prove something to ourselves, whatever… But we've never pretended with each other."

"No."

"I love being with you, I do."

"I swore to myself, when I was a kid, I'd never have sex again," I confess. "I'd never *ever* do those gross, disgusting things with anyone ever again, and then you… and I… I never thought I'd ever *love* sex."

"I never loved sex until Christmas Eve," Tammy murmurs. "I mean, I had a lot of sex, Jamie, you know that. I wish I could have been like you, but… Anyway, I never l*oved* sex, until you, because it's so much more…"

"It *is* so much more. I love being close to you. I love the way you crush me close to you after, and it's so warm, wet, sticky… and the way it s*mells*…"

"Why don't you call in sick already!" he grumps, then his voice lowers enticingly. "You *know* you want to."

My knees don't have cartilage holding them together anymore. All I want is for him to drive his ass back over here and fuck me silly. "Honey, I have to go. I'm so late."

"Seriously, Jamie. I'm worried."

"Please, Tammy, don't worry anymore."

"I…"

"You're the best."

"Jamie…"

"For the last time, I'm going to be *fine*. I love you."

"I love you too. Don't forget to call me!"

"I won't. Promise."

"The very instant you walk in!"

"The very instant. I promise, Tammy."

"Okay." He's relaxing a little. "I love you." I hear a kissing sound on his end.

"Love you too," I say, and kiss my cell phone.

I gather up my keys and the kitchen garbage. I remember the

towel rack I tore off the bathroom wall. I scoop it out of the tub, mindful of the reeky puke splattered and drying all over the white fibreglass. I say another rushed goodbye to the kids and lock the front door behind me.

thirty-three:

tammy
(december 29 and 30)

He didn't want me to go to work with him.

It's not that I believe Jamie's going to off himself as soon as he's out of my sight. I do believe he loves me. I do believe he wants to live.

But… I can't shake this feeling as I drive home.

Mom's sound asleep, so I move quietly as I microwave some leftover vegetable beef soup and settle in front of the TV.

I can't eat. The soup is tasteless. I shove it away.

I'm upset, that's all. I'm upset over the events of the day— the video, Yvette's deplorable behaviour, the fight Jamie and I had, the threat of suicide…

The *Bugs Bunny* cartoons aren't helping a bit. I can't get this nameless fear to disembark. I snatch our portable house phone and call Jamie's house again. No answer. By now he must be on his way. I dial his cell. No answer. Shit! He's either got the damn thing turned off or it's on vibrate and he can't hear it because he's got the radio blasting.

The prayer bursts out of me. *Please God, please get Jamie to work safely, and make him remember to call me when he gets there. Please…*

Fifteen minutes go by, and I can't settle down. I call St. Paul's and ask for three south, where Jamie usually is stationed. I know he can't be there this soon, but I want to leave a message for them to remind him to call me. The nurse who answers says, "I haven't seen Jamie up here."

"I know. He was running late tonight, but he's on his way now. Just have him call me, please."

"Okay," says the surprised nurse.

I go back to watching *Bugs Bunny*. Okay, now Jamie's had more than enough time to get there.

I fall asleep waiting for his call.

I dream of Jamie, or rather, his voice, calling to me from a dark echoed place, a place I can't see, no matter how I squint. *"Tammy? Tammy, where are you? Tammy? Tammy, Tammy, when are you coming?"*

I leap to full alertness. The clock says five-thirty. I curse myself as I grab my phone and dial St. Paul's again.

"No, Jamie's not here," a new nurse says. "Haven't seen him all night... isn't he off tonight, Linda?"

A voice nearby asks, "Is that the guy who called last night?"

"Yeah!" I say. "I called last night. Didn't he show up?"

Linda gets on. "I think Jamie is off tonight, sir."

My heart is pummelling. "No, he's supposed to be there. He was on call," I say rapidly, frantically. "They called him at about ten last night to come in at eleven! He left the house at around ten-thirty or a quarter to eleven, so he was running late, but he should be there!"

"Just a sec," says Linda.

A familiar, deep, brusque voice suddenly snaps, "Who is this?!" It's that fat old hag, Paulina, a.k.a. Nurse Ratchet.

"I'm a friend of Jamie Pearce's," I try to explain. "He's supposed to be there working tonight. He was supposed to call me and let me know he got there okay, but he hasn't called. Is he there?"

"He's *supposed* to be on the fourth floor!" she snarls.

"Oh! Can I have the number up there?"

"He never showed up!"

My heart lurches against my Adam's apple. "What?! Are

267

you sure?!"

"I *am* the super tonight!" she declares in her haughty nurse voice. "So, yes, I'm sure! I've had to rearrange my entire staffing roster because he no-call, no-showed!"

"He was supposed to be there," I pant worriedly. "He was running late, but he was on his way there!"

"Well, he didn't make it here, that's all I know," sneers Nurse Ratchet. "He'd better not make this a habit, or he'll be looking for a new job!"

Throttling the urge to cuss her out, I hang up, spring into my car, drive like a demon across town, out to Jamie's house. It's dark, lonesome, isolated, too secluded. The only lights are the muted orange of the streetlamp about fifty yards away, and the weak yellow of the porch light. His car is gone from the drive. I park along the curb in front, near the bins. There is no answer at the front door.

I call the hospital again, this time asking for the fourth floor.

"No, he didn't come in," the nurse says. "He was a no show tonight."

"Are you sure? He was going to come in. He wouldn't just no show! Has he ever no showed before?"

"Here, let me have you talk to the supervisor."

"No! I..."

Too late. "Who is this?!" Paulina again.

"I'm still looking for Jamie Pearce."

"I told you not a half hour ago that he's not here! He skipped!"

"He wouldn't *do* that!" I shout. "I know that for a fact because I asked him to call in sick tonight and he wouldn't. He said he promised to work tonight and that he couldn't back out!"

"Well," she scoffs, "There's always a first time! Now, if you'll excuse me, we're *busy* up here!"

"I'm telling you, he's not playing hooky! He's *missing*!"

"That's not my problem! Why don't you try calling the queer clubs!"

"I'm reporting you for that!" I snap. "Count on it!"

"Do whatever you want. Just tell your little *friend* he's being written up for the mess he's created for me tonight!"

268

"I'm wasting time talking to *you*. I need to call the police!"

"You're wasting *my* time," the bitch grunts, and I hang up on her. Too bad it's only my cell. If it were a big, heavy landline receiver, I'd break her eardrum slamming it down. I'm in tears of outrage. She's such a cold, callous, mean old bitch!

The sky is lightening. I go to every window, trying to see into his house, shouting, "Jamie!" The curtains are all drawn, the blinds all closed. I can't even see if any of the kitties are in there. I try the front and back doors, both are locked. I crouch down and open the cat-flap Lloyd installed in the back door. "Jamie? Jamie, are you home?" No response. None of the cats appear either.

I have no choice. I take a loosened brick from one of the flowerbeds and hurl it through a back window, expecting an alarm to shrill at me. It's completely still. I wonder if he has a silent alarm. I hope so. I want the cops here immediately. Hoping none of the cats were near the glass, I climb through into the dining room.

Please, God, if someone's hurting him, please make them stop! If he's dead, please let it be he didn't suffer long! He's suffered enough! I sob in a rage at the remembered and the unseen and unknown. No. *Let it be Jamie's okay. Please don't take him away from me!*

His cats are all fine, but my sudden anxious movements and my sobbing shouts disturb them as I dart from room to room, searching, and they file out their little pet door.

There is no sign of Jamie, and other than the damage he did in the bathroom and what I did to the window, no sign of disorder.

The police haven't been lured here by any silent alarm, so I go out in the front yard and call. The sky is icy, mother of pearl, as the sun slowly ascends. I suddenly notice how the cold is biting into my hands, turning them red, chapping the skin over my knuckles.

"Has he been missing for twenty-four hours?" asks the officer.

"No, he's been missing since between ten-thirty and eleven last night. He didn't show up for his job in Sac."

"Are you sure?"

"Sir, I've called twice, and they insist he never arrived last night. That's not like him at all."

"Has he ever done this kind of thing before?"

"I just told you, no," I sigh.

"Does he make it a habit of being late to work?"

"Not that I know of."

"You don't sound like you've known him that long."

"Well, I've known him for many years, sort of."

"Sort of?"

"Listen." My patience is wearing dangerously thin. "I have a really bad feeling. I think something's wrong!"

"Where does he live?"

"I'm at his home now," I say, feeling sheepish for not knowing his address by heart, for having to look up above his front door for the number. "2507 Willow Road, Somerville. His car is gone and he's not answering the door. I broke his dining room window and went in to look for him. He's not here."

"Sir, you *broke* in?" the policeman asks sharply.

"I had to. I'm *scared*!"

"Hmmm… Aside from you breaking in, any signs of foul play?"

"Not that I can see."

"Well, sir, I'm really not sure what's going on, but we'll send a unit to the residence in just a moment. Stay on the line with me."

"He wouldn't ditch work, officer! He *never* misses work!"

"Just try to remain calm…"

"He *never* calls in sick, even when he's sick as a dog!" I insist.

"Alright, sir, calm down."

"I have a really *bad* feeling!"

"I need you to calm down, sir."

I've been shouting, but I can't help it!

"We've got a car on the way. But I have a feeling that if you would have just waited it out, given him a chance to call you and explain…"

"He was supposed to call me when he arrived to work!" I

bellow. "He *promised* me!"

Maybe he's trying to call me now, I should be keeping this line clear.

But if he were trying to get through, or Mom, to let me know he's called the house, my cell would tell me that!

"He'll probably find his way home this morning," the officer says cheerfully.

What is Jamie, a lost *dog*?! A barfly who can't find his car?!

As if the cop can read minds, he asks, "Does your friend drink?"

"Not when he's supposed to work."

"And where does he work again?"

"St. Paul's in Sacramento!" I repeat as patiently as I possibly can.

"Was he upset about anything last night?"

My heart palpitates painfully. "We had a... disagreement... but it's resolved."

"Resolved," parrots the cop. "Are you sure?"

"Yes!" If I don't have to disclose any of the private tidbits about our difficulties, I'm not about to. All it would do is give the policeman ammo to construct a petty gay love-spat theory.

"Maybe he's not as sure as you are about that," offers the officer. "What did you two fight about?"

"It wasn't a fight, it was a *disagreement*," I snap. "Huge difference."

"Okay, what was your *disagreement* about, then?"

"It's very complicated," I say cautiously. "The *important* thing is, everything's okay between us. And yes, he knows it as well as I do."

The way I've worded my last sentences has clued him in. "Are you his domestic partner?"

His calm disarms me. He's not being catty, not insinuating. Only asking. "He's my boyfriend, yes," I reply.

"Alright, sir, I understand why you're worried. You're really sure he's not angry at you, that he didn't leave you?"

"No sir, everything was fine when I left him last night. I know it was fine. He was just going to take the trash out, and then he was supposed to go to work." I'm fighting not to start

271

blubbering like a baby.

"Listen," the policeman says in a mild voice, "There's not a lot we can do at this time. Perhaps he's on his way home now. He might arrive in the morning…"

"It's already going on six-forty! It *is* morning! He's been missing for at least seven hours!"

"Can you tell me why you didn't call us last night, if he's been gone that long?"

"I didn't *know* he was missing till this morning!" I'm screeching again. "He promised to call me when he got to his job. I even called ahead when he was supposed to be en route, asked the nurses to remind him to call me the minute he got in! He never called!"

"That doesn't explain why you waited until *now* to call us," the officer says gently. Now his soothing manner is inciting me to riot.

"I fell asleep waiting for his call," I admit. Why did I have to fall asleep?! I don't give a shit how exhausted I was, from the fight, from the video, from all the emotional upheaval. How could I just fall *asleep*?! "When I woke up, it was five-thirty. I called his work twice, and both times they insisted he'd never shown up for his shift. I just *know* something's wrong!"

My cell phone beeps… only to tell me that the battery is getting low.

"You're *sure* he didn't leave you?"

"I'm sure!"

Am I? Did he coddle and promise me just to get me out of his hair?

Maybe he did leave me. Maybe he went to the coast to cool off, to visit Lloyd.

Maybe he checked into a Travelodge or a Motel 6 to commit suicide…

But he wouldn't leave his kids!

Unless… unless he left instructions about them, like he said…

But I didn't see a suicide note anywhere.

So what? Lots of people go out without leaving a note!

"I'm sure," I say again.

No, he hasn't left me. He hasn't gone to end himself.

Two black and whites pull into Jamie's empty drive. The four cops walk the perimeter of the house. The first is short and chubby, with brown hair. His badge reads, "O. Deming". He asks, "Are his cats inside?"

"They have a pet door. They're in and out."

"Well, aside from the window you broke out, we don't see any signs of struggle out here." Three of them clamber through the window I broke, scrutinise the inside of his house. One officer, a blonde of medium height, stays with me as the other three go inside.

"You think maybe his car broke down on the highway?" This officer, whose badge says, "S. Cantrell", is casual, friendly, just making conversation, trying to put me at ease, the way cops do when they're trying to spearhead a negotiation with a lunatic.

I'm beyond fracas at this juncture. "He'd call me to come get him."

"Maybe his cell phone died or something."

"He would have found a payphone somewhere," I argue. "No… no… something's *happened*." And I can't say the word "bad". I just can't do it. My heart is in the cold, quiet clutches of terror, and to use the "B" word would send me over the edge.

"Why'd you break the window?" he asks me, his tone a little harder now.

I respond with indignation. "I thought he might be in there *hurt*! I thought someone might have forced their way in, attacked him, taken his car!"

"Alright, alright, sir, calm…"

"Don't tell me to calm down!" I snarl at him. "I'm *worried* about Jamie! He's very small. He's only about five-five, he weighs probably a hundred and ten, maybe a hundred and fifteen pounds. He's no match for anyone who'd attack him!"

"Sir, I can see you're under duress."

"I think someone rushed him as soon as he opened his front door to go to work. I think someone…" My voice dies as visions of Jamie being attacked and left by the side of the highway mingle with the brutalities I watched in that horrid video. "We're *gay*," I emphasise. "When you're gay, you're a

273

target!"

"I think you're overreacting."

"No, I'm not!" I scowl, my forbearance in real jeopardy now. "I think they rushed him, attacked him, when he was taking his trash out. That's the last thing he was going to do before he left, he told me."

We walk over to the two large bins sitting at the curb. He opens them both. One's empty, the other's got a single white bag. He removes it, opens it, sifts through it. Empty cat food cans, empty corn and green bean cans, a couple of egg shells, wadded napkins, empty washing-up bottle, food wrappers, a couple of cartons of spoiled Chinese food...

"Nothing out of the ordinary in here," he remarks, and puts the trash back in the bin. "Look, sir, give your friend a little more time. If he's had car trouble, he might have been able to get someone to help him get it to a shop. He might still be waiting."

"No, he would have *called* me!" I squawk. Nobody fucking *listens* to me!

"I think you're overreacting, seen too many scary movies, or gay shows, or whatever..."

"You're not fucking listening to me!"

"Sir, please don't use that kind of language with me."

"Who *cares* what kind of language I'm using?!" I shriek. "My boyfriend is in trouble, I know it, and you're talking down to me like I'm a five year old!"

"I'm trying to help you."

"You're doing zilch to help me!" I can feel steam jetting from both ears. The other three officers exit Jamie's house and walk up. "We found vomit in the bathtub," says Deming, the short, stocky brunette. "Can you tell us anything about that?"

"Jamie was sick last night," I say tiredly. "He threw up in the bathtub."

"It also looks like someone removed something from the wall by the tub, a bracket or a rack or something," says the third officer, who is tall, with chunky thighs and a masculine face. His badge says, "C. Howard".

"Jamie did that," I say, and suddenly, I'm afraid. How do I

explain how upset he was, so upset that he mustered enough physical power in his slim arms to wrench a towel bar off the wall? "He took it off because... he... it was messed up. He's planning to put a new one up."

"Well," says Officer Howard, "Other than those things, and the broken window, nothing's been damaged or disturbed. You say your friend was sick last night, threw up in the bathtub?"

"Yes," I nod.

"Have you called all the area hospitals? Maybe he checked himself in to one of the emergency rooms with a stomach flu or something."

"No, I don't think it was the flu." It's becoming more and more evident that I should probably just tell them *everything* that happened last night, no matter how embarrassing, private, morbid. The video, how it upset me, how it made me ill. How the resurfacing of his past made Jamie mortified, sick, enraged, suicidal. Do I *mention* that he was suicidal? Will it help? Will it get them moving to try and find him quickly? Or will it slow them down? Will it cast shadows onto *me?*!

"If I were you I'd call a repairman to fix that window ASAP," Officer Mendoza, the fourth cop, says. "Otherwise, you'll lose your stereo, DVD player, VCR..."

"Yeah, sure," I groan in exasperation. "What about Jamie? It isn't the flu."

"Are you sure? It's going around right now."

"No! It isn't the flu!"

"Maybe food poisoning," Cantrell suggests. "Call the local hospitals. See if he's been checked in."

I make for the broken window, and Cantrell calls after me, "Sir, you're not part owner of this house, are you?"

"No."

"Then we can't allow you inside. You'll have to go home to make your calls."

They start towards their patrol cars. "You're just *leaving*?" I say incredulously. "That's it?!"

"There's nothing we can do here," Deming replies. "There's no sign of foul play."

"I can't believe this!"

Cantrell grins at me condescendingly. "Sir, just call the local hospitals. You'll find him."

And they get into their cars and drive off.

I make sure all four cats are okay, each spending this brisk, misty morning in his/her own way—dozing on a soft rug on the back porch, hunting for rodents in the flowerbed, inspecting the trunk of one of the small plum trees and contemplating whether to climb it, watching a sparrow fluttering and fidgeting, peering longingly at the solidly frozen water in the pretty metal birdbath Lloyd placed in the centre of the lawn some years back, wishing it was sun-warmed so he could take a bath.

I return home. As much as I hate to concede to the police, there really is nothing I can do at Jamie's house. I should have preferred to wait there, but somehow, being in his house without him, not knowing where he is or what trouble he's in, with the draft of the broken window chilling my back.

I put my cell on its charger.

Utilising my home landline, I phone every hospital I can find in the phone books, from Sacramento to Vacaville. When I come up empty-handed, I try the hospitals in Stockton, Yuba City/Marysville, the East Bay. I know I'm on a wild goose chase. Nobody has admitted or heard of a patient named James Pearce. "What about John Does?" I urge. "Have you had any patients admitted unconscious?"

"Sir, there are so many of those around here," says one nurse in Sacramento. "We couldn't possibly try to track all of them down when you don't even know for sure if there's been an accident."

Accident, nothing, I think dourly. He's been attacked. *He's been…*

I'm barely registering what the nurse on the phone is saying now. "The best thing you can do is try to remain calm. If he's a John Doe, someone will find ID on him sooner or later."

"But he has no family. His dad died earlier this year."

"What about you? Aren't you kin?"

"No. I'm just his friend. I don't know if he has my number in his wallet. How will they know who to call…" I begin to cry, and the disconcerted nurse tries to pacify me. "Sir, all you can do is wait to hear something."

After I've exhausted myself calling hospitals all over the state of California, I check my cell. No new calls. I tell myself that I need to keep off the landline just in case Jamie calls. I need to keep off both the landline and the cell.

But the waiting is killing me.

I call the police again. I'm not going to stop bothering them and be a good little boy. "Something has happened to my boyfriend and I *demand* that you start searching for him immediately! I don't care if you think I'm a lunatic or not, just start looking for him! He's in trouble!"

Officer Cantrell interrupts me, "Mr. Mattheis, a car has been found, about a half mile outside of town... a Mercury Cougar, dark blue."

"Shit!" I whisper.

"We're running the license plate and we have a unit en route right now," Cantrell says. "We'd like you to come down to the station and give us some more information, if you would please."

When I get there, the collective of law enforcement personnel is glaring at me, and I'm dragged into the interrogation room, where Howard, the craggy-faced, masculine cop, and his partner, Cantrell, begin the first in a series of inquests.

thirty-four:

jamie
(december 29 and 30)

The distant streetlamp yields a poor orange glow to the short walk to the curb where my bins sit. I toss the white kitchen bag full of rubbish in, and I'm about to toss the towel rack.

Strong hands grab me from behind, and the metal bar makes a musical *clang-clang-clang*! as it lands on the cement. Another pair of hands clamps over my eyes and mouth before I can scream for help. A male voice grunts, "Where are your keys?"

The fear I suck into my lungs freezes me as I stutter, "M-m-m-m-my p-p-p-p-pocket!" I cannot see them, but there are at least two people. I fight to free myself but I can't even move. One pair of arms ropes around my upper torso. One hand remains fastened over my face like one of those hatchlings in *Alien*. I try to bite, but I can't even open my jaws. The other pair of arms takes me around my legs. A hand quickly dives into my pants pocket and fishes out my cell. Another hand removes my wallet. I'm lifted into the air, carried. I hear the creaking of hinges.

Someone is binding my legs and hands behind my back. I'm hogtied. The hand over my mouth lifts, and I gurgle and gag hard as a cloth is pushed into my throat.

I'm tossed into the black trunk of a car.

Neither of them could have opened the trunk just before throwing me inside, and in spite of my kicking and fighting, they succeeded in trussing me like a pig. There are at least three assailants, not two.

After the beatings I endured in high school, I've always imagined what I would do if confronted with violence again... what I would say. I'd remain calm, level-headed... I wouldn't scream, I wouldn't be hysterical or terrified out of my wits. I've rehearsed them many times, the serene negotiations that would render my attackers disarmed, baffled into releasing me.

I can't remember my script, despite how I'm urging myself not to panic, and I am hyperventilating in the deathly dark of the trunk they threw me in, gagging on the cotton they forced into my throat. I have no idea whose car it is. I can't get my eyes to work in this blackness. How long have we been driving? Where are they taking me?! *Calm down*, I beg myself. *Calm down! Don't lose your shit now!*

But the wheels in my brain spin in super-speed panic. *If they wanted to rob me, they would have simply taken my wallet. If they wanted my car, they would have taken the keys and left me standing in my front yard.*

Am I in my own trunk?

It feels like hours. The car slows to a creep. I don't hear the *whish* of passing cars anymore. They've taken me somewhere dark, remote, private.

The trunk opens with a subtle whine. "Get him out," mutters the male who ordered me to surrender my keys. He's got his dark hoodie pulled up over his lower face.

"Come on, faggot!" another guy snaps, grabbing me hard by my shoulders, and hauling me up and out. His face is hidden as well, by a puffy black or dark blue jacket. A third person silently observes nearby, identity concealed by a light coloured sweater.

It's freezing. Their breaths condense through their facial disguises. The three of them, looming over me in the dark, are horribly reminiscent of Klansmen, or mediaeval executioners, or fire-breathing demons.

Supported only by his arms, I wait as the guy in the hoodie severs the ligatures from around my feet and pulls the rag out of my mouth, damp with my saliva. I lean against my car, weakened and wobbly with unspoken terror, and I recognise the car as Lloyd's. I whisper, "Please, just take the car."

"Shut up!" the man in the hoodie spits. "How about in there?" He juts his chin toward the naked vineyard to the right of the dark gravel road we're parked on.

I would run, but I'm so afraid that I can't move. "Please, where are we?" I ask meekly.

"I said, shut up!"

"I don't think it's dark enough out here," speaks the muffled voice of the party in the light sweater. "Let's keep driving." Hoodie shoves the cloth back into my mouth.

I feel something—a silent pop inside of me. Warm tears begin to run down my face. The chilly night air freezes them in streaks. I still can't see who my enemies are in this gloom. The moon is almost eclipsed by our shadow.

Stop it, I scold myself. *It can't be happening.*

Instead of putting me into the trunk again, they toss me like a sack of fertilizer into the backseat of my car. Puffy Jacket and Light Sweater get into the front seat, while Hoodie sits and re-ties my feet. When I try to kick him, my shoe barely scraping over his forehead, nearly dislodging his disguise, his fist smashes into my nose. I feel the warm trickling of blood. "Do that again, cocksucker, and you'll wish you hadn't!"

I beg them, but nothing comes out of me except buzzing moans through the gag. I can't scream, I can't fight, I can't even move. The rag in my mouth, the blood drizzling down my throat, make me feel strangled, smothered.

And yet, I can cry. I can fucking *cry*. I can do something completely worthless. I can cry. That's what I can do.

Puffy drives and drives, my surroundings grow darker still. My abductors are beginning to argue. "Come on, this is far enough!" Hoodie barks above me.

"Well, there might be a house out here, or dogs," says Puffy Jacket.

280

Hoodie snorts, his voice chilled with hatred. "So what? Nobody's going to find him out here for at least a day or two. Right over there! Park!"

"But…"

"No, come on! It's almost one o'clock! Let's do this!" Hoodie opens his door, jumps out, grabs me roughly by the legs and pulls me out. A muffled squawk escapes me as my upper body plops on the ground.

"Come on!" Hoodie roars at Puffy Jacket. "Grab him!" I'm yanked up by my shoulders.

We're on another lonely road, this one unpaved. I haven't the faintest inkling where. They carry me into a sizable orange grove to the left of where they've parked the car. The trees are loaded with fruit. Thick, tangled yellow and green grass grows at the base of each tree. It's isolated, shadowy, and I can see no lights indicating civilization, not for miles and miles. My heart is whacking painfully. I'm dizzy with terror.

About ten rows or so in, they deposit me to the muddy ground and let me lie there. Hoodie kneels and unbinds my feet again, then my hands.

"Why you untying him?" asks Puffy.

"Got to give him a fighting chance," sneers Hoodie. Then, he growls at me, "You know what the bible says about faggots, don't you?"

I can't answer, even after they've taken the rag from my slobbering, bleeding mouth.

"It says you're an abomination," Hoodie says. I can practically see him leering at me, but I can't see what colour his eyes are. I can't see anything that will help me identify him. "You're disgusting!" He lowers his disguise just long enough to hock back and spit into my hair.

"Come on, man," Puffy Jacket says uneasily. "You're wasting time!"

Hoodie raises something above his head, something long, shiny, metallic. I scream and curl into a ball, waiting for a squall of bullets to begin ripping into me. Instead, I hear and feel the dull crack as something slams into my right shoulder. I scream again. Puffy Jacket exclaims keenly in reaction. I launch myself forward, trying to yank the towel bar away from Hoodie's grip. He easily pulls it out of reach of my fingers and brings it down, hard, on my right arm. I howl again as the weight of the blow reaches deep into the weather-sensitised bones that were broken sixteen years ago. Hoodie backs away for an instant and then hurls another strike at my left shin.

"For fuck's sake!" Puffy yells. "Someone's going to hear him screaming!"

"Nobody's going to hear anything," retorts Hoodie, admiring his handiwork, me, cowering in the damp soil, writhing in agony.

"Why are you doing this?" I sob.

"Shut the fuck up, faggot!" He hits me again, across the left thigh. I grunt in pain as I lunge again, my right hand closing around the jagged, twisted end of the broken towel rod. My right shoulder is on fire, blazing its protest of what I'm doing. I employ my left hand as well, desperately attempting to yank the weapon away from my hooded nemesis. He swears at me again and gives a tremendous pull. Another shrill scream echoes in the darkness as the razor-sharp metal gouges deeply into my right palm and my torn fingers uncurl involuntarily. The metal bar slams down on my shredded right hand. Bones crunch and I scream so high and loud my voice breaks. I recoil, cradling my broken right hand in my left, my eyes facing the leaf and grass littered floor of the orchard. "Please," I whisper. "Please stop. Please stop…" The blood in my nose and mouth tastes sticky and metallic.

"Come on," Puffy Jacket says, reaching out to Hoodie. "Let's go. Let's just go."

"I'm not finished," Hoodie breathes.

"You've done enough. Let's leave him here. I think we've made our point. We don't have to…"

Hoodie swings the length of metal and it smashes against my left flank, forcing the air from my lungs in a *whoosh*. I can't even gasp.

"Dammit, Ray!" Puffy Jacket says.

"Stupid fuck, I told you not to use our names!" Hoodie says and takes a hostile step towards Puffy, brandishing his weapon.

282

Something is popping, bubbling inside of me when I'm finally able to re-inflate my chest. I roll my body up again, gasping with each stabbing inhalation, trying to stop the warm, strange pain spreading up into my back. My forehead touches my knees.

"Now he can ID us, asshole!"

"This has gone too damn far," Puffy mumbles.

Ray... Ray... it's Ray. I don't believe it. I don't understand it. *Please, wake up,* I tell myself. *This is a dream. A nightmare. Wake up. Wake up.*

"Tell me. Is it true?" Ray asks me, advancing on me again. "Do you like to suck cock?"

I struggle to sit up, folding my knees beneath me.

"Are you a porn star?"

How am I going to survive this? I look up into Ray's eyes. They glint with sick thrill. I'm garbage to him. *Lloyd, what happened to me?* I ask the sliver of moon above. *You saved my life. I love you so much I couldn't even be mad at you for getting to me before God did. You saved my life, and I wanted to kill myself tonight. What happened to me, Lloyd?*

"Yeah, he's a star," floats the sinister, feminine voice of Light Coloured Sweater. "He's famous." Now I know who she is. "He *loves* cock. He loves taking Daddy up his ass."

"My dad is dead," I gasp through my swollen, tacky lips. "He's dead. He raped me for years. Then he killed my mother and then blew his fucking head off."

"Should have shot you too, faggot," Ray scowls. "No matter. You'll finally get what's been coming to you."

"You're just like them." I spit blood at him. "No, you're worse!" I'm going into shock, imbued with a paradoxical audacity as I whisper, "I punished myself for everything they did to me. I even pretended I liked it. I punished myself, because if I was the bad guy, they could make sense to me. But they never made sense. They were evil and you can't make sense of evil. I can't make sense of what you're doing now, *Ray*," I stress his name, so he'll know I know it's him. "Evil makes no sense."

"Ray, for God's sake, let's get the fuck out of here and go

home! Leave him!"

My need to survive is as strong as it was the day I watched Lloyd grieving over what my monsters did to me. I'm kneeling in the mud, so weak I can scarcely hold my head up. "I didn't deserve what they did to me, and I don't deserve this."

"We're not leaving until we exterminate this little piece of vermin! Besides, he'll only tell the cops. He knows me, thanks to you! I'm not letting him live now. As for *you*," Ray leans over me and grabs me by the hair, shakes me back and forth, upsetting my re-broken right arm and making me screech silently, "You deserve worse than I could ever do to you! You've turned Tam into a flamer. You're both goanna get it from God!"

"You don't have to kill him," Puffy groans.

"I do now, dumbass! Blame yourself for this, not me!" The metal rod lands against the left side of my body again. I try to deflect the next strike with my left arm, but I'm too slow, too weak. I feel ribs cracking, splintering, under its force.

"You're the one who's goanna get it," I whisper when I'm able to draw in a few gasps of iced oxygen after a very long moment. I'm nauseous, dizzy. My blood pressure is falling…

I'm wandering off. I can feel myself floating. I'm weightless, as I was in my deathbed before Lloyd came to save me. *Tammy, Tammy, where are you? Tammy? Where are you? When are you coming? Tammy?*

"Tammy's not here!" shouts the female. "Nobody's coming to help you!"

I fight to keep a hold of solidity. With my good hand, I reach into my scrub top to clutch my little pewter angel on the silver chain Tammy got me the other day. "Please call 9-1-1," I slur. "I think I'm dying."

"Yeah, I hope so!" Ray raises the metallic rod above his head.

"Please… call 9-1-1," I beg again. "I won't tell. I won't tell who did this."

"I *know* you won't," he nods ominously at me. "What are you holding in your hand so reverently?" he snarls. "Oh, how cute! An angel!" His hand twists into the chain cruelly, like he

284

wants to strangle me with it. The metal pinches me as he rips it from around my neck and drops it, scowling at me evilly, raising the towel bar again.

"Please, Ray... I won't tell," I bargain in a hoarse, bubbly whisper. I see micro-drops of red spraying from me as I talk.

"Ray, just hurry this along," the female I know complains nonchalantly. "It's cold!"

"Please don't leave me here." My hopeless sobs infuriate me. That they've reduced me to a bloodied pulp, *begging* for their compassion! "Please don't leave me here."

With every ounce of muscle he has, Ray brings the rack down on to my head.

I watch as I slump over, the right side of my head split open, a slow, black stream of blood beginning to ooze. My hair begins to harden into dark spikes.

Everything gets black and quiet.

"I was born this way! God does not make mistakes!" I say with a booming authority that should be impossible given my physical condition.

Now I know what to say? Now?! *When I'm exhausted and on death's porch? Now my voice returns?!*

It's silent. My tormenters say nothing.

I come to for a moment. My ears are ringing. They shove me up against the thin, gnarled trunk of one of the orange trees. "Gimme that garbage bag," Ray orders Puffy Jacket, pointing to a large square of black plastic laying next to another tree.

I still can't see any of their faces. Is it the Ray I've known for years?

"It's torn!" he grumbles as Puffy hands the bag to him. He throws it at me and it floats, making its crackling plastic sound, down over my face and chest.

"Think he's dead?" the woman asks.

"My head hurts," I murmur, but my lips aren't moving. They're glued together with blood.

Ray picks up my left wrist, palpates with his thick fingers, unable to detect the threading pulse that yet sustains me. He then prods at my neck and shrugs, "I don't know. No, I hear him breathing. But it won't be long. It's cold. If the freeze doesn't finish him, I'm sure I've ruptured him somewhere. Little piece of shit's as good as dead sooner or later."

I slip away again. *"And do you really believe your God is pleased with you kidnapping me, dragging me out here, beating me, spitting on me, leaving me to die alone... in an orchard?!"*

They ignore me. They simply turn and walk away.

I reach for them. I want to call them back.

My lips are numb. I watch blood seep from under the nails of my broken right hand.

It's dark and silent in the forest.

I'm alone again.

My ire soars to life as they stand before me, more rotten and vile and grotesquely disfigured than I imagined they could be. They're not glorified or pretty, they're ugly, presented to me as they truly are. Mom's eyes are swollen closed, her long black hair twisted and tangled, her skull exposed, stained with blood and decay. Daddy stands beside her, his head mangled on one side from the bullet he gave himself.

"What you did to me makes you evil first and mentally ill second," I sternly assert. *"You made me do horrible things. You made me feel worthless! You slowly killed my spirit, or you* tried *to. Lloyd saved me! I beat you!"*

Like Ray and his companions, my parents say not a word. Why aren't they speaking? Why aren't they upholding themselves against my judgments? Why aren't they laughing and hooting at my predicament?

What gives me so much power now?

I rally just enough strength to open my eyes, open my one functional hand, close it around the pewter pendant laying beside me. I'm shocked they didn't take it from me. I bring it up to my chest.

The cold penetrates every layer of me.

My hand tightens around my angel.

God, how I love you, he'd said that day.

I love you, Tammy, I said tonight. *I'll love you always. All my life.*

thirty-five:

tammy
(december 30)

Jamie's car is found abandoned, just outside Somerville's town limits, at approximately 8.20am. The police search the area around Solano Street, which isn't far from the high school, on the other side of town from where Jamie lives. My ears can only snatch small doses of information as people pass by the open door. No body has been found, no clothing, no spoor they can follow. Nothing.

In the interrogation room, I'm asked about my association with Jamie, but I'm too freaked to do anything except ask over and over, "Have you found him?! Have you found him?!

"No. Where is he?" Officer Howard asks tolerantly.

"I don't know! Why are you treating me like *I'm* a suspect?!"

"Let's start with your relationship with Jamie Pearce," Officer Cantrell says.

How do I begin to talk about the complexities that have made up our relationship in these past days? I tell them I met him in high school, that I moved to L.A. for a long time, and when Mom fell and got hurt, I came home and became re-acquainted with Jamie, who is a nurse at the hospital Mom

287

stayed in.

I tell them that we recently began a sexual relationship, and I hope to leave it right there. How can I talk to these strangers about Jamie's sexual hang-ups? About how the trauma he suffered with his parents has affected both of us? About how he spoke of suicide last night?! *Threatened* suicide?! How can I broach this stuff with them?! Do I mention the video?

My disinclination to describe the awe and woe of our affiliation predictably fuels the suspicion I'm now under. I ask for a phone call and Cantrell smirks, "Sure you can make a call. You're not *under arrest*, we're only questioning you. Didn't you know that?"

I call Stacy. "Jamie's missing. He never made it to work last night. They found his car. He's missing…"

When she arrives, Officer Howard leaves the questioning room to meet with her. I can't hear them. Cantrell stares at me until I'm ready to jump from my skin.

Howard comes back in without Stacy. "Miss Pendleton says you dragged Jamie out of The End last night. Is that right?"

"I didn't *drag* him. We left together. I was upset and I… told him I wanted to leave. He went with me. I didn't *drag* him." My eyes narrow in defiance of their allusions.

"Why were you upset?"

"It's… private." A still, small voice tells me I should tell them everything. Tell all. I try to speak. the words are clear: *Yvette Feldman—you probably know her from town—sent me a pornographic video of Jamie being raped and tortured as a child by his own parents. Yvette told me about it at the bar. I don't know where she obtained that video. Her sending it to me was a gesture of hostility. In high school she spread rumours that Jamie was gay. She hates him. I pulled Jamie out of the bar because I wanted to get him the hell away from her.*

The words are there. My mouth opens, but nothing comes out.

Howard sighs, "Sir, you reported your friend missing. You came to us. Now, the best thing you can do to help yourself is to *talk* to us."

"Unburden your soul, so to speak," adds Cantrell, his eyes

288

twinkling

His merry little quip unhinges my tongue. "I have not done *anything* to harm my boyfriend!" I shout at him.

"I warned you before. Settle down! Keep your temper in check. Now, Miss Pendleton tells me that Jamie was upset at you last night," Howard says. "She says he was very distraught, that there was something wrong between you. She believes you two had an altercation, a fight..."

"It's hard to explain," I pant. "It's..."

"It's private?" asks Howard.

"It's difficult... private... so hard to explain."

"Well, I suggest you explain anyway, because you're fast moving from a person of interest to the chief suspect!" Cantrell snaps.

"We didn't have a fight, we had a... discussion."

A loud pounding snaps my head toward the tinted window of the interrogation room. I hear Stacy screaming faintly on the other side, "Where is he, you son of a bitch?! What did you do to him?!"

Cantrell saunters out into the hallway. I can't hear what he's saying to Stacy. I can't even see them.

I turn back to Howard and appeal to him. "I swear... I didn't do anything to him! I love him! He's out there somewhere! Why aren't you looking for him?!"

Cantrell returns, closing the door softly behind him.

"We *are* looking for him," Howard says almost kindly. "But we need your help. Talk to us. Tell us what happened. You'll feel so much better."

"I didn't hurt him," I cry. "I didn't!"

"When they found the car, they found blood in the backseat, Mr. Mattheis."

The nausea is potent and instantaneous. I lean over and puke splashes on the floor beside my chair. "No, no. God, please, no..."

"Where is he, Mr. Mattheis?" Howard asks softly. "Help us out."

"Please, please, please, God. Please..."

Howard leans over to Cantrell, whispers, "We need a

warrant."

At the spot where Jamie's car's been discovered, they search for the car keys and can't find them. They find several strands of long, dark hair clinging to the headrest of the passenger front seat. They dust Jamie's steering wheel with black powder and find a lot of fingerprints, none of them matching mine (I volunteered mine immediately). That doesn't convince them. "You could have wiped them off," says Cantrell. "*CSI* has made our lives a lot harder, lemma tell you!"

They search *my* car for traces of blood, clothing threads, bits of hair, anything that would be hard evidence—and find only a couple of longish blonde strands of hair. "Jamie's been in my car, many times," I tell them, "Including when we went home from The End last night."

Now they're flummoxed. Surely I couldn't have vacuumed that well, or found someone to detail it in the middle of the night.

Still, they believe that if they keep at me, I'll eventually break, or they'll catch me in a lie.

At about nine-thirty, they bring Mom in and chat with her in another room. She can't give them an airtight alibi, but she tells them that although she was in bed when I came home from Jamie's house, she knows, "My son didn't hurt Jamie. They're like best friends. Tammy wouldn't hurt him."

"How long have they known each other?" asks Officer Cantrell.

"Since high school, I think," Mom replies. "Jamie's a nurse. He took care of me when I broke my pelvis. Tammy's his friend. My son wouldn't hurt a fly. He's a good boy. He used to be angry, but, he's a good boy."

"What do you mean, angry?"

She tells them about my boyhood, how I never knew my father, how I resented her for the mistakes she made that resulted in me not having a father. She tells them I was angry and rebellious and wayward during my early teen years, but that after high school, I seemed to "mellow out and calm down".

"Describe his childhood. What kinds of activities was he

involved in that you didn't approve of?"

"He hung around a few boys that were troubled. They drank, smoked dope… played with guns, acted up at school—that sort of thing. I was pretty worried about him, so I had his father talk to him," Mom says.

"His father? I thought you said he didn't have a father," Cantrell says, eyeing her suspiciously.

"Well, of course he has a father. We're not together…" Mom looks away, embarrassed as always when this chapter of her biography comes up.

"But he spoke to your son… to straighten him out?"

"Yes, and I think it worked. After they talked, Tammy mellowed out quite a bit!"

"Who's his father?" asks Howard.

Mom bristles. "Do I have to answer that? That's really none of your concern, and what's it got to do with anything?"

"Well, perhaps we'd like to speak with him, get *his* take on Mr. Mattheis."

"I'd rather not discuss Tam's father," Mom says flatly. "He doesn't have a relationship with him anyway."

"I thought you just said his father straightened him up," puzzles Cantrell.

"Well…" she hesitates.

Cantrell snorts, "Perhaps we should charge you with obstruction!"

Mom tells them who my dad is. "It was a mistake," she sighs irritably. "He was just as at fault as I was."

"Alright, Ma'am," Howard says. "We're not concerned with that. We just need to speak to him." But their looks don't miss her.

At a little after 10.30, Pastor Asshole waltzes in and tells them all about what I did to Cotton. He doesn't stay long, just long enough to rub my nose yet again into the most humiliating, stupid thing I've ever done. Just long enough to fan the fire under the ignorant, widely held estimation that gay men, all gay men, are perverts in one form or another. Having a gay son, an illegitimate gay son to boot, can be quite embarrassing to any man whose life endeavour is to be holier than anyone else.

291

It's almost noon by the time I'm released to go home, with a cordial, "Don't go anywhere, Mr. Mattheis." Both Mom and I are wrecked by the resurfacing of the travesty of her association with the Asshole and my implied proclivities toward bestiality.

"I'm going to look for Jamie," I voice my plans. Mistake. Officer Howard adamantly says, "No, you're not."

I want to say, "The fuck I'm not! He's out there, hurt, maybe dying! I'm not sitting on my ass while you waste time investigating me!"

But something tells me to keep still. I watch a black and white slowly roll by our house. I'm under surveillance. I'm too exhausted to scream at Mom for blabber-mouthing to the Asshole years prior about the Cotton matter. Instead, we sit together on our couch and cry.

I endeavour to explain my childhood viciousness to her.

And finally I tell her, about what Uncle Price did.

"A pervert!" she cries. "My own brother!"

"Jamie's out there, somewhere, probably hurt! Dead! Fuck Uncle Price!"

She stares up at me. "Is it true, Tammy?" she asks. "Are you and Jamie…"

"Gay?!" I thunder at her, leaping to my feet. "Yes! We're gay, Mother! We're a couple of flaming faggots! Queers! Queens! Pussies! Fairies! Yeah! We're a couple of fucking queers! Who cares?!"

"Tam… I'm just *asking*…"

"You think Jamie's a bad person because he's gay?" I surmise with a shout. "You think *I'm* a bad person?"

"No." Her lips press together firmly.

"Tell the truth," I snap. "You're just like all of them. You think we're perverts."

"I love you, Tammy," she says. "I want you to be happy in life."

"I've *never* been happy… all my life… until Jamie," I say tiredly. "He makes me happy, Mom. I don't even recognise myself anymore, and I'm glad of it. I'm proud of it." I underscore the word "proud" and dare her to condemn me.

She says softly, "I love Jamie, you know I do. I love that kid.

I'd never want harm to come to him! Don't you think I have any heart at all?" She begins to cry again.

I sit back down with her. "I'm sorry, Mom," I sulk.

"I had no idea," she sniffles. "I want you to be happy, and if Jamie makes you happy... you never *could* talk to me." She's disappointed.

"You're kind of a bigmouth," I say as nicely as I can. "And you're a Christian."

"What difference does that make?" she bristles.

"Well, we didn't really feel free to come to you and say, 'Hey, Mom! We love each other and we're having sex!'"

"Alright, Tammy, alright," Mom sighs.

A loud banging on our front door jolts us up. It's the police again. They've got a warrant for the house now. They look for blood, in the trash, on my bedding, in my bathroom. They remove my shoes and fail to find blood on them. They're still not convinced. "You could have burned whatever clothes or shoes you wore last night," says Howard, "To get rid of the blood.

"I'm wearing the same shoes I always wear," I bark at him. "And the clothes I wore yesterday were in the hamper you searched!"

As they raid my bedroom, they ignore the black rectangle hanging out of my VCR like a tongue, seeing no cause to collect it. A man in a dark coat comes out of my room, his arms full of marble note pads.

He's unearthed my journals.

For a few minutes, Officer Cantrell and the man in the dark coat flip through them.

Mom says angrily, "I've told you officers, my son didn't hurt that young man. Why aren't you out looking for him?!"

"We've got lots of people looking for Mr. Pearce right now, Ma'am," Howard assures her.

"They have a wonderful relationship," she says, trying to be helpful.

"Hmmm..." Cantrell says thoughtfully, not taking his eyes off the violence scrawled across the lined paper. "How about his relationship with *you*? What's that like now?"

"Much better than when he was a boy," Mom answers. "Officers, please! I know Tammy didn't do this. Maybe he was angry as a child, but he's changed. He's not a violent man."

"I disagree," Cantrell says. "And we're thinking Mr. Mattheis is the perpetrator."

"Why?!" cries Mom.

"Because," says Officer Howard, "A: he's the last person to have seen Mr. Pearce alive. Several witnesses saw Mr. Mattheis dragging Mr. Pearce out of the End bar last night."

"Including me!" Cantrell interrupts. "I was there. I saw him do it too."

Officer Howard turns to his partner, looks embarrassed. "You never mentioned that *before*, Steve."

Cantrell shrugs a little sheepishly. "Yeah. I was there. I saw."

"We'll talk later," Howard continues, unruffled. "B: Mr. Mattheis hasn't been very forthcoming during our investigation. We believe he knows where Mr. Pearce is, and isn't cooperating."

"I do *not* know where Jamie is!" I shriek.

"We have no direct evidence incriminating you at this moment," Howard says, nodding at me. "But when we find Mr. Pearce, we think everything will fit together quite nicely. A lovers' quarrel, a crime of passion. The evidence we found in Mr. Pearce's car indicates that he's been attacked. We found blood, tears and saliva."

He's so cold.

Jamie is out there, hurt, dying.

Blood, tears, saliva.

He bled, cried, drooled all over the backseat of his car.

Someone took him somewhere and hurt him.

He must have been so terrified. My chest seizes. I wonder if I'm still too young for a heart attack.

I should have gone with him. I should have insisted.

He must have felt so alone.

This bastard is cold as ice.

I can feel my stomach turning itself inside-out again. "Someone's done something horrible to him," I sob wretchedly.

294

"C: these journals are rather revealing into your character, Mr. Mattheis."

My saliva thickens. I feel the retches building. My stomach is tender. "I wrote those a long time ago. I'm not like that anymore."

"We're eager to discuss them with you."

I'm driven back to the station in a squad car. They don't handcuff me, but the looks they give me immobilise me like Pavulon. Mom follows in her car, wiping her glasses with her fingers as tears splatter the inner lenses.

It's about one o'clock.

A faint odour of puke from when I was here a few hours ago lingers in the interrogation room. Cantrell has been taken off the case, replaced by Officer Lord, Howard says. "We didn't know he'd been at The End last evening. He's likely to be a witness for the prosecution if the D.A. decides she has a case against you."

"I didn't hurt Jamie," I maintain, by now utterly done in by today's horrific turn of events. I want to kick everyone aside, bash all the doors down, and run, run, out into the open, and scream into the sky.

In the grey room, Officer Howard reads aloud three stories from my anthology of gore. The anger is candid, the hatred is authentic. Still, the macabre tales are those of a boy who no longer lives on this earth.

It doesn't matter to Officers Howard and Lord, who now gaze at me with repulsed, fascinated disdain.

It doesn't matter, even after I regurgitate swallowed saliva in the middle of the third story and beg, through sickened, sobbing hiccups, for Howard to stop reading.

thirty-six:

jamie
(december 29 and 30)

For brief moments, I return to my flesh, regain my mortal lucidity, able to employ the organic matter between my ears. I attempt to raise from the position they left me in, try to fold my legs under me and lift my body up, but a huge, stabbing sensation along my left side steals my breath and sends me sagging against the orange tree again. I'm in such misery I can't even pant for air. The spirit is willing, but the physical strength is bleeding out of me in a warm gush. My strength, my bodily warmth, desert me slowly and surely.

As when I was alone in that dungeon my birth parents bequeathed to me, time has no meaning. I have no knowledge at all how many minutes, hours, or even days, might be passing as I sit, my body broken, smaller than I realised, my shoulders slumped forward, my head bowed over my chest, my legs curled beneath me.

God, please let me live. Let me live. If you're a loving and merciful God, please let me live through this. Let somebody find me and help me. Don't let me die here alone.

The night is long and cold. My bodily fluids have slowed to

a crawl within me. Slothful tears are frozen along the arcs of my cheeks. I no longer see my breath misting before me. My wounded head, once throbbing hotly, is slowly, gently pulsing under the matted tangle of my hair and a thin layer of red ice. I watch myself languishing, longing to join my foster dad, but reluctant to leave Tammy behind. Cold condensation accumulates over every inch of skin uncovered by clothing.

He loves me. I know he does. I used to go on and on how if he broke my heart I'd die. If he loses me like this, he won't get over it. He won't. It will kill him.

Lloyd's here.

I'm sorry I never called you 'Dad', I tell him. I just never wanted to call you what I called that evil man who raped me. I never wanted to associate you with him, in any way.

He stands before me, the only anything I can see in this leafy darkness. He's healthy again, olive-skinned, shaggy-haired, quietly handsome, the way I remember him best. I know, son.

I never kissed you—at least not that often—I just wasn't like that, Lloyd. It isn't because I didn't love you.

I know, son, he says again, his face calm, peaceful, happy.

You know I loved you, I say. I still love you.

I know. And you know, I still love you too. Bet you didn't know that. When we die, our bodies stop, but we don't. Our love lives on.

I want to stay with you, Lloyd. I do, but... what about Tammy?

That boy loves you, Jamie, Lloyd says. I'd like you to stay with me, of course I would. I miss you.

Oh, I miss you too, Lloyd. I feel like I took you for granted all these years, and you died so suddenly. I begin to weep. I feel like I never let you know how much I loved you. I never said it enough. You saved my life, you gave me a new one, and I don't know if I ever said thank you.

You were my sunshine, Lloyd smiles. You said thank you by getting better and becoming the most wonderful son I could ever have wished for. I wasn't even worried that you were going to be a brat or a delinquent. You were my boy. I never thought

297

about having children, Jamie, but when you came into my life, you were such a blessing to me.

I feel the same way about you. I should have said thank you every single minute, I whisper. You were my guardian angel.

And you were mine. You always took care of me after I got sick.

I didn't do enough. I should have made you go to the hospital. I should have known that morning. You needed to go in right away.

Jamie, I was a grown man. I was responsible for my health. You couldn't make me do anything I didn't want to do. Remember?

"Hey! Hey! Sir? Can you hear me?" The voice reverberates in the distance. I can sense without seeing what the man is doing. I cannot feel his hand shaking my shoulder and jostling my poor re-broken right arm. If I was there instead of up here, I would be squalling in pain. I watch from this height, as a troupe of farm labourers, having stumbled upon me while searching for frost damage, gathers around me, their hands over their mouths. One of them dials his cell phone. I can hear him weeping…

…another stranger crying for me, Lloyd. What a world we live in, huh?

Yep, says Lloyd. People who don't even know you calling 9-1-1, kids you grew up with bludgeoning you and leaving you for dead. Oh Jamie. When you get out of here, you do something with this too, just like you did when we got you out of that room they locked you in. Do something with this, son.

I will, I promise him.

My skin feels the subtle sting of settling dew.

"We found a body out here," the labourer cries. "He's dead… yeah… we're in the orange grove off Delta Road… about three miles west of Winters… just off the highway going into Vacaville… I don't know… no the body is fresh… it hasn't been long… maybe yesterday… yeah… fuck, it's a mess…" he sniffles loudly. The other men are crying too.

I love you so much, Lloyd. I'm telling you that right now. Always know I love you.

I do know, son. I do know. But I don't want you to leave Tammy behind. I'm worried about him. He won't stand it if you die.

I know.

Go on back to him, Jamie.

I'm watching, floating someplace above, as policemen in dark blue uniforms kneel and inspect me. I'm still leaning against the orange tree where Ray and the others dumped me. Under the shredded black trash bag Ray half-covered me with, I'm wearing my dark teal scrub top over my white pullover turtleneck, stained dark red. My left arm is folded against my chest. My broken right lays limp, flush, against my thigh. I'm still in a wacky sitting/kneeling position. My legs are twisted beneath me where I tried to stand and fell back. My shoulders are slack, my head slumps forward, my reddened, sticky, spiky hair in my eyes. One of the cops gently lifts my head up. "Shit," he swears into his walkie-talkie. "I think it's the guy from Sommerville alright. He's dressed like a nurse."

"Is he dead?" another cop asks from inside the walkie-talkie.

"I'm pretty sure." He pushes the fabric aside and feels for a pulse in my neck.

He stops cold, his fingers swiping up and down my skin. "Sweating! I've got a weak pulse too! Let's move!"

Two other policemen are talking, indicating the bloody, misshapen towel rod that Ray used to beat me with. Another officer points at the rag they crammed down my mouth.

I'm with Lloyd again. How do I get out of here?! I ask him in a bursting of panic. It's so dark! I can't see!

Feel your way, Jamie, he says. Feel your way out. God'll show you. He'll get you back home.

Lloyd. I don't know. I've been fighting so long. I'm so cold. I don't know if I can keep holding on like this.

You've got to hold on, Jamie. You've got to. Just a little longer... just hold on...

I'm so weak, Lloyd.

I know, but this isn't your time. Not now. You stay with them. I'm going now.

Don't go, Lloyd! Don't leave me!

They're here now, son. They're going to get you through this. Just hang on.

I love you. You were my dad. You were always my dad. You're my family. You're my friend. You're very important to me, Lloyd. Always know that.

Hold on, son. Just hold on.

I'm lingering here, still watching, as they gently position my neck into a brace. They place me on a stretcher, load me into the ambulance. I hover above them, watching as they pierce my arms and the fluids begin to dribble into my shrivelled veins. They shout at me, shake me as gently as they can in their urgency. My left hand falls open a little, and I see my angel keychain, sticking to the centre of my palm, glued with my blood. *Oh, shit, it's gonna fall onto the floor of the ambulance and get kicked around and lost forever. Please, oh, God, please don't let them lose my angel!*

One of the paramedics then takes it from my hand and carefully slips it into a ziplock baggie.

Please, don't lose it, please...

My ears begin to ring again. I can't hear.

"He's crashing!"

They get the paddles lubed and ready. I recognise that chaotic green electronic zigzag as v-fib. They shock me. Zap! I feel it, even up here... painful... my heart lurches... sputters... dies again. Zap! Now I'm in v-tach. Zap! I'm in sinus rhythm, but it's very tachy, about 170.

I'm back, and I'm displeased. Not only am I in the worst pain of my life, but I'm not floating up above myself. I'm no longer free and weightless. I'm strapped to this damn stretcher.

I'm enraged.

I'm tied to a bed again.

Lloyd, I think I'd rather have stayed with you.
Then I remember.
Tammy's waiting.
I have to do this.
It hurts like hell, but I have to.
I have to...

thirty-seven:

tammy
(december 30)

I'm slowly taken apart, dissected, deconstructed, examined, studied, like a frog in biology class is scrutinised by a sadistic teacher and his little pupils.

It was about 10am when Jamie was found by a bunch of farm workers in an orange grove near Winters, which is about fifteen miles west of Sommerville. At first, he was taken to the hospital in Woodland, but when they deduced that he needed more care than they were equipped to give him, he was hastily flown to UC Davis.

It is now about 2pm. I've been held as a suspect and questioned now for only a little over an hour, but my ordeal has been going on since five-thirty this morning. Nobody will tell me anything, whether he's alive, dead, or hacked to pieces in the black garbage bag I keep hearing about.

Stacy refuses to leave the station, determined to find out the truth. She also refuses to speak to me, until I ask where Jamie is, then she shrieks at me from her side of the tinted glass, "You're not going anywhere *near* him, you bastard!"

The cops leave me alone again. They're gone for almost another hour, and when they return, they regard me with burning hatred. Officer Lord shakes his head at me. "Why would you do that to him? You're twice as big as he is! If I could *just* get you alone, you piece of shit! You rotten fucking coward!"

"No! I didn't!" I sob as I pace the interrogation room, wringing my hands, crying, crazy and exhausted, long past the point of a psychotic break. "Please, is he alive? Is he dead? Is he injured? What's happened?!"

"Why don't you tell *us* what happened?" Officer Howard asks icily. "The sooner you fess up, the sooner we'll be done. I'll bet you could use some sleep. Let me guess. He got too needy for you? I've heard tell you don't like long term engagements."

Lord snickers bitterly and adds: "You had quite a reputation in high school, from what I remember. I was a sophomore when you were a senior."

"No! It was nothing like that. I love him."

"I have a scenario, and I want you to tell me if I'm close," Howard says. "You got sick of him being clingy and jealous and needy, so you told him you needed to talk to him alone, somewhere private…"

"We talked at his house," I say, and Howard shushes me, "Whoa… whoa, wait, let me just finish this first. And you had him follow you out to Winters, to a nice, quiet, private road where nobody would bother you. Maybe you two talked, maybe you didn't, but I think you sucker-punched him and knocked him into the backseat of his car. His nose bled, and he cried and asked you to stop. You really gave him a good one too, I must say." Howard scowls at me. "His lip was split—probably why we found drool all over the seat."

"You're wrong!" I sob, spraying tears and spittle all over myself and them.

"Then you grabbed him and dragged him into the orchard, and you beat him with that towel bar!"

"The towel bar?!" I shriek.

"We found it when we found him. I'm surprised you didn't stab him with the sharp end!" snarls Howard. "Oh well, I suppose you did plenty of damage. I've never seen a more brutal beating in my life!"

I lunge, at nothing, set free my anguished screams. "Jamie! Jamie! Jamie! JAMIE!"

Howard and Lord stare at each other as I sink to my knees and dry heave. "Is he dead?!" I beg between retches. "Please, just tell me! I can't take any more! Please tell me if he's dead!"

Officer Lord puts his hands on his hips. "He's alive, Mr. Mattheis. They had him out at County in Woodland, but they had to fly him to Davis. He was a John Doe—nobody knew who he was, till we got there—he's in surgery. They're not sure he's going to pull through. And I'll tell you this, my friend," he adds, "If he dies within a year of this beating, you'll be charged with murder."

I begin to hyperventilate. "G-G-G-G-God help-p-p-p m-m-m-m-me! P-p-pl-pl-please! Pl-pl-pl-please, G-G-G-God!" I weakly beat my fists onto the dirty floor. "Did-did-did they r-r-r-r-rape him?"

They stare at me with something funny in their eyes, like they never expected me to behave like this. "No, Mr. Mattheis," sighs Howard. "He was not sexually assaulted."

Relief avalanches onto me, the one relief I can glean from this madness. *They beat him, almost to death, but thank God, they didn't rape him.*

And no, it's not the kind of sickening, possessive crap you hear about with boyfriends, husbands. That *someone else inside my wife* shit. I'm thinking about Jamie, how atrocious it would be for him to relive being raped *and* beaten. It was awful enough they beat him. They didn't rape him; they spared him that.

"Come on, sit down," Lord says calmly. "Tell us about the towel bar." He offers me a paper bag to put over my face.

It takes a few minutes for my breathing to normalise. "Jamie pulled it off the wall," I tell them. "He was upset… angry… and he ripped it off the wall."

"Did he threaten you with it?"

"No!" I bluster incredulously.

"Then why?"

"He just tore it off… he wasn't really thinking about it, he

304

was talking to me while he was doing it. He was upset, like I said."

"How about that mark on your face?"

My hand flies to cover the small red bruise on my left cheek. "Jamie slapped me."

"So you *were* fighting."

"No! I didn't hit him back. He was upset, like I said."

"Yes, you told us. Hitting you. That's, uh, that's pretty serious."

Last night was probably the only time I'll ever see Jamie possess enough physical strength, to pry a towel rack from a wall, to hit me hard enough to leave a bruise. He's not a violent person. It was the insanity of having to relive his childhood, of having to deal with the fact that I had just watched his parents raping and abusing him.

"What exactly were you two talking, fighting, discussing, whatever-ing about?"

Now comes the hard part. I sigh, "Okay. It's a very long, complicated story."

"And we need to hear it," Howard nods at me.

"We were at The End. Jamie sings karaoke there with Stacy."

"Miss Pendleton tells us that Jamie was angry at you... you hadn't called him all day yesterday, she says. He thought you were planning to break up with him. Do you see where we're coming from, Mr. Mattheis? About him being needy?"

"He's not needy, and I wasn't going to break up with him! It was nothing like that! Something... happened. I was upset yesterday, not at Jamie, but..."

"But what?" prompts Lord.

"This... this is so hard." I see Jamie in the video. I can't believe I watched that thing. I didn't *need* to know how it ended! What, did I think maybe they'd all smile and have a group hug and say, "Just kidding"?

Did I think Jamie would live happily ever after?!

"We're waiting." Lord is doing a poor job masking his impatience.

"Somebody sent me a video," I say hoarsely, still holding

down my nausea. "It was a video of Jamie. He was very young, about seven or eight, and he was being sexually abused."

The room becomes deathly silent, then Lord clears his throat. "Continue."

"His parents. His own parents!" I say wretchedly. "They forced him to make pornographic videos with them. They made him perform oral sex. They raped him, they also used foreign objects. His mother beat him, and burned him with cigarettes. They did it for years and years. And not only that, they starved him and kept him chained in his room... Don't you remember? Officer Tafford and Officer Bloom found him in his room. His parents were dead—murder/suicide. He was nothing but a skeleton. He almost died!"

"Yes, I remember that," Howard says thoughtfully. "Now, how did *you* get this video?" His eyes narrow.

"When I got home yesterday," I say, afraid of the new look in Howard's eyes, "My mother handed me a package. It was the video. There was no return address. I didn't know who had sent it to me."

"So you didn't know about this seedy video until you received it?" asks Lord.

"No! I *didn't* know!" I yell angrily. I know what they're insinuating now! "I'm not a paedophile!"

"But you watched it?"

As calmly as I can, I tell them what I told Jamie: that I kept forgetting it was an image, that Jamie was no longer there in that prison, being sodomised and tormented.

Amazingly, they seem to comprehend what I'm saying. "Please, go on," Lord requests.

"I didn't call Jamie all day because I was so ill, so traumatised... that video was horrible. It made me so *sick*. I couldn't talk to him... couldn't call him... I was just so..."

"Were you angry at him?" Howard guesses.

"I was hurt. Traumatised... seeing him doing those things... I know he didn't want to, but... it's so hard to talk..."

"Mr. Mattheis," Lord says gently, "Did you punish Mr. Pearce because of that video?"

"No!" I scream. "Listen to me, goddamnit! I did *not* do this

306

to Jamie! Someone else did it. I'm beginning to think I know who!"

"Alright, then, who?" asks Howard.

"Yvette Feldman. She's the one who sent the video. She told me last night at The End. She came up to me and said, 'Did you get your package?'. She said a friend of hers, here, at *this* police station, gave her the video. She told me she sent it to me because 'Jamie is a pervert and he's corrupting me'!"

Lord and Howard stare aghast at me. "Mrs. Feldman sent it to you? You're sure about this?"

"She *bragged* about it!" I snap. "And she said, 'Tam do you really want that faggot to drag you to hell with him?'"

"But she didn't write her name or address on the package?"

"No."

"Hmmm." Lord ponders for a moment. "If she did this, we can pick her up for distribution of child pornography, but we don't know she did it—it's just your word. In fact, *you* could be charged with possession of child pornography."

"She sent it to me! I didn't know what it was!" Then I sob, "Please, I want to see Jamie."

"He's in surgery, I said. Can you think of anyone we should be talking to about Mrs. Feldman's involvement in this? Anyone at the bar aside from Miss Pendleton?"

"Talk to Stacy again! Maybe she remembers how Yvette talked about it, bragged about it."

So they go out into the hallway and interview Stacy again. "She didn't hear what you and Mrs. Feldman talked about. All she says is that Mrs. Feldman sat at a table with you for a few minutes. She says Jamie was very upset about that, that you didn't even invite him to sit with you, that he was wondering what was such a big secret that you couldn't include him, and that he suspected you wanted to end your relationship with him."

I shake my head violently. "No. Yvette said, 'I'd like a word with you'. I told her to fuck off—we've hated each other for years—but she said it was very important that she speak to me. She took me over to the table and told me she was the one who sent the video. When she did, I grabbed Jamie and took him out of there. I didn't *drag* him away. I was sickened! I wanted him *away* from that bitch!

"When we got home, I told him what Yvette had done, and we… we got into it. I said things… he said things… we were hurting, do you understand? …and he slapped me. I apologised about watching the video, and he told me everything. He told me his parents abused him, made videos of it, and sold them to their friends. He was crying, he tore the towel bar off the wall, and… he was going to slit his wrists with it…"

The two policemen both sit back suddenly. "He was suicidal?"

"Yeah," I reply softly. *Jamie, forgive me.*

Howard leans forward again, "And did you help him accomplish…?"

"No!" I spit at him. "I did not!"

"It is a bit brutal for an assisted suicide," Lord observes wryly.

"I did not try to kill him, and I did not assist him to kill himself," I sputter. "We apologised to each other, for everything we said, for my stupidity. I never should have watched that video. I felt like I was no better than one of the freaks his parents sold to! But we made up. Everything was okay, he promised…"

"He has a funny bite mark on the back of his neck," Howard says, his usually squinty eyes widening curiously. "Like a hickie or something. What's that from?"

"I really don't think it's any of your business!"

"Maybe *you* raped him."

"I'd like to put your lights out right now!" I snarl.

"But you won't," Howard says lightly. "You know better. Cowards like you never take on someone their own size."

"I wrote in those diaries a very long time ago," I say, weary to the bone. "I would never harm another living being. I write articles against animal cruelty. I volunteer at an animal shelter in L.A. I'm ashamed of what I wrote. I'd like to say I didn't write it, but I did. Or at least someone I used to be. I've changed."

"People don't change," grunts Officer Howard.

"Yes, they *do*. People *do* change. I know. I'm one of them."

"That's what they all say."

"You're testing me," I mutter.

"I'm trying to find the truth."

"The truth?" Alright, fuck it! "Jamie asked me to bite his neck the night before last."

"Was it a sexual thing?"

"It was," I reply, sitting straight and defiant, waiting for them to smirk and grin. "We had rough sex. He asked me to spank him and to bite him, and I did."

They say nothing. I think about Jamie, alone in a frozen orange grove, left for dead. I think about whoever did this to him. I think about his parents, how they left him alone to die.

And I say, "If Jamie dies, I'll never forgive myself. I begged him to let me go to work with him—I had a bad feeling—I didn't want him by himself." The tears roll down my face. "I shouldn't have listened to him. I shouldn't have let him be alone. If he dies, I don't think I can live. I've loved him all my life. I'll never love anyone else."

It begins to dawn on them.

"Mr. Mattheis," Howard asks, his voice shockingly gentle. "Do you still have the video that was sent to you?"

"It was horrible. It was evil… it was so evil, what they did." My stomach cramps again.

"Mr. Mattheis."

"Yeah?" I reply weakly.

"You still have that video at your house?"

"Yeah. It's at my house, in my VCR. I wanted to throw it away, break it…"

"You didn't, did you?" asks Lord.

"No."

"What about the package it came in?"

"It's there somewhere. I didn't toss it."

"Good."

It's been three or four hours since Jamie was found, and the cops cannot find anything solid against me. The diaries are not even close to pertinent, nor are the statements given by Mom,

Stace and the Asshole. The D.A. refuses to press any charges. For a while, I'm terrified she's going to charge me with possession, but once I tell her how I received the tape, and how shocked and horror-struck I was, and how Yvette behaved that night about it, I am released.

I'm not going home. I can't possibly sleep until I see Jamie for myself, see if he's alive... breathing... and I'm sure once I've seen him, once I see what they've done to him, I won't be able to close my eyes anyway.

Officer Pete Bloom, Lloyd Tafford's old partner, comes to them, having just heard about Jamie's attack. He's retired from the police, but he still likes to drive around in his civilian car at odd hours, looking for suspicious activities or characters. "I saw three people, walking down Solano right about where Jamie's car was found. I recognised them, so I didn't think anything of it, except... it was strange, how they were walking around at two in the morning."

They ask Yvette to come in and talk to them. She admits she sent the video, and that she got it from one Officer Steven Cantrell. She bribed him with sex, she says, and he gave it to her.

"You have a bunch of them here at the station, Steve told me. Ever since they found the kid's parents dead and all that."

"Why would you do a thing like that?" Lord bemoans. "Why would you deliberately send Mr. Mattheis a videotape of his boyfriend being raped and abused?"

Yvette shrugs nonchalantly. "I thought he should see what his boyfriend is..."

"And what is that?"

"A cocksucking little fag!"

Every cop within earshot is taken aback. "He was a little boy!"

It doesn't phase her a bit.

"Are you involved in this beating, Mrs. Feldman?"

"No," she responds flatly. "I'd like to throw 'em parade though."

"So you know who they are?"

"Maybe..."

310

"Why don't you tell us?"

"So you can punish *them*?" she jeers. "They did the world a favour! They exterminated a disgusting little insect! I'm only sorry they didn't kill Tam too, that overgrown, bleeding heart faggot!"

"They didn't *kill* Mr. Pearce, Mrs. Feldman."

"Too bad," she shrugs arrogantly.

"But he may die... It sounds to us like you knew about this attack before it happened," Howard snarls at her. "That makes you an accessory. We can charge you with conspiracy and depraved indifference. You could go away for quite some time."

Yvette gasps and says, "Steve... he was going with them to do it."

"With whom?" Lord asks.

She won't say a word more, until she sees an attorney. They arrest her, for distribution of child porn.

They know something's off. The station doesn't keep items from cases on the property longer than five years or so. The child porn videos found in Jamie's childhood home were either erased, destroyed, or warehoused somewhere off site.

"Try again, Steve," snaps Officer Lord. "Where did you get the video?"

Very clumsily, Cantrell states that he got it from his cousin in Davis. "He bought it off the guy's parents back in '87 or '88. I found it and recognised him. Then I told Yvette about it. She wanted a copy so she could see for herself. I told her I got it from the station and that I couldn't share it, but... I went ahead and gave it to her."

"Did you participate in this beating?" they ask him.

"No. I was just out with them for drinks last night," stammers Cantrell. "Then they started talking..."

"Who started talking?"

"Yvette, and her brother Ray, and her husband Benny, and some other people. They started talking really loudly—we were all wasted—they asked me to come along. They were going to find James and Tam and just... razz them a little, just for fun. I didn't want to get involved. I'm an officer, after all."

Not for long. Having nothing to prove he's directly involved, depraved or indifferent to a violent crime, they fire Cantrell, then charge him, too, with distribution. It's a paltry victory, but it still gives me a lift.

At my suggestion, the police locate the three dudes who bashed Jamie twice in high school. Guy number one now lives in Davis, works just a few blocks from the UC Medical Centre. But he's got an alibi. When they reach him on his cell, he's at Pismo with the wife and kids, and has been there for almost a week. Guy number two was killed in some accident in Sacramento in 2002. Guy number three now lives in Utah.

In the presence of their lawyers, Yvette and Cantrell backstab each other. She names him as one of the three who abducted Jamie. He names Benny. When she calls Cantrell a liar, he too names her as one of the three kidnappers. She emphatically denies it.

Then, Mrs. Cooke, the lady who runs the bakery on our main drag in Sommerville, calls in with a tip: her very first customers upon opening her door at six the morning of the beating were Ray Battle, Steven Cantrell, and Lydia Rocha, a friend of both Stacy and Jamie, who, like Ray and many other "friends" of ours, is now living away from Sommerville but back in town for the holidays. The three came in, ordered some maple bars with chocolate milk, and talked in hushed tones about "Jamie". Mrs. Cooke says she heard Lydia speak threateningly to Cantrell, and the words, "the little queer won't be found until it's way too late".

It doesn't take much effort to get Cantrell to rat Lydia out, as long as it's understood that he "really didn't want any part of this thing. I only drove," he whines.

"Lydia's been mad at them for years. And she's been hot for Tam since high school," Cantrell reveals. "She once had a crush on James, but it was brief, and then she liked Tam—she couldn't believe they were spooning. She thought it was disgusting. She was the mastermind. She's the one who wanted them dead—both of them. But when we got to James's house, Tam had left, and it was only James."

thirty-eight:

jamie
(december 30)

In the ER at County Hospital in Woodland, the docs insert a pleura-vac tube to siphon the blood out of my chest where my ribs have punctured my left lung and caused it to collapse. When they realise I have internal injuries and their CT scanner is on the fritz, they put me in a chopper and fly me to Sacramento, to UC Davis.

In the OR, they lay me on my side and stitch up my ruptured left kidney, then they flip me over and stitch up the laceration along the right side of my head, By the grace of God, the MRIs reveal no brain injuries or other internal trauma. Miraculously, my spleen wasn't touched. They put my right arm and right hand back together and encase them in plaster. They ease the arm into a sling because my collarbone is broken in half.

I've lost so much blood that they have to give me four or five units of PRBCs. I observe the chaos from up above, once again pivoting between the doors of life and death.

My lungs are horrible, torn up and tired, they say, and need a good rest, so they intubate me and let a ventilator do the hard work of getting oxygen into my traumatised tissues.

Every now and then Lloyd shows up, but he says little.

Mostly, he's like me, quietly witnessing.

Tammy arrives at last, and when he tells the hospital staff I have no remaining blood or legal family on this earth, that I only have my emotional family in himself, Stacy and Peggy, they hand him my angel, thickly coated in a tacky mixture of mud and blood. He sobs quietly, his shoulders shaking.

Poor Tammy. I wish I could talk to him, tell him that I'm alright, in some peculiar, quiet way. I look awful lying there, a snarled plethora of tubes running through every orifice, my right eye so black I look like a pirate, the slits in my head and flank held together with ugly black nylon and silver stitches. He cries and cries. I want to go to him, but I can't move. I can't speak, can't let him know I'm alright.

Stacy comes in, finds Tammy sitting there with me. "I'm so sorry, Tammy," she weeps. "Please forgive me."

"Why'd you change your mind?" he asks her coldly, not taking his eyes from me. "You saw me 'drag' him out of The End. I was the last one with him, so I *had* to have done this, right?

"The way you've been acting—you can't fake that—I know you didn't do this."

"No, I didn't," he says, his voice splintered.

"How you holding up?"

"I'm not," he sobs coarsely.

"I'm sorry. I'm sorry I accused you."

"I wasn't the last one with him," Tammy sputters. "They were, whoever they are."

"It's going to be alright, Tammy," Stacy says.

"Not if he dies," Tammy shakes his head. "I can't... I won't be able to live without him. I can't..." Peggy comes in a few minutes later. Stacy pulls a picture from her wallet.

It's me, sitting in front of the Christmas tree at work. Stacy took it a day or so before Peggy came in with her fractured pelvis. "Isn't he sweet," Peg exclaims.

Tammy takes the photo and holds it for a long time.

"He looks lonely there, doesn't he?" asks Stacy, watching him.

"Can I have this?" he begs her.

"Of course."

"That smile," he cries. "That sad, beautiful smile. I've never known anyone as beautiful, or as sweet. I've never loved anyone this way. I've never loved anyone, period. I was never happy, until him."

"He loves you, Tammy," his mother says. "I know he does."

"I know he does too. I mean to tell you guys, that man loves me. He wears me out!" Tammy laughs a little. "He takes, and takes, and takes love from me, then he gives me his love. So much love... sweet, dirty love."

God, I love him.

And I don't even mind him using the "D" word. In fact, I love it.

He sighs, and Peggy blushes, "Tam!"

"But he's not dirty. Not at all! He's so good to me. So pure, beautiful... so good inside... so wonderful."

Stacy kisses Tammy's cheek. Peggy holds on tight and kisses his other cheek.

I'm loving this. I'm not there, so I know he is being real. I'm not present to cause him to censor this affectionate vernacular.

He sobs anew. "Hasn't he been through *enough*?! Who could do this?!"

"I think it's going to be okay, son," Peggy tells him.

"I'm praying, but I have a bad feeling, Mom..."

I feel that premonitory tickling sensation in my chest. *I'm going to crash again. I've got to concentrate! I can't do this to him!*

"Code blue, ICU," the speaker announces below me.

"He'd want you to go on, Tammy," Stacy says, and immediately, she looks like she could kick herself.

"I can't, I can't!" Tammy screeches. "Please!"

I'm still breathing, that is, the vent is still breathing for me, but my heart is exhausted and trying to give out. My skin is deathly grey again, like it was in my bedroom the day Lloyd found me. Now my telemetry monitor shows v-tach again. I watch, furious at myself, as Tammy clings to Stacy and Peggy, and the three of them cry as the doctors and nurses shock me once, twice, three, four times.

Finally, my heart is restored to normal sinus.

But now I'm deeply asleep. I'm so deep, so far down, or up, that I don't return to my bed, to my flesh, like I did in the ambulance and in the orchard. Everything I hear is in faint, surreal echo, dreamlike.

"He's in a coma," the doctor tells my friends. "We'll just have to wait and see."

"Do you think he's brain dead?" asks Tammy. I know neither Stacy nor Peggy would have dared ask it.

"The scans show brain activity, so no, he's not brain dead. However, we don't know if... when he'll wake up. It may be days, weeks, months... we just don't know."

"How did he live?" Stacy asks tearfully. "How did he live after all that happened? He must have been lying there at least nine hours!"

"It was freezing," the doctor says quietly. "His systems slowed down. It bought him just enough time until those men found him. If they hadn't..."

Stacy nods jerkily.

Tammy either won't or can't say anything now. It's like the tears are never going to stop. Then the doctor says, "You're his power of attorney."

"What?" Tammy's eyes flood over again.

"He made you his power of attorney," the doctor says. "If he doesn't recover—if he doesn't awaken, if he continues to decline—you have to make decisions for him."

Tammy sobs into his mother's neck. Stacy runs to the restroom, probably to throw up.

It's true. Only four days ago, on December 26th, when I was suffering in the ER with hypoglycaemia, Stacy helped me fill out paperwork with routine questions like, "Who will make your healthcare decisions should you become unable to make them yourself?" I made Tammy my DPOA.

I don't think he's taking this too well.

After a while, he raises his head from where he's soaked Peg's shirt. "I deserted him. I wasted all those years and now that we've finally gotten together, this happens. I've loved him forever. He doesn't believe me when I tell him that we met the first time in a supermarket when we were little."

"What are you talking about, Tammy?" asks Peg.

"Don't you remember? A long time ago? We were in Sacramento, getting groceries, and we got in the checkout behind this woman. She had the prettiest little boy in her cart. Beautiful, big blue eyes..." Tammy sobs.

"You can't remember that far back!" Peggy exclaims. "Can you?"

"I didn't, until one night after a football game, when I saw Jamie eating red liquorice," Tammy says. "He looked at me, and I knew it was that little boy from the shopping cart. I know it's him, Mommy." Tammy nods, tears spilling again, like Niagara Falls. "I know it's him. And that woman... that woman he was with was that evil woman in the video!"

Peggy looks at Stacy.

"Fuck," Stacy whispers harshly, and they hold him.

I am not solid. There is no matter to me. Now I *want* to be in that bed, but I want to be *awake*. I reach for Tammy with arms that are made of nothing. I can't get to him. Nothing has ever hurt as bad as this.

"That little boy was eating red liquorice, remember, Mommy? And I kissed him and he kissed me. Remember Mommy? Remember?"

Peg and Stacy go home, but Tammy demands that a cot be brought in. "I'm his power of attorney," Tammy says so endearingly and importantly that I wish I could tease him about it. When it's brought in, he doesn't bother lying down and putting it to use. He's so tired. He sits in one of the ubiquitous beige vinyl chairs, leans over me, strokes my hair, caresses my face, winces at my black eye and cloven head. "There won't be too bad of a scar, Baby," he whispers to me, twirling a lock of hair over the ugly gash. "Your hair will cover it... you'll still be pretty... nothing will ever make you ugly."

Tammy, how do I get down from here?

"Come back to me, Jamie," he begs me. "Come home. It's so lonely without you. I miss you."

I can't find my way. I'm lost. I'm alone...

You're not alone, he says. I'm here.

Keep talking, Honey. I'm looking for you. I can't see...

I'm praying for you, Jamie.

You're praying?

Yes, I'm praying. Come home to me, Jamie. Come home...

I fight through the black forest, swatting the limbs as they slap my face...

I'm back in my body, but it's a different body... a different me. I'm two years old, sitting in a shopping cart, my legs kicking and dangling, and I'm resplendently lacking in any clairvoyance of the abuse the dark-haired woman accompanying me will inflict on me in less than a year.

A boy with dark brown, almost black hair and fathomless greenish-blue eyes looks up at me. He seems so familiar...

I reach out, my fingers wrapped around my Red Vine. "Come here," I beckon him. He stands on tiptoe and says, "Look at you! You have the biggest eyes I've ever seen!" He looks back at his mother, who smiles at him and then me.

"What a sweetie!"

Peggy!

I look at the pretty boy...

Tammy!

I squirm between the bars of the baby seat on the cart. I want to talk to him so badly, but as yet, though I'm past my second birthday, I haven't learned to say much more than Dada, Mama, Baba. My babbles translate silently, only to me, "You mean you don't have to sit in your mom's cart? No fair!"

"How old is he?" the boy asks my mother.

"Two!" Mom barks in her raspy voice. I jabber to my new friend, "Don't mind her. She's a grouch."

"You don't say!"

I giggle at him. "Yeah. She's even crabby to my daddy!"

"Is that right?" the boy gasps.

"You better believe it. I try to stay out of her way."

"What's his name, please?" Tammy asks my mom. But she pretends she doesn't hear him. She treats all kids like this. At stores, at libraries, at the preschool/daycare centre she takes me

318

to on her way to work.

"Come on, Jamie," she mutters grumpily. "Let's get out of here!"

"See what I mean?" I coo to Tammy. "Grouchy!"

Tammy laughs. "His name is Jamie?" he asks my mother.

She gives him a mean look; she's an unhappy person. She never smiles. She acts like she's too good to smile or talk to people. She says the most hateful thing to him, "Yeah, Jamie! What do you care? You'll never see him again anyway!"

Awww, Tammy's eyes moisten and he appeals silently to Peggy, who shakes her head sadly. I wish she'd tell my mean mother off!

Poor Tammy! I reach for him again. "Come here."

He comes to me, stands on tiptoe.

"Don't you even mind her," I gurgle.

He reaches up and kisses my cheek.

I kissed your cheek, Tammy says. And you kissed my mouth.

My baby eyes wide open, I lean as far over as I can go, and babble, "I love you, Tammy." My tiny red mouth touches his. We kiss each other goodbye.

I'm deeply asleep, but I taste the liquorice. I do... I taste it...

The story is true.

It was our first kiss. And we've loved each other almost our whole lives.

This old, new, wonderful memory dispels my fear, my loneliness. All memories of being savagely beaten are erased, and replaced by the softness of Tammy's lips against mine, the taste of him.

Of liquorice.

I've always loved you, he says. Since this day...

His face begins to distort.

"Don't go, Tammy," I cry plaintively. "Please! Where are you?"

"I'm here. Come to me, Jamie. Come back to me. I miss you." I feel his lips. He kisses me softly, again and again. "Come back to me, come back..."

He knows I love him. I know he loves me. Our love has grown. In the measly five or six days we've been together, in the

319

sixteen years we were apart, in the thirty years since we met, it's grown. It's grown from the innocent affection between two toddlers, from the crushing teenage lust of two high schoolers, from the sexual discovery of two thirty-somethings, to this, this absolute need and belief in each other. It's matured into something bigger, stronger than the fear, the anger and the hatred, both internal and external, that has tried to vanquish it.

I feel the anger, the bitterness, the self-hatred I've always toted with me, draining away, dying, melting like the witch in The Wizard Of Oz, *replaced by this amazing strength, this love, pouring from Tammy's mouth to mine, like synapses swapping neurotransmitters, like water into a dry chalice.*

The kiss of life.

His voice, his lips… he's charming my tears.

I'm getting a hard-on, and, oh! It feels so good! Oh Tammy. Where are you?!

I try to kiss him back, but my lips won't cooperate.

"Nurse?" I hear him shout. "Come here, please!"

I hear the scuffing of nurse shoes on glossy linoleum.

"Look at this. What…?"

The nurse studies me for a moment. I can't *see* the nurse, but I hear him. I feel him touching my arm, checking my IV.

I'm back… in my thirty-one year old body.

"Is he crying?" asks Tammy, his voice thickening.

I feel a warm wetness, a trickling…

Tammy. I'm trying to find you, I'm trying. Help me…

My sobs begin to shake my body as I wander in this pitch black. I hear him cajoling me closer. I feel him kissing me. I taste his wonderful essence.

But I don't see him.

"Is he crying?" Tammy sobs again.

"I don't know," replies the nurse.

"I think he's crying. Jamie! Come to me. Come on, come to me. I'm here… I'm waiting. Come on…"

The tears course down my face steadily. "Come on, Jamie. Don't be afraid… I'm here. Come back to me." His lips touch mine again. "Come on… come on… please come to me."

320

White begins to bleed into the black. Now I can see. I see myself, lying in the cot. I look like a ghost, my skin like dingy sheets.

"Please, Jamie, come home. I can't do this without you. I need you. I need you, Baby, come home…"

I open my left eye to a world opposite the one I've just stepped from, of stark whiteness. I'm reminded of the time Tammy took me to the ER after those assheads beat me up.

There they are, the symbols of persecution: the IV dripping clear liquid, the big cast over my twice-busted right arm, the dried blood from cuts and scrapes too gently cleaned, the damned Foley catheter they stuck up in my dick to collect my urine.

Ugh! If I recover from this I'll get those motherfuckers! I'll get them!

Do something with this, Jamie, Lloyd says. Take this and do something.

I'm going to get better. I'm going to live. I'm going to walk out of this hospital. They aren't going to have the last damn laugh!

I look down to find my Tammy draped across me, asleep, the tears still wet on his face, so close I am able to touch him with my nose. I kiss the two or three inches of air between my mouth and his cheek. Frustrated, but undaunted, I gently inch myself down. I can't raise my right arm. It's weighted down by that cast. My left arm is taped to a board so the IV doesn't come out if I were to move suddenly.

I inhale his scent.

Yes. He's here…

My lips won't stop until they've found his.

I open my mouth to say, "Wake up."

But no words come out.

Oh, yeah! I'm on a ventilator.

Even when I look to my left and fail to see any hissing, humming apparatus doing my breathing for me.

When did they take me off the vent?

How long have I been out?

321

How long was I in the supermarket with Tammy?

I can't believe, I *refuse* to believe I've lost the power to speak. I kiss Tammy again, again, again…

He moans and raises his head.

I smile at him.

"I'm home," I want to say.

His gorgeous mouth spreads horizontally. He fumbles for the call button and presses it.

thirty-nine:

tammy
(december 30 to january 14)

When he crashes in his ICU bed, I'm sure he's going to die. His heart is failing because he has "fluid overload" and it's building up in his lungs. He lies there, inert, his skin ashen, like a corpse's. The room thunders with the shouts of doctors and nurses who surround him, jabbing him with more needles, shoving diuretics to regulate his fluids, epi to kick-start his heart, bicarb because he's "out of balance". I have no idea what they're yelling about. It's like a scene from *House M.D.*: the music in the scene is the ominous beeps and chimes of the alarms on the monitors above him. I should be grateful he has such a vigilant and hard-working team caring for him, but after five minutes of chest compressions, syringes, IV bags, yells and musical alarms, I only see Jamie's doctors and nurses as another pack of bullies, torturing him, beating him, making him miserable. I want to charge them and chase them away, but Mom holds me back, using all of her strength, and I beat my fists on the vinyl chairs.

Stacy has been apologising every twenty minutes or so for the way she was treating me when Jamie first vanished. She'd better be sorry! The most calculating killer could not fake the way I wail and flail as they resuscitate him.

When at last his heart rhythm is regulated, they hook him up to antibiotics to prevent infection and as abruptly as they show up, they disperse, all talking at once.

I won't leave him, not for one minute, unless it's to use the bathroom that adjoins his room to another.

I dispense liquid soap all over the pewter keychain I got him, use my fingers and nails to peel and scrub away the layers of dried blood and soil and bits of grass that hide its sweetness. It slips from my hand and my whole body leaps as I rescue it from being lost forever down the drain.

And that's when the fatigue sets in and the numbness wears off, and I lean over the sink, tears rolling down my face, down the pipes.

Why couldn't I have saved *him*?!

I refuse to shower, because that would take longer than one minute. Mom stays and fretfully hobbles on her cane, back and forth from Jamie's room to the cafeteria to get me drinks, food, whatever. When she gets too tired to hold her eyelids up, Stacy comes in and assumes go-fer duties.

Jamie shows some improvement over the next few days. The chest tube collects blood and drainage from his punctured left lung and the lasix (diuretic) helps Jamie drain the excessive fluids into his urine bag. His lungs sound better, the doctor says, and they begin to "wean" him off of the ventilator until he's able to breathe on his own. Satisfied with what the chest tube has done for him, they remove that too.

An article about Jamie's beating appears in the *Sacramento Bee*. It describes his injuries in grotesque detail and accuracy. At press time, "no suspects have been arrested".

Reporters try to sneak into the ICU to spy on us, to ambush us and try to gather juicy info for their rags and their six and eleven reports. Thank God for the nurses. They're like dogs with bones.

During these several days, I talk to him constantly, wondering if he can hear me. I pray to God that these medical efforts aren't all in vain, that he hasn't suffered some irreversible brain cell death from all this trauma. He looks so

324

small. He looks *dead*, lying there. Is he really in that shrunken grey shell before me? What's on his mind as his body struggles to recover and mend? What was on his mind during those long, cold hours in that orange grove?

Why wasn't I there for him? Why did he have to go through this *alone*?!

Unable to stand another minute without some respite, I decide to take a walk around the ICU floor. But that's not enough. *Please, God,* I pray continuously, *don't let him die while I'm gone… and if he wakes up, keep him awake until I get back.* I have to stretch my legs. I have to move. I feel grimy, my own body ash a second skin holding in my heat. I need a shower in the worst way.

In the main lobby, I spy two elderly women, one small lady with short, curly silver hair sitting in a wheelchair, the other, taller, white-haired, kneeling before the wheelchair and stroking the silver-haired woman's face. I think they're lesbians, but they might just as well be sisters or close ladyfriends. I pretend I know for sure, because I like to imagine they're in love, and in it for life, whatever life has in store.

Mom limps up beside me and takes my hand. "How's Jamie?" she asks.

"Same," I murmur, my eyes not leaving the lesbian couple.

"Do you know them?" Mom asks.

"No, I think they're lesbians."

"Aw, you don't know that for sure, Tammy."

"I'm pretending that I know for sure," I say softly.

Mom watches the two women for a long time. Then she says, "That's what it's all about, honey. Staying together through it all, never giving up."

I'm never giving up.

If… when Jamie wakes up, I'm going to marry him.

Around January 8th, I get a call from my landlord in L.A. I haven't paid January's rent and it was due on the fifth, so it's either pay or get out. I hate the idea of leaving Jamie, but the doctor says Jamie can only stay the very same or improve. I know better. I may not be a nurse or a doctor, but I know anyone can suffer sudden reversal and die. I've listened too closely to Jamie's horror stories to be naïve.

Stacy and Mom both promise to keep a close eye on him, that one of them will be by his bedside at all times. Stacy gives me her key to Jamie's house, and on the ninth, I drive down to my apartment and pack my things together. The stuff I can't take with me, like furniture, I donate to the Salvation Army and to the Purrfect Peace Cat Sanctuary. As I help them unload the van I've rented, I ask them how my old friends Wonka and Teddy are doing. Neither of them have been adopted, so I buy two cat carriers and adopt them both.

But Teddy has attached himself to a pretty female cat named Pepper, a long-haired tortoise shell who looks like Mom's cat Tillie. It doesn't matter that Teddy and Pepper are both fixed. They're inseparable, so on the eleventh, I bring all three kitties home. Between the gas, the van rental, the adoption fees, cat food and cat caddies, I'm out at least six or seven hundred dollars, and just about as broke as the ten commandments. Mom can't stop laughing when I call her to tell her about adopting three new "children".

I call a guy to come change the locks and have new keys made. I am moving in without asking Jamie first, but there's no *way* I'm letting him stay alone after this. Besides, his house is perfect for us. It's two bedroom, one bath, with a nice, fenced-in back yard and a secluded front yard. There's hardly any traffic on his street.

I carefully introduce our new family members to Misty, Sam, Tigger and Ginger, and linger a little while, watching how they interact. The two "groups" are receptive, but not overly friendly to each other. Tigger and Ginger lie together on the couch. Misty and Sam, as always, hog the two beige recliners. Teddy and Pepper, anxious over the smells and sights of their new home, retreat under Jamie's bed. Wonka, the odd man out, is as confident and easy-going as I remember him. He decides the coffee table is his domain, and proceeds to stretch out over the autumn leaf table runner that, according to Jamie, has been there since before Halloween.

When I'm satisfied our family of seven will coexist without tearing each other to pieces, I head back out toward the hospital. On the way, I stop at Wal-Mart and spend my last hundred dollars on a bill of groceries. His cupboards will be full for the first time in ages. I also buy a soft, plushy, light blue velour throw blanket that catches my eye.

I return to his side and beg him to wake up. For three days, I talk to him, inveigle him, even browbeat him a few times. When he begins to cry while still in the invisible fist of his coma, I mutter to him, "Jamie, if you think I'm mad at you, I'm not. I'm not! This isn't your fault. Don't pay any attention to me. I'm tired, that's all. I want you to come back to me, but if it's too much for you..." I can't bear what I am about to say. "If it's too much, if your body is too damaged... go where you need to go... I don't want you to suffer. I don't want you to hurt anymore..."

I stop and let a huge sobbing jag pass over me. "...but Jamie, if you die now, after all we've been through... I don't know if I'll make it."

It's a good old fashioned guilt routine, and I'm a shithead for using it. He's had enough guilt in his life without me adding to it. But I can't help myself. "If you die, I won't make it, Jamie. I can't lose you now. Besides, I moved into your house without your permission. I adopted three kitties in L.A. They're waiting to meet you. They get along real well with Tigger and Ginger and them! Please come back to me, Baby. Please..." I kiss and coax him. His mouth is gummy and his breath is stale, but I don't care. "Come home. Come back... come back to me..."

Three days after my return from L.A., my prayers are answered.

forty:

jamie
(january 14 to 27)

My surgeon, and a throng of doctors and nurses gather around my bed excitedly as I gaze into Tammy's eyes. I can't stop smiling. I'm so happy to be home, I just kiss him over and over, clasping his hands, refusing to let go. Not being able to talk doesn't matter to me at the moment. I can't stop touching him as I make inaudible little "Mmmm, mmmm" vibrations in my parched throat, swollen and raw from the breathing tubes.

It matters to everyone else, including Tammy, and as they pipe one question after another, I notice that I still have pain, an ache, a spasm, inside of my neck, in the membranes and muscles. They're so sore I can picture them, blood red, raw, like a fresh slab of steak.

They do swallowing tests and though it's difficult, I'm able to gulp both solids and liquids without choking. They check for vocal cord and nerve damage, and find nothing.

"Do you know where you are?" they ask loudly, thinking maybe my hearing is damaged, and I nod, but I can't tell them.

"Do you know your name?" Again, I nod.

Tammy asks me, "Can you write, Jamie?"

I nod *yes* and he gets me a notebook from the nurse's desk.

My right hand, arm and clavicle are broken, along with my right wrist. I can write very sloppily with my left hand. "What's your name?" asks a nurse.

James Michael Pearce, I write.

"Do you remember what happened to you?"

A jumble of transient faces and words... I see people with half their faces covered... I hear someone telling me Tammy's not coming to help me.

But he's here. I smile up at him.

I write, *I don't remember.*

"What's your last memory?" my surgeon asks.

I happily scribble, *Tammy is right. I met him in a grocery store when I was a baby.*

The doctor steps back in confusion. "What's he talking about?" he asks Tammy.

"Baby! You remember now?"

I think I dreamed it. When I was out.

"What's your latest *real* memory?" a nurse asks flippantly. Tammy scowls at her.

That <u>was</u> a real memory, I write. As for my latest waking memory, I put down, *Tammy and me eating breakfast. We had toast and jam. We talked about him having to go to L.A. soon to get his stuff moved up here.*

"That was the morning of the attack," whispers Tammy to the doctor, but I hear him. *Attack?* I envision faces, half-covered in the collars of sweaters, jackets, hoodies. I write down what I see and everyone nods thoughtfully. That's it.

"What do you do for a living?" asks my surgeon.

Nurse.

They all nod at each other, looking relieved. *Yes, I'm in here. My brain isn't damaged. I just can't talk.*

"Why?" they ask.

I don't know.

Just to be absolutely certain, they give me vision tests to see if I can correctly identify colours and shapes. They have me do basic and intermediate math problems. *Don't bother with calculus*, I write, and they chuckle. They do a CT of my brain and see no bleeds, no herniations, no lesions.

Having to use my left hand to write and do calculations, I tire easily. Actually, *everything* is wearing me out, ergo my temper is volatile. I spend most of my days and nights trying to sleep on the inhospitable hospital bed. I bitch at the nurses nonverbally when they wake me up to get my blood pressure, to walk the hallways or to take a shower.

I try to be nicer to Tammy, bless his heart, but when my right arm throbs or my head aches, I answer more snidely than intended. When a nurse tells me my IV is infiltrated and I have to be stabbed with another damn needle, I throw things—empty kidney basins, a hairbrush, my notebook a few times—-and aim silent screams at the ceiling. I get overly hysterical when Tammy tries to be of help by raising the head of my bed and all it does is make me feel dizzy and nauseated. When I'm particularly tired, my left leg drags, and the doctor says that might be from brain injury. So they take me all over again to do a CAT scan of my head and of course, they find nothing.

Please get me out of here, I write.

Tammy says, "Soon, Baby," in his sweet, saintly way. Argh!

The day I'm discharged to home, January 27th, they sit all of us down, me, Tammy, Stacy and Peggy, and tell us that aside from some short term memory loss, they deduce no discernible permanent damage. I've simply become a mute. "We're pretty sure the cause isn't physical or organic," they say. "We may be wrong, but we believe the cause is psychological."

I keep seeing a towering figure with a face obscured by a dark-coloured hooded pullover. I keep seeing flashes of light in a dim background, like lightning in a coal black sky. I write all this down again, but again, no-one remarks.

"It's likely he'll speak again," the doctors say. "But it will have to be in his own time. With the emotional trauma he experienced, his muteness might be elective."

"You mean he *wants* to be like this?" Stacy asks.

What are you guys talking about? I write, and hand my scribbles to Stacy.

But they go on talking like I'm not there. I cut my eyes in silent outrage and resolve not to communicate with any of them

330

for the rest of the evening.

"Not necessarily," replies the doctor. "The mind is tricky, delicate. More than likely, Jamie will be able to speak after he processes what happened to him."

"He can't even *remember* what happened to him," Tammy sighs.

He's wrong. It's coming back, in jigsaw pieces.

"He's probably repressing," the doctor says, his voice low, but I hear him. How noisy does he think this office is anyway? "In which case, you," he indicates Tammy, "Need to be prepared for him to need your emotional support. He's probably going to have nightmares, night terrors, hallucinations... He'd benefit from counselling. There are wonderful support groups too, for gays and lesbians who have been harassed."

"Harassed," Tammy snorts bitterly. "He was bludgeoned nearly to death!"

I simply sit there, seething at them. Physical therapy for my smashed right hand, wrist and arm is arranged, and I fume all the way out to the car. I won't even talk to Tammy, and naturally, he keeps asking me what's wrong. Finally, I take my pad and pen and write, *Why should I talk to any of you? You all acted like I wasn't there every time I asked a question!*

"You are a firecracker," Tammy chides me, hoping his smile will enchant my anger away. "You don't remember what happened to you, Jamie, so anything we said probably didn't make sense anyway."

You're an ass, I write. *I suppose remembering some creep in a hoodie means nothing to you?*

"Oh, Jamie. Please don't be mad at me. It's so awful, I don't even *want* you to remember."

It's coming back, sorry.

"I know, and I'll tell you everything when the time comes."

Why not prepare me <u>now</u> so I don't have to be so traumatised?!

Instead, he invites Stacy and Peggy, who I'm going to call Mom—no, Ma, from now on, out to eat with us at the Sizzler-type restaurant. Then he has them stay all evening with us at the house. He rents a bunch of dumb new movies that Stacy thinks

331

will be great. If we were alone, we'd be watching *Father Goose* or *Arsenic and Old Lace*.

I ignore all of them and spend the night silently pouting and petting our new kids, Wonka, Teddy and Pepper, who are crowding around me adoringly. Misty, Sam, Ginger and Tigger sulk over in the corner for a while, then decide to join the family.

Halfway buried by seven fluffy felines, I look up every now and again to see Tammy smiling at me, sadly, hopefully. "I love you," he mouths.

I snub him.

He begins flicking peanuts, M&Ms, and Crunch 'n Munch popcorn at me. I bite off a hunk of Red Vine and sling it at him using my good arm, putting remarkable strength behind my throw.

"Ouch!" he grins.

I stick my red-dyed tongue out at him.

"Mustn't fight, children," Stacy mutters.

"Don't be mad at me," mouths Tammy, his eyes drilling into me.

I respond by looking back down at Wonka, who is purring like an outboard motor, snuggled against my breast. I stroke the rich, coffee-brown fur over his face and kiss his forehead softly.

"You know?" Tammy muses boldly. "I wish I was a cat. I wish I was a furry brown and white cat right now. And I wish a certain someone was doing to me what he's doing to that cat!"

Ma laughs. Stacy grumbles, "Hey, we're trying to watch a movie here!"

Tammy winks at me, and my mean determination to give him the cold shoulder disintegrates. I smile back at him and shake my head. No fair.

That night he gives me a present. It's the softest, cuddliest, most luxurious little velour blanket in the world. It's baby soft as I brush it against my cheeks, and I knead it like a contented cat. In fact, I'm sure the kids would love to confiscate it.

"You can lie on it when your elbows are sore, and when those scars on your back hurt. Sheets can be kind of abrasive," he says gently. He looks a little leery, as if he expects me to lash out at him for mentioning my scars. I grab him and hug him hard, and cry a little.

Why are you so good to me? I ask him.

"Because I want to be."

I'm rotten. I never do anything nice for you.

"You do lots of nice things for me," Tammy whispers. "Especially in bed."

I mean I never buy things for you!

"Well, then, buy me stuff!"

I don't know what you'd like. I'm a very un-creative shopper.

"Get creative. Surprise me," he murmurs, kissing my ear. "I'll love anything you get me."

I never shopped for Lloyd either. I barely even told him I loved him. I'm awful. I don't deserve you.

"Oh, shush," Tammy says into my hair. "You loved Lloyd and he knew it."

I think I saw him when I was out, I write. *I think he talked to me.*

He smiles, "Maybe."

I love this blanket.

But with my right arm in a sling, I'm in no mood or shape for sex.

"I'm not either," Tammy agrees. He laughs very softly. "But soon—very soon—and this blanket… it's sooo soft! It's better than velvet."

I can't wait. I'd love to lay my bare ass on that velour heaven. I want to feel it against the back of my balls while Tammy's fucking me.

But tonight, we watch an old VHS of *Our Gang* shorts instead, and I comb my fingers through the blankie's obscenely soft fur while I swallow two Tylenol with Codeine, prescribed for the painful, fragmented mess of bones inside my plaster cast.

Pen and paper are inadequate media, to explain to Tammy that I'm recalling it all now, and that what happened to me in that orange orchard literally scared my voice away.

It's returning to me, swiftly, tumbling onto me, overtaking me, like a rogue wave.

forty-one:

tammy
(january/february)

The nightmares are terrible, and useful, and Jamie names Lydia Rocha as the woman in the white sweater who was in that orchard on December 30th. He recognised her voice, he says, and when her apartment in San Ramon is searched, they find not only Jamie's car keys, but his cell phone and his wallet. The dumb bitch didn't even bother to hide them. Jamie says that someone named "Ray" carried out the physical beating. Ray Battle denies it of course, but Lydia, in hopes of getting a lighter sentence when trial time comes, fingers Mr. Battle none too subtly. As Yvette did with Steve Cantrell, Lydia and Ray turn on each other, each naming the other the "mastermind".

Yvette and Cantrell both plead guilty to possession and distribution of child porn, but nobody is going to cop to the abduction and attempted murder without trying to reap whatever benefits are available to them. Ha! The D.A. isn't interested in lightening anyone's sentences, for any reason. She's disgusted with every last party who had any knowledge of, or involvement in, Jamie's bashing. When Lydia talks, she weeps big crocodile tears about having been in love with me since high school, and how Jamie made her feel stupid for once having a thing for him.

334

"They're fags!" she sobs. "I liked both of them and all this time, they're fags!" Though she pleads "not guilty" to the charge of kidnapping and conspiracy, her statements incriminate her as a bitter, bigoted bitch who orchestrated this, along with a pair of chicken livers who hate homosexuals.

They all plead "not guilty", but the D.A. tells us that the evidence against them, along with their hateful, vindictive attitudes about Jamie and me, have pretty much fucked them. Along with kidnapping and attempted murder, they will all be charged with depraved indifference. Whether Yvette came along for the ride or not, whether Lydia struck Jamie with the towel rack or not, they all talked, they all laughed, they all conspired, and they all knew Jamie was going to be attacked that night. Everyone will be indicted: Ray Battle, Yvette Feldman, Steve Cantrell, Lydia Rocha, and Benny Feldman. Mrs. Cooke's statement has established beyond a doubt that Cantrell is the man in the "puffed jacket" who drove the car that night. Benny might not have "done" anything per se, but he most certainly is not off the hook. He is guilty of knowing that a crime was going to be committed, and not informing the police. I'd like to lose my shoe in his ass just as much as in all the others'.

Almost every night following Jamie's release from the hospital, he wakes up, crying voicelessly. One morning at about two o'clock, I get up to pee. En route, I get distracted by my stomach rumbling, and I stop at the fridge to snack on the remains of one of Jamie's famous chocolate mousse pudding pies—sex in a graham cracker crust. I am about to resume my original itinerary to the toilet when I see his tiny figure, barely throwing a shadow behind him, in the hallway. He lost a lot of badly needed flesh while he was in his coma, and he looks fragile, adorable, in his white t-shirt and long pyjama bottoms.

"Hey, Sweet Thing," I murmur to him.

He just stares—stares at me with those big, lost eyes. I go to him and kneel so that our eyes are level. "Are you okay?"

It's clear he's not. He's shivering.

"What is it? Tell me."

He moves closer to me, his eyes silently appealing me to

touch him.

"Did you have a bad dream?" I finally ask.

He nods, tears splashing on my chest. I hold him. "It's okay now."

He shakes his head, still quaking turbulently. His nails dig into the back of my neck. He won't let go. Whatever he dreamed about scared the holy crap out of him.

I read his mind then. "Did you think I left you?"

He shrugs, his eyes shimmering in the quiet dark. I can *hear* him shaking.

"Oh, Baby. I only got up to go pee, and I was hungry. I was eating some of your chocolate pie, that's all."

He doesn't move. His face is buried against my throat.

"I'll never leave you alone," I whisper. "Never, ever. That's why I moved in. I can't have you being alone right now."

He begins to sob. He's mute, but I know his thoughts. "What happened to you wasn't your fault, Jamie. I'm not mad at you. But I'm never leaving you alone again, not even when you insist that I should." I don't want him feeling like a prisoner or a helpless child either. "I love you."

He nods, kisses my neck softly.

"I know you're afraid," I murmur. "It's going to take a while for you to get through this, but they're not going to hurt you again."

He lifts his face. He glances around, juts his chin towards the front door.

"I changed the locks, Jamie. *Nobody* is coming into this house unless we invite them."

He sags against me, limp with relief.

"Let's go pee, then we'll watch *Our Gang* and go back to bed later."

As Chubbsy Ubbsy duels with Jackie Cooper over the affections of pretty Miss Crabtree, Jamie falls fast asleep in my arms. I stare at his beautiful face, stroke my fingers over his cheekbones, through his soft, curly blonde hair. He's so pretty... no scar will mar that.

He's here, he really is. God answered my prayers. I'm so thankful.

336

But I miss his voice. I miss that so much. I wonder if when we're able to make love, he'll make any sound at all. He has no idea how I love the sounds he makes when I'm inside of him. We used to "talk" to each other while we fucked. He'd make the sweetest little squeals and grunts, "Mmm-hmm? Mmm-hmm?" while he rode my dick, our lips fastened together, our tongues dancing, my answering groans vibrating into his mouth...

I'll never be able to explain it better than this. It's like part of him is still missing. I haven't heard him speak since before he vanished and was found fighting for his life, under a black garbage bag. It's like his voice is still out in that orchard, trying to find its way back to me. I know it sounds stupid. I know I should be grateful that Jamie is alive.

And I *am* grateful. I'm nothing *but* grateful.

Thank you, God, I meditate, and then my tears flow. *Oh, God, I so appreciate you for letting him live. I really do. You know I'm thankful.*

But please, let Jamie's voice come home too.

I urge him not to think about the ordeal he's survived, but he scrawls, *I have to deal with it, Tammy. It's not going to go away. I wish I could forget about it. I wish I could pretend it never happened. I almost wished I had permanent memory loss, but I didn't want to lose memories of us, memories I love.*

He adds, *I'll be alright. Just give me time.*

Time. That's something I need practice with. Time and patience.

He's taken an extended leave of absence from work. One day, he receives a get-well card from his co-workers at St. Paul's. His friend Marilyn Medrano writes, *Angel, it's such a slice of heaven working with you on the noc shift. It's so dull around here without you to make us laugh. I love you, because it's such hard work but you take delight in it. Hurry back!*

"I told you people *love* you!" I say.

He nods solemnly, and writes, *You're right.*

And to our astonishment, Paulina, that crotchety old Nurse Ratchet, writes, *You're in my prayers.*

What a world, Jamie writes.

He fills his considerable idle time with writing thank you notes, to every person he can think of who has been kind to him during this mess. He writes cards to me, to Stacy, to my mom, to Patti and Deanna, to Mrs. Cooke from the bakery, to Mr. Bloom, to the staff at UC Davis, and he also tracks down and writes to the four guys who found him in the grove and called 9-1-1.

February arrives, and it takes my proposing marriage to get him to speak, though only in a whisper, and only a few croaking words. He writes that his throat is weak and something keeps getting in the way when he tries to make words. We talk to his doctor again, who reassures us that there is no damage in Jamie's trachea or voice box.

When I pop the big question, it's spur of the moment, my emotions coming to a head after nearly losing him. I don't have a ring or any token of commitment, and I feel bad, but Jamie writes, *The angel you gave me.* He pulls it out of his t-shirt and stares at it. *I kept it close to me that night. I thought of you, and it kept me going. You're my angel, Tammy, not the other way around.*

"Oh yes, you *are* my angel," I say sternly.

OK, we're each other's angels.

"Alright, then."

On every calendar in the house, Jamie writes, *Get married!!!!!!* We're not waiting. What's the point of waiting? I ask him, "Are you *sure* you're ready to be married?" He nods, scribbles, *I'm sooo ready to marry up with you!*

"We're going to do it for real... we're going to go somewhere where gay marriage is recognised, and if we can't, we're going to have the commitment ceremony with every friend we have to witness it!"

They recognise in Canada, writes Jamie. *Patti told me. I want her at our wedding. Sylvie is a lesbian, by the way! We could go to Vancouver or Toronto.*

"It seems sudden, in a way, but then, we *should* have been
338

together all those years. I love you. I want you, nobody else."

You're the only one for me, Tammy, he writes. *There will never be anyone else in my heart. You're <u>everything</u> to me.*

I know, we're making you nauseous. I'll stop for a while.

forty-two:

jamie
(january/february)

My voice continues to elude me. But we try to get on with it the best we can. I want to get back to living as though nothing happened to me, to us. They almost killed me. They almost took me away from Tammy, and that would have killed *him*. My love for him is undiminished, and I have never been more certain of his love for me. Nobody else would put up with the mood swings that grab me out of nowhere, the frustration of not being able to express myself verbally, the irritation of being unable to articulate, the supreme annoyance of having to fucking *write* everything I can't communicate with nods, shakes or gestures. The spasm in my throat is long gone, but when I open my mouth to try and speak, there is nothing. I don't moan when I turn over in bed, I don't groan when I stub my toe against the coffee table leg. When I sigh, when I laugh, when I cry, it's in whispers, with no musical quality at all.

Will I ever sing with Stacy again?

Sometimes, Tammy acts like he thinks it's all by choice, and it makes me feel both guilty, and angry at him for *making* me feel guilty.

One night at The End, Pete Bloom stops by our table, tells

me he's going to testify about the three people he saw walking not far from where they found the cougar.

A few minutes later, a couple of our old high school friends, Patti and Deanna, come to our table and ask me how I'm doing.

"You know he can't talk," Tammy says protectively, and I cringe.

Deanna sits down and puts her arm around me. "I'm so sorry about what happened to you, Jamie. I can't understand how Lydia could do this to you. I can't understand it!"

I just nod. I don't know whether to trust Deanna or not. I never would have guessed Lydia had so much hate in her heart towards me, and look what happened.

Patti pats my shoulder. "I'm happy for you and Tam," she whispers discreetly in my ear, even though she doesn't have to because, after all, we're at The End. "And I hope Lydia, Ray and all the others who did that to you get what they deserve."

I write on a napkin, *You wrote that on my cast, remember? In high school?*

"I did, didn't I?" she smiles. "Well, they fucking deserve the death penalty. I don't think they're Christians at all. Besides, Sylvie is a lesbian! Did you know?"

Are you serious? I ask.

"Yeah. She lives with her girlfriend in Alabama," says Patti. "They're going to get married in a few months. She just told me last week!"

That's awesome!

"They get all kinds of shit, living in Alabama—the Bible Belt, you know, but they're determined, they're gonna get married. They're going to Canada!"

Maybe Tammy and I will do that someday.

"I think that would be awesome, Babe. You're both so gorgeous and look so right together. I mean it. You're the hottest twosome I've ever seen."

Deanna doesn't say much. Do you think she thinks it's wrong?

Patti ponders for a second. "I think she's fine with it, but you shouldn't care who likes it and who doesn't, Jamie. It's your life. We only get one life, and we should do what makes us

341

happy."

I'm just afraid it'll happen again. I can't go thru that again!

"I know, Babe."

I look around, and I see faces that are friendly and non-threatening. But I also see a few frowns directed my way. Some guy, about sixty years old, and very drunk, comes walking up after a few minutes, and snorts, "I hope you're happy! A good cop went to jail, and for *what*?!"

Patti stands up just then, and cements my faith in her sincerity. "That *good cop* shouldn't have participated in a hate crime! Not to mention distribution of child pornography!"

The man reels drunkenly away from her, then slurs, "You don't know nothin'! You don't know what you're talkin' about!"

"Why don't you take your smelly, drunk ass away from our table before I have you bounced?!"

"Fuckin' faggots," the asshole mumbles, and staggers a little. "Sendin' my nephew to prison!"

Well, no *wonder* he's pissed.

Tammy stands up. "Sir, you either take yourself away from our table or I will physically bounce you myself!"

Someone from a nearby table says, "Get lost, fudge-packers!" Raucous laughter ensues.

My heart quickens. Now I remember every minute detail of being beaten in the orange grove. My lynch mob of three, standing around me, looking down on me. The towel rack flashing in the moonlight, plummeting down onto my head. The stitches have long since been removed, leaving behind a scar that is still vivid dark pink. It begins to burn. Tears blind me.

Another voice shouts, "Shut the fuck up! Fucking hillbilly bigots in this town! Hope they give those haters the gas chamber!"

Cries of ascension come from all directions:

"Go home, bigots!"

"Haters, get lost!"

"Yeah, bounce! Or *be* bounced!"

"We're in the twenty-first century now, bigots!"

"God loves *everyone*! And He hates people who hate!"

"Fuckin' A!" screams Patti. "Haters aren't welcome in Sommerville!"

I inhale deeply. In through the nose, out through the mouth. My heart resumes a slow and steady thud.

Tammy smiles at me.

And I smile up at him.

We have allies. Lots of them.

But I write, *Please, let's go. I think there's going to be a fight!*

I don't think I'll ever be happy here again, if I was ever happy before. And now, everywhere we go, I'll be the reason for bar-room brawls and verbal wars. I never wanted this kind of attention, to always be reminded of the bashing. I'll never be able to remove from my brain the knowledge that people in this town now know about the videos my parents sold.

I want to leave. I want to take Tammy and go.

I want to start my life over again.

On a Sunday in February, we make love for the first time since the beating, in our laundry room. Tammy's just put in a load and added detergent and closed the lid. I come in to add a shirt and I don't know what comes over me, except that I'm horny as hell seeing him standing there with nothing on from the waist up and his long, white PJ bottoms.

I want his hands on me, all over me.

"You're frisky," he laughs as I kiss him all over his face and neck. I nod eagerly and grab his cock through his pants.

He lifts me, sits me on the shimmying washing machine, grabs my legs and lifts them up over his head. I'm folded like a paper clip, my ass on the lid of the washing machine, my knees bent over his shoulders, my fingers raking through his short hair, pulling him as close as I can, my tongue assaulting the inside of his mouth as he hammers into me, his pyjama pants down around his ankles. The vibrations coming from the washer below me enhance the experience.

Tammy pants, "God, I hope Mom doesn't come over for at least twenty minutes." (She has a key now.) I give my usual raspy laugh. Tammy slows from his frantic thrusting to a gentler rhythm. "Tell me you love me," he whispers to me. "Tell me. Tell me you love me."

I moan and cry soundlessly, open my mouth, wanting something to come forth, even a hoarse, squawked version of my original tenor.

"Jamie," he pleads, "Say my name. Tell me you love me."

My heart is bursting with frustrated love. I can't do what he's asking. I just can't. I can't make the words. I just yawn my maw over and over, like a dog trying to rid himself of a foul flavour. Finally, I clasp his head and pillage his mouth with my own, sucking his breath away, gasping and sighing silently as my tongue and lips and teeth try to convey what he needs to hear. "Oh… Oh, God," he cries. "Yes, Jamie! I know you love me. I know. I know, Baby…"

No fewer than ten minutes later, his hands stroking the sweat-soaked hair curling around my ears, Tammy asks me, "Will you marry me?"

Before I even feel them, tears are streaming down my face. I nod so energetically that my head might fly off. I open my mouth again, struggle to say, "Yes! Yes! I'll marry you!"

I just don't seem to have any strength in my throat to bring my voice to life. Like a fish out of water, I gape and suck in deep, ludicrous breaths, trying to get the air, the power, the muscles together. At last, in a rough whisper, "Y-yes."

Tammy smiles, laughs tearfully. "Jamie. You talked!"

I nod. The single, stuttered word has taken every bit of power I've had, for the moment. I huff and puff and open my mouth again, but it takes almost another full minute before I croak, "I… love… you… Tammy."

Still no actual voice, just a whisper.

It's good enough for Tammy. He grabs me and bear hugs me, forgetting my still-sore ribs. We make love again, and I replay the words over and over in my mind, "We're going to be married! We're going to be married!"

On the calendars in our home, I write, "Get married!" on February 14th, Valentine's Day.

There is one remaining obligatory yet unwanted event in our

344

timeline, casting a dark, monolithic shadow: the trial.

Yvette Lard-Ash doesn't have to suffer a public examination. She's plea-bargained her way down to two and a half years for sending Tammy the video, but when it's discovered that she's gone and made *copies*, nearly twenty copies, that have been passed around at parties, given to known "Christian" gay-haters who no doubt watch the pornography, get off on it, and then sit in judgment of *me*, the D.A. is so mad she's foaming at the mouth, and she slaps Lard-Ash with no less than six years.

Cantrell is the one who's committed the most crimes, introducing the pornographic tape to Yvette, and participating as the most important player in my abduction. After all, if you have no driver, you have no kidnapping. Not to mention the fact that he obstructed the investigation by not admitting outright that he was at The End that night, that he knew the whole plot against us. His being a cop on top of it all has been a major embarrassment to the Sommerville Police. He's been fired without any severance pay, and all he has to look forward to now is the trial and a long prison term.

Benny pleads guilty to being indifferent. He admits, "Yeah, I knew they were going to do it, and no, I didn't care. He deserved to die and I wish they had killed him!" He gets off pretty light, with a year in jail. Then his lawyer says that isn't fair, and when all is said and done, Benny only has a year of community service.

If I had any kind of power, I'd fix them. I'd fix them all.

But…

Do something with this, Jamie, Lloyd said. Take this and do something.

Alright then. I won't waste my time on revenge. I may have a few battle scars, but they didn't win. They didn't kill me.

I have neither the time, nor the desire, to dwell on the unfairness of it all, how my trauma will outlast even the longest sentence passed down to those fuckers. We're getting married. We're not waiting for the trial to be over.

I want to live *now*.

On the plane to Vancouver, I unbuckle my belt and droop my head and hands over the back of my seat. Watching Stacy watching the snowy Cascades thousands of feet below, I love her with all my might and silently adopt her as my sister, once and for all. I write to her, *You're giving me away*.

She blinks away tears of joy and nods, rendered as mute as I am. Tammy tells Ma, "Okay, then you're walking me down the aisle then, Mom." And of course, Ma starts boo-hooing happily.

When we're checked into our modest, mid-range hotel room, we ask Ma to entertain Tammy while my sister and I steal away to the shops. I have to get Tammy a ring.

And it has to be *perfect*.

forty-three:

tammy
(getting married, february 14)

We fly to Vancouver, B.C., accompanied by Mom, Stacy, Patti, Deanna, Sylvia and her partner Alice, Mr. Bloom and his wife, Mrs. Cooke (dear old lady!), Marilyn (Jamie's friend from work), and my boss from the Davis station, who I invited, but was pretty sure couldn't come. We're surprised and pleased that these people, most of whom are only acquaintances or business associates, plunked down money out of their own pockets to join us.

And unbelievably, from our old church, one of the assistant pastors shows up, a guy who has always been friendly and receptive to me in the past. Since we've been left thin-skinned and wary by Jamie's near-death ordeal, we think he's gotten wind of our wedding and has come to condemn us, but he hasn't. "I want to celebrate this with you. I don't condone what was done to Jamie, and I'm not here to preach. I have a cousin who is gay, and I love him very much. You and Jamie were always a part of our family, in my opinion. I'm sorry that others have taken a different view."

He's so nice. We would ask him to officiate, but we didn't know he was coming and we already have a judge.

We *do* have friends. There *are* good, supportive, decent people in the world.

After getting my approval, Mom has also invited Aunt Sharon and my cousin Natalie. My cousin, who once made me green as Vulcan blood with jealous hatred. How can I face her, after I hated her so much just for being born? How can I ever stop hating myself for butchering her Barbie dolls? How can I live with myself after seeing Uncle Price messing with her and doing nothing?

Does she know what I'm guilty of?

Does she remember?

Does she wish me well, or does she hate me?

Outside our hotel room, I gingerly approach her and say, "Hello."

She looks away and I feel my stomach drop like a bomb. But she does say, "Hello," back. We talk. She wishes me well. I give her a delicate hug. She hugs me back.

I'm going to make amends. I'm going to. It's too late to do anything about Uncle Price. Aunt Sharon says she had to put him in a nursing home in Elk Grove just a few weeks ago because he was leaving the burners going on the stove and nearly setting their home on fire, and he thinks Natalie is his wife, not his daughter.

But it's not too late for me to have a relationship with my cousin. I doubt she remembers me standing there watching her dad molest her. She was only a baby then. But maybe Aunt Sharon knows that I hurt Natalie's Barbies. Maybe Aunt Sharon put two and two together and knew I was the reason some of the dolls came up missing.

One day, maybe I'll forgive myself for that, and for not reporting Uncle Price. Jamie says I was only a boy, and that I didn't know how to assert myself and have Price stopped. But I'm an adult now, and I still feel like I should have done something.

It's true. I'd rather feel bad. I'd rather feel the guilt. I'd rather feel like shit about something I did or didn't do, than be like Uncle Price, just going along, never knowing the damage he's done to us kids.

348

Thank you God, for changing me, for never letting me become more vicious than I already was, for making me aware of the wrong in what I did. Thank you for helping me. God, thank you for everything!

Late in the afternoon the day before our wedding, as a gift to Jamie, I take him to a professional photographer down the street from our hotel, and we have private photos taken of us naked, wrapped only in diaphanous white satin.

Jamie is apprehensive. I can see the memories in his eyes, the way he looks at the man behind the camera. "This isn't pornography," I inform him gently. "These are portraits, private portraits, of you and me. And the only ones who will share them are you and me."

"Don't pose," the photographer says as he adjusts his settings and zooms. "Just be yourselves. Just do your thing."

I drape the sheet of white satin, so snowy pure that the folds and shadows appear light blue, over Jamie's head. "Little White Riding Hood," I chuckle, kneeling naked before him and listening to the hisses and clicks of the camera. Then I pull it away from him and wrap the gossamer fabric around myself like a cloak. A single picture is snapped of Jamie, standing naked before me, shivering, so vulnerable and beautiful it makes my heart (and other places) ache. I wrap my arms and the satin around his body and pull him to me until he's sitting on my lap, his cool buttocks against my hot thighs. We kiss, nuzzle our noses, gaze deeply into each other. My lips drift over the graceful, pale curve of his neck as he stares into the camera for one photo. We go on kissing until we begin to make out. The photographer exclaims as he leaps back and forth, "Beautiful! Beautiful! You're a gorgeous couple. Very beautiful. Beautiful shot!"

The photos are so intimate, so sexy, so beautifully done, that I hire the guy to do our wedding pictures too.

"Look at you," I croon to Jamie that evening. My favourite shot is the one where I'm kissing his neck and he's looking right into the lens. Every line so clearly etched, every curve caressed by the lens. And those eyes! Lord have mercy.

Me?! You're spectacular, writes Jamie, staring at the glossy images. *I don't think our wedding pictures will be <u>this</u> good, even if it's the same dude. Even if you're a <u>vision</u> in that tux!*

"How can you hate looking at yourself in a mirror, or in a picture?! How can you feel ashamed? How can you feel dirty? *Look* at you!" I groan. "You're so gorgeous. Damn, these pics are making me hard. I think I'm going to have to pin you down on that bed before I can make an honest man of you tomorrow!"

I pause before soberly adding, "I did this for you, Jamie. I did this so you could see how wonderful you are. I don't *ever* want you to feel dirty about yourself again."

He scrawls, *I don't feel dirty. Except in a <u>good</u> way.*

In spite of how the photos arouse us, we somehow manage to abstain from sexual gratification the whole night before our wedding, taking titillating pleasure instead in acting like two chaste virgins who have never known one another. I stay with Mom in one room while Jamie stays with Stacy in the other.

Yeah, right! We all crowd into one suite for half the night, watching movies on TNT, ordering in three loaded pizzas, drinking beer and soda, munching on nacho chips, burping, farting, guffawing loudly (all except Jamie, who whisper-laughs) and gabbing about how nervous we are about the wedding.

I'll probably trip and fall right on my face, Jamie writes to me.

"I'll probably rip an extra loud cheer the minute I get up there… all this shit I'm eating!"

Aunt Sharon snorts, and I'm not sure if she's laughing or disgusted. Natalie giggles.

"Oh, Tammy, for pity's sake," Mom protests.

"Pizza? Bean dip? Beer?" I howl. "I didn't even think to bring any Beano with me!"

"It's going to be fun, no matter what," Stacy says, her mouth full of pizza. "We'll all no doubt be honking like seventy-six trombones!"

In the morning, we split into two teams. Jamie, Stacy and Natalie vamoose to their room to get ready for our one o'clock ceremony. Mom and Aunt Sharon fuss with me over my hair, my teeth, a single zit which, thanks to the pizza, has sprouted on my chin overnight, my black tux and how to tie the perfect bow at my throat.

"He sure is a pretty thing," Aunt Sharon remarks when I ask her if she likes Jamie. "If I was about thirty years younger... He's a nice boy. I like him."

"When I first found out about you and Jamie," Mom murmurs as she works with the tie, "I thought it was weird, I just couldn't picture it—you being in love with another boy. Then, the day he woke up, I saw how he looked at you and you looked at him. It was the sweetest thing I'd ever seen."

My eyes burn and my throat tries to close. I pull my mother to me and whisper, my voice thick with emotion, "I love you, Mom." She nods, begins to cry. Aunt Sharon stands aside sheepishly, but I grab her. "Get over here."

It feels so good to be loved for who I am. It feels so good to have a family. I'd thought I didn't need these people, but I was wrong. I do need them. I've always needed them. They were there for us when Jamie was attacked. They're gonna be here when Jamie and I get married. They're going to be here when we need them. They're going to make us strong.

Just as Jamie does, these people make me real. They make me *me*.

We have an outdoor ceremony at a modest chapel only three blocks from the hotel. The patio is completely shaded, and there's still snow smashed up against the fence. It's almost too cold for what Jamie is wearing, a beautiful white shirt, as snowy as the satin we took photos with, and white jeans.

As I wait for my cue to march with Mom, my boss hugs me. "My son is gay. We had a fight when he came out to me three years ago, and we haven't spoken since... I said things I shouldn't have, but I still love him. I want to call him." He struggles to keep his voice steady. "How do I call him, Tam? How do I tell him that I'm sorry, and that I love him for who he is? I'm so afraid he'll cuss me and hang up."

"You just gotta take that chance," I tell him. "Do it. I'll bet he wants to talk to you just as badly."

We have family that has nothing to do with blood or heredity. It's such a wonderful, happy day for me, but I'm sad too. I'm sad that Ray and Lydia were people we never really knew. They won't be sharing this important day with us. Instead, they're going to jail. I'm sad because my biological dad is ashamed of me, ashamed of the way I live and love, and doesn't care to know me. I'm sad because if I had stayed in town instead of moving to L.A., I would have known Lloyd as the dad I never had. I feel like he's up there watching us as Mom walks me down the aisle. When I see Jamie and Stacy coming, I almost lose it. He looks like a spectral waif in all white, his big, wide eyes set off by eyeliner and mascara, his plump lips lightly painted in an earthy, rosy-brown. He got his hair cut a little before the wedding, and his honeyed locks are flowing and curling softly just past his ears.

Stacy and Natalie, who also has a pretty voice, sing our wedding songs for us: "A Groovy Kind Of Love" and Elton John's "The One".

I've written out my vows to him. "You and I have been through hell and back over the past few weeks, over the past sixteen years... I know we can do this. I *know* it. I know I can love you forever, whether we're rich or poor, healthy or sick, for better or worse, whether you're sweet or in a foul mood... I can love you."

Jamie cries because the judge has to read his vows. When he slips the ring he got me, a simple, wide gold band, over my finger, I cry too. Later, I take it off and read the tiny inscription:

To my husband, my friend, my lover, my soul-mate. My dream has come true, because you love me. I'll love you forever, Jamie.

I've given him a ring too, of course, but my real gift I want to give him tonight. It's something I've wanted to do *for a long, long time*.

I'm as patient as I can be, but when the sun goes down and they're still hanging around our room, I have to shoo Mom and

352

Stace out. There's no point in trying to be demure, so I just say, "Mom? Stace? Go home!" They chortle and stare from me to Jamie. "Let's go eat!" Mom says to Stacy.

"Sounds good to me!" Stacy chirps. "Sure you two don't want to come along?"

"No," I answer for both of us. I see the anxiety creeping into Jamie's eyes already.

I temper my impatience, trying to be forbearing for as long as it takes for me to talk him into letting me do it. And I know it's going to take a while. "I don't blame you for being nervous," I growl as I slip my arms around him from behind. "I'm planning on giving you a night you won't forget." I turn him around in my arms and he shyly touches my tie, still tied in its perfect bow. The tiniest brush of his fingers against my neck makes me shudder. Slowly, we take off each other's clothes. I can feel my eyes smouldering like coals as I stare at him.

It's like he is a virgin all over again as he plants both hands on my chest and tries to put some distance between us. "I want to taste you, Jamie. I want to taste you tonight, every part of you. You know what that means, don't you?" He quivers as I nibble his neck, but I feel the struggle.

"Please, Jamie, let me. Let me do this for you. Let me show you how *wonderful* you are."

Only if you let me do it to you first, he scribbles on his notepad.

"I'll let you do it to me, then you'll say you're too tired to let me do it to you." I argue.

You've given me more gifts than I've given you, he insists. *Let me give you my gift first.*

I don't argue. After all, I'm a man. What man do you know who would refuse a blow job? Sigh! Except *Jamie*?!

By the time he's finished with me, I'm panting and wheezing, spent, and very happy, unsure of whether or not I'll be able to muster up the oomph I'm going to need for him. I've never gone down on a man before, but this is something I want as much as my next breath.

And of course, he tries to back out. *If you're tired, you can do it some other time. I don't mind*, he scrawls dubiously.

Yeah, uh-huh! He wouldn't mind if I *never* did it to him.

I'd say, *Oh, he's so unselfish... to be willing to suck me off and then forego being sucked off by me.*

But that's crap.

He's afraid, that's all it is...

I've *got* to show him what he's missing.

I want to take him to a place he's never been.

We end up having a terrible episode with him locking himself in the bathroom and crying. I coax and encourage him for at least half an hour before he begins talking in a croaking frog's voice about feeling like a child molesting pervert.

From my side of the bathroom door, I gently scold him, "You're *not* a child molester. I've seen *your* soul too, Jamie. You would never hurt a child. You're not evil, you're a good, beautiful person..."

"Am I talking?!" he suddenly cries.

"Yes," I answer. "You're talking."

He bursts out of the bathroom and throws his arms around me, and I exhale in relief as I tenderly lay him down on the sea-green satin comforter on our king-sized hotel bed. "Do you want your blanket?" I ask him. He nods, frightened into immobility again, supine, his hands raised over his face as if to prepare for an attack, or to cover his eyes like he does whenever I attempt something sexual he's afraid of.

Well, he's letting you do this, I tell myself. *He might be scared, but he's trying. He's trying to make you happy. That's* something.

I hand him his blue velour blanket. "Do you want it under your bottom?" I ask softly. He nods, and I lift him and slide it into place. He grasps a piece of the velour softness in each hand, holds on for dear life.

"I can talk to you all through this, Jamie," I whisper. "I don't want you to be afraid. The last thing I will ever do is hurt you."

He nods, tears slanting towards the green pillowcase.

Remembering the lessons I've secretly taken from him every time he's given me head, I nibble and kiss my way up and down his body, slowly. There's no rush. "We have all night," I tell him in a smoky whisper. His body shakes as I gently bite his

354

nipples, kiss his belly, feeling the muscles jerking and quivering under me. I divert from my due south direction to taste the pale silk of his inner thigh, the soft blonde hairs tickling my lips. "Okay, now remember, I'm not going to hurt you."

And I go for him, gently, softly. He's so pretty down there, so firm yet so soft, the very tip of him flaring out, like a roseate mushroom, the warm, frenzied blood congregating readily. His mind is reluctant, but his body can't argue and it can't hide from me. I can sense the tiny seedlings germinating within him as I kiss him, like I kiss his mouth, my tongue gently dabbing and sponging over the little cluster of nerves just beneath the pink velvet tip. My own cock throbs joyously against the crook of his knee, in time to an entrancing, ethereal music playing, vibrating in my soul like a bell.

I hear him sobbing. "It's okay, Baby," I sing between soft, sucking kisses. "God made you, Jamie. He made *every part* of you. No part of you is dirty. He made the human body to *enjoy* sex." I suck hard against the side of him, suck his skin against my teeth. His lungs sob deep. I feel him tense like a rope pulled taut. "In fact, this is the holiest place on your body. Did you know that, Baby?" I taste the clear, salty nectar weeping from him like tears. It's sublime. "That's why you thought you were dirty, *because they sinned against you.* You're delicious, not dirty. You're beautiful, Jamie. You're the most beautiful thing I've ever seen in my life."

Now my mouth closes over him to take him deeper, and I say no more, too busy revelling in the taste, the heat, the *life* of him. *He's alive!* I cry inside. *He's alive...* the way he fills my mouth and throat, the way he pulses and swells as more blood fills him, finds its way into the millions of tiny caverns and crevices of him. I feel his hands playing with my hair. I hear his hoarse sobs of anguish and rapture as I increase both the tempo and the vigour of what I'm doing. He squirms and claws at me as my tongue flickers savagely over that little bundle of nerve endings. I hear him beginning to whisper, "Please... please... please... please, Tammy..."

"Please what?" I ask sweetly, menacingly, loathe to stop, my mouth watering the instant I release him to ask the tiny question.

He lies below me, chanting, sobbing, "Please... please... please... please..."

"I want you to cream right into my mouth," I snarl gently, my greedy tongue lapping, dragging, curling around him. "Come on, Baby. I know you're ready. Come on. Come inside my mouth..."

He pants and convulses and silently wails as I work him over. He arches his back so high he nearly snaps his spine. "Please Tammy... Please..." And he begins to scream shrilly as I gulp the honeyed essence of him down in warm, hungry, luscious swallows.

When the last weak little spurt of semen has left his body, I release him and hastily crawl up to gather him up against me.

I had known he'd cry the minute I'd decided I wanted to do this to him, *for* him. Now I hold him. I don't ask questions, I don't tell him not to cry. It's taken real courage for him to allow himself to be this vulnerable with me, and I'm so humbled and awe-struck I can't speak right now anyway.

I let him cry as long as he needs to, and finally, he raises his head, shakes it sadly.

"Are you okay?" I whisper, brushing my lips against the damp tangles of his hair.

He looks around frantically for his notepad and scribbles, *I'm trying, Tammy. I'm trying to get over what they did.*

"You're *not* your father," I tell him as sternly as if I'm talking to a child, maybe a little too sternly. "You are not a dirty perverted creep who rapes children! You are my husband. *That's* who you are! God, Jamie. If only you could see yourself the way I see you. If only you *knew*..."

With an aghast frown, he touches his finger to my chin. "What?" I ask softly. When he brings it away, I see he's dipped it into a dollop of creamy, iridescent sperm that's still sticking to my chin. I take his finger, my eyes on his, and suck it into my mouth, onto my tongue, moaning at his pungent taste. "I'm telling you, you're not dirty, you're delicious. And you're mine." I catch the tender pad of his finger between my teeth and bite softly, smiling at him. A gasp escapes him, and his eyelids

356

droop almost sleepily, over eyes glazed with pleasure, the pupils opening, dark and languid. His breath comes in warm, excited bursts. His perfect mouth quivers east and west into a smile that makes my cock throb harder as he pulls his hand away and attacks me so wildly I don't even have time to utter a cry of surprise. His tongue plunders my mouth as we roll all over the bed. I barely have time to arrange his soft little blanket under his ass before his legs are spread-eagle, his body bent into a "V" beneath mine as I fuck him like a jackhammer.

He screams again as we come simultaneously, his voice feral and keening. Our orgasm lasts a small eternity, leaving my cock both tingly numb and chafed and hyper-sensitised.

Jamie lies in my arms, mute again, but smiling so blissfully, so radiantly, that I know there's hope for him.

After a little bit, he writes in his notepad, *I thought I was the wife*, and giggles in his throaty way.

forty-four

jamie
(getting married,
february 14 and 15)

Our budget isn't very big, and after we book our flight, the hotel, and the chapel, after we order our cake, lemon flavoured, with white and yellow buttercream frosting, we're practically out of money.

"Leave it to me," says Ma.

"Me too," adds Stacy, and they hurry down to a cute little market where they buy enough chicken breasts to feed fifteen to twenty people twice, three big loaves of sourdough, some fresh veggies, sour cream, sprigs of rosemary and other herbs, butter, and three bottles of pink and peach champagne. "Okay, *now* we're broke," Ma laughs.

You guys are so great. You shouldn't have done all this, I tell them when they're done slicing and sautéing and cooking. *You shouldn't have spent all your money.*

"You'll change your mind when you taste it," says Stacy.

We use the nice copper pots and pans and casserole dishes from our hotel rooms to carry the food in. The menu is chicken breasts cooked in butter and sour cream with rosemary and baby portabella mushrooms, sourdough toast with garlic butter, a simple mix of cooked vegetables, and cake and champagne.

The chapel is decorated in red and yellow roses and white ribbons and bows. Stacy wears her prettiest red dress and sparkly red shoes, like Dorothy's ruby slippers, as she takes me to Tammy. Ma, wearing a dress printed in red and black flowers and leaves, sits down, having delivered her son to the front.

Tammy's in his black tux, and I'm too nervous to process how good he looks until we look at our wedding photos later on. I wear white tweed pants and a bright white filmy shirt, its collar lapels embossed with flowers, butterflies, and other pretty things in white thread.

Stacy gives me to Tammy, then she and his cousin Natalie, twenty-three years old with dark hair and emerald eyes identical to Tammy's and Ma's, sing the songs we picked for the wedding. The girls' voices are gorgeous, and they both look beautiful, Stacy in her red frock and Natalie in a simple little black spaghetti strap dress.

I thought this would be the happiest day of my life, but I hate this. I can't say my vows to Tammy. I have to let the judge say them and all I can do is nod. It doesn't feel right, and my emotions are so tangled up that I angrily stamp my feet. It's pure stress, and I'll be glad to have it over with, at least *this* part, standing in front of our family and friends, my voice lodged, my head pounding, my heart slamming, my bladder suddenly full.

Tammy's eyes never avert from mine as he recites his hand-written vows. My ears are ringing. I hear people laughing lightly… I just smile, my eyes darting around like those of a trapped rabbit. I don't hear the judge telling us we're married. I wanted to hear those legal words out of his official mouth. Suddenly Tammy's bowing to kiss me. My lips are numb again. I hardly feel it. We turn to face our family and friends, having just crossed the line in the sand from Single-pore into Marriedland. My knees are like water. I need to sit down.

Marilyn comes up to me afterward and hugs me. "Angel, I'm so glad you found someone to love you. I always noticed the sadness in your eyes and I don't see that anymore. I think you will be very happy. You deserve happiness." She looks over at Tammy. "He sure is a good-looking babe," she exclaims. "You're lucky!"

She turns to my husband and says, "You take good care of this little angel. You be good to him."

"I will," Tammy promises.

We're both naked less than ten minutes after Stacy and Ma leave to go eat. I wish like hell we would have gone with them. Tonight, he wants to go down on me, he says, and he won't take no for an answer.

I don't want to hurt his feelings tonight. Tonight is our first night of married life.

Cold shivers run down my back as I sit gingerly on the still-made bed. Tammy sits close to me, expectantly, tentatively stroking my shoulder and kissing the back of my neck.

No. I'm not agreeing to this. I *can't*.

I don't want it.

I just plain don't *want* it.

I can go my entire life without this. I offer to do it to him first, easily convincing him by telling him that it's only fair I give him a gift first, since he gives and buys me twice as much as I do him. If I can tire him out, or myself, maybe I can get off the hook.

Nope. In spite of how happy Tammy is when I'm through, he's not going to forget it. Quietly, we bicker, Tammy with his voice, me with my stupid damn notepad.

I can't just miraculously erase my association of studded belts and glowing cigarette tips with what Tammy wants to do to me.

But he won't let up. "Please, Jamie. Please let me... Let me. I want to show you how beautiful, how wonderful, I think you are."

No! I write. *Please stop asking me, Tammy. Please. This is our wedding night. I want it to be beautiful.*

"It will be, Jamie, if you let me love you. Please..."

By this time, I'm crying. I'm not going to let Tammy have his way. I'm not going to put myself through that...

360

…and yet I still feel guilty.

And it makes me so angry.

At him.

I shove him away, run to the bathroom and throw up in the toilet. *Why can't he leave me alone about this?! Why is he doing this to me?!*

He's on the other side of the door, rattling the locked knob frantically. "Jamie! I'm sorry! Please let me in! Please let me in!"

I roll into a ball on the bathroom floor.

You're always crying, I think to myself. *You're always so sad. You're always so fucking* sad.

"Please, Jamie. I'm sorry! Come out. Forget about it. I won't make you if you don't want to, you know that. Come on, please. Come out, or let me in. Baby, please?"

Now he's crying again too, of course.

I'm not doing this to be *cruel* to him!

Why can't he *see*?! Why can't he *understand*?!

I remember the things he said to me the night I was attacked and left for dead. *"Let me love you. Let me care. Let me in. You haven't let me totally in."*

I recall the first time he had attempted to make love to me with his mouth, and I had screamed bloody murder, had curled my body up, such horrid images before me that I covered my eyes.

"Don't you trust me?" he had asked.

Trust.

Well, there it is. Do I trust Tammy? Do I?

I love him, yeah, but do I *trust* him?

Why did I marry him, if I can't put my trust into him?

"Jamie? Jamie?"

It's not about Tammy, I argue with myself.

Are you a porn star? they had asked that night. *Do you like fucking your daddy?*

No! I had never *liked* it!

But you're such a good actor… could have fooled me.

I was doing what Mommy told me to. I didn't want her to…

"Jamie, please open the door…"

But she did, didn't she? She did it anyway. She hit you and burned you every single time. You did exactly what she wanted, how she wanted. You did it perfectly, like a little porn star. So if you knew she was going to hit you anyway, why did you do it?

Because I always thought, maybe this one time, she'll hug me and kiss me and tell me what a good boy I am.

She never did. *All I ever wanted was for them to love me.*

Tammy pounds harder on the door. "Come on, Jamie! I'm sorry! Please!"

You were nothing to them. You were garbage. That's all you were. That's all you'll ever be. Don't ever decide to have a child... don't even bother. You'll just become your own daddy.

No. I could never do that to a child! I'd rather die!

It runs in families, that kind of thing...

I'd rather have been beaten to death! Why did they have to find me?

Because I prayed. I prayed for you to come home to me.

Maybe you shouldn't have... I don't want to live if I'm a bad person... I don't want to be a child molester! I'd rather die!

Stop it!

I mean it!

You're not a child molester.

I'm not talking to the Accuser anymore. *Every time you ask me to let you do that, I feel like I'm going to become Daddy.*

You're not him!

I can't believe him. I can't trust him. He's only saying these things to make me feel better, to trick me into giving in to him. *How do I* know? *How do I know I don't have the same compulsions, the same perversions? I'd rather die than hurt a child! I'd rather go through it again* myself *than do it to anybody.*

That's why you're not him. I've seen your soul too, Jamie. You're not an evil person, you're not. You're good.

I stand up, wipe my eyes.

You promise?

I promise, Baby. Open the door. Let me in.

I blink. *Tammy?*

Yeah.

Am I talking *to you?*
Yes, you're talking.
I'm talking?!
You are.
I *am*!

I open the door to him, walk right into him, throw myself against him, cling to him. His arms rope around me, crush me against him. His lips ravage mine. "Jamie… Jamie… Jamie…" Immediately I'm sinking, drowning. He kisses my neck, my chest, my tummy. I'm throbbing, I'm erect, I'm burning in a sea of magma. "Tammy… Tammy… Tammy… Ohmygod!"

But as soon as I realise he still wants to do it—that thing I don't want— I begin to freeze.

I can't let it go. The fire crystallises as Mommy's gravelly voice sweeps over me. *You're a dirty boy, Jamie. You're filthy dirty…*

Now my body won't respond. I'm cold, numb, flaccid, lifeless. I'm not even shivering. I'm cold as death.

Don't turn off your feelings, Jamie, he had pleaded on Christmas Eve in my living room, frantically searching my eyes…

I'm frozen, unresponsive. "Please… Jamie, please…"

He kisses my cold, numb lips. Come back… come back… please…

I'm afraid, I whisper, paralysed, cold, in the dark.

Look at me, Tammy whispers.

I can't. Even my eyes are frozen.

Please… look at me, Jamie.

I let out a small breath. It's frozen too.

Look at me, Baby.

His voice… God. I can't ignore it. I never could! My eyes stab into his angrily. "*What*?" I sob. "What do you *want* from me?"

"I want you to let me in. Let me in…"

"I have!"

"More, Jamie, more. I want to be so close to you that you'll never, ever be afraid again. I want to erase every horrible thing they did."

"You won't!" I hiss.

"Let me try, Baby, please!" His eyes delve deeply into me. "Please," he whispers. "Let me try. Let me try…"

I'm paralysed. I can't move. To reject him. To permit him. *I can't move. I can't move…*

"Push me away," he croons, and my breath deserts me.

"Go on. Push me away," he repeats.

"I can't," I cry in anguish. "I can't!"

I can't help it. He sees my eyes, how much I adore him, how much I want to let him do whatever he wants, how much I want to let go of this terror. His voice melts the steel around my heart. His lips touch mine, Mommy disappears and the flames leap again. Tammy's hands clasp around my ass as he grinds against me. "You're so beautiful," he sobs as our mouths come together noisily in those sexy, nakedly honest, scorching closed mouthed kisses. Slowly, my body warms, and the same crushing lust-love that has forever kept me at Tammy's mercy makes my tummy liquefy, my thighs tingle, my pelvis clench, my asshole pucker, my cock swell and throb in time with my wildly beating heart. His whispering pleas caress me inside, "Please, Jamie. Let me love you, let me… let me show you everything I feel. Please… please…" I gasp as he lifts me into his arms, beyond helpless and struck dumb again, the only sounds from my lips being voiceless, feeble sobs as he carries me to the big bed and lays me down. "I'll talk you all the way through this, Jamie. I'll help you. Just please… please… let me show you… let me…"

And so I lie, flat on my back on my security blanket, motionless and dizzy with desire and terror that are equally relentless. My body screams for his lips, but the fear is right there, tainting it, the fear that once my body does what Tammy wants it to do, I'll be ashamed… I'll be strangled with shame.

He loves you, I tell myself as his lips begin to travel down my body. *He's not trying to hurt you.*

He's not your mother.

He's not your father.

He's not you. He's not a child at all.

And you're not your father.

You are you and he is he. This is love. This is your miracle.

This is the miracle you've always hoped for. Tammy loves you.

Slowly, I try to feel what Tammy feels. I try to feel the love he has for me. I try to feel why he thinks this is so important.

Don't turn off your feelings, Jamie, Tammy whispers.

I try to feel.

I begin to feel.

The horror that has kept my skin numb and asleep begins to thaw a little.

I begin to come out of my own head...

...and I feel it, his hot, moist breath melting the frost, searing my skin, his voice, teasing, demanding, promising, sending bolts of lighting crackling through every re-awakened, quivering nerve. In spite of how hot I burn, my body, alive and shining, shivers uncontrollably as I lie beneath him, writhing, helpless, lost, my eyes closed tight.

"You're not dirty," he rasps as he swipes his rough tongue tirelessly over me, his hunger rapacious, terrifying. "You're delicious. You're beautiful... you're mine. You're so precious to me, Baby. You're so wonderful, you don't even know. You have no *idea* how much I adore you..."

The dam inside my heart blows apart. The pillow under my head becomes soaked as I suck sobbing breaths into my lungs.

"Don't be afraid of your body, Baby..."

I'm being loved, I'm being worshipped, I'm being controlled, I'm being possessed. I'm completely his. I'm afraid. I feel it coming, and I'm afraid. I'm so afraid and I love it... I love it...

"This is the holiest part of your body, did you know that, my Baby? Did you know that? No wonder you've felt so dirty. They sinned against you. They tried to make you ugly, like they are..." He kisses and gently sucks my most secret flesh, and under the pounding waves, I cry for mercy, but he doesn't hear me. He's talking again. "They didn't win. They'll never win, Jamie. They can't, because you'll always be beautiful. You're *so* fucking beautiful..."

They'll never win, I cry inside. *They'll never win...*

I struggle to hold onto that as Tammy stops talking and his mouth becomes more loving, more ardent, more relentless. The sheets scrape roughly against my back as I dance and twist and buck into his mouth. I can feel it breaking… something is breaking… as my orgasm begins to come to the surface, ready to pull me up through the whitecaps on this boiling, churning sea I'm lost in.

Why?! I ask furiously. *Why did they do it to me?! Why?!*

There's no answer to that. And I've known it for years. But I keep asking, don't I? I need to stop asking.

I need to let it go.

I want, I need, to wrest myself free…

Let it go…

A hot wave is rolling up my body, crashing onto the shore, into my voice. "Please," I begin to cry softly. "Please, Tammy… please? Please? Please?"

He sucks me hard, and the sound his mouth makes when it parts from me nearly ends me. "Please what?" he growls so silkily in his throat that I almost orgasm again. I lay beneath him, my chest heaving. I can't answer. I want his mouth back on me. I want it back. I can't believe how close I am to him while I'm inside of his mouth, how warm, how safe, how utterly *loved*. I can't explain this oneness. Where do I end? Where does he begin?

I'm afraid of this total loss of control, this possession he's taken of me. I'm afraid of what's breaking inside of me because when it's out, I'm going to shatter into a million sparkling pieces and be scattered all over the universe.

I don't want to surrender. I don't want to let it out, but how can I hold it in?!

You're not dirty, you're delicious. The sordid images seared into my brain my whole life long burn away brightly in the unbearable heat. "Please? Please? Please…" I beg as Tammy devours me like a lion savouring the pulsing blood of an antelope.

My body clamours for release, twists itself into knots, screams for an end to this horrendous, beautiful torment.

He takes his mouth off of me again, just long enough to say, "I want you to cream right into my mouth, Baby, come on… come on, Baby… I know you're ready. Come right into my

366

mouth..." His voice strokes me inside, fanning the already monstrous fire, then his mouth returns...

It breaks. I can't stop my body's response to his beguiling voice. I thrust, sobbing, my back arching painfully, my soul separating with a soft ripping sound...

...and floating, like an angel, above my flesh.

The chains snap from around my ankles.

Let it go... let it go... just let it go...

A brilliant light strobes before me, and I scream, hoarse and shrill, in agony and pleasure as my body empties itself into Tammy's willing mouth.

This is different. Usually when I come it's hard and quick, over with too soon, or slow and rich and wet, my entire pelvic region clamping, releasing, clamping, like our first time or the day he gave me my angel.

Right now I can't describe it, except it's not so much physical. It's all *feelings*. It's like everything is leaving me and I don't know if I am comfortable with everything I've ever known leaving me. All my fear, all my anger, all my hatred. It's seeping swiftly out of me. It's like pain, but it feels so good.

I slowly come back to myself, and, like the vulture that waits for a last dying gasp, it's there again as my body softens and my heart bridles itself from a gallop. It's there, hideous, hateful, persistent, the voice of Satan, the Accuser, the Liar. That's who it is. That's who it's always been:

You're dirty. You're nasty. You're just like your daddy...

They were Satan's disciples. They were doing Satan's work when they raped me. When they beat me. When they tortured me.

You're a pervert. You're dirty. You're just like him.

Shut up, Liar! I retort in a soundless screech.

I turn and tell myself, *He's a liar! He's the father of liars, remember?*

Tammy thinks I'm strong. And he's right... I'm strong...

But I'm not as strong as I'd like to be. I never *have* been as strong as I'd like to be. The visuals crowd in on me, corner me, queued up, raising their clubs, attacking, and all I can do is cower, cry, cover my eyes...

367

But then, Tammy is here. "Come on," he says, and he takes me and holds me and lets me cry. I cry for a long time, because it hurts.

It hurts to let it go.

But I have to. I have to let it go. Forever.

And I have to let Tammy love me.

He holds me close, talks to me. I feel the strong, solid thud of his heart against my cheek, and I know I trust him. Abruptly, I'm all over him again, like syrup on a hotcake, kissing him everywhere. He bends and folds my body like origami. My heels dig into his ass, pull him to me, and we laugh as he mounts me and fucks me like there's no tomorrow.

After hours of dozing, eating cold leftover pizza, and fucking our brains out, he finds me sitting out on the balcony at four o'clock the next morning. He asks me if I'm alright and I nod, *Yes*. "Can I come out there with you?" he asks. *Of course*, I nod.

Cooling tears are still dangling from my chin as he whispers, "Penny for your thoughts?"

I shrug. "I'll go get your pad," Tammy says. Then he halts just as he's about to open the sliding glass door into our room. "You're not going to *do* anything, are you?"

I can't believe he can still think that.

"I'll get your pad," he says again, and dashes inside, returning only a few seconds later, stumbling clumsily, nearly stubbing all ten of his toes on the heavy iron patio chairs, obviously terrified I'd thrown myself to the ground below. When I shake my head sardonically at him, the dam *he's* constructed over the past several weeks begins to crumble. "I'm sorry, Jamie… I almost lost you… twice!" He sits and pulls me into his lap, and we hold each other. Instead of writing, I force the words through my mouth: "I… love… you… Tammy."

Unable to speak another word, I scribble, *I'm crying because I'm so happy! I don't want to die!*

Tammy cries on. "My worst fear is losing you," he sobs.

You didn't lose me, I write. *I'm here.*

"I'm never lonely when you're close to me. I couldn't take it if I lost you…"

368

I'm the one who was attacked and left for dead, but Tammy was nearly killed too. I know that. As physically big and strong as he is compared to me, sometimes he seems the more fragile of the two of us.

"I'm here," I whisper, nuzzling my nose to his.

"Yes," he whispers back. "You're here."

I lost another kind of virginity tonight, I write.

"Me too," he sniffles. "Thank you, Jamie. Thank you for letting me in."

You know I love you. And I trust you, I add.

"You do, don't you?"

Yes. I lay my head on his shoulder and gaze over it as he gazes over mine. We each stare out into the sparkling skyline of Vancouver stretching up into the inky, starry firmament. We hear the whispers of early morning traffic. I feel a gentle, cold wind lifting and ruffling my damp hair. The gold band on my finger flashes in the dark.

forty-five:

tammy
(life goes on...)

...but I'm with Jamie. The trial, which is coming up in June, is in the way of us really *living*. We return home after our wedding, try to settle into domestic life. I go back to work at the UC Davis station with my show, my hours now from six to ten pm so I can be home at night with my husband, but I feel a restlessness. I want to do something *more* with my life. The job's been fun, but it seems I'm about more than just fun nowadays. I want to concentrate more on writing about animal cruelty, and focus a lot more energy than ever on the fight against it. I've read a lot of articles in the PETA magazines about the mistreatment of everything from snakes to ducks and geese, and I feel like I'm sitting and doing nothing about it.

Eventually, Jamie returns to Saint Paul's Hospital. His peers and superiors accept that sometimes he cannot speak (*I feel like my throat is <u>stuck</u>, it's so weak*, he's tried to explain to me.) and has to rely on a notepad or gestures to communicate with the staff and patients. But he, too, has felt a big sea change. *I want to work with AIDS patients*, he tells me. *I'm going to go into hospice nursing. I want to do something real—really help people. I don't feel like I really <u>help</u> people when all they did*

370

was break their leg skiing. He mentions a cat sanctuary on the coast again.

Deep in the wee hours one night, I begin to cry while feverishly typing out an article about an animal "hoarder" who was recently busted in Michigan. She had upwards of two-hundred cats and dogs living in squalor in her barn, attic and basement. They were crammed into cages, sometimes two animals in one cage with barely enough room to turn around. The cages were encrusted with filth and waste, and there were corpses in many of them. Several cats and dogs were covered in skin infections. Some were half-starved. Some were so far gone they had to be humanely put down.

Crying's not an unusual thing for me. I cry all the time when I hear bad things on the radio, or see them on the news. It's not just animals I care about. I cry over the poor little kids from Somalia who are being driven from their homeland by drought and al-Qaeda terrorists. I cry over the atrocities committed by the drug cartels. I cry over a lot of things that I never used to think twice about.

My heart is tenderised.

I still won't watch crush videos, but the other day, I was on a website, a good and sincere website trying to bring awareness to the world about this evil, and I saw a couple of still captures from a crush video—just still captures, not moving video, but they were horrible—a man torturing and murdering a puppy, oh God…

Why are these kinds of people allowed to live among the rest of us? Why are they allowed to live *anywhere*?! They should be taken far away from any living creature, put on an uninhabited desert island (get all of the animals safely away first!) and left to their own devices!

I usually weep quietly and then wipe my tears and press on, but tonight, it's just so overwhelming, all of it. It's like the weight of everything that's happened to us, the weight of evil in this world, is finally caving in on me, for real. I break down, sobbing all over Jamie, and he scribbles, *You've been so strong for me, but you have to take some time off. You've been doing so much*, he insists. I'm sitting up at night on the computer, researching, still writing articles for the Glendale shelter and Purrfect Peace, and now contributing my time to an animal rights group in Vacaville.

I'm overtired, Jamie says. I cry so easily and feel everything so intensely.

"Excuse me for caring," I snap at him quietly.

I know you care, he gently writes. *But you're going to make yourself sick and burnt out and useless if you don't take a break.*

"I know that," I mutter irritably.

All you can do is pray, Tammy, Jamie writes. *You can't be there for every single cruelty case. The world is too big and too evil. All you can do is pray about it.*

I sit and tearfully glower at my screen, trying to ignore him.

Let's go to Fort Bragg.

"Now?!" I exclaim.

Yeah, why not? We can be there by dawn. We can dig our toes in the sand, watch the sun come up.

I shrug carelessly, but the thought of the ocean is beginning to lift my ass out of that chair already.

You need pampering, he writes. *In two days, you'll be refreshed and ready to take this on again.*

God, I love him. It's like a second honeymoon. We sit on the beach, take deep breaths, let the cold, salt spray hit our faces, bury our toes in the sand, close our eyes, open our hands, and just let our bodies relax. After a while, we abandon our meditations and play in the surf. I pick him up and carry him out to where the breakers are curling into white foam and I toss him in. He leaps up at me and silently screams, *"It's cold!"* He tries to grab me and pick me up, but I'm too heavy, so he grabs my legs and shoves at me until I lose my balance and tumble in.

When we return to our motel, we take a warm shower and watch the sand swirl down the drain. Jamie obviously means to pamper me. He gently and firmly massages my feet, my back and my neck and shoulders, and his warm hands melt the tension away. He holds me close to him, softly kissing my face, whispering to me, making me relax. My eyes drift closed, and I dream sweet dreams. The motel room has blackout curtains, and

372

we spend most of the day just sleeping, with the TV playing on low volume.

We wake up in the middle of the night and make love. I beg him to top me. I want to feel him inside of me. I want to feel what he feels. I want him to feel what I feel. He shakes his head.

"Please, Baby."

He writes, *I can use my fingers*. And I accept.

He's very shy, because he has to look, really look at my body in order to use his fingers.

I remember watching Uncle Price molesting Natalie, an infant. I remember violating my dog Cotton. How wrong it was. I still feel so ashamed, so shitty, about all of it. Jamie says he'd rather die than ever become a child molester. I feel the same way. How could I have *done* that?

Children do weird things, Jamie said once.

I could never do it again. I will never, ever hurt or molest a child. Nor will I ever hurt or molest another animal. And I know it.

People *do* change. Children do grow and learn right from wrong. I have a conscience.

Jamie's movements are gentle, tentative... Is he thinking this is wrong? Is he worried that he's molesting me? Is he still having those fears about becoming 'Daddy'?

And I do everything I can to remind him that we are *not* our fathers; we are *not* our uncles. We are Tam Mattheis and James Pearce. We are two adult men. We are a loving, married, committed, consenting couple.

I do everything in my power to let Jamie know that I love him... that I trust him. I whisper and writhe my encouragement as his fingers speak to me.

This is intimacy.

We grow closer with every new experience.

I want him inside of me.

But he's not ready right now, he says.

It's okay.

It's going to take a while. It took him so long to let me do what I did on our wedding night. And I can wait for him, as long as it takes. I know one day, he'll make this latest wish of mine come true.

We talk and talk, and a new life, even beyond the completion of being married, calls to us. For weeks, we both sort of push the little voices into the backs of our minds.

But what are we *waiting* for?

Mom is always here, cooking, cleaning, fussing over both of us, and Jamie knowingly says, or rather writes, *She's lonely. Let's have her move in with us.*

"I don't think she'd want to give up that house... it's hers, free and clear."

But you're not there anymore, writes Jamie.

"I wasn't there for sixteen years and she did okay, didn't she?"

She's getting older. She's lonely, I can tell. She needs us. Besides, you said yourself you get along better with her than when you were a kid. She loves you, Tammy.

Unexpected tears gather in my eyes. I didn't realise how much I missed her when we were so estranged, how cut off I felt when she put that wall between us after what happened with Cotton.

Jamie's right. It's not easy to let go of your guilt. It's not easy to ignore the Devil when he taunts and torments you about things you can't change. You have to rebuke him every time he comes around to bully on you.

We've both been seeing Doctor Halliday once a week for therapy as a couple, and twice a week individually.

She's nice. It helps. We learn...

She suggests that an antidepressant might help me to better cope with the things I encounter in this difficult calling I've followed. I listen as she explains that it can help me focus without feeling so helpless and angry and tortured. "It won't make you stop *caring*," she stresses.

It's with some trepidation at first, because I worry about "needing" antidepressants, and I worry about the stigma, the ignorami who think they're for "crazy" people. But after six weeks or so, I can see that they're working, and I know neither Jamie nor I have any reason to be ashamed of them.

374

I've helped Jamie with his demons, and he's helped me with mine. I know I've said a million times that I wasn't sure there was a God up there looking after everything, but I'm changed. No, I'm not into radio preachers or people telling me my marriage is a sin, but I do believe in God. I've been raised to believe in Jesus Christ, and I still do in a lot of ways, but I admit, I'm not sure exactly what I believe in. I'm still learning. I only know that there is a God. I asked Him/Her to save Jamie's life, and Jamie was given back to me. I don't rely on manmade books to help me figure it out. To me, God is a Great Spirit, something beyond my knowledge, but always there for me, always with an answer, even if it's not the answer I want or expect.

I'm still in the process of forgiving myself for all the wrong things I've done. God forgives. Once I asked Him/Her to forgive me, He/She did.

Forgiving myself: that's harder.

In April, Jamie turns thirty-two, and we celebrate by going to The End.

He still can't bring himself to try and sing. *I can't!* he writes on his pad.

"Just try. Maybe your voice is just hiding. Maybe it'll come back!"

No! I can't sing!

"Maybe it will come back once you're up there!" My frenetic optimism kills him.

It won't just come back! It doesn't work that way!

So I get up and sing with Stacy, "Our Day Will Come" by Ruby and the Romantics, a sweet, antiquated tune that saves us from a night of sullen silence.

At the trial in June, Jamie's three attackers sit stone-faced and unrepentant as the damning evidence is presented one piece at a time: the blood-encrusted towel bar, the cotton rag with

Jamie's blood and saliva on it, copies of the fingerprints belonging to the three defendants that were found inside and outside of Jamie's car, a shredded black garbage bag with both Cantrell's and Ray's fingerprints on it, and the testimonies of Officers Howard, Lord, and of course Bloom, along with Mrs. Cooke's invaluable information about what she saw and heard in her doughnut shop early that morning.

In spite of our air-tight case against them, the defence tries to call my dad, Pastor Asshole, up to the stand, hoping to get him to speak about my violent past and the Cotton matter and smear me with the jury. They also try to mention the journals when Officers Lord and Howard are up there. Each time the defence brings up something completely irrelevant to steer suspicion away from their clients, the DA hollers, "Objection!" The judge ends up reprimanding the defence attorneys very severely.

Anyway, when Jamie gets up on the witness stand, which he has been dreading for months, he uses a computer keyboard and overhead projector because of his inability to speak. When he does open his mouth, the jury cringes at his screechy, tattered voice. I've never heard his voice sound so exhausted. They see the scar on his forehead and he lifts his shirt to show the dark pink scar sprawling from the left of his chest all the way into his middle back, where they had to repair the kidney Ray ruptured with the towel rack. The jurors get angrier and angrier as they read what Jamie's attackers said and did to him. His memories of that awful night are crystal clear, and I both appreciate and hate that as I watch him cry silently.

When he's not testifying, he'd rather not be there at the courthouse if he can avoid it. He thinks he will either cause a riot or be traumatised all over again by the details of the police testimony, or worse, be peppered with obnoxious comments by the hate-mongers roosting outside the Yolo County courthouse, those who support and condone what Lydia, Ray and Cantrell have done. Asinine as it sounds, it looks even worse. Demonstrators from various churches and groups can be heard shouting their hate-filled slogans, holding up signs saying the same. "God created AIDS to kill faggots!" "Death to faggots!" and of course, "The BIBLE says to put them to death!" Rage boils my blood as I think of Jamie, as I think of how these insane, evil idiots believe Ray and the others were right!

He stays with Mom, Aunt Sharon and Natalie at Mom's house, and spends all of his time cooking wonderful meals and desserts for all of us, and cleaning and scrubbing the house over and over, to thank all of us for being there for him.

But he does show up the day the jury returns with a "Guilty" verdict for all three of the kidnappers. I've asked to speak to the court, all my thoughts handwritten on a wrinkled page from a notebook of lined yellow paper, my hands trembling and staining the sheet with sweat:

"I met Jamie sixteen, almost seventeen years ago. We were in high school. It was on a Sunday in church. I wasn't much on church. I would rather be anywhere else, even having a root canal at the dentist's." The court laughs quietly. "The pastor asked everybody to hold hands together while we had prayer. Jamie was holding my right hand. I looked over at him, and there was just... something so familiar about him. Not long later, I began to remember who he was. He was the little boy I talked to in line at a grocery store when I was no more than four years old. I know that's hard to believe, but it's true. And now Jamie remembers that day too. I loved him and wanted to be his friend forever, but I didn't think I'd ever see him again. The supermarket was in Sacramento, and I lived in Sommerville. It's like hoping to run into the same person twice in Los Angeles or New York. But we met again in high school.

"I don't want to talk about how Jamie came to live in Sommerville. It's a very sad story, but what matters is, he was adopted by a very kind gentleman named Lloyd Tafford, an officer of the Sommerville police. He began high school when I was a senior, and that's how we met again. It really happened, and it shows me how God, or fate, or whatever, works.

"This is not the first time Jamie has been beaten because of who he is. It's not even the second. It's the third."

The jury shakes their heads, not having been privy to that knowledge. It was not allowed during the trial because it was "irrelevant". That's what the pond-scum defence lawyers thought, anyway.

"I was in love with him, but for reasons you can probably guess, I was afraid. I didn't have the courage I needed to be with Jamie, so I ran away. I couldn't face who I was—who I am. I deserted him and ran away from home, and I stayed away for sixteen years. Sixteen years squandered. I was a coward, simple and plain."

I'm not afraid to admit it now, because my cowardice is a thing of the past. I look outside now, and separated by a human buffer of the Davis Police are our supporters, local chapters of groups like GLAAD, PFLAG and the Human Rights Campaign. They are using bible scripture too. Their signs say, "God said thou shalt not judge", "God said thou shalt not kill", "Love thy neighbour as thyself", and the Golden Rule, "Do unto others…".

They're giving me strength. I'm feeling the strength in their numbers. I feel empowered. I feel alive. I feel proudly gay today. When I have a moment, I'm going to take Jamie, Mom, and Stace out there, and we're gonna let them know that we are so grateful for what they're doing.

"In December," I continue, my hand more steady around the yellow paper I'm clutching, "My mother fell and broke her pelvis and had to be hospitalised. It's how I met Jamie again. For weeks he took care of Mom and I fell in love with him all over again." My voice begins to catch. "No. I had never *stopped* loving him. I had never stopped thinking of him, all the time I was gone from home.

"We spent about a week—just a few days—together. We were happy. We were so happy, and it was like, this is meant to be. And then, they…" I point at Lydia, glaring at me through obsidian eyes, Ray sitting silent and expressionless and Cantrell, forever the ambiguous one, eyes flitting from me to the jury. "They grabbed him in his own front yard, tied him up, threw him into the trunk of his car, drove him out to an orchard on a dirt road, beat him with a broken towel rod, and left him to die.

"Let me tell you, really, who Jamie is," I sob, my eyes never leaving the three accused. "Because you haven't heard it yet, really. Jamie is absolutely the last, the very last person on this planet, who deserved to have that done to him! I'm not going to

378

go into detail—I keep arguing with myself about whether or not to tell you what this young man has lived through, but you need to know who he is. Forgive me," I say softly to Jamie, who is sitting in the back between Mom and Stacy. "When he was little, his parents abused him. You don't need to know the details, and I'm sure some of you know already. They abused and starved him, for seven years. Imagine. Seven years, from the time he was six till the time he was thirteen, seven years, of abuse, of starvation, of not even being let out of his room to go anywhere. They locked him in his room!

"Nobody knew he was alone," I shudder, vicariously feeling that for the first time. "He was alone, crying, begging, praying for someone to help him. None of us can begin to imagine what he went through, how he lost any hope for escape or rescue.

"Finally, somebody called the police. And Jamie survived. Officer Tafford rescued Jamie and adopted him.

"Jamie is a survivor. He's the strongest person I've ever met. He has to be, to put up with *this* kind of crap," I flick my hand at the defendants. "The only—the *only* consolation I have right now is that Jamie's attackers are going to be punished.

"A survivor. But that's not all Jamie is," I continue. "He's smart, funny, gentle, kind, loving. He loves to sing, but when this happened, he lost his voice. He loves to cook. He loves to take care of sick people. He loves cats. And he loves me. We love each other. He's my lover and the best friend I've ever had. We could have been together, all these years, but because certain people think that he and I are evil, that our love is evil, we've had to hide our feelings, deny our feelings. It isn't fair. It isn't right. I'll tell you something: evil is sitting right over there at that table. And they've put us through hell...

"And those picketers outside with their ugly signs saying, 'God kills fags'. How dare they think that kidnapping Jamie, beating him, and leaving him to freeze and bleed to death *pleases* God?! How can they have the gall to profess to be Christians? What sort of God do they worship anyway? Sounds to me like they worship Satan, not God!

"Look at those other signs out there. The God we know is about love, not hate. There were a few times when Jamie struggled, as I used to struggle, with whether or not our love angered God, and I am the one who reassured him that if it is God's will that we live alone and miserable and unhappy, that we deny the fact that we are soulmates, just because we're both men, then He isn't a God I care to worship.

"But I know better. I love God. And I believe God loves me, a lot! God made Jamie for me and gave him to me. God orchestrated everything, right down to how we met each other.

"I've spent much of my life believing that this world is a cold, dark, cruel and evil place. That's one of the hazards of my side profession, working with homeless and unwanted animals in shelters. It gets to me so much sometimes that I have to take breaks from working with them. It seems endless sometimes, the helplessness and hopelessness I've felt as I've written articles about animals who are homeless, beaten, stomped on by the world.

"The world is cold, and cruel, and evil, but when Jamie looks at me, when he touches me, or kisses me…" (I don't care what anyone thinks of my out-loud love for him.) "…when he simply talks to me, I know there is goodness and love in this world. I know it, and I know there is a God, because I see Him or Her in Jamie. I was a lonely child, and I was an even lonelier adult. Except when Jamie was there. I've never been lonely with him near me.

"Jamie is a person, a human being. He's somebody's son, somebody's brother, somebody's husband. He is my family, and my mother can say the same. He's her son. Try to imagine your own child, your own brother, your own husband or wife in Jamie's place. Don't insult Jamie by giving these murderers, because that's what they are, even if they failed to kill him, anything less than the harshest sentence allowable."

When we exit the courthouse, Jamie hugs me and croaks, "Thank you."

"I didn't say too much?"

"No," he whispers. "I loved what you said."

I curve my arm around him, shielding him from the surging reporters thrusting their microphones into his face, asking ridiculous questions. Mom and Stacy cover us from the front and back, screaming, "Let us through! We're done!"

The rallies of hatred with their heinous signs and venomous shouts don't escape Jamie. One deep, harsh scream rings out, "God spared you so you can repent of your filthy sins, you sodomite!" I hold him closer to me, eyes closed tight as I fight to hold down the volcano of rage, and my tears of fury and despair roll down.

But I hear Jamie say, in his croaking frog's voice, in audible, musical notes I've never before heard, "Look, Tammy!" He points to our supporters, who are shouting, "God hates hate!" and proudly displaying their rainbow-coloured signs. The spirit of love in this side of the courthouse crowd banishes my fear and fury as Jamie walks over to them, reaches out to them, shakes outstretched hands.

For a long time, they talk to him, and to us. Mom, Stacy and I introduce ourselves. Their hands clasp around mine and I feel more of my strength returning. I see tears in their eyes as people gently push back Jamie's hair and look at his healed scar. He hugs some of them. They call him a hero, and he says, "No, those men who called 9-1-1 and stayed with me, the police, the paramedics... they're the heroes. And this guy right here..." He grabs me. "He's a hero. He prayed for me to survive."

They surround us almost worshipfully, their eyes glistening as Jamie introduces his family. I'm his husband, Mom is his "Ma", Stacy's his sister.

By the time we get into our car and ride away, we've each gotten a long list of names, numbers and invitations to meetings and functions, all within driving distance.

We return home, to a life that mirrors the life before the attack.

Except that the phone rings several times a day with callers asking how Jamie is doing, and now and then, a caller who has nothing better to do than condemn us and call us hellbound faggots.

Except that Jamie is mute most of the time, with a fading scar above his right eye and a little gold band around his left ring finger that says, deep inside, in tiny, engraved fancy script:

I've loved you almost all your life, and I'll love you for the rest of your life and beyond. Your husband, Tammy.

We've changed so much, but at the same time, we haven't changed all that much. We're like an old couple. After we come in from work, we spend our evenings cuddling in front of the TV, wrapped in Lloyd's old quilt, the cats all around us, Mom sometimes snoring in one of the beige recliners, Stacy stretched out on the other. Sometimes we leave them, to be alone in our room. Sometimes we just sit there, watching really old shows on Antenna TV and MeTV. Stacy thinks we're ridiculous. She'd rather be watching *CSI* or *NCIS* or *Law & Order LA* or something made in the twenty-first century. Nope, Jamie has really been enjoying black and white episodes of *Bachelor Father* and *Dennis The Menace* while I've been into *Good Times*, *Sanford & Son* and *The Jeffersons*. Since Mom likes old stuff too (her favourites are *Maude*, *Three's Company* and *Married, With Children*), it's three against one.

In July, the jury gives Lydia, Ray and Cantrell each a sentence of twenty-five to life. Lydia will be going to the women's facility in Chino. Ray will be incarcerated up in Susanville and won't be eligible for parole until 2023. Cantrell will serve time in Corcoran, but his lawyer has appealed his sentence, saying that since he didn't swing the towel bar, he shouldn't be treated "so unsympathetically". The D.A. reports that the judge told Cantrell that most of his sentence is based on his being a pornography touting pervert. Eh! Neither Jamie nor I care much at this point. Even if Cantrell ends up getting a lesser term in prison, we won't worry. We'll be long gone.

Yes, we're leaving. We're not sure when, but soon. Someone drives by a week after the sentencing, and shoots through our living room window. A couple of days later, I find hate mail in our box, someone threatening to kill our cats. I keep all seven of them inside for the next couple of weeks. When I tell Jamie why

I don't want them outside, he's mad. *You should have told me!*

"I didn't want to upset you."

I'm not a baby!

I respond quietly and firmly. "No, but you've been through enough."

As boring as the snowless California winters are, they're preferable to the summers. It's been so muggy and sticky lately that I feel like I need to shower five minutes after I've taken one. Thank God Jamie has central air rather than a swamper.

But the weather's different one evening in late July. Jamie and I fall asleep on our couch watching one of our old VHS tapes, relieved by a pleasant San Joaquin Delta breeze coming from the south, wafting through the locked screen door. During *The Jack Benny Show*, Gisele MacKenzie begins to sing, "Smile, though your heart is breaking…"

In his sleep, Jamie begins to sing, "Smile…" Not in the deep, croaking, broken voice he's been using lately, but in his real voice, the one he lost seven months ago. "Smile, though your heart is breaking… smile… smile…"

"Baby, wake up," I whisper to him. "You're singing."

"Hmmm?" he asks sleepily.

"You're singing. You're *singing*, Jamie!"

"I'm singing?" He blinks slowly. "I was dreaming of Gisele MacKenzie, that we were watching her on *Jack Benny*."

"We were. You were singing in your sleep!" I can't stop the tears. His voice is back. For real. I know it. It's back!

"I was getting used to talking like Rochester," Jamie says.

I blubber, "I missed you so much, Jamie. I feel like you're really *home* now, like you're really back. I know I should have been grateful that you lived through what they did, and I was—I am—but I missed your voice so much!"

"Tammy?"

"What?"

"Please, let's have Ma move in with us. Ask her if she wants to. She'll say yes. She needs us. I love her. She and Lloyd should have been married. They would have been perfect together. The perfect parents…"

"What?" I laugh.

"They would have."

"I have absolutely *no* desire to be your brother," I cackle.

"When we move to the coast, we have to take her with us," says Jamie.

It bubbles out of me. "Jamie, why don't we move there now? Let's take Mom and the kids and just *go*! Let's just move to our cottage! What are we waiting for?!"

His eyes are shining. "And Tammy?"

"Yeah?"

"Can we get married again?"

I cup his chin. "You want to get married again?"

"Yes," he cries, tears beginning to shimmer. "I want to *say* my vows to you."

"Oh, Baby," I murmur, "You did perfect that day."

"No," he insists. "I want to do it right. I want to say them. It doesn't have to be formal. We can do it at the coast, after we move, on the beach, with just you, me, Ma and Stacy. We don't need a judge or anything. I just want to say them to you. I *need* to say them to you. I mean it, Tammy. I'm serious. Please, let's *please* get married again."

"Okay," I smile. "Let's do it."

forty-six:

jamie
(life goes on...)

We put Lloyd's and Ma's houses up for sale, and in the autumn following the trial and convictions of Lydia Rocha, Ray Battle and Steven Cantrell, we move to the coast, to Fort Bragg, where my beloved Lloyd's ashes were scattered. We all go, Tammy, me, Ma, her cat Tillie, and our seven kids, Ginger, Sam, Misty, Tigger, Wonka, Pepper and Teddy.

We find the sweetest old farmhouse, painted a soft grey-blue with a strange but not unpleasant dark coral trim, four bedrooms and two bathrooms, sitting on nearly twelve acres of gentle, rolling hills covered in waving golden grass. It's everything I imagined and more. Everything is delightfully old. The kitchen has one of those old-fashioned sinks that you have to bend down to get to. The hardwood floor is beautiful and shiny. Even the doorknobs are old, round, with old-fashioned key locks that require skeleton keys. It sits about half a mile from where the water crashes against the edge of California.

A few days after we're settled in, Stacy comes up to visit, along with Tammy's Aunt Sharon and cousin Natalie.

They like this town. My sister hasn't been here ten minutes when she announces she's moving here too. Aunt Sharon and

Natalie say they might just do likewise. I love it.

I'm not sure if Tammy or Ma has ever really talked with Sharon about what her husband did, but Sharon's a lot nicer to everyone than she was when I first met her. I wonder if her daughter has discussed Uncle Price with her. They both seem lonely.

"Everyone's lonely to *you*!" teases Tammy. "You'd love it if the Blooms and Old Mrs. Cooke came up here, wouldn't you?"

"I'd probably love it, yeah," I admit.

So Tammy and Ma urge Sharon and Natalie to join us. They're overjoyed, all huge smiles, eagerly gabbing and making plans, and under that thrill, I can see the exhaustion in the dark circles under their eyes, the gladness that Price is pretty much out of all our lives. He's staying in Sacramento forever, and we are going to be here on the coast, a family. I can feel the same "new lease on life" euphoria in Sharon and Natalie that I had when Lloyd gave me his heart and home, and again when Tammy came home to me.

Yeah, he teases me, but he can't pull the wool over my eyes. He wants everything I want, family: friends and love.

We pick a day, and we all walk out beyond the Glass Beach, to a place where the waves are exploding against flattened rocks.

"You're my friend, my lover, my husband and my soul-mate," I tell Tammy, raising my voice above the crashing surf, thrilled to have it again. It's my real voice, not the barking croak I'd grown accustomed to, the real thing, the smooth, soft, medium-deep tenor I haven't heard since that awful night last December. "You put up with things nobody else would ever put up with. You're the very definition of love, Tammy. You're patient, kind to me, long-suffering. And you never give up. You know what I'm talking about," I wink at him. "This began with a crush, but what we've lived through, what we've experienced together, makes it far more. I don't know why God gave you to me, but I'm so glad He did, and I'll never take it for granted, I promise."

After we've renewed our vows, we walk back to the house, damp and chilled from the spray of salt and foam. We towel-dry

386

ourselves, make hot chocolate, and chatter on the porch until the sun is down and we can only hear the faint roar of the ocean.

Before we moved, I was shocked when Tammy had announced he wanted to give up his job as host of the college rock radio show. "Don't you have fun with that show?" I had asked in surprise.

He said he had a lot of fun with it for many years, but now he wants to write full-time about the plight of mistreated animals. He begins travelling and conducting exhaustive research, his quests taking him (and me too, when I can go with him) as far away as rural France, to scrutinise the repugnant methods of factory farmers who provide ducks and geese for foie gras. I don't understand how Tammy can stand seeing the things he sees, how he can keep his sanity, and I worry about him.

But it is a calling for him. When you're called, you have to go. No matter how hard it is. One night he sees images from an awful video of a man killing a little beagle puppy, and I've never seen Tammy so broken and torn to shreds. Just a glimpse of that puppy's terrified brown eyes and I scribble, *How can you look at that?!* Instantly I regret writing this, because I know he feels ashamed of watching the entire video of my parents hurting me. How can I let him know I understand why he watched it now? How can I let him know that yes, I realise he watched it to understand just how evil they had been? And that in some weird way, he forgot that I really wasn't being hurt anymore, that I wasn't that seven year old boy anymore?

I feel an unholy presence wafting from those motionless images, and I write, *Some people have no souls. It's like they've given their souls to Satan.*

Tammy turns to me and smashes me against him, crying so hard he blows a vessel in his left eye. I suddenly feel the burden he's carried with him for all these years. He clings to me, sobbing, "What I did to Cotton was nowhere near as barbaric as this. And I was a kid, right?"

That's right, I tell him. *You were a child, Tammy.*

"I can't forget what I did! I had no reason to hate him so! He was a tiny, sweet, little white dog. He never hurt anybody!"

I feel the scald of Tammy's shame radiating off his skin. "I'm not a saint. I'm nothing. I'm just a reformed abuser myself."

I have to tell him. *We're all evil, Tammy, in some way or another. We all have evil in us. Because we are a lost, lonely species. Only God can bring out the good inside of us. We have to let God take control and make us as good as we can be. And you've done that, Love. You're not that angry boy anymore, Tammy.*

"No." He's shaking.

You were a boy.

"I wasn't little though. I was eleven, twelve, thirteen…"

You were a tiny, lonely, lost little boy, Tammy. You were a baby. This person is no younger than thirty, twenty-five at the youngest! You changed! You'd never hurt a dog, or a cat.

"I'd never hurt any living creature, not even a spider. I just can't!"

You have to stop beating yourself up, Tammy. You have to. We can't change the past. I wish we could, but we can't. You're a good man. God helped you to change. He gave you the miracle you prayed for. Don't forget that.

"He needs help too. He never got it, and now maybe it's too late for him."

Maybe, I'm forced to agree. *Maybe if we pray, he'll change. Maybe he'll see. Maybe he'll turn his life around. Maybe a miracle can happen for him.*

His arms tighten around me. "How did you live through what they did to you?"

"Who?" The word pushes past my lodged airway.

"Your parents, Ray and Cantrell, all of them…" His body shakes and I hear an unspoken request for me to give him another crushing bear hug. He needs it and I use all of my strength to give it. "It's okay," I whisper roughly. "It's okay, Tammy."

After that evening, he decides to take Dr. Halliday up on her offer to put him on antidepressants and anxiolytics. She tells him that she's concerned about the emotional damage that watching those terrible videos might be doing to him. She is kindly adamant in her explanation that she doesn't think the videos will turn Tammy into some kind of hardened wacko, but that rather, he is the owner of an especially sensitive heart, that he absorbs the pain of others far too well, and that the mental torture involved in investigating such heinous crimes could literally kill him. She urges him not to watch them anymore.

I agree. He won't let *me* watch them, so I shouldn't let him either. He doesn't believe it, but he needs protection too. He's said before that he doesn't need to be emotionally rent apart by visual evil in order to be against it. Finally, he decides he can stand no more, and heeds our advice.

In time, he will join the editorial staff of the *Mendocino Vegan*, an animal rights magazine based in Fort Bragg, and both of us, along with Stacy, who has also become a vegan, will be speaking at different functions on behalf of the animal kingdom.

I'm soon on my way to being a vegan gourmand, studying under Stacy, who is a genius in the kitchen. After she moves into an apartment nearby, she talks about starting her own vegan restaurant, or at least writing a vegan cookbook. Either way, she wants to call it, "The Garden of Eatin'". We plant a big garden outside our kitchen window.

In the meantime, Tammy and I have another issue we speak passionately and candidly about: being gay. It's not enough that I have survived being beaten three times and that we now live in peace. We felt forced to flee the town that we grew up in when it decided it could not accept us. We know there are others like us, lovers in hiding, people who, in spite of how civilization has advanced since the 1950s, do not feel free to hold the hands or kiss the lips of their beloved in public. Every time we see a heterosexual couple slobbering all over each other, Tammy and I sneak a soft, lingering kiss, and when we see the dirty looks given us, we get angrier still at the double standard. It isn't fair, how we're treated, and since meeting a lot of great new friends during the trial, we've begun frequenting gay and lesbian organisations in the Bay Area and throughout northern

California, speaking, giving our testimonials, reaching out.

We're *not* alone. We're loved. People come up to us after we've spoken about our lives together, and they tell us we're loved.

Tammy begins churning out articles for several local gay publications about violence, legislation, and other issues that concern us. We both get a huge thrill when *Out! Magazine* publishes one of his pieces.

We have family. So do Ma, Stacy, Sharon and Natalie, who have discovered countless new friends at the local chapter of PFLAG. At the Gay Pride parade in San Francisco, Natalie meets a couple from Idaho who married several years ago. She often visits them, and becomes such a great friend of theirs that they will eventually ask her to surrogate a baby for them!

We get birthday, Easter and Christmas cards from Marilyn, Sylvie and Alice, Patti, Deanna, Tammy's old boss at the Davis station, Pete Bloom, Mrs. Cooke, Officers Lord and Howard, and even ol' Paulina Holstein, if you can believe that.

We meticulously plan our cat sanctuary. All around the property, we build runs that allow cats to flee from the always possible coyote or hawk and take shelter in a covered kennel, while letting them choose between sleeping or dwelling inside or outside. We stock up on food, litter boxes, medicines, beds, and catnip toys. We name the shelter the Lloyd C. Tafford Cat Sanctuary and we adopt every starving stray and condemned-to-death shelter animal we can until we have nearly eighty cats and twenty dogs within the first year. Tammy decides to write a book about our brainchild. His second book is a work of fiction based on our lives and the inspiration for our shelter: Lloyd.

We all take care of the sanctuary during the day, and three or four nights a week, Tammy, Stacy and Ma take over while I minister to hospice patients with HIV and AIDS along the Mendocino coast. I have a pager on me at all times, and frequently, I find myself driving late at night to sit by a patient and their grieving partner until the sun is up and the patient is either feeling better for the moment or lying peaceful in his bed, his body still, his skin translucent. It's a job that leaves me sad on some days, but it's rewarding in ways I've never dreamed.

I also work one weekend a month as a telephone counsellor for gay youths who are suicidal. Tammy feels the call and comes aboard a short time after. We collaborate on everything, Tammy and me, and we're doing God's work. We both feel the call to help, to reach out to people who are going through what we've been through.

We're accomplished. We have love and purpose.

I wake up every morning with a reason to get up and out of bed with him.

He's my strength as much as I am his.

I've finally learned to harden myself against those who hate me and Tammy and everyone like us, spewing their scriptures of damnation. I've learned to use their own tactics against them. "Well, some religions don't believe in eating shellfish", and "Some churches are against blood transfusion and life-saving surgeries", and "What about hermaphrodites? They are both male and female. What if a hermaphrodite went to one of those churches that don't believe in cosmetic surgery? What if a hermaphrodite had surgery to become a man and later discovered "he" feels more female than male? Is he going to hell too?". And, "We're all female at the beginning of gestation... can it be possible that some of us men still have 'female' brains?". The dogmatics I try to talk to won't listen, but I'm not going to keep silence. I'm tired of being bullied, and I'm tired of being lied about by people like James Dobson, Dubya and the charming people behind California's Proposition 8.

I've learned that sometimes anger can make me stronger, if it's the right kind of anger. I get mad at the way some people think they know more about God than the rest of us, the way they think they're more entitled to God's love than others. Tammy and I are like any family. We pray. No, we don't get down on our knees together and pray for hours, but we do pray, almost every night before bed. We know God listens, and that He/She cares.

I've quit smoking, so needless to say, I've quit burning myself. I've replaced tobacco with red liquorice. And I blow bubbles. I take a little bottle of bubbles with me wherever I go. The clean scent and the white film of soapy dish bubbles permeates our home.

I've become accustomed to eating more than just one small daily meal. I've gained a little weight—maybe seven pounds or so—Tammy seems to like it, a lot. He can't keep his damn hands off me!

And he's been wanting something new from me that I haven't been too comfortable about. One night, he asks once again if I'll "top" him.

"Trade places with me," he whispers.

"Oh, Tammy. I can't. It seems too *mannish* for me."

"You *are* a man," he reminds me with a smile.

"I know," I sigh. I've just never felt like I want to do that. A while back (actually, it was during a little excursion to the coast, before we moved there for good, a badly needed getaway after Tammy's horrified reaction to those terrible photos), I appeased him by using my fingers. It was wonderful, watching him, feeling that little gland swelling as my fingers grazed against it. He began to touch himself, and I grabbed his hand, gesturing, "Let me."

I do that again tonight. One hand caressing him in front, one hand manoeuvring my fingers, I watch him writhe and thrust restlessly, wordlessly begging me for more. I love the faces he's making. "You're so beautiful, Tammy."

He smiles, closes his eyes, and watching his amazing, erotic dance, watching his soft lips parting as sighs of pleasure float past them, watching his dark green eyes open halfway… my heart beats harder in my throat, so hard, I can barely speak as I pull my fingers away and cry, "Tammy, I want to be inside of you…"

"I want you inside of me," he answers desperately.

"I don't want to hurt you!"

"I don't care if you hurt me," Tammy moans. "All I care about is whether you love me."

"I do love you, Tammy."

"I *know* you do."

As I put on a condom for the first time in my life, I'm so scared I'm going to be clumsy and hurt him, and the old terrible fear that I'm turning into my own father tries to snatch the moment away from us, but I rebuke it, like I always have to, and shove it away.

As I gently enter my husband's body for the first time, I watch his face below mine, feel his body around me. He's the most beautiful, selfless person on earth. I feel so safe, so warm. I feel so loved, within him. His body belongs to me as much as mine belongs to him. I know that so acutely at this moment... *Does he have any idea how much he's given to me? How much he's giving to me now? Does he know what he's sharing with me?*

Of course he *must* know, because he loves me, and wants me to feel what he feels when he's inside of me. I do. I feel it... *Does he know how much I love him? Does he know, really, how important, how utterly priceless he is to me?*

There's nobody like him, nobody in the world. He wanted me to feel what he feels, and now I know. "You're so beautiful," I tell him. "You're so wonderful."

His body contracts around me, bear-hugs me, crushes me, loves me.

"I love you, Tammy," I gasp.

"I know you love me, Baby," he whispers.

He *knows*...

We're one flesh...

He calls me, "Baby," and I call him "Tammy", or "Sweetie", or "Honey". Now, unbelievable as it seems, I can play with him, and call him "Daddy", without feeling guilty or dirty or disgusting, without giving my biological sire more than a perfunctory mental blink.

I can play with my husband, because I know he loves me, and he knows I love him, and what we have is honest and beautiful and healthy... We're part of something wonderful.

We're happy. We're happy at last.

We're on a journey that will never end.

This is part of the testimonial we give to our community.

No, it's not perfect every single minute. When you're a victim of hate, it's never easy to sort through all the shit and recover yourself. You're in pieces and it takes the whole rest of your life to find each one and bring it back into you. Unlike in fairy tales, true love cannot totally erase everything I've suffered. I still have nightmares, but not as often now. I still struggle with bitterness and doubt. I still have trouble with that pesky shame I've known all my life. It pops up when my guard is down, and Tammy helps me with it, and I help him when his guilt rises out of nowhere and tries to slap him down.

I stopped asking my parents, "Why?" after my wedding night. I actually stopped.

Because there is no why. I have to accept that.

And I have to forgive them.

Forgiveness. It took nearly dying for me to realise that I have to forgive those who have hurt me, that only forgiveness can free me of my hatred. It's for me, not them.

It's taken a long, long, time, but I finally realise my parents had something terribly wrong in their souls. I loved them so much... then I hated them. Now I simply pity them. I have a life. They don't.

As for forgiving Yvette, Benny, Lydia, Ray and Cantrell... well, I'm still working on it...

Tammy often says he feels that Lloyd is looking down from heaven with love and pride and happiness, and sometimes I find myself almost believing it, believing that our loved dead watch over us as we struggle through life. The day I married Tammy in Vancouver, I wondered if indeed Lloyd was up there watching us, overjoyed, knowing that we're both safe, and happy. And I wondered if, at last, my dad was able to breathe a sigh of relief before retiring to a silver cloud he now calls his bed.

But I keep remembering that passage from the Bible about the dead knowing nothing, and it gives me solace when I ponder the visions I had of Lloyd, as I fought for life in that orange grove. The apparitions of Lloyd and of my attackers and my parents, well, they might have been real, in their way, who knows? And naturally, I'd love to believe Lloyd was there to comfort and encourage me as I tried to find my way in the dark.

But when I think of him actually witnessing the gruesome, indefensible way in which I was beaten, the nefarious things that were said and done to me, the long, frigid night I spent in that orchard, when I imagine how helpless and angry and terrified he felt while he beheld the events of that horrible night, I truly prefer believing that my visit from Lloyd was a mirage, a reverie, completely hallucinatory, and that in actuality, he's asleep, safe in God's arms, blissfully unaware of the course of my life since his death, even if I am happy now.

To be absent from the body is to be present with God. And years from now, when Tammy and I are separated by death, whoever dies first will float in that warm, welcoming womb of darkness, asleep, oblivious to the world below, in the presence of a loving and merciful God. When we're both deceased, I don't want us aware and missing each other. I don't want us wandering in the dark, calling for each other, receiving no answers, lonely, traversing the universe alone…

I think we'll be sleeping.

And waiting.

My voice did return, for good, that breezy, twilit July evening during *The Jack Benny Program*.

On the blackened, industrialised coast of downtown Fort Bragg sits a warehouse-turned-bar and grill. It's called The Wharf, and now we, Old Reliable, Stacy, Natalie, Tammy and I, have found a new place to indulge our karaoke fetish. In the dimly-lit room filled with drippy white candles and waitresses who wear hairnets and smell of fish and frying grease, Ma and Aunt Sharon sit at a table in the front, munching on garlic bread and crispy French fries, falling off the wagon and dipping them into the most delicious non-vegan buttermilk ranch dressing in the world, using almost an entire bottle until there's barely any left for the big green salad.

They sit, eating until they're both ready to pop, cheering us on, along with a houseful of old, salt-coated fishermen who've found that they love New Wave and Jammin' Oldies.

Love
Yourself

3/25/2010

acknowledgements:

My sincere thanks to my cousin, Leslie Purkey and to my mother, Joan Johnson, for being the first readers of Crush and providing your honest feedback.

To Sean Jones and Jacob Woods for reading advance copies and giving your invaluable critique and feedback.

To my friends Becky Baron, Joel Moran, Patsy Moran, Bonny York, Heidi Rose, Sherrie Harris, Annie Kelly, Cheryl Headford, and Cathy Witbrodt, for your enthusiasm and support. I know I've missed a few others who also deserve recognition.

To Mark Coker and the amazing people at Smashwords: thank you for publishing Crush as an eBook and for tirelessly working to help dreamers like me share our work with the world.

Thanks to Debbie McGowan and the staff at Beaten Track Publishing in England for reading, proofing and helping me to spread the word about Crush.

Thanks to Carol Lynn Pearson for her gracious permission to use my favourite poem of hers in this book.

To Lulu.com for making it possible to produce a beautiful, professional looking hardcover.

To my family: I love you.

To my "kids", who I will always love and miss wherever they go, and wherever they are:

Ted, Sals, Sam, Toby, LeeLoo, Sylvester, Ginger, Pepper, Sugar, Patsy, Misty, Mollie and Baby.

resources for lgbtq youth and adults:

The Lesbian and Gay Foundation
lgf.org.uk

Queer Youth Network
queeryouth.org.uk

Schools Out
schools-out.org.uk

London Lesbian and Gay Switchboard
llgs.org.uk

Lesbian and Gay Christian Movement
lgcm.org.uk

Coalition for Equal Marriage
c4em.org.uk

Stonewall
stonewall.org.uk

OutRage!
outrage.org.uk

resources for
animal rights:

People for the Ethical Treatment of Animals
peta.org.uk

Royal Society for the
Prevention of Cruelty to Animals
rspca.org.uk

Humane Society International
hsi.org

Dogs Trust
dogstrust.org.uk

about the author:

Laura Susan Johnson was born in California in 1970. She lives back and forth between California, Idaho and the coast of northern Oregon. She began writing stories at the age of eleven and was a staff journalist in high school. First and foremost, she is a writer, but she is also a nurse, a web designer, a quilter, a traveller and a wanna-be vegan gourmand.

Her other written works include the short stories: Burdens, Our House, and Old Cars

She is currently working on her second novel.

Her website can be found at:
http://peachhambeach.jigsy.com

CPSIA information can be obtained at www.ICGtesting.com
Printed in the USA
LVOW12s1818090114

368771LV00001B/74/P